Afterlife

JOEY W. HILL

ELLORA'S CAVE
ROMANTICA PUBLISHING

An Ellora's Cave Romantica Publication

www.ellorascave.com

Afterlife

ISBN 9781419964138
ALL RIGHTS RESERVED.
Afterlife Copyright © 2010 Joey W. Hill
Edited by Briana St. James.
Cover art by Syenca.

Electronic book publication November 2010
Trade paperback publication 2011

With the exception of quotes used in reviews, this book may not be reproduced or used in whole or in part by any means existing without written permission from the publisher, Ellora's Cave Publishing, Inc.® 1056 Home Avenue, Akron OH 44310-3502.

Warning: The unauthorized reproduction or distribution of this copyrighted work is illegal. Criminal copyright infringement, including infringement without monetary gain, is investigated by the FBI and is punishable by up to 5 years in federal prison and a fine of $250,000.
(http://www.fbi.gov/ipr/)

This book is a work of fiction and any resemblance to persons, living or dead, or places, events or locales is purely coincidental. The characters are productions of the author's imagination and used fictitiously.

AFTERLIFE

ฒ

Trademarks Acknowledgement

The author acknowledges the trademarked status and trademark owners of the following wordmarks mentioned in this work of fiction:

Boy Scout: Boy Scouts of America Corporation

Cinderella: Disney Enterprises, Inc.

Corolla: Toyota Jidosha Kogyo Kabushiki Kaisha Toyota Motor Co., Ltd

Dunkin' Donuts: Dunkin' Donuts USA, Inc.

ESPN: ESPN, Inc.

Godiva: Godiva Brands, Inc.

Hallmark: Hallmark Licensing, Inc

Limoncello: B M Distilled Spirits, LLC

Molly Maid: Molly Maid, Inc.

National Guard: Army National Guard Agency of the Government United States

Nike: Nike, Inc.

Obi-wan: Lucas Licensing Ltd.

Oz: Turner Entertainment Co.

Superman: DC Comics E.C. Publications, Inc.

The Mummy: Universal City Studios LLLP

Weather Girls, The: Rhodes, Dynelle Individual

Chapter One

ဆာ

"I better get a good report on you today, Sergeant. Any whining and you'll get your ass blistered soon as we get out of here. Maybe sooner."

Rachel sucked in a surprised breath as Dana's white cane shot out toward Peter's unprotected shin with impressive accuracy. Despite his formidable size, Peter sidestepped it with practiced grace, tossing Rachel a grin as he slid an arm around Dana's waist, drawing her to his side. Closing his hand over her slim fingers, he plucked the cane from her. "And I'd best hold onto this for you."

"Chicken," Dana retorted. She turned her face up to him. "Afraid a little blind girl's going to take you down with a plastic stick."

Rachel pressed her lips together against a smile as Peter used one arm and a quick move to hoist his petite fiancée over his shoulder. Though Dana threatened to dismember him in creative ways, he simply steadied her with one hand spread across her attractive bottom. When he hooked his thumb in one of the pockets of her snug jeans, that intimacy alone was enough to make Rachel ache. "Where do you want her?" he asked. His storm gray eyes lingered on Rachel's face, his brow creasing thoughtfully as if he saw something there he shouldn't.

Snapping her gaze away from the placement of that large hand, she nodded toward the usual cot for Dana's physical therapy. Since she was standing at her corner desk in the therapy room, Rachel shuffled through her calendar, pretending to finish up some things before they got started.

In reality, she was breathing through that sharp twist in her lower belly, the one she recognized as yearning. It was a far-too-frequent feeling since Peter had started bringing Dana to her PT sessions. It wasn't their teasing loveplay. They were being a little more blatant than usual today, but since they were engaged, it wasn't unexpected. Their romantic vibes fairly oozed out over everyone around them. The only reaction it should have triggered from her was indulgent amusement, maybe a touch of motherly exasperation. But there was an additional component between them.

Most people would miss it, though they might pick up on something about Peter and Dana's interactions that mesmerized or made them feel inexplicably uncomfortable. Unable to place what it was, they'd call it something else, or shrug it off as those engagement vibes. She'd done the same thing, but she'd known from the first she was fooling herself. Even after all these years of trying to mute her desire, she seemed to have a radar for it.

It was in the way Peter followed Dana's movements, tracking her facial expressions, picking up everything she was feeling and anticipating it so well. He was as aware of Dana's physical and emotional state as the woman herself. Probably more. Each word she spoke, every syllable of her body language, elicited some type of response from him. Pure, monitored attention.

Rachel had convinced herself men like that didn't exist. Another of the many lies she'd told herself for way too long. When Peter made that sensual threat to blister his fiancee's ass, the faint tinge under Dana's mocha skin said she knew he'd live up to that promise. And she'd welcome it—as a reward, not punishment.

Their weekly visit was both the highlight and curse of Rachel's week.

He was carting Dana back to the cot as if he was carrying a grain sack. "Got to get you back in shape, soldier. I expect you to wait on me hand and foot like a proper wife should. I'm running out of patience with this coddling."

"I'll be happy to put my fist or foot right where it'll do you the most good," Dana returned sweetly. She had her right elbow propped on Peter's wide shoulder, holding herself up. Rachel noted she was guarding the left arm. They'd need to do extra work on that today. However, the stomach muscles were admirably strong.

Peter slid Dana off his shoulder and onto her feet, as smooth and gentle as if she were a porcelain doll, belying his words. It was in his face, every time he looked at the black woman who barely came up to his chin and yet had the force of personality to match his larger-than-life presence. There was nothing he wouldn't do for her. Except let her give up on herself, which Rachel knew was why he came to every session with her.

Dana wasn't a complainer. She was always stoic and cheerful, such that Rachel was sure she and Peter were the only people who knew how hard these sessions were. Before the end of it, Dana would have her teeth gritted against pain, tears running down her face as she pushed it a little further. Like so many patients, she also waged a mental battle against despair, confronted with a body that would never be the same again.

Dana had been injured in Iraq, losing her sight, most of her hearing and some mobility and strength in her left side. Not only had she required multiple surgeries, she'd needed physical therapy to regain flexibility. PT was never easy, but Dana's had been rougher than most because she'd battled post-traumatic stress disorder and its attendant deep depression for over a year, letting the already damaged muscles atrophy. That said, over the past three months, Dana had made tremendous progress. She was a strong, brave woman, but Rachel also knew a great deal of it had to do with the man who encouraged, bullied and stood by her, no matter what.

He'd bring her to the therapy area, but typically he'd return to the waiting room during the first part of the session, when Dana would insist she didn't need babying. However, with uncanny timing, whenever the session reached its worst point, Peter was likely to wander back to see if Rachel wanted a soda from the vending machine. When she'd decline, he'd take a seat nearby with a magazine he wasn't reading. Even without sight, Dana's other senses would align on him like a rifle scope, and things would get better.

Like most healthcare professionals, Rachel knew family support for meaningful recovery was immeasurable. Fortunately for Dana, her fiancé was also very affluent, and he didn't let her pride stand in the way of using his resources. He'd already facilitated a cochlear implant surgery that used enhanced hearing technology. It had reduced Dana's hearing loss to a mild hardship, mostly exacerbated by her inability to see people's faces as they spoke. The cosmetic surgery that had been done since they were engaged was handled by the best plastic surgeon in the country.

Peter Winston was part of top management at Kensington & Associates, one of Baton Rouge's most prestigious corporations, a manufacturing and acquisitions concern. Since Rachel was sure Peter's role as operations manager for all their domestic and overseas plants had to be a busy and difficult job, the fact he didn't miss a single PT appointment spoke volumes to her. Despite Dana's insistence that he didn't need to be such a mother hen, there'd been days he'd flown back in from a job only for this, having to leave again that evening. It not only told Rachel how devoted he was to Dana, but that he knew, despite her spirited banter, how hard this was for the determined young woman.

"Why don't you go away and flex your muscles for the nurses up front? Show them your tattoo. They can coo over you while Rachel and I get some real work done."

"What if one of them wants to stroke my impressively large ego?"

10

"Give me back my cane."

Chuckling, he bent and caught her mouth, which softened under his. Though Rachel stayed ostensibly occupied with her calendar, her ears caught his quiet admonition to behave and work hard, that he'd be close by. Dana's serious response was a bare whisper Rachel nevertheless managed to hear.

"Yes, Master."

She gripped the edge of her desk, hard enough that the rough underside cut her hand, but she bit her lip to keep from making a noise of distress. The cut was the least of it. Yes, she'd been sure for a while, but it was the first time she'd heard it confirmed so baldly. The painful vindication had her floundering in an appalling swamp of self-pity, envy and an old fury that welled up to choke her.

Damn it, Rachel, stop it.

To hear it, to know it existed in such a desirable form, didn't just double her over in pain. It thrilled her with a charge of sensual lightning through her extremities. She'd have to ground the energy into the solid earth beneath her feet—or in this case, the beige tile floor—because it had nowhere else to go.

That had always worked in the past, but maybe it was how much she genuinely liked these two that made it more difficult to ignore the effect they had on her. From the moment they arrived for each appointment, she strained for every word between them, absorbed every touch and gesture, as if she was living vicariously through them, and maybe she was. Recently, she'd been waking from dreams that left her thighs damp with perspiration, her gown knotted up around her waist as if a man had pushed it there.

While Peter and Dana might keep those old demons awake and tormenting her, they hadn't resurrected them. It wasn't Peter who'd invaded her dreams. It was the man who'd referred Dana to Rachel's PT practice.

Jon Forte.

* * * * *

When not doing physical therapy for the hospital, Rachel ran a small yoga studio. Jon had started attending her classes once a week almost a year ago. Because of his work schedule, he came to different classes, varying his attendance, but she suspected that was a good thing. If he was a dependable regular in any of them, that class probably would have had a mile-long waiting list for female attendees.

There was a different kind of beauty to him. Unlike Peter, who was a broad mountain of muscle, Jon had the build of a Baryshnikov, all compact strength. Though not overly tall at around five-ten, it made him quite a bit taller than Rachel's five-three. His eyes reminded her of striated sodalite, the vivid blues infused with the fire of the earth that had created it. His hair was thick, black silk that feathered temptingly over his forehead.

Like everyone else in her class, she'd done a double-take the first time he spoke. Not only did he possess the velvet tones of a late night DJ, spinning languorous R&B tunes in the loneliest hours of night, but it was impossible to imagine arguing with him, doing anything to interrupt those fluid, resolute syllables from flowing over the skin like the reassuring brush of angel feathers.

He was always courteous, talking to each woman in a way that suggested he took a personal interest in her life and how her day was going. He had that still, attentive way about him as Peter did. If another male attended her class, he handled that interaction in a relaxed, friendly way, seamless male bonding amid a sea of estrogen.

He was a K&A management scion as well. Following impulse rather than good sense, she'd looked up articles on the company. Like Peter, he was one of the brilliant five-man team that ran K&A. They'd been given various nicknames in both the business and society pages, including the *wunderkind*, because of what they'd accomplished at a relatively young age in the manufacturing world.

12

However, one gossip columnist gave them a different name. *Knights of the Board Room.* With the calculated indiscretion that a gossip columnist could dare, the reporter had noted they had a closely bonded intuition usually shared by fetuses in the womb. Another reason for the nickname was that they were well known for their support of charitable efforts, both with money and hands-on time. They'd been deeply involved in relief efforts for Katrina and supposedly always had personal bets running between them where the winnings went to the charity of the winner's choice. In the pictures taken of them at different functions, she knew they were all handsome as sin, though her gaze always strayed to Jon's face, and sometimes her fingers, slipping over the image with guilty shame at the girlish act.

With his mechanical aptitude and inventor's spirit, Jon was called the "boy genius" of the group. He held dual financial and engineering degrees and already had multiple patents for innovative manufacturing processes and gadgets. He also had impressive diplomacy and negotiating skills, and was considered the calming yet irresistible influence of the group. Business rivals had dubbed him "Kensington's Archangel" with grudging admiration.

Knowing he was an engineer and inventor explained why the knuckles of his long-fingered hands were often scraped, his palms calloused. She'd not only had the shameful, secret pleasure of touching them, but some of the rest of him as well. Enough to know firsthand his trim frame truly was solid muscle. Because his upper body strength made the more extreme positions easier for him to execute, she'd fallen into the despicable habit of using him to demonstrate those. Despicable because she used those innocuous visual cues as an excuse to make contact.

Note how Jon has his weight balanced. A quick touch of his thigh, braced and holding in Warrior One. *Pay particular attention to the position of the neck here, the angle of the hips...* She'd almost gone too far that day, because when she'd stepped up behind him to lay her hands on his hips, she'd accidentally brushed the upper rise of his taut buttocks with her thumbs. She'd blushed like a girl. Thank heavens for the dim lighting, the flickering candles that created a tranquil environment and hid such reactions. His skin was fueled by a heat that warmed her whole body at the casual touch.

She assumed he came to the class for the camaraderie of others, because he was more proficient in the ancient practice than Rachel was. Some days she wished he would stop coming; other days she could hardly wait to see which day he turned up. In less rational moments she blamed *him* for reviving all these feelings.

He'd given her direct permission to touch him, after all.

* * * * *

It was a ritual she performed with all her new students. At the beginning of a class, she would take a seat on her mat and ask the first-timer the same question. "May I touch you?"

The reason for the question was innocent enough. At the end of each session, they would perform the yoga *nidra*, the students lying on their mats, entering a state of deep relaxation. She would visit each one, kneel at the crown of his or her head and massage the temples with herbal-coated hands, her thumbs slowly rotating over the third eye, spiritually located above and centered between the eyebrows.

When she'd met his gaze that first day, at the beginning of class, those blue eyes had been deep and mysterious in the candlelight, almost causing her to lose her train of thought.

"May I touch you? Jon." She added the name as an afterthought, but it felt wrong, as if an honorific was needed instead. Particularly when something indefinable entered his gaze as if he heard the pause and—unlike her—had no doubt about what should go in that empty space.

"Yes, Rachel. You may."

14

No nervous half smile and quick one-word assent, as often happened with a new student, surprised by the question. Those four words, uttered in that velvet tone, had brought back to life dangerous fantasies she'd kept quelled for so long. She had the crazy thought that it wouldn't matter when or how she wanted to touch him. He would always require that she wait for his permission. It made her palms dampen and her pulse flutter.

Maintaining her focus that day, staying centered in her practice, had been all but impossible, because all she could think about was touching him at the end of it. She'd lectured herself, messed up right and left cues about twelve times, until her students were teasing her good-naturedly. However, when she finally knelt at his head, her hands scented with lavender and eucalyptus oils, she'd tried to keep her eyes on the gold band of her wedding ring, the protection that illusion gave her. Instead, her gaze strayed to his closed eyes, the set of his firm mouth, the slope of his jaw. The way his hair brushed her skin as she laid her fingers on his temples.

She imagined what would happen if he lifted his hands, closed them over her wrists, holding her manacled there as he opened his eyes, looked up at her and made entirely different demands. Just the vision made her wet, a shocking development. It had been quite a while since anything had caused her to have that response.

As if some kind of devil on her shoulder was determined to make things worse, Jon had lifted his chin as she settled her fingers on his brow. Though he kept his eyes closed, his nostrils flared. "I like this scent, Rachel," he said, his voice low.

Of course he meant the eucalyptus and lavender. Right?

* * * * *

Of course he did. He was a business executive who had the confidence to handle people well. For heaven's sake, he'd never made a single inappropriate move toward her. She needed to put him out of her mind. Particularly right now, with Peter and Dana here. It made thinking about him all the more hazardous. The idea that her small world had rolled into the trajectory of *two* full-blown sexual Dominants was an irony that smacked of the Universe's cruelest sense of humor. It was best for her to pretend she'd never heard that powerful word fall from Dana's lips, a word that unlocked all sorts of wild things in Rachel's soul.

The same word she'd been certain had belonged in that empty space when she'd asked Jon if she could touch him. And how insane was that?

Jon Forte. Just saying his name in her mind made her breath shorten and crazy things happen to her body. Things that her body didn't do, hadn't done, for a very long time. Unlike Peter, he was not engaged and therefore far too tempting. He might as well have been happily married though, because he was no less off limits, for a variety of reasons. She reminded herself of the least painful one, that the man was at least ten years younger than she was. Probably fifteen, though she winced to push it that far. He was closer to her son's age than hers.

The age her son would be now, if he were still alive. Another sharp hurt came with that thought, even higher up. In a moment, she was going to be as rigid with pain as one of her new patients, fresh from a car wreck.

Damn it, she was done with all the things that Peter and Jon represented. She'd tried to go down that road and ended up nearly destroying herself. Squaring her shoulders, she turned away from her thoughts, her desires and her memories, and gave herself the here, the now and the realistic—a much safer trinity.

Chapter Two

so

"All right, there you go. Take a deep breath. Think we can go a bit further?" Rachel leaned on the triceps, ready to push the arm back another notch if Dana gave her the slightest indication she was ready for it, though she was pretty sure the woman had reached her limit.

Dana gave her a quick jerk of a nod and closed her eyes, focusing. Watching the tension throughout the rest of Dana's body, Rachel cut the hold time down to half before she released. "I think that's plenty for today. You've made progress since last time. You're doing your exercises religiously."

"Try getting out of them with an ex-captain who wants to be a drill sergeant when he grows up." Dana managed a wan smile.

Reaching into the drawer next to the cot, Rachel withdrew a gold-foiled chocolate and put it in Dana's hand. "Your reward. You did really, really well, honey. I know it's slow, but you're improving your flexibility at the rate someone like me wants to see."

"Improving, but it will never be the same as before." Dana pressed her lips together, showing the strain behind the words, but then she sat up with a quick snap, a shake of her head. "Sorry. Weak-assed thing to say."

Rachel put a hand on her shoulder, but merely said, "You're still doing the Iyengar poses I showed you, with the straps?"

"Yes." Dana nodded, offered that half-smile again. "Peter likes the straps."

17

Rachel normally would have managed a witty comeback, but it caught in her throat. She couldn't joke today. She was too full of envy for what Dana had.

"Hey." Dana moved her hand to Rachel's knee. "You okay?"

"Yes. Definitely. I was just...smiling at you two. Being so in love and all. It's a nice thing to see."

"It's a nice thing to feel." Dana cocked her head. Rachel's left hand was resting on her knee, so now her patient was touching the gold band on her ring finger, a plain contrast to the diamond engagement set that flashed on Dana's. "I hope you're going to tell me you still feel that way about your husband. It might keep me from bashing in Peter's big rock head before we even make it down the aisle. Or are you still newlyweds?"

It happened on occasion. Rachel would never lie about it, but she did everything to avoid being asked. "I'm not... I'm divorced."

"I'm sorry." Dana's fingers tightened on her hand, over that ring. "Was it recent?"

Dana was planning to attend seminary. Though she'd only just begun prep courses for it, Rachel could tell she was going to be a good minister. She already had that quiet, soothing way of talking that made it feel like she was inviting a confession and forgiveness, instead of being intrusive or nosy. Of course the idea of forgiveness for a passionless crime...

She didn't want more questions, so it was best to get it out, rip the bandage off fast. "No. It's been a few years. I wear the ring so I don't have to fend off male attention." She forced herself to sound light, breezy. "It's appalling how few men are deterred by it these days, but it does help some."

Rachel was far more curvy than Dana's regal Ethiopian physique. Full-breasted, with a generous ass and hips that didn't bother her, because the yoga kept it all firm and healthy, even if she didn't match the standard for thin. She knew from experience she was far more likely to catch the eyes of passing males than the pencils in designer wear a couple decades younger. She did understand that about men, that they liked a woman to hold in bed, liked the way clothes could be made to amplify those fertile attributes of breast and backside. But it was bolstering knowledge only, not designed to catch the passing fish who couldn't meet her needs. She'd learned it was best not to cast the line.

"So no one in your life now?"

"Do I detect a matchmaking note? If so, remember I can actually tie your body in a pretzel shape and leave it that way."

The problem with having this kind of conversation with a blind person was they couldn't be thrown off by visual cues — the false smile, a casual shrug. Rachel tried hard to make her tone teasing, relaxed, but the crease across Dana's smooth brow said she wasn't fooled.

"You feel like a woman who has so much love to give a man, Rachel. I never would have guessed you didn't have one. Do you have other family? Children?"

I had a family. And one beautiful child.

"Oh heavens." Rachel gave a strained laugh, one she was sure sounded fake, but she was out of courage to handle the conversation. She was too fragile today. That word kept running through her head. *Master, Master, Master...* With each beat of her heart, she felt anew the thrill that had run through her vitals when she'd heard it. Only now it was starting to feel like an electric shock applied to the soles of her feet. "It's almost eight o'clock. I have to run an errand upstairs before my next appointment. I'm sorry, honey, I don't mean to cut us short..."

Withdrawing her hands with a quick pat of Dana's, she rotated on her stool and jumped, surprised to see Peter leaning against the wall a few feet behind them. She hadn't heard him enter, so she guessed he'd arrived during their brief, far-too-intimate interchange.

Dana rose then, gesturing as if she'd give Rachel another reassuring touch if she was still in range. "I'm sorry, Rachel. I didn't mean to get too personal. You don't have to pretend. You can tell me not to be such a nosy bitch, I can tell you to bite me and we'll be square again."

The warmth that welled up in Rachel now was real. She liked this woman and her fiancé, so very much. There were too few people like them. Since she had no trouble being physically demonstrative in such circumstances, she was able to put her arms around the slighter woman and give her a pure warm energy hug, rubbing her back a moment before letting her go. "Okay. Nosy bitch." She laughed as she stumbled self-consciously over the rough language, but then added, "Remember to keep up with your exercises and I'll see you next Tuesday. Ice pack and heat when you get home."

"Bite me. And no problem." Dana gave her another squeeze. When she reached out, Peter was already there, putting her cane back in her hand and giving her his arm.

"How'd she do?" he asked.

"Exceptionally well," Rachel said.

She meant it sincerely. However, looking at the two of them, another impulse gripped her. Something needy uncoiled in her belly, a desire to connect on this level, even if it was only in some miniscule way.

Knowing she could be risking a vital faux pas, she added, "Except she was a little tough on herself at the end. Thinking her hard work didn't deserve praise because it would never restore her to what she was. Just a brief moment, but I thought you should know about it."

"Really?" Peter arched a brow, holding her gaze an extra minute before glancing down at his fiancée. "Well, I guess we'll have to go home and deal with that attitude, won't we?"

He gave Rachel a significant nod then, an expression that made something quiver inside her. Her hands closed at her sides, terror at her own daring. "Most illuminating," he murmured. "Thank you, Rachel. See you next week."

She was relieved to see the smile playing on Dana's lips, and accepted the additional press of the woman's hand before it slipped away to rest on Peter's biceps, trusting him to lead her wherever she needed to go.

* * * * *

By the time she finished the week's appointments and three yoga classes, Rachel decided she needed to start the weekend with a stiff drink and a serious reality check. She'd been oddly euphoric right after that little interchange, but ever since, she'd been unbalanced, raw. She knew better than to go down that road, even with a seemingly innocuous tease. But for one solitary second, she'd put a foot inside a circle in which she'd longed to be all her life. Though it was only as a pathetic side character, a walk-on part where she facilitated something for the main players she couldn't share with them, it had felt so damn good.

Of course, like most things that felt that way, it came with a crash like a sugar high. *Damn it.* She'd been vacillating between reliving the moment and being depressed over it for most of the week. It hadn't helped that Jon hadn't showed for any of the week's classes. It just underscored she needed to have herself committed.

As she slid into her car outside the hospital, she saw her cell had a voice mail waiting. When she listened to the recording, she didn't know whether to laugh or cry.

"Rachel, this is Jon Forte. I'm sorry I missed class this week, but we had an engineering prototype due and I was burning the midnight oil. Would you be free to do a private for me on Sunday? Give me a call and leave your preferred time on my message service if you miss me. Sorry for going the impersonal tech route, but I'll look forward to seeing you Sunday if you can do it."

The impersonal tech route had given her a permanent recording of his voice. She could listen to it whenever she wanted, unless she made herself delete it. *Yeah, right.* That would happen after she got herself sloppy drunk, which she never did.

She needed to make up a lie, tell him she wasn't available for a private this weekend. Indulging in a one-on-one class with Jon would be the height of foolishness after the way she'd been raking her emotions over the coals and dredging up dark memories that really needed to stay buried. Next week would have been her twenty-fourth wedding anniversary. The small gumball of nails rolling around her belly grew into something like a spiked mace at the thought.

Knights carried maces, right? *Knights of the Board Room.* Even her colorful self-deprecations were making her think of him. *Great.*

When she hit the button to reply to the call, she didn't know if it was a positive or negative sign she reached his voicemail. Instead of telling him she wasn't available, she opened her mouth and something else entirely came out. "Jon, thanks for your call. I'll see you at 10 a.m. Sunday."

A time most people were in church. Choosing to ignore the significance of that time choice, she snapped the phone closed. Who really cared if she stood on the slippery bank of a lake in which she could drown?

No one. Especially not her.

* * * * *

Despite a glass of wine, maybe two, she rocked herself to sleep Saturday night, her thighs pressed together over that sick, unabated throbbing. Every reformed drug addict knew you couldn't indulge even a taste without awakening the horrible, must-have-it-or-die craving. But still, she got up the next morning, put on her yoga clothes and went, anticipation making her knees wobble, her stomach flutter. Her hands shook on the steering wheel of her battered old Corolla, fingers cold.

She'd spent a lot of time creating a peaceful environment in her yoga studio, which was an add-on room to the local fitness club. Rice shades, oak wood floors and a high ceiling with a slowly rotating fan. Bamboo plants and bonsai were displayed on a few artfully placed pedestals.

He'd arrived early, of course. With his masculine grace and inexpressible beauty, Jon looked like he belonged here, though the feelings he evoked this morning were anything but peaceful. During those few moments before he noticed her arrival, she hung back in the doorway of her studio, remembering all the guilty scenarios she'd played out in her mind.

At appropriate intervals, she joined other female rehab professionals for lunch. Since they were all of a similar age, occasionally there'd be jokes about "cougars", women who preferred younger men. Women who fantasized about those strong agile bodies, someone who would make them feel in their twenties again, males who could match their surprisingly expansive forty-something sexual appetites. Though she enjoyed the harmless frivolity of it, that wasn't what she felt for Jon.

She wasn't seeing herself as the older, wiser woman, taking him over like some kind of Mata Hari, guiding his steps in her bed. When she looked at him, instead she sensed his ability to take *her* over, guide her steps. Why couldn't she say it, even in her mind? She'd already opened that can of worms, hadn't she?

Jon was a sexual Dominant, the same as Peter was. A Master. Now that she knew it about Peter, she was certain of it for Jon. In between the lines of that gossip column, there'd even been a couple of snarky hints about certain sexual tendencies the Knights shared, but nothing stated overtly enough to invite problems for the paper or confirm Rachel's suspicions. But now she was sure, and wondered that she'd ever doubted it.

Though being a Dom didn't make a man more mature, Jon gave her that feeling. She responded to him, far more than she had to any Master close to her age, those few she'd encountered on her Internet forays. It was as if whatever his particular brand of Mastery was, it was calling to her, and her alone.

Foolishness. The K&A men had never lacked for female companionship. They were regularly paired with Louisiana's most beautiful women for large charity events or other prominent social occasions. But always different women. As if it was more for show than a real relationship, no commitment or meaning.

Oh God. Was she really doing the rock star groupie thing? All those other women mean nothing, because he hasn't met *me* yet. The real me. For the millionth time, she reminded herself all he'd ever been toward her was warm, cordial. Anything else was her, reading things into his behavior. The few times he'd tried to draw her out about her life beyond the studio or PT, she'd firmly discouraged that. He'd been enough of a gentleman to take the hint, mostly because she'd seen his eyes fall on the wedding band she wore. She liked that about him, that he respected that, no matter how false a signal it truly was. However, now that she knew what he was, she thought it was even more than a respect for the institution.

In his world, a man did not encroach on what belonged to another man. When she thought of it in such an archaic way, a way that would appall most modern women, it sent that inappropriate thrill through her again. Men with such a code might demand a woman obey their will, but they considered that a gift that should never be abused. Their dominance wasn't a lack of respect, but rather an acknowledgment of their responsibility to care for that woman.

Yeah, right. Damn it, she never learned, already tripping along in a romantic fantasy land again. People were far too messed up to figure things out like that. Those who understood it, on both sides, were too few. Instead, they usually crossed the lines and abused the boundaries, making it all pointless. She knew, from trying with her husband. She hadn't known how to articulate what she needed, and Cole...

It didn't matter anymore. She'd enjoy her avid fantasies from behind the safe gate of her mind. It was a torment she was obviously willing to endure, because she was here, wasn't she?

He was wearing natural cotton drawstring trousers, soft and worn, like the white tank tee that showed off the well-muscled arms and chest. After class, if it was a weekday, he would shower in the locker rooms and change into his expensive suit. His dark hair would fall in sexy disarray over those thoughtful, incredibly intelligent blue eyes, the cut emphasizing the slope of cheekbones, a firm jaw and mouth that would actually cause her to stammer if she made the mistake of looking at it while she was addressing the class.

He was sliding off the shoes he'd worn from the locker rooms. As he straightened, he saw her. She couldn't speak, looking at him there. When he walked over to her, he passed through shafts of early morning sunlight, filtering through the rice paper shades. Shadows and light.

"Good morning," he said, and it echoed through the empty room, a resonance that enchanted the senses. She wondered if it was the same kind of voice the Virgin Mary had heard when an angel appeared and told her about her divine fate.

Okay, just because she was meeting him on Sunday morning didn't mean she could intertwine sexual yearning with biblical passages. She'd be on a one-way course for hell for sure. She already felt the flames licking over her body, and the fact they felt good wasn't reassuring.

As he stopped in front of her, she still hadn't said a word. She couldn't. Particularly when he slid a knuckle along her cheek, catching a loose curl of her blonde hair and tucking it back into one of her hair clips. They all laughed about her wayward hair that she French-braided along her nape for class. More than one student had done the same thing he'd just done. Only it meant so much more when a male hand did it, a hand attached to a body like that and intense eyes like those.

Snap out of it, Rachel. You're making a damn fool of yourself.

The words came straight out of her dead marriage, in the same abrupt, impatient tone. They propelled her back a step, the startled jump of her heart making her clear her throat with a rasping cough. "Good morning," she said, though "Good" broke into two syllables because of the catch in her voice. She shrugged her shoulders, a mental shake that might look odd, but it helped get her mind back in the right place. Or at least turned in that direction. "Do you have anything in particular you want to practice today, or should I follow our usual class format?"

She should have indulged in more inane conversation. How was traffic, how was your week, the weather? *Did you have a Danish for breakfast? Because your breath has a sweet iced sugar scent that makes me want to devour your mouth.*

However, since the rest of her class wasn't here, she needed to get this progressing forward, before she really *did* do something foolish.

"You already know what I want, Rachel." As her stomach lurched, he gave a half smile. "I prefer the more advanced sessions. Are you up for it today?"

Her advanced class met on Friday mornings. He often couldn't make that one because of the executive staff meetings he'd told her were held on that day. When he attended her basic and intermediate classes, he chose the more intense modifications of the *asanas*, but he rarely had the opportunity to do some of the truly advanced positions.

"Yes, that will be fine." She nodded like her head was jerked by a string. "Let's get started."

Since he was studying her curiously as they moved to their mats, she tried to relax her shoulders, loosen up some. Then his next question coiled her up like a spring again.

"What are you doing on the last Saturday of this month?"

She blinked. Was he about to ask her out on a date? The very idea could make her legs buckle beneath her, even as her mind scrambled for a way to deal with it. Saying she was knitting boots for an expected grandchild might be sufficiently off-putting, except of course she didn't have one of those. And she didn't know how to knit. "I'm not sure. Why?"

"There's a Tantric yoga workshop for couples at Independence Park that weekend. If the weather's nice, they'll have it in the botanical gardens. It's going to be taught by a visiting guru from Bangkok." At her nonplused look, he lifted a shoulder. "You mentioned that some of your married students have been asking you to teach that form, but you needed to brush up on it. The setting is beautiful, of course, and we could go have a coffee at a café afterward, maybe somewhere on the riverfront."

She didn't know what to say to that, but Jon shrugged casually at her silence, offered her that sleepy smile again. "Just give it some thought. You can tell me your answer at the end of class. Though I'm not taking no for an answer, so you might as well say yes now."

She didn't know how to respond to that either. However, his easy manner about it helped make her noncommittal nod feel not so awkward. Still, to discourage further conversation, she folded herself into a sitting position on her mat and initiated *pranayama*, the breath control exercises.

In through the nose, pulling energy up, then out through the mouth, trying to release tension in her shoulders. Though yoga required focus and concentration for maximum benefit, within three breath cycles she knew that was a lost cause for her today. But an intensely physical workout would be good. She'd work both their asses off, and then she'd be too exhausted to think. Saying no to that Tantric class would be automatic, no more than a reflex she'd conditioned and used countless times to maintain her privacy and solitude. That was best.

They went from breathing to standing and stretching *asanas* as warm-up, and then from there she worked them into the more difficult poses. Unfortunately, it was hard to let exertion numb her when Jon gave her a yoga experience like she'd never had before.

Even in advanced classes, she couldn't move at this pace, not at this level of difficulty, because the class couldn't read her mind. But he seemed to anticipate her every choice and moved easily with her, so it was almost as if they were bridging the gap between a *hatha* approach and *ashtanga*, which used flowing, dance-like movements to transition between postures. It was exhilarating.

And no level of exhaustion could help her overlook how well those poses displayed the male body. It made one that was already beautiful even more so. When they transitioned into Sleeping Thunderbolt, she found herself studying him in the corner of her eye. As he folded himself to the floor on his knees, he aligned his feet on the outside of his hips, planting that fine ass on the floor between his calves. His torso elongated in mouthwatering display as he arched back, his knees remaining on the floor as his upper body became a crescent and the back of his head touched the floor, his hands settling into a prayer pose on his open chest.

She'd put herself at a diagonal position to him so that she could watch his posture as his teacher, but that was an unnecessary adjustment, because his form was flawless. Watching those taut buttocks resting on the floor, she wished she could see the strain of his thigh muscles beneath the loose pants. She was all too aware of the camber of cock and testicles emphasized by the upwardly canted position of his hips. She wanted to crawl over there, slide her hands under the baby soft cotton of the tank, caress his abdomen, follow it with mouth and fingers...

Sleeping Thunderbolt was a misnomer, because it awakened a storm inside her. Giving herself a fierce internal shake, she brought them out of that for the next phase, the inverted *asanas*, head and handstands. When she used the wall for hers, he waited until she pushed up and balanced. It was the only time during the class he hadn't been in sync with her, and she realized he was spotting her, ready to catch her if needed. It wasn't one of her personally easier moves. Though most of her students wouldn't have noted that, he obviously had. While she was qualified to teach yoga, yogis could spend decades perfecting the moves, and she'd only been doing this for a few years.

She'd turned up the room temperature to maximize the benefit of body heat for their practice. It had put a loving sheen of perspiration on his muscles, which became more pronounced as he stripped off the shirt, put it aside and then pushed up into a full handstand. He had no need of the wall, those gorgeous shoulder muscles creating a work of art as he held his weight and balance on his mat.

The ache in her limbs after that sequence and a glance at the clock, showing they'd been going at it for ninety minutes, told her it was time to take it down. She moved them back into a few sun salutation repetitions, then down for some floor stretches, easing into the closing *nidra*. Her limbs had turned to spaghetti, such that she wobbled when she went from a standing pose into a half-lotus.

"All right?" He was watching her so closely. That, plus the gentleness of his tone in the quiet room, made her feel like his question was directed to something far beyond her mere physical state. She had to swallow before she answered.

"Yes. Just overdid a bit. Joints aren't as resilient as they once were."

"You look superbly flexible to me. But sometimes we push ourselves too hard when we're trying to outrun things."

He had a way of saying things like that, with such unruffled calm, as if it was completely normal to venture past the intimate edges of a person's psyche.

"Like time?" The halfhearted joke, the attempt to turn him away from the sharp boundaries, didn't do the trick. His attention didn't waver.

"Things you're afraid to want."

Candlelight, heated room, heart rates slowly evening out. At his words, hers stepped up a pace, making her feel a little lightheaded, though she was already sitting down. She made what she hoped was a noncommittal noise, gave him her practiced distant smile that warned he was stepping over a line. As she put her hands on her knees, she adjusted the fake wedding band with one finger, knowing the sparkle would catch the candlelight. When his attention went to it, she shut him out further by closing her eyes, starting their breathing sequence again.

She kept her ears attuned to it, knew when he was matching his breath to hers, following her deep inhale, the slow exhale. She focused on her posture, on grounding and centering herself. Supposedly yoga practice helped a person connect to divine energies. Today her focus cavorted outside her grasp like a not-so-playful poltergeist. The demons she'd hoped to leave behind had only swelled in size, such that instead of peace and calm, her stomach had been invaded by flesh-eating beetles from *The Mummy* movies.

All because of one simple, utterly truthful statement. *Things you're afraid to want.* Damn him. Didn't he understand she couldn't afford these types of games? She'd long ago lost her ability to risk the playful nature of romance. Like a child who pretended to play dead during heroic games, but then saw actual death, she knew what such games meant now. The reality of love was dark and damaging, a morass she couldn't face again.

When she lay down on her back, straightening out her arms and legs for the *savasana*, the Corpse pose, the sad irony wasn't lost on her. She refused to let herself look toward him, until she heard the shifting of his mat. She cracked open an eyelid to see that he'd aligned his mat next to hers and was now lying down, emulating the stretch. His spread fingers were within an inch of hers.

She wasn't sure how to react, what to do. He was doing nothing at all wrong. Maybe he was inside the personal space margin, considering there was the whole classroom floor to use, but he wasn't touching her. Not technically. In the space between their parallel bodies, she felt the compressed heat of two auras, and was hyper aware of every long, lean portion of the body next to her.

"Having trouble hearing?" Another weak joke, delivered with a touch of desperate acid. She wished she could take it back, because she didn't want to be mean to him. She just needed him to leave her alone. But she also needed him to never stop coming to her class, so she could still have the guilty pleasure of dreaming impossible dreams.

"I wanted to be closer to you."

She turned her head then, but he had his eyes closed. "Walk us through it like you normally do," he said. "I want to hear your voice."

Rachel resolutely closed her eyes. She took them through the steps of putting the body in a neutral position, pushing out the legs, lifting and flattening out the pelvis, softening the groin area. Lifting the skull to push the neck toward the tailbone, then bringing the head back to the floor, in all ways easing the body. Then she enhanced the effect by mixing it with a relaxation exercise. "Starting at your feet, relax your toes, one by one. The arches of your feet, your ankles..."

She progressed up the body, one muscle group at a time, and for each he relaxed, she was sure hers tensed and quivered further, because her mind was following that progression up every inch of his body. Things were throbbing between her thighs that never throbbed. Or hadn't in recent memory. She wasn't going to survive this. She became vicious with herself, imagined the humiliation of jumping him like some sex-starved spinster... She wasn't able to be anything like what he would want. She wasn't young, beautiful. Her breasts weren't bad, but they certainly didn't sit up high and firm as they once had. She had stretch marks, as well as the soft pouch at her stomach many mothers and post-forty women had, only she didn't have the child to show for it.

Most importantly, she wasn't able to have an orgasm. That cinched it, right? Faking one for her fantasy would shatter her soul.

Thank God, the five minutes were up. Rolling away from him, she went into the fetal position. It was supposed to comfort, a symbolic return to the womb, a lovely way to finish a practice and come out of it energized, as if newly born. Instead, it reminded her of the many days she'd spent in that position beneath her covers after Kyle was killed, after Cole had left her for good. She hadn't bathed, hadn't brushed her teeth. She'd embraced her malodorous self. A shower was an offensive mockery, a dead heart pretending to be alive.

A few more minutes and it would be over. She'd thank him for coming, offer the *namaste*, say she had an appointment of some vague origin and make her escape. She'd go home to her sanctuary and pull it back together again.

Then he shifted on his mat. He was right behind her, his arm sliding around her waist, his body curving in behind hers, that incredibly emotional spooning position, her bottom cradled in his lap as he brought his knees up behind hers. His chest was against her shoulder blades, his breath on the back of her neck. He was so close to her, he had to have his other arm crooked beneath his head.

"What are you doing?" She didn't pull away, despite the alarm her tone revealed. He was firm in all the right places, strong and male. Rather than a frontal attack, a kiss or a pass she could rebuff, he'd chosen this, something warmly intimate.

What she'd assumed were fanciful imaginings might be frightful truth—that he could read her needs so easily it was like breathing.

"What I want. Sssh. Be still. And I mean that at all levels. Still your mind, Rachel, the same way you just stilled your body, one tense bundle of thoughts at a time, and give yourself to me. You don't need to think."

In truth, all she could think about was that arm around her waist, his hand against her abdomen, the fingers spread so his forefinger rested right below her breast, his smallest finger on her lower abdomen, near the crease of hip and thigh that made a lap. With her backside nestled into his lap, she felt the shape of him, the way his cock stirred against her. It made her worry, her hand closing over his anxiously.

"Sssh. Obey me, Rachel. We're going to lie here. That's all I'm going to allow to happen."

Not, "I'm not going to ask or demand anything of you". This was all he required and would permit. It amazed, aroused and soothed her at once, a peculiar triad that made her hand tighten over his further until he loosened her grip, reversed it so he had her wrist manacled, their two hands tangled beneath her breasts. Then he touched the wedding band. When he pinched it between his thumb and forefinger, taking hold of it, her hand curled into a defensive ball. He stilled.

"Open your hand, Rachel, and stretch out your fingers."

A simple command. No coaxing, no reasoning. She closed her eyes. She couldn't get lost in this. She couldn't. But her fingers were listening, straightening, no matter the rapid-fire protestations from her brain. Whoever said the body couldn't function separately from the mind was full of crap.

When he slid the band off, she looked down at it. A fifty-dollar wedding band from a jewelry store. Cheap, yes, but she'd still felt like a liar when she'd bought it, knowing it mocked something supposed to be sacred. It was why she'd put her own wedding set away and then ultimately pawned it, though it had torn something loose in her soul when she did it, all that symbolism now up for sale.

He set the fake ring on its side on the wood floor in front of her. With a deft flick, he sent it rolling. She watched the candlelight flash off it as it traveled a few feet away and then toppled on its side, rocking back and forth, devolving into that tinny vibration as it settled.

"What do you want, Rachel?" His voice was a breath in her ear. "Tell me."

Had he known this was the best time to ask a person for a truthful, painful answer? There were no lies during yoga *nidra*, because there was no room for artifice. Of course, what she wanted was a tangled mess. "I don't know," was a pitifully inadequate answer, but what she wanted had been buried under others' expectations and her own disappointments. Nearly twenty years of them.

Yet she knew something was still buried alive under all that. There'd been a time when she'd woken from nightmares, imagining it screaming with terror and need, afraid that it wasn't being heard or—even worse—heard and ignored. But she'd learned her needs weren't relevant, and never had been. There was nothing so pathetic as a false sense of importance in the universe.

Rolling away from him, she got to her feet. As she did, she stepped on the wedding band, which made a harsh squeak against the wood floor. Bending, she picked up the ring. As her fists clenched, it cut a circle into her palm. It was a pose more suited to a self-defense class than yoga, but the body adapted to what was needed, a preservation instinct.

"I can't do this, Jon. I appreciate it, but…" She shook her head, started over. "I've learned not to want things, at least not so fiercely. I don't have that kind of energy anymore." *That kind of strength.*

Settled wasn't as horrible as it sounded. Like sediment at the bottom of the lake, she could look up and appreciate the sparkles of sunlight on the water, the change in seasons. The things that flitted by so fast, so vibrantly, leaving her behind, she'd accepted. There was no getting it all. She'd traded everything for peace, because her life had literally depended on it. She refused to regret it. Couldn't afford to regret it.

He was still lying on his side, his head propped on his hand, and it flustered her, that he could lay there, looking up at her, and still seem so in control. That steady gaze was taking in every detail of her flustered condition, lingering over her breasts, their rise and fall betraying the shortness of her breath. Then he rose, one graceful flow of motion that nevertheless had her skittering back two steps as if he'd leapt toward her like a wild animal. He cocked his head.

"Do you want to know what I want?"

She couldn't answer, but it didn't matter. He took silence as assent.

"I'd like to do that routine we just did, but I'd like to see you do it naked. I'd like to see you in that Sleeping Thunderbolt pose, make you hold it while I stroked your thighs, and let my fingers stray up your body, from your clit to the base of your throat. I want to feel you quiver under my touch."

Her mouth opened, soundless. But he was continuing. "I'd do that for as long as I liked, then I'd take you into the shower. I'd blindfold you, make you kneel in the corner where the steam would keep you warm. I'd enjoy looking at you while I washed myself. You'd sit up straight, your hands clasped at your lower back, your breasts thrust out for me. Your knees would be spread, steam teasing your cunt lips, making you even wetter. You'd stay in that position, knowing nothing was required but to sit like that while I took my fill of viewing what was mine. And it would drive you as crazy as it would drive me, until I'd be so hard I'd have to fuck you against the shower wall."

As he'd spoken, he'd started moving toward her. Slow, deliberate steps, and it wasn't until her back hit two walls she realized she'd matched his pace, letting him back her into a corner. He laid a palm against one wall, then the other, so she'd have to duck under those long arms to get past him. Nothing was touching her, but she could feel every plane and curve of him, wanted all of it.

When she moistened her lips, she could tell his eyes registered not only the motion but the thoughts behind it. It wouldn't surprise her if his mind could follow hers like a hound tracking a scent, see what she was imagining in such detail.

I want to be on my knees in that shower. If I stayed very still and on display for him, he might give me permission to taste his cock, make him even harder. And when he came, I'd take every drop down my throat. Then he'd lift me up on the wall and pin me there, take me hard as he said, until I screamed out with every raw, painful need bottled inside for way too long. I would die that way, and that would be okay.

He leaned up close, breath a heated touch on her face like the imagined shower steam. "Your eyes are so hungry, Rachel. You hear what I want and you tremble, your skin flushing and nipples hardening." His body was against hers, a brush of contact against the tight points, and she bit down on a moan. "You say you've learned not to want things so fiercely. Next time I see you, I dare you to say that to me again."

She closed her eyes. His mouth touched hers, another featherlight contact. Then coolness enveloped her, a draft of air. When she opened her eyes, the heavy sense of loss warning her, she was alone. Her body was doing everything he'd said it was, but it was her heart that reacted the most strongly.

It ached, as if engulfed in an oil fire that would never stop burning.

Chapter Three

ᔕᑡ

She did her job on Monday, but it was like a hive of bees had been loosed in her head, driving her to distraction with their frenetic buzzing. As the day progressed, they migrated out through her body, crawling under her skin until she wanted to scream and claw the incessant irritation away. Sunday night she'd put her hands between her legs, rubbing uselessly, nothing there responding, even though she was wet just from the memory of Jon curved behind her, his cock against her ass. She'd known this would happen, hadn't she? She was back in that place where her whole world seemed to be narrowing, darkening, and it scared her. She had so many feelings running through her she didn't know whether to eat a consolation tub of ice cream or throw up what little she'd been able to eat.

All through her morning therapy sessions, she had a steel spring in her lower belly, tight enough to launch a cannonball. By lunch, she couldn't handle anymore. She had to act or she would go insane.

There was a BDSM club in Baton Rouge. She'd found out about it a long time ago, when she'd lurked on D/s sites. Places where the open chat rooms felt like virtual meat markets, and the Doms' online personas made her feel small and shrinking. She hadn't been to such sites in a very long time, but during her sleepless Sunday night, she'd searched on the name of the club specifically—Club More, Baton Rouge. Perversely, she hoped it had closed down, putting it beyond the reach of temptation, but it was still there, with a current revision date for the website. Very little other information was provided, except the cover charge, operation hours and an offer to join the club mailing list she declined.

Regardless, the name—*More*—felt like a sign, an arrow demanding she go in that direction. She knew she was feverish, manic and it was the wrong thing to do, but no one would know her, and if it was a complete disaster, she could put this to rest once and for all. Jon called late afternoon when she was handling another appointment. When she saw the message show up on her cell phone, she forced herself to hit the delete button, even as her heart screamed at her as if betrayed.

She had to get herself back in control before she exposed herself to more of his irresistible persuasion. He didn't understand that she couldn't do this. Unfortunately, the rest of her didn't understand either, and she had to fix that. Prove it was a mistake or see if she was strong enough to go down the path he'd re-opened in front of her. And she wanted to take that test alone, away from the eyes of anyone who knew her.

She had no idea what to wear. When she got home, she settled for a pair of dark slacks she thought hugged her curves in the right places and a thin white blouse. Under it, she wore a sexy black demi-cup bra. Severe blacks and whites, like her severe state of mind. Until she'd pawed through her mostly mundane underwear drawer, she hadn't realized she still had the bra. It was something she'd worn for Cole a few times. It seemed patently appropriate to wear something of that life, so that she could remember why she couldn't do this. Which of course didn't quell her wary anticipation, her determination to go forward with it, test it under extreme circumstances. She didn't know if she wanted to pass or fail this test, or if it would be the same thing either way. God, she was a pathetic fool.

It was in a seedy area of town, but that didn't concern her. She knew as well as anyone that adult clubs weren't accepted by the mainstream, fetish clubs least of all, and so they were relegated to industrial districts and trashy areas frequented by the criminal element. She had a Taser and pepper spray in her purse, and she knew to stay alert. There were about fifty cars in the parking lot, and at least there was a doorman. She saw him when she pulled up, a bouncer type all in black, with the club logo on his shirt. It was reassuring, but it was the only thing that was. She sat in her car, staring at that door. A black, one-story rectangular building with metal sides, like a squat warehouse. No windows of course. The chat rooms had said the appearance of such places could be deceptive, right?

That doorman was approaching her car. She had a flash of panic, then she rolled down the window. His day's growth of beard made him look even more intimidating. Before she could speak, he assessed her in one glance. "You here to find a Master?"

She moistened her lips. "I...yes. I think so. I've never — "

"Shut up, slut. You'll speak when spoken to. Give me twenty dollars for the cover charge."

She pulled it out with shaking fingers. There were safe words, boundaries. They would observe them. This was part of the role playing, getting into the atmosphere. She got out, prudent enough to lock the car, but then she gasped as he shoved her back against the closed car door. "Put your hands on your head. I'm going to frisk you for weapons."

Okay, now she wasn't sure. Her mind wasn't keeping up though. He took hold of the front of her blouse and ripped it open with one jerk, his gaze crawling over her breasts, quivering in the demi-cups. "Nice tits. They'll like that. Want to clamp those babies, make them black and blue." He put his hands on them, squeezing them as if they were market produce, in an efficient, functional manner, then worked his hands down her body, over her hips, bringing one large hand up between her legs. "Spread them," he barked. "This cunt is up for grabs tonight. You keep these legs open for any Master who wants to feel."

He spun her then, ran his hands over her ass. Her heart was rabbiting in her throat, but she couldn't stop him. She didn't know how to say no. Which was exactly what she'd feared, right? She'd wanted to bring this into her life so badly, she would take even this in silence, for the hope that something better, something more "right", was behind that door. She yelped as he snagged the upswept twist she'd done with her hair and dragged her by it toward the door. "When we walk in, you get on your knees, in line with the others. You're late. You must not have gotten the latest from Mistress Natasha about the time change. They're about to assign the meat for the night. You almost missed your chance."

There was no time to stammer out a reply or question. She was thrust into gloom. Sweat and alcohol permeated the atmosphere, as well as a dank underside, perhaps from a past flooding that had gotten into the carpet, seeping under the cheap metal walls. She had a brief impression of a narrow stage, where a naked girl was suspended by her wrists. She cried out as she was tapped by what appeared to be a cattle prod. Sparks flew from it, and there was a fresh brand on her flank, the skin red around it and the brazier still set up with ominous intent in the corner. A Master fucked her with a large vibrator. The girl was crying, yet shuddering with what appeared to be an impending climax.

"Knees," her keeper barked, shoving Rachel down so she not only landed on her knees but fell forward. Before she could rise, a foot was on her neck. At close range, the vile-smelling carpet added a combination of cigarette smoke and other unthinkable bodily functions.

"You'll obey instantly, slave, or you'll be up on that stage next." A new voice, deep and gravelly, issued that terrifying prediction. It was underscored by the icy trill of a woman's cruel laughter.

"This one's new. Turn her over and let's see what we've got."

She was rolled over by rough hands and pulled to her feet. Her hair had fallen out of the polished sticks she'd used to make the style appealing, exotic. But now it was disheveled, a rat's nest falling around her shoulders and in her eyes. Tears she couldn't stop were probably making her mascara run. With her blouse torn open, she probably looked like an attempted rape. Even as she recognized that seemed like the preferred dress code, her chaotic needs ignored it, kept clawing at her, making her helpless.

"Nice." The gravelly voice belonged to a man dressed in only a body harness. His cock was cinched tight in a leather and silver sleeve. Even semi-erect, the organ seemed thick as her forearm, and just as long. "It'll be my pleasure to break this one in for you, Mistress Natasha."

The woman standing next to him was clad in latex. She had fire-red lips and kohl-rimmed eyes, and fingered a whip coiled around her waist. "Give her a good ass fucking for me, Milo. I want to hear her scream when you're deep in her hole, then we'll put her on the flogging post and I'll make that lily white skin red as a split strawberry."

"No..." She was breathing fast. Hands came out of the darkness, holding her arms, pulling at her clothes. "No, I don't want...I need to go, I—"

An explosion of pain and her head snapped back on her neck. She stared at Milo, stunned, as he followed through with the backhand. She'd never been hit in the face in her entire life, and it hurt more than she could say, that searing pain across the cheekbone and lip. She tasted blood. He kept the hand lifted. "You want to sass your Mistress or me again, little slave cunt?"

Something burst in her then, a volcano erupting. The docile and helpless side vanished and she was fighting, snarling in terror. She'd known this was a mistake, but this was beyond a mistake. It was blatant, staggering proof that what she wanted was beyond her reach, that she'd devolved into the most unimaginable, idiotic folly.

So what the fuck's your fantasy, Rachel? Letting me and my golf buddies gang rape you in an alley? Leaving you in some bum's vomit and piss? Is that what gets you hot?

"Stop, stop, stop." She was screaming at the top of her lungs, and the hands unexpectedly released her. When she stumbled against heated bodies in various states of undress, by some miracle she found her way through them to the heavy metal door. She pushed out of it with both hands, the doorman staring at her as she staggered onto the broken and uneven pavement. She'd left her purse in her car, with her pepper spray and Taser, but she didn't think she could have used them anyhow. She was shaking so badly, she stumbled and fell, scraping her hands and ripping her slacks. It was her favorite pair, because they'd always made her feel sexy and feminine when she wore them. She was going to burn them as soon as she got home.

When hands closed on her arm, she shrieked and rolled to her back, striking out.

"Easy there, it's okay. Calm down. I'm a police officer."

The voice was a new one, and unlike Milo or the doorman, it projected firm, steady authority. Not a roaring bark that made her stomach jump as if it had been goaded by that cattle prod. When she managed to stop thrashing, she blinked up at this man. Built with the broad, solid lines of a football player, he was clean shaven, with shrewd, cynical gold-brown eyes. After taking in the jeans and dress shirt, she zeroed in on the shoulder holster for his gun beneath the open coat. Recognizing he probably was what he said he was brought knee-shaking relief, as well as mortified horror, imagining herself on some evening news program.

"Are you all right, ma'am?" He asked it in a tone that, to her way of thinking, sounded like "another twisted deviant hanging out where no decent person went". She stared up at him and didn't know what to say.

No, I'm lost. So lost, I'm not sure I'll find my way back this time.

He studied her, then crouched to a squat. "This is my badge," he said, pulling it out of the inside pocket for her to see. "I just went off shift and changed into my street clothes."

She should have asked for that proof herself, but she wasn't thinking clearly enough to manage it. When the doorman strode toward them, she shrank toward the cop, though she despised the weakness of it. The hand he put on her shoulder was surprisingly reassuring, as were his words. "It's all right, miss. Cyrus, what the hell's happening here?"

Cyrus stopped, gave her a look that was a mixture of disgust and exasperation. "Natasha's having one of her private parties. Ten girls. I was told to give them the full treatment when they pulled in. I didn't know she'd freak out. Natasha usually goes for the really hardcore ones."

"I...I didn't know it was a p-private p-party... I just c-came... Website..." Rachel shut her mouth, closing her eyes. She wished she was back on her cushioned mat in her studio, Jon behind her. His simplest command had made her feel quiet and still. Unsettled, in a good way. Not frightened and humiliated, not like this.

"Oh fuck." Cyrus swore. "Keller, come on. I didn't know she wasn't one of the guests."

"Goddamn it, Cyrus, we've discussed this before. You guys take way too many fucking risks. She has every right to bring assault charges against you and anyone else in that club who manhandled her, and it would serve you right. I'd love to throw your asses in that jail cell."

"I don't w-want...I j-just w-want t-t-to go..." She was fast losing the ability to talk, and the policeman seemed to realize it, because he curled a strong arm around her, rubbing her back in easy, firm strokes.

"You're going to come with me, calm down and then we'll talk and see what you want to do, miss. For right now, you take it easy." He threw a glower at Cyrus. "You tell Natasha to keep her floor show inside from now on. She damn well better have an acceptable vetting process at her door by tomorrow night, or I'll find every possible freaking code violation in this cesspool. I suppose if someone's grandmother had pulled up asking for directions, you'd have mauled her as well?"

"Fuck, she was dressed for it, Keller. Maybe not as blatantly as—"

Rachel had her forehead pressed into Officer Keller's lapel, so she felt a hardening of impressive chest muscles that matched the sudden, deadly tone in the cop's voice.

"Trust me, Cyrus. Don't go down the 'she was asking for it because of the way she was dressed' road. I'll run your ass over."

He didn't wait for a response, not that she ever heard Cyrus give one. Though her teeth were chattering, she was cognizant of Cyrus thankfully retreating to the door, muttering. The officer helped her to her feet, keeping a supportive arm around her.

"Here we go." He was directing her toward her car. "Ma'am, my name is Sergeant Leland Keller. I don't have a vehicle here because I just got off shift. We're near my place, and I was picking up dinner at that corner deli over there. But I tell you what we're going to do. We're going to take your car to our precinct and I'm going to get a cup of coffee into you. We'll let you clean yourself up and then we'll talk, all right? And if you want a female officer, we have plenty of those."

She shook her head. "Want to go h-home."

"Well, you're not doing that until I'm sure you're okay, so there's not going to be any arguing on that point, all right?" With that unrelenting assertion, he took her keys from her, still somehow clenched in her fist, so tight the metal had left impressions in her palm. Opening the passenger side, he folded her into the seat, secured her seatbelt around her and then closed the door. As he maneuvered his long frame into the driver's side, sliding back the seat to accommodate him in the little compact, he gave her a penetrating glance. "Besides, I don't think you want to go home to your husband looking like that."

"Husband?" She followed his look to her left hand, the pale band of pigment that stood out so starkly there. She hadn't put the ring back on once Jon had taken it off, a significant statement of its own. However, at the sergeant's assumption, a hard spike of sobs tried to choke her breath again. "I'm not...married. Long story...but not married. No one. I have no one."

It sounded so pathetic, said like that, but she laid her head back against the seat, too tired to say anything else. She didn't want anything now except numbness.

Mission accomplished, right? In spades.

As Sergeant Keller put the car into drive, she stared into the side mirror at the retreating club. It looked like a demon crouched underneath a moonless sky, satisfied that it had devoured another soul.

* * * * *

The police precinct was as cheerless as she expected. Dingy tile, fluorescent lighting. Sidelong glances from jaded eyes that had seen it all. Sergeant Keller continued to be kind and attentive, however. Rather than fishing through the lost-and-found, he brought her a clean T-shirt from his own locker and a washcloth to use in the bathroom. Once there, she took one look at her face in the mirror under the harsh lighting — blood on her mouth, tear tracks, smeared mascara. All of it accentuated the crow's feet at her eyes and stress lines around her taut mouth. She didn't look again, except to steal quick glances to ensure she'd wiped all of it away that she could.

She'd been so rattled she'd left her purse at Leland Keller's desk, but it didn't matter. Any touch-up would look like clown makeup. Milo apparently had a hand the size of a tennis racket, for her cheek, eye and lip on the right side were swelling. The blouse had been stained with blood from the split lip.

The cotton T-shirt fell to her knees, almost hiding the rip in her slacks. Because one of her heels had broken in the parking lot and the other had been left behind, they'd also given her a pair of sneakers from the lost-and-found that were only about one size too big. She stuffed the broken shoe in the trash along with the blouse and came back out, following an officer's direction to Sergeant Keller's area.

He rose at the sight of her, gestured her to his guest chair. "You look better. Hot compresses and a good bath should help, a few aspirin." He touched her face, tilting it away from him, and his jaw hardened. The way he touched her, so easy and confident, made her go still. Desperately, she told herself it was a police thing, the female perception of safety, protection. Believing anything else meant that she was going to have to tear out her mind, because it seemed the only way to stop it from going down this path over and over again.

While she believed in Fate, karma and the forces that drove destiny, she couldn't possibly believe that suddenly Doms were everywhere, like a damn convention was in town. She'd gone years without meeting a single one outside of the Internet, after all. It was far more likely she was starting to hallucinate, like a crack addict snorting up everything from salt to talcum powder, or ground glass.

He released her at last, gave her a nod. "Yeah, you'll be all right. That would be Milo's handiwork there. They're a hardcore pain club, miss. They dish it out without causing ER visits or police reports, mostly, but they sure as hell don't observe enough of the rules for the things they do. It results in what you experienced tonight, among other things. I know you were pretty upset when I found you. Were you checking out the club...or were you lost and seeking directions?"

He asked it with a carefully straight face, giving her the out for her dignity, but she thought lying to a cop would be far more humiliating. "I was checking it out. I thought..." As her voice quavered, he pushed a hot cup of coffee into her hands. She clasped the warmth to her, inhaling the familiar scent of coffee beans. Something normal. "I made a mistake, is all."

"That's as may be, but a mistake shouldn't lead to this." He gestured to her face and general state. "I wasn't just trying to spook Cyrus, miss. You have every right to file assault charges. They didn't ask you for your consent, did they? Didn't have you sign anything coming in the door or go over any safety restrictions, health issues?"

She shook her head. "He asked for twenty dollars. I gave it to him. I guess a court would say that was consent. It doesn't matter anyway. The fact I sought out a club like that would tell a judge or jury everything they'd want to hear. I'm not stupid, despite the fact I did something very stupid tonight."

"Now, miss—"

"I overheard two of the female police officers talking about me when I went into the bathroom." She made herself say it aloud. She needed to hear it, needed to write it on every mirror in her house, to remind her of the way it had felt, the way it all felt. "'Stupid bitch wanted a man to beat her like a dog, and then chickened out. I'd have left her there.'"

Drawing a breath, she straightened in the chair, though every bone in her body wanted to slump in defeated dejection. But she managed to sound calm, meet his gaze. "I have no desire to expose my life to public ridicule, and this is the kind of story that court reporters love to stumble upon, don't they?"

Leland's eyes had flashed, his glance snapping toward the exact two female cops, alarming her. But registering her tension, he spoke mildly, his shoulders easing a fraction. "They shouldn't have said that. It's just that a lot of people don't understand what it is you're seeking."

She nodded wearily and rose, fumbling for her purse. "I'm one of them." Drawing her pride around her as best she could, she extended a hand. "Thank you for your help, Sergeant Keller. I don't care to file charges, and you won't need to rescue me from such a place again. I can promise you that."

He rose as well, clasping her hand rather than shaking it. He had golden-brown hair to go with those golden-brown eyes. He reminded her of a bear. A handsome, appealing bear, capable of impressive ferocity but also tenderness, like his touch now.

"I've tucked my card in your purse. If you need anything, or reconsider, you give me a call."

She nodded again, but she was already pulling away. The need to get to her haven, to close the door on the whole world, was a steady cord reeling her toward home. She'd take a couple days off, have her backups fill in for her appointments and classes. She'd give herself forty-eight hours under the covers, with the drone of daytime TV and the stifled sound of her own sobs, and she'd pull it together again.

Then she'd renew her personal vow to herself. She'd never, ever go down this road again. She'd known better from the beginning.

* * * * *

After the pretty blonde left, Leland sat back down at his desk. It wasn't exactly protocol to go through a victim's purse, but when he'd tucked his card into the side pocket, he'd seen another card. He'd been bothered by her broken admission that there was no one else in her life, and so he'd sneaked a glance. After tonight's events, it was the last name he would have expected to see there. When he dialed the number, Jon picked up before the second ring finished.

"Leland. What the hell? You know it's one in the morning, right?"

"Don't hand me that shit. You're in that mad scientist home laboratory of yours, breaking all sorts of hazardous material laws to figure out how to turn the universe inside out. Or tuning up a device to give a woman so many orgasms in one go you'll never lack for pussy again."

"Been there, done that."

"Oh yeah? Which one?"

"Both, of course. What's your excuse for being at work so late? Shouldn't you be in that dump apartment of yours, drinking your once-a-night beer and eating your convenience store nacho package before you go to sleep to ESPN recaps? Can't imagine why some woman hasn't snapped your exciting ass right up."

"Blow me. No, I'm up because I just pulled a woman out of a tricky situation. A woman carrying your card in her purse. Rachel Madison?"

Jon's tone went from lazy insult to sharp attention, a knife striking stone. "Is she all right? Where is she?"

"She's fine. Gone home and will likely sleep it off." After a considering pause, Leland gave him the immediate details. There was the code he observed as a cop, and the code he observed as a Dom, and he didn't mind bending the rules a bit in either direction when it made sense. When it was to protect someone who obviously needed some help.

"She said she had no one. Which I expected was true, since if I had a girlfriend and she went off to a place like that at all, let alone on her own, she wouldn't sit comfortably for a week." He let the statement hang out there, intending the mild note of accusation, but Jon's instant response reassured him on that score.

"We're not involved like that. But I was headed that way. I didn't know she was there. It's not going to happen again."

The man typically emanated tranquil vibes like a damn lava lamp. The whip-taut tension Leland heard was a radical change. "Hmm. When I saw your card, I thought she might be one of your occasional sub-with-benefits friends. But you usually pick them smarter than that."

"She's smart. Just hasn't figured out that part of things yet. You know how that can be, at the beginning."

"Yeah." Leland sobered. "Classy lady. She belonged in that crowd the way a swan belongs among a bunch of carrion eaters."

"That's been Club More's MO since they opened. Don't worry about them, Leland. I'll be passing on this tidbit to Matt tomorrow. By the end of the week, Ben'll have dug up so many legal problems with the place they'll have to convert to a Dunkin' Donuts."

"Good. I like their coffee."

"Damn it. This is my fault." The sigh on Jon's side was followed by an ominous tone. "It's a mistake I'm going to fix."

"Sounds good. But give her the night, Jon." Leland paused, hesitating over the other part. Weighed the pros and cons, what he knew of Jon, what his gut told him, and said it out loud. "I ran a check on her. Pretty standard thing in this situation, but came up with something that happened four years ago. She was cleaning a gun and it went off. Grazed her neck, the bullet went through her window and lodged in the outer wall of the adjacent building. It was called in by a startled landlord when he heard the shot, saw her come out onto her balcony with blood on her neck and the gun in her hand. She looked a little out of it. It all got worked out, of course, and was logged as a simple accident, no harm done."

Jon's voice was tight. "She's thorough and careful. Detail-oriented."

"Yeah, well, everyone can make a mistake. But you're already following the right track. The officer who was called out, a rookie, had a different take. No proof, so no action taken on it, just a sticky in the file. Anyhow, the kid thought it was an attempted suicide. Powell has good instincts. He's in narcotics now. He took it upon himself to check on her a couple times after that, noted she seemed on a more even keel, had opened a yoga studio, so over time he assumed he was either mistaken or she'd gotten herself straightened out."

The silence was long and weighted, and Leland's brow creased. "You okay?"

"She's a friend, Leland. And more than that."

"Yeah, I get that impression." Knowing the man's nature as he knew his own, Leland had a pretty good idea what might be roiling in Jon right now. It was probably best for Rachel not to be exposed to it tonight. "I know you want to go be with her and take care of this, but trust me. If you don't have a relationship in play between you yet, you'll want to give her about a day. She's pretty damn raw and vulnerable right now. She didn't strike me as someone on the suicidal edge again, but she needs time to pull herself together, feel like no one knows except a nosy cop in the wrong place at the right time."

"Thanks, Oprah." But Jon blew out a breath after another long moment. "I know you're right. I need to get my mind wrapped around how to handle it. She's complicated. A lot of layers I don't yet understand, and you gave me a missing piece I should have taken the time to see before I... Goddamn it, I don't want her to be alone with this. *Fuck.*"

Leland didn't bother to suppress a grim smile at the sound of something crashing, perhaps accidentally knocked off a table—or knocked off deliberately—and the stream of curses that followed. Despite the serious circumstances, he wished he had a recorder so he could play this for the other guys of Jon's team who were used to him being so irritatingly placid under pressure. Now that he figured the woman was in good hands, Leland could enjoy the break from pattern, though he was smart enough not to goad. Much.

"Try some of those 'ohms' you do," he said encouragingly. "You know, that lotus thing, with the fingers all arranged in a circle."

He chuckled as the phone disconnected with a definitive click, and replaced his own receiver. Damn, it was late, and he'd volunteered to take Ramirez's early shift tomorrow. Maybe he'd get one of the guys to drop him off at the corner, so he could get some more packaged nachos from Raj. Checking his watch, he thought he could still catch the two a.m. ESPN wrap-up, after all.

After tonight's events, he thought he'd be dreaming of the curvy, perfect submissive he'd yet to find. The one who would wear his collar and nothing else to bed. He'd curl his large body around her like a protective panther and know she was

51

all his, one hand cupped around her generous breast, the nipple teasing his palm as he nested his cock in the crevice of her soft ass. They'd dream the night away together.

He hoped Jon was on the way to finding a similar treasure. Something in the serious hazel eyes of the blonde, the set of that pink mouth, the dignified way she'd managed to straighten up at the end, said she might be the kind of pure gold every man sought. That every Master needed.

Chapter Four

❧

When she got home that night, Rachel took a thorough shower, knowing it would be her last one for a while. She woke briefly in the early morning to call in a replacement to her PT appointments and yoga classes for the next two days. Since she had two reliable backups who were always looking for extra money, they were eager to take the slots and didn't ask her many questions, letting her get off the phone as quickly as possible. The relief that she'd be missing Dana's appointment was tangled with a disappointment that only made her more viciously ashamed of herself.

For the next day and a half, she buried herself under her covers, left the TV on and slept. So very, very tired, she didn't care about anything. But she'd been down this road before, and she knew how to manage it. She'd give herself the two days for uninterrupted numbness and self-pity, but on Day Three, she'd make herself get up and resume her life, no matter how impossible that sounded from the dark cocoon of her comforter right now.

Tears spilled out now and again, as she drifted back in time and sobbed for all the losses that had led to this, as if the pain of what had happened at Club More wasn't excruciating enough. Every time she thought about it, she cringed, trying to block the humiliation and fear she'd felt. Once, long ago, she'd called her cravings a harmless fantasy. Not only had what she'd experienced from Milo and Natasha been far from harmless, but in truth, the fantasy that had driven her there had been part of the barbs that tore at the fabric of her marriage, helping to unravel it.

She took aspirin and put compresses on her face, but more often than not, she just slept. She thought about Jon, cried about what he represented. Of all the things she'd have to face on Day Three, he was the one that frightened her most. Maybe she should go ahead and take her full two weeks' vacation. It wasn't like she was going to use it for anything else. If she could afford it, which she couldn't, she'd take a whole month. She wished she could get caught in a time vortex like in the movies, where she could sleep for days and days and then wake up at the same date she'd gone under, not having been missed or harassed by anyone who wanted something from her.

Still deep in that mode, it irritated her intensely when, on the afternoon of Day Two, there was an insistent knocking on her apartment door. She ignored it at first, because she didn't have friends close enough to visit her at home, and the time of day ruled out any of her working neighbors being home and needing anything. So all that left was the rare door-to-door sales attempt in the apartment complex, and she for sure wasn't dealing with that today. However, when it continued, became more insistent, she stumbled out of bed, swiping her hair out of her face. Making her way to the door through the living area and kitchen, she peered out the peephole.

Oh God. No way was she opening the door to him, not looking like this. And why the hell was he here?

"Rachel." No question in his tone. He knew she was there. "Open the door."

"I...I have the flu, Jon. Whatever you need, I'll help you whenever I get back to class." Which was a ludicrous thing to say, since he could hardly be here for some mundane reason. He shouldn't know her address or anything else about her.

"You don't have the flu. Open the door. Now."

He didn't raise his voice. The words were quiet, smooth, yet there was that note in them she'd never experienced in such a targeted way. This was an undeniable command, and it shot through her chest, sending an unusual tremor through her limbs. Definitely not a good idea to answer the door.

Oh for God's sake, she was a grown woman. "Jon, I don't know what this is about, but it's not appropriate for you to be—"

"It's not appropriate for you to be going to some sleazy dive where you could get yourself raped or worse. You'll open this door right now, and I wouldn't suggest you make me repeat myself again."

Shock took over, followed by an uncertain spurt of anger, but it was enough to have her unlatching the door and pulling it open, heedless of how she might appear. "How did you—"

When she opened the door, he was standing almost in the threshold. The recalled violence of nearly thirty-six hours ago was enough to make her step back with a startled cry, her angry words caught in her throat.

A range of expressions crossed his face. First, he registered her fear. Then his gaze covered the bruise on her cheek, the swollen eye and lip. The one brought a look of gentle caution, the other a flash of fury that he tamped down with obvious effort.

He took two steps inside. She backed up but gripped the door, dizzy because of the shock of seeing him, and because she'd stumbled out of bed with very little on her stomach. Before she could evade him, he slid an arm around her back to hold her in place. Then he bent to put another under her knees and lifted her off her feet.

Just like that. Like instead of a woman who hadn't showered, who had oily, limp hair and was wearing her warmest, thickest flannel pajamas that caught under her heels and flapped over her wrists, she was some fragile, beautiful heroine with flowing hair and silky lingerie. A heroine who could trust him to carry her to safety. She could curl her arms around his shoulders, which seemed broad enough, his lean frame notwithstanding, and bury her face into his shoulder, reassured by his male scent. And not just any male. A male who would protect a woman, who would care for her, no matter what. Who didn't question or resent that but considered it a duty, a privilege and, beyond that, a deep, abiding desire.

She was embarrassed that he was seeing her small apartment like this. She usually kept it clean and cleansed, a tranquil space for reading, meditation, regrouping. But the clothes she'd worn to the club were still crumpled beside the coffee table, her purse left there. In the kitchen, dishes piled in the sink and dirty countertops showed the remains of the lackluster meals she'd made. Though he seemed to take all that in with a quick glance, his steps didn't falter as he headed for her bedroom, following the easy-to-discern path to it.

She'd never had a man carry her. Didn't even remember her deceased father doing that, because the last time it had happened she'd likely been too young to remember it. She'd scoffed at the way they did it in the movies, so smooth and easy, even if the woman wasn't expecting it or resisted, which would, in reality, result in an awkward flurry of limbs, a hitch in his movements to handle her weight. With her yoga muscles, heavy breasts and curvy hips, she was a solid one-thirty, but he'd plucked her off her feet as if she weighed much less. But of course, this was a man who could easily hold his own weight on his arms.

She'd started shaking again and she didn't want to fall to pieces. But it was as if her body and mind had been waiting specifically for this. While she was apprehensive, she couldn't deny pretty much every part of her was glad to have him here. And that was bad.

Laying her down in the rumpled nest of covers, he planted his very fine backside on the edge of her bed, keeping her hemmed in. He glanced at the side table. "Aspirin and compresses?"

She shrugged. "It's the best thing for helping it do what it needs to do. What are you doing here? And how did you…"

"I came to check on you. Leland and I know one another. He noticed my card in your purse and assumed something about you that I was more than pleased to have him assume. That you're one of mine."

Digesting the mortifying shock of him knowing Leland Keller took a moment. Then she blinked. "Excuse me?"

He put a hand on her face, the uninjured side. "Rachel, why did you do this?"

When he was little, her son had taken martial arts training. For some reason, at Jon's direct look, the firmness in the hand on her cheek, she remembered one of Kyle's instructors. He'd been gentle, careful, intelligent. Yet when he helped the boys spar, there was a concentration in his gaze that suggested it was best not to underestimate the power of a gentle, focused man.

She closed her eyes. "Jon, we can't have this conversation. I can't have this conversation. It was stupid and pointless. That part of my life was over a long time ago. I'd accepted it. It was just..."

"I started something I didn't finish, and left you nowhere else to go."

"No." She opened her eyes immediately. "This was my stupid decision, Jon. You weren't responsible. I appreciate you coming by to check on me, but..."

It was as if he were weighing the significance of every word that came from her mouth, noting every minute change in her expression, the uncomfortable shift of her body. Since he was sitting on her bed, his hip brushing her thigh, he now slid his hand from her cheek to her shoulder, his thumb resting on her collarbone. It effectively stopped her babbling. She couldn't seem to continue, to tell him she was fine, that he needed to leave.

"Breathe," he said. "Like when you start your class. Three count. And keep your eyes on mine."

His thumb shifted so it was on the pulse in her throat, making short strokes there as she drew in a breath. She felt foolish, but she took that deep breath, drew it in for a count of three, even as she remained conscious of those two points of contact, his hand on her throat, his hip against her leg. When she let it out, emotion welled up in her chest, making it tighter. She got the second breath out, and it got worse, such that more tears spilled forth.

"I don't want you to see this." Her voice broke. "I can't—"

"One more," he said, not unkindly, though his hold on her throat increased, underscoring the relentless command.

It was a shudder of sobs, more than an indrawn breath, and as it crested, they broke. She'd cried a lot over the past day and a half, but this was different. This was the way a person cried when someone was there to hear, to help. Pulling her into his arms, he turned them so they were stretched out on the bed together, one of her arms wrapped around his back and the other around his neck, her face buried into his chest. He stroked her, crooned to her as she shook and cried, until she'd cried out the fear and shame, and was left limp with exhaustion.

If she was going to experience soul-deep weariness, she couldn't have asked for better immediate surroundings. He smelled like sage and sandalwood aftershave, and beneath that, more faintly, something that was like motor oil and burning wood. His hair was under her fingertips, silk she was able to stroke in nervous movements, trying to regain her composure. Since he was wearing slacks and dress shirt, his tie loosened, she realized he'd come from work. Because she'd had her cheek pressed to the tie, it was now water spotted. Drawing back enough to see it, she saw it had a subdued silhouette pattern of dark blue dolphins against a deep ocean blue, like seeing the magical creatures leaping through the waves at night.

"I like your tie," she rasped. She smoothed her hand over it, the man beneath. "What you said, 'one of mine'. I don't understand. I can't—"

His hand closed over hers, held it still. "I want to know more about you before we start talking about me," he said.

That velvet voice became irresistible when it dropped to a rumble, like now. "What did you mean when you said this part of your life was over a long time ago? Have you served a Master before?"

He made it sound so normal. Of course, it was part of his life, like yoga class or going to work. It made her want to cry again, but she had no tears left.

"No. My husband…he and I divorced some time ago, and he wasn't into that. I've never been able… I'm not really, either. I got confused. Chalk it up to midlife crisis." Her other hand pleated and worried at the tie under his grasp. Her fingers were cold compared to his.

"Hmm. So if it's never been a part of your life at all, why did you say this hasn't been part of your life in a long time?" Catching both her hands now, he brought them into a prayer *mudra* and folded his over them, giving her warmth but also bringing her gaze up that pointed direction of their fingertips, to his penetrating gaze.

"Jon." Why was she saying things she couldn't possibly explain, to him or anyone? "It was a mistake. Can we please leave it there?"

"The only mistake you're making right now is not trusting me."

"I'm not going to tell a man young enough to be my son that sex hasn't been part of my life for nearly six years." Longer, if she counted when she'd stopped being able to enjoy it.

Then she realized what she'd said, and panic clutched her stomach. If he asked her about Kyle…

"All right," he said gravely. "You don't have to tell me that. But maybe you could tell me why. And I'm only old enough to be your son if you had me when you were barely a teenager."

The relief that he hadn't taken it as a direct reference to her being a mother was quickly replaced by another sick feeling. He was going to make her say it. Despite the blow to her already nonexistent pride, maybe it would push him the necessary step back from her. It still shamed her to speak the words.

"I can't do it. I don't get...excited. Not the right way. And the things I want..." She sat up, pulling away, and huddled on the edge of the bed. She felt so worthless, used up. A whole cauldron of emotions she couldn't handle was bubbling up. Why the hell was she saying these things? Because she'd dreamed of having someone understand. No, she'd wanted someone she *loved* to understand. But no one loved her. And she was having to explain it to this handsome, charismatic man, a Master who could have anyone. Multiple anyones, such that a cop had thought she was "one of his".

The bed shifted as he rolled off the other side and came around the end of the mattress. Any other time, she would have watched him, because she loved to watch him move. But today, seeing such a thing could lacerate her heart even more deeply. She wondered if a cardiac surgeon had ever been asked to do a heart transplant merely because the heart had been slashed to ribbons from too many serrated emotions.

When he stood in front of her, she kept staring at the floor, her bare feet beneath the floppy cuffs of the pajamas braced on the bed railing. "Jon, I know this sounds so ungrateful, but can you please go? Just leave?"

"Do you want me to leave?"

"Yes." She forced it past the hard lump in her throat. *No, no, no.*

Reaching out, he stroked his hand through her limp, unwashed hair. She closed her eyes, not wanting to revel in the male strength in that touch, but unable to keep herself from turning her head into the stroke, pressing hard into the heel of his palm, holding there while his fingers made short caresses of the area around that pressure point. It was a long moment before he spoke.

"For a year, you've kept me at arm's length with that wedding ring, making me believe something that's untrue. I should have followed my intuition sooner, because I knew it didn't fit. I don't pursue married women, and yet I kept coming back to your studio, unable to stop seeing you. I asked you a question just now, and you lied to me as well. Rachel, look at me."

His fingers dropped to her chin. When she couldn't manage the motion herself, thinking of how swollen and blotched her face must look, no makeup, he forced her face up to meet his intent gaze.

"You won't lie to me again. Do you understand?"

With that trace of steel in his voice, her reality shifted. She was standing in an open doorway, and he was ordering her across the threshold. Her trembling soul recognized it, even as the rest of her wasn't yet brave enough to wrap her mind around it.

"Do you understand how to answer me, Rachel?"

She swallowed. She couldn't. He didn't know how often she'd stood here. Her dangerous decision to visit Club More had been evidence of what taking that step could do to her. There'd never been anything across that threshold except a sickening drop into disappointment, humiliation and a complete loss of self-worth. She was at the bottom of that well now, with nowhere left to go unless someone gave her a shovel to start digging. And she was terrified that was what this was.

He dropped his touch from her chin, but only to turn his hand over, offer it to her. When she placed her hand in it, his fingers closed over hers.

"Rachel."

"I can't, Jon. I'm afraid."

"Good. An honest answer." Tugging her off the bed, onto her feet, he walked backward toward her bathroom, bringing her with him. As he studied her features, his serious mouth curved unexpectedly. "You have such thick lashes," he said. "A doll's lashes. And a mouth so soft and pink, it makes me think of your pussy, how soft and pink it must be."

Words so sensual and graphic at once. Though she knew men still saw her as a sexual being, there was a significant difference between recognizing it and letting it in. Responding rather than blocking it off or neutralizing it. Her reservations, all the reasons she shouldn't be doing this, were going down the drain as if Jon had reached inside her and pulled that plug.

He switched their positions, so he was backing her over the bathroom tile, cold on her soles. Then she was on the lavender bath rug, which she scented with that herb so that the movement of her feet over the pile brought the aroma to her.

Stepping away from her, he nevertheless held onto her hands until their fingers were templed against one another. Sliding free, he turned her vanity chair around and straddled it to face her, his forearms crossed on the top and thighs braced out wide.

"Take off your clothes, Rachel."

"Wh-what?"

"You heard me." That same tone of gentle steel and steady unwavering gaze. He was pushing that door open wide inside her and she lacked the ability to shut it, to refuse him. "Remove your clothes and get in the shower. Leave the door open. I want you to wash yourself thoroughly. Do you shave your pussy?"

When a doctor asked personal things, there was a clinical detachment to it that saved it from being inappropriately intimate. The way Jon was asking her this, it was in-the-deep-end-of-the-pool intimate, but his confidence made it appropriate, as if he had every right to demand answers. Her quaking stomach wasn't disagreeing, even as her knees were beginning to wobble at what this was doing to her. As he'd proven already, this was normal for him. For her it was a dream, one that she'd had for so many years it had become a painfully obsessive addiction. Her breath was coming short again, and she reached out for the shower door to steady herself.

In an instant, he was back beside her, pressing her against the wall, holding her to him. "I'm sorry," he murmured. "You're so new to it, aren't you, beautiful?"

"I'm hardly beautiful," she managed. "Especially at the moment."

He cupped her face in both hands, and he was *so* close. "Yes, you are. Now, back to my question. Do you shave your pussy?"

"Yes."

"I thought so. Some of the leotards you've worn are pretty formfitting."

"You must have been straining your eyes."

"What good is being around lots of women in snug clothing if you don't look?" A glint of humor in those blue eyes gave her a shard of reassurance, then it broke into butterflies as he brushed her temple with his lips. "And since the teacher is the best looking one…"

She had a good amount of twenty-somethings in her classes, with figures much better than hers, but she decided she would believe him, just for a second. She wasn't up to arguing.

"No more procrastinating. I want you to bathe and shave yourself." Reaching in the shower, he turned on the hot water. She was leaning against his hip as he kept his other arm around her waist. His throat was within a breath of her mouth, so tempting. She closed her eyes to quell the urge, then opened them as he stepped out of reach again, only this time he leaned against the sink counter. "Clothes, Rachel," he said firmly.

She swallowed. She couldn't possibly, not while he was watching. "You know, formfitting or not, those leotards cover a lot of things."

"I know. That's why I want to see it all." His gaze roamed over her then came back up. "Lower your eyes, Rachel. To your feet. You'll keep your attention there unless I give you permission to look at me. Now take off your clothes."

Her stomach clutched at the order, delivered in that even, formidable tone. "Jon…"

"Obey me, beautiful. I promise it will be all right."

Unbuttoning the flannel pajama top, she slid out of that so her hair brushed her bare shoulders. He could see her breasts, the pink tips drawn tight from the chill, though she wondered if it was also the heat of his regard affecting them. Pulling the drawstring loose on the bottoms, she let them drop so she was standing in her plain cotton panties and socks. Then she slid them off, balling them up and putting them in the hamper behind her. She turned toward the shower. She would not think about the fact she was standing naked in her bathroom, in front of Jon Forte. She would jump in the shower and —

"Stop. Put your hands behind your back, fingers laced, and spread your legs shoulder width apart."

Her breath caught in her throat. It was a standard submissive pose, allowing the Master access to his slave however he wished. It made those butterflies in her stomach go wild, even as that throbbing tightness in her chest and throat started anew. It wasn't real, it wasn't true. It couldn't be, because she'd wanted it for too long. She was playing a game that had already passed her by.

She shook her head, fumbled for the towel on the bar. "Jon, this isn't going to work. I can't—"

His hand closed over her wrist. He shut off the shower, then he wrapped his other hand in her hair, pulling at the scalp in a near painful way, though his movements remained calm, unhurried.

"Down."

She wasn't sure at first what he meant, but the pressure of his hand, moving to her shoulder, made it clear. She couldn't resist him, and suddenly she was kneeling on the lavender carpet before him, his hand tethered in her hair keeping her up on her knees, her buttocks brushing her heels. The steam created by the shower caressed her bare skin with heat.

His fingers flexed. "Do you want to kneel to me, Rachel? Have you fantasized about it? Don't think, just answer."

"Yes." Her throat was clogged with tears again.

"And what did you do when you were on your knees?"

"I...put my mouth on your... You put your c-cock in my mouth."

"And what did you call me? What name did I demand you call me when you begged for more?"

Once again, it was stymied, too much debris washing in with the very thought. She couldn't speak.

"Did you masturbate when you fantasized about me like that, Rachel?"

He'd let her have that one, a pass card. She got the feeling he wouldn't give her another. "Yes."

"And did you ask my permission to come?"

"Yes." She licked her lips. He'd told her to keep her eyes down, but she was very aware that if she looked up she'd be staring right at his cock, beneath the fabric of his trousers. She wanted to see him hard and thick, swipe away the viscous fluid collected at the slit with her tongue.

You're a fucking whore...

She flinched, pulling back from his touch. "No," she said brokenly. "Please don't." *Don't ruin this.*

"Rachel." Jon was kneeling with her then, his hands on her bare shoulders even as she tried to get away from him, mortified, vulnerable beyond repair. "Ssshh. Listen to me. Hush and listen."

She stopped only because it was clear he wasn't letting her go, and he was far stronger and more determined. He had one knee on the carpet by her right knee and the other bent leg hemming in the opposite side.

"We have a long way to go, don't we?" That firm mouth had a kind curve now, his eyes compassionate. However, the intensity remained, indicating his compassion wasn't the pity she dreaded.

"You know that place of utter stillness, the one you find in meditation?" When she managed a jerky nod, he continued. "It's a place where you've let everything that burdens your mind free. All those thoughts, good or bad, peaceful or disturbing, can wander in and out of your mind like an open room. You don't try to hold onto anything or push it out. You release your will and simply be. Take a breath. Slow, even, deep. Let it go."

She managed it, though her fingers remained clutched on his forearm. Her gaze stayed on her knees, lowered as he'd demanded.

"You've been a submissive for a long time, haven't you?"

He didn't say, "you've wanted to be a submissive". He acknowledged that she was one. He spoke it as truth, validating it, pulling back every doubt, fear, accusation and ugly word as if it were rusty barbed wire that had been bound around that part of herself. Now he was pulling the barbs out, making her bleed.

"Yes. I think so." Her voice broke.

He put his mouth on the tear rolling down her cheek. It had reached the corner of her mouth, but she couldn't turn her head, make it into a full kiss. She was paralyzed, not knowing what to do.

"Yes. You are. And as far as you're concerned, from here forward, you are 'one of mine'. You understand?"

She shook her head. "You never said what that means."

"You know what it means." He straightened up so she only saw his legs, clad in the tailored slacks. Despite his command, she couldn't help letting her gaze lift when she saw he was loosening his tie further and unbuttoning his shirt. "It means I'm your Master and I'm going to take care of you, starting right now."

As the buttons were slipped, pale marble skin was revealed. A thin mat of black hair on his chest artfully narrowed to that silken line over his striated abdomen and disappeared in his slacks. There would be a tangle of black coarse hair around his cock, a light layer over his heavy testicles, unless he shaved that area. Despite her words earlier, trying to push him away, this was a grown man, not a boy. And it was clear exactly which one of them held the reins.

"Didn't I tell you to keep looking down?"

"Please, let me look." The whispered plea came before she could stop herself. "I've wanted to look at you for so long."

As he rested his hands on his belt, her attention zeroed in on the diagonal lines of muscle at his waist. "You have looked at me, Rachel. You and that wedding ring hoax put me through hell, every time I'd catch you checking me out with those hungry eyes. I had to exercise some serious mind games to keep from reacting. Those cotton pants don't hide much."

"No, they don't." A tiny smile bloomed in her heart, then on her lips, surprising her. "Particularly during Sleeping Thunderbolt."

He gave a snort. "Well, everything is wide awake now. This time, you may look. But only if you get into a submissive kneeling posture. Hands laced behind your head, ass on your heels, knees spread shoulder width apart."

She complied, mouth dry once again. He didn't give her long to look, moving around her, pausing outside of her range of vision. One fingertip drifted up her spine, a tingling sensation that made her shiver, arch.

"Better. Some Masters want the back ramrod straight. I like this, where your breasts are tilted up and there's a strain in the muscles, keeping your mind focused. I want your mind only on my desire and will, nothing else. Until I release you, there's nothing else but that. Understood?"

"Y-yes."

A pause. "I'll let you get away with not addressing me properly for now, but only because I want the pleasure of hearing it come spontaneously from you the first time, when your mind truly lets go."

She was thinking her mind had let go already, but she was willing to embrace the temporary insanity. When he stepped back in front of her, he unbuckled his belt, unhooked the trousers. She could tell he was already aroused, because the smooth pleated line of the linen was no longer smooth. She didn't know a body could reach a starvation point so quickly, but it was a ravenous ache in her stomach, the strain in her thighs and arched back intensifying as he toed off his polished shoes, removed his socks with the slacks low on his hips, the tongue of the belt hanging loose, the buckle making a faint clinking noise as he lithely bent to set the footwear aside. If he'd let her, she'd take down that zipper with her teeth, use the excuse to mouth him even through the cloth.

But apparently allowing her to look was as generous as he was getting right now. He slid the zipper down himself, hooked the snug boxers beneath and skinned them off at the same time so she saw the pale hip bone, the light layer of black silk over the pubic area. Then she saw his cock, hard and so remarkably virile a whimper came from her throat. Even if she couldn't have an orgasm, she prayed for enough moisture to let that slide deep inside her. Maybe she could get a moment in the bathroom alone to slip some oil inside her, to be sure it would work...

Bare, muscular and beautiful, he was now standing in front of her. When he extended a hand to her, she couldn't help that her fingers were still trembling. Heavens, she hadn't stopped shaking since he'd come into her apartment, but it seemed to be getting worse now. Making a noise in his throat, he closed the warm strength of his hand around hers. He kept her on her knees with its pressure, a wordless communication. It reminded her of how he anticipated her yoga moves during class. He could be mute and still speak to her more eloquently than anyone she'd ever met.

Pure, painful, irresistible insanity.

She licked her lips, her gaze coursing over the muscles at calf and thigh, the compact strength of his arms, the way his hair brushed his neck. Back down the slope of his chest, over the ridged abdomen, the descent a roller coaster rush that brought her back to what had saliva gathering in her mouth. The desire to suck a Master's cock had perhaps been the first sexual indicator of what she was. She'd longed to do that to the male who claimed her, have him push her to her knees to service him, give him prolonged pleasure with the sucking, skillful pressure of her mouth.

Her PT lunch friends had once brought up blowjobs, such a crude term. They'd joked about them, most only mildly enjoying or putting up with the act. Some strategized to do it in the shower, so they could more easily and discreetly spit out the release.

She wanted Jon's come on her tongue, shooting down her throat, his hands flexing in her hair, pulling hard on her scalp as she gave him the orgasm he'd demand from her. Goddess, her breath was getting shorter, and she couldn't help but sway forward on her knees.

He caught her other hand. "Easy now. You made my cock harder by looking at it with those greedy eyes. It's so obvious what you need. What you crave."

She closed her eyes. His voice was husky, but she was afraid of what he must be thinking. "Are you teasing me?"

"I hope so. In all the right ways."

He lifted her up then, turning the shower back on. Testing it first with his hand, he then guided hers in, circling her wrist and turning her palm up to the spray. It aligned their bodies, the point of his hip into the top of her buttock, his chest against her back. She shuddered again then, the hitch in her throat close to a sob. A bare male body against hers, his erection pressing against her soft, willing flesh. She was torn between arousal and something very like grief, gripping her heart in a fist so tight, she couldn't draw in a breath. "Jon…"

"I've got you. Sssh…" He slid his arm around her waist, his other across her shoulders, above her breasts. Seeing those overlapped forearms, sprinkled with black hair and the veins prominent and smooth on the track up his biceps, made it worse and better at once.

"I can't—" She cut herself off, twisting in his arms to slide both of hers under his, pressing her palms flat against his back and her face into his throat. His half foot of height difference fitted them together perfectly. Every marvelous inch of his body against hers, hard and soft together. "I'm sorry, I'm so sorry…"

"What are you sorry for, silly girl?" He didn't push her away, instead holding her close, the shower misting her skin along her back.

Sheer bliss, this offer of comfort to cocoon the disturbing power of her arousal. And he saw her as a girl. *Silly girl.* "I'm…sorry… You didn't tell me I c-could…h-hold you."

"No, I didn't. I'll punish you for that later. For now, you stay right where you are." She heard tender humor, laced with something else. Again, not pity, but something more devastating. An intuitive caring that saw to the bottom of her soul.

Brushing the crown of her head with his lips, he cupped one palm over her shoulder blade, the other molded into the small of her back, his thumb tracing her spine. His cock pressed into her stomach, his thighs against the tops of hers. Her breasts were mashed against him, a burning need centered where her nipples made contact with his chest. When she shifted, the base of his cock, his testicles, brushed against her mound, her clit. Her breath left her in a short gasp as the feeling rocketed through her, constricting the grip of her arms.

She knew thoughts of him had made her moist the other day, and she wondered if she was getting wet again, if something so unlikely could be happening.

Still holding her close, he eased them into the shower, turning her so she had the benefit of the spray. He let her hold onto him as he cupped her face, threaded his fingers in her hair so the water could saturate it. She closed her eyes, tilting her face back, wanting to fully experience the way it felt, those strong hands taking over, taking care. After two days, the cleansing had an emotional as well as physical effect.

He washed her hair. Put in the shampoo, worked it in, rinsed it until it was all out. But when it came to the soap, he gave her the lavender cake and stepped back, leaning against the wall. "I want to see you wash. I want to see how you touch yourself."

She was steadier on her feet, enough to be self-conscious. But now that her hair was clean, she wanted the rest to be too, to be ready for wherever else this might lead. She rolled the soap in her hands until she had a lather. Usually, she started with the neck and worked downward without lingering, then applied the razor in quick strokes wherever needed with the pink shaving gel propped in the corner. She was glad she had a roomy shower, though not too roomy. She could reach out and touch, but she'd regained enough composure to know she shouldn't do that again without permission. His proximity had to be enough.

"Stop."

She'd made a cautious pass over her sternum and the tops of her breasts with the soap, a motion as functional as a paint brush passing hastily over a wall's unprotected surface.

"That lather is my hand, Rachel. Show me how it will touch you." The look out of his blue eyes was an unexpected blast of undiluted male lust. "You know exactly how thorough I'll be."

She gave a quick nod. Since she knew she wasn't brave enough to follow that command while looking at him, she lowered her gaze. Making uncertain circles high on her chest, she started to move lower.

"I'm sure I would cup your breasts as I washed them, pinching the nipples to make sure they were lathered properly."

He was guiding her, instructing her on how to self-pleasure. While she wasn't an inept teenager, she was revisiting that awkward uncertainty right now. She quelled the embarrassment, closing her hands around her breasts. It made her thigh muscles hum as he continued. "That's it. I want to squeeze them, Rachel. I want the nipples to get hard, the areola getting dark and flushed. You have beautiful, large nipples."

His cock, semi-erect during her minor meltdown, was rising once again, and under her avid gaze, it looked as if it would soon be brushing his belly. He wasn't modest about it at all, leaning there against her tile shower wall, arms crossed over his chest, all his attention centered on her. When she pinched her nipples, rolled them between her fingertips, aided by the slick soap, a whimper caught in her throat.

"There you go. Keep doing that. I'd keep doing it until you were rocking forward in a fucking rhythm against my touch, because your body is gravitating toward what it wants. To be spread on my bed, those legs wide open for my cock. Your breasts tilted up, offering themselves to my mouth. Or maybe you'd like me in your mouth, straddling your neck while your pussy weeps for me. And when I came, I'd move down, clasp those heavy, gorgeous tits around my cock, fuck them as I came, spilling myself on your chest."

"Oh God," she whispered. "Yes."

Her gaze flickered up, just a quick look, to see blue fire. Then back down, to receive more direction. "Your nipples are nice and stiff now. Move down your stomach, wash everything else, but not your pussy or between your buttocks. Not until I say you can."

She obeyed. He had to remind her twice to keep her pace slow, lingering. As a result, for the first time in a long while she was aware of the feel of her own flesh, the length of thigh, the softness of her skin, the curve of hip. The line of her ribs. Back up to her throat. The sensitivity of that area made her close her eyes briefly, and she could tell his attention sharpened on her reaction. She shaved her legs, bracing herself against the wall as he continued to watch. His gaze lingered between her legs as she had to brace her foot against the porcelain rest provided in the corner.

At that angle, he could see her pink, flushed sex. In the shower, it might look moist and ready, whatever its true state was. She wanted to find out, but he'd told her she couldn't touch herself there. Plus, she was afraid she would find what she usually found. A bare hint of true lubrication, but something dammed up inside her, holding the natural fluids back.

Uneasy now, she placed the razor back in its cradle. She'd done her pubic area and armpits, which had brought her self-consciousness back, since those areas required less elegant contortions than the legs. He'd noted every shift of her muscles, the creamy track of soap, the water pattering down upon her. Five minutes had passed since he'd said anything. His focus was unnerving, yet also captivating. Then she was rinsed and clean, all of her but those two parts he'd specifically forbidden her to wash.

"Soap." When he put his hand out for it, she hesitated. She hadn't showered in two days, after all.

"Maybe I should—"

When those three words left her lips, something changed. Like the strike of a cobra, it wasn't something she saw happen. His countenance, the arrangement of muscles in his face, the posture of his powerful, shamelessly naked body, all told her she would obey him in this. The weak protest died in her throat.

She remembered those Internet sites she'd visited, with Doms who came down on any show of resistance or disagreement like a snarling tantrum, making her wonder if that was what most submissives craved. Or oddly, if they were truly Doms or just pretending, because somehow it felt forced, even on their side.

Even more oddly, it had made her think of a section of one of her favorite childhood books, *Black Beauty*. How some humans thought, to make a horse do their bidding, they had to jerk his mouth, dig their heels into his sides so hard. In reality, if the horse was trained correctly, he would respond to the lightest guidance of the leg and rein without question, because he wanted to serve his Master, was eager to do so.

She placed the soap in his hand.

Curving his other hand under her hair, he turned her toward the wall. "Lean forward and take hold of the safety bar. Spread your feet out shoulder width, and lift your ass toward me."

The quivering was back in full force, but she managed to obey. She was partially under the spray, but she still felt the pressure of his fingers, sliding over her shoulder blades, gathering up her hair and twisting it so it fell over her right shoulder. Then he smoothed his palm down the curve of her back. As he did, he picked up the long-handled scrubbing brush she kept in the shower for cleaning it once a week.

"Eyes forward, Rachel."

She obeyed, imagining all sorts of things, not so sure now, but then—

Thwack!

She yelped as the flat of that brush hit her with precision at the most generous portion of her right buttock. It stung, but it didn't overwhelm her with pain. Instead, something rocketed through her, head to toes, making the latter dig into the wet tile.

"That's a reminder," he said, his voice enhanced by the water's rush. "Do you understand?"

She nodded. "Y-yes." Why couldn't she say anything to him without stammering?

"Be still now. Feel."

From the change in water flow, she knew he'd directed the spigot away from them. In the blurry reflection on the glossy tile, she knew he was lathering his hands, setting the soap aside. Then he put his hands on her waist, lingering there. The gesture made her feel feminine, an hourglass cinched in the middle by those long, elegant fingers and large palms. As he moved downward, the soap made his passage slippery, heated. He braced one of those palms on her left buttock as the other slid between her spread legs.

She jumped, she couldn't help it. Cursing herself, she went rigid, trying to hold the posture, fighting the panic that leaped into her throat at such an unwelcome reaction. "I-I'm sorry."

"Rachel." He continued his movements, his knuckles brushing the delicate crease between labia and thigh, and then his palm sealed itself over her pussy, his fingers settling with possessive skill on either side of her clit, applying the lightest of pressure.

A convulsion—no other word for it—vibrated from the soles of her feet, all the way to her stiffly held neck. "Oh..." The word was a strangled syllable, echoing in the enclosed space. "Oh God..."

It wasn't a climax of course, but something as intense. A need that held her prisoner in its grip.

"Rachel." He repeated himself, patient, but there was a thickness to his voice that told her he wasn't unaffected by her reaction.

"Y-yes." Thank heavens he'd known her for a while, or he really would think she had a stutter.

"Don't apologize for anything again, unless I demand an apology from you. The fact a man has not touched and pleasured you in such a long time that it's strange to you," his palm moved, an easy movement that sent his soapy fingers gliding over the petals of her sex, and then an intimate dip inside, rubbing, cleaning, "is nothing to apologize for. That's for damn sure."

The last four words were spoken with visceral male satisfaction. It helped, because she couldn't stop making those gasps and whimpers as he stroked and probed, cleaning her. It felt...maybe, like she was slippery, but that could be the soap. When he removed his touch from that area, he kept his palm curved over her mound as an anchor point as he used the other hand to clean between her buttocks. It kept fountains of glittering sensation shooting up into her body.

She'd thought a lot about anal play, had explored herself there and been startled by how erogenous a zone the rim area was, but to have it actually massaged by a male hand, her bottom still smarting from the strike with the brush, was stunningly different. With his other hand still stimulating her pussy, it was automatic to moan and lift her ass even higher to his touch, taking herself to her toes, hands clutching the safety bar.

"None of that now." He pressed on her lower back, putting her flat on her feet again. "You stay in the position I've put you. No begging for more. That's for me to say."

He cleaned her, then took the shower head off its mount and rinsed her as thoroughly, passing his fingers more intimately over her than her husband had during all their years together. Throughout it all she stayed still, though she quaked and shivered, and made those cries. She thought she sounded like a lost lamb, those tiny bleats of emotions, and she pressed her forehead to the wall, familiar despair sweeping back in with the thought. She wanted the next step, wanted to be clean and see what would happen, but she was afraid of it too.

Maybe he'd cosset her, tuck her back into bed, and that would be the end of it for now. She'd be left feeling as loose and wild as she had when he left her studio that day. She couldn't bear that. He was a man, he was naked and aroused. Surely, if nothing else, he would simply fuck her while she was still slippery with soap. Then it wouldn't matter what she could or couldn't do. She could hold onto the feeling of having him deep in her body. Of being joined, however briefly, to another soul. She could feed herself on that for a long, long time.

How many times had she explained to Cole that, even without the orgasm or natural lubrication, she needed that connection, the feeling of being desired, needed, filled? Jon had already made her feel that in spades, without even touching her, really. She could pay him back by giving him what he wanted, and what she needed.

She wouldn't leave it to chance. If she persuaded him to do it now, up against the shower wall, he might not notice whatever deficiencies she had in the response department. That spiked ball in her lower belly stabbed her with desperation, told her she had to clutch it now, before the chance slid away like a slippery fish.

Spinning around, she intended to move into him, be blatant about what she was offering. But when she lunged at him, he caught her by the waist. In one astonishingly deft move, he'd flipped her around so her back was against his front. He held her immobilized as he braced his body against the shower wall.

"Rachel, sshh. Easy. No." When she struggled, he made it clear how easily he overpowered her. "Settle now. Stop."

She bit her bottom lip, squeezing her eyes shut. One hand had landed on his thigh, her nails digging in, the other clawing his forearm. "Let me go. I want you to do this. I need you to go ahead and do this *now*."

"No you don't. That's the very last thing you need. All right, that's *enough*."

When she hesitated at the sharpened tone, startled, he shifted, taking her arm from his thigh. She gasped as he pushed open the shower door, pulled her out and in the same smooth movement, bent and hefted her over his shoulder in a fireman's half-carry. His hand landed on her bottom, holding her there, her wrist firmly in his other grip. "You aren't ready to let me do anything for you, Rachel. You're still too wrapped up in your head."

"No…" She gasped it. If he left her now, just left her here, she couldn't bear it. "I'm sorry, I didn't mean—"

"Be quiet. You need a Master with a strong hand, Rachel. One who's not going to *let* you do anything. You'll do as I command and that's the end of it."

Chapter Five

‍ℬↄ

She was still whirling over the meaning of that when he took her through her bedroom in a few determined strides. How a man could be bare-assed naked and appear so in control, like a warrior striding across his camp, she didn't know, but he accomplished it. She'd been vaguely aware he'd been carrying a briefcase when he shouldered into her apartment. Now he took her to her foyer and barely paused in stride as he picked it up. As he pivoted, she noticed he was careful to protect her head and shoulders from the tall lamp next to her end table in the sitting room before he headed back to her bedroom.

"This can't work," she said, even more panicked. "Please, Jon..."

He slid her off his shoulder, pushing her to a sitting position on the bed. Bracing a long arm on either side of her, he clamped his hands over her wrists, keeping her palms flat on the mattress. Then he put his mouth on hers, in such a strong and penetrating kiss that her head was pushed backward and the muscles of her arms flexed against his hold, trying to stay upright. What little rational thought she had scattered beneath that demand, her whole body shifting focus to the heat of his mouth, the tangle of his tongue with hers, the moisture between their mouths. When he lifted his head, she felt dazed, staring into his eyes.

"Why won't it work, Rachel?"

"I...I told you. I don't...I can't..."

"You can't have an orgasm. And it's hard for you to get wet."

She nodded, telling herself she wouldn't humiliate herself with more tears. And she couldn't lie, couldn't pretend it was early menopause. Despite being naked and dripping from the shower, as well as completely out of her element, she had to strive for maturity here, to face reality. Maybe he *could* get her wet between her legs, but there was that hard knot low in her stomach that would remain there, a knot that had been weathered by so much disappointment and so many salty tears there was nothing that could untie it anymore. And that knot stood in the way of any type of release.

"All right then. Fair enough. You've told me, now we'll do things my way."

"But I can still... I have lubricant, and anything you want..."

He didn't move. "So if I use you like a whore, all for my own benefit, that's all right?"

"I didn't mean it that way." Stung, she tried to pull her hands back, but of course his grip was immovable.

"I think it's time for you to stop talking." A gentle note re-entered his voice, unexpected, as was the hand that cupped the back of her head, fingers diving into her hair as he changed the angle of his mouth. Now he laid his lips over one eye, which closed at his approach. She felt his tender caress there, a small touch of his tongue at the corner, absorbing her tear. Then he did it to the other side. "Keep your eyes closed and I want you to go back to your breathing, only more in-depth this time. Through the nose for three seconds, hold three seconds, out through the mouth for three seconds. Focus only on that, and I command everything else. Do it, Rachel."

Even though the idea of anything calming her down at this point seemed incredible, she knew it couldn't do her any harm. And maybe it would block the flood of all those other distressing thoughts his far-too-sharp observation had brought surging forth. She drew in the first breath, leaving her eyes closed.

When he drew his touch away, she heard the briefcase opening. "Keep them closed and keep breathing. Three, two, one…" He counted it off slow, as she did during class. He kept counting, so she focused, following him, wondering what he was doing.

At the beginning of her classes, she used *pranayama*, the yoga breathing exercises, to still other external forces. To help her students leave behind their worries, focus only on their practice and make the most of it. She knew he was likely using it for the same reason here, helping her set her fears aside to experience this. But as she kept breathing, she found he had other equally powerful ways of turning her attention only to what was happening in the here and now.

Putting a knee on the bed, he slid his arms under her knees, her back. He turned her, so her head was partly off the foot end of the mattress, and guided her hands out to either side of her. A padded cuff was wrapped around one wrist, and then tension was put on that arm as he looped some type of tether through the ring of the cuff. She heard the faint metallic ring of contact with the bedrail as he secured the tether there.

Her lashes fluttered, but before she could look, he slid an eye mask on her face, a ribbon tie securing it, his fingers lingering at her hair line. She shuddered. "Jon…"

"Keep breathing. Three, two, one…"

He restrained the other arm the same way, then he was moving down the bed. When he cinched her ankles down, he spread them wide. He knew within an inch the limits of her flexibility, so she was incredibly vulnerable, her muscles straining. That knot in her stomach moved lower, burning.

"Since you can't climax, I guess we don't have to worry about this pretty comforter." She imagined him looking at the Monet print pattern as he continued in that mild tone. "Though if you did climax on it, gushed hard, it would darken the pale pinks of Monet's flowers. The same color your cunt looks now. You're glistening, Rachel." When he dipped his finger into her, she mewled, twitching her ass against the cover as he explored. Then he was back near her head, though he didn't touch her. He was shifting, doing something, because she could feel his movements on the mattress. Then he answered her curiosity.

"I'm looking at you, naked and bound, and rubbing your oil on my cock."

She imagined those elegant fingers, soaked with her arousal, sliding along the broad head. Her stomach muscles contracted.

"Do you want to taste it, Rachel?"

"Yes." She rasped it.

"You're going to have to ask for it the right way, aren't you?"

She'd told him she couldn't. But he'd known the blindfold might make that barrier a little less daunting. In that opaque world, she could answer the dangerous desire she'd nursed. For once in her life, she could not only speak the words but mean them. All those years, she'd longed for the one who would coax it from her, and here he was. But he wasn't coaxing at all. He was demanding and she couldn't deny him, because it was merely an echo of the truth.

Her voice shook so hard, she could barely get it out. "Y-yes, M-master. Yes, Master. I want to taste. Please."

Having her head tilted over the end of the bed increased the sense of exposure and vulnerability. It also put her in a perfect position to service him with her mouth. Since she was tied down, he had full control of how powerfully he thrust, how deep.

When he put his cock against her parted lips, a growl of pure hunger came from her throat. He gave her just the head, pressing it against the flat of her tongue to let her curl around him, taste and swirl along that firm, heated skin. She tasted him as well as herself, and knew the tip of his organ had already been wet, his arousal joining her slippery honey.

Though she hadn't done this in quite a while, she'd once been good at it. Since most men enjoyed oral sex, this was a part of her subservience Cole had embraced, at least at first. She didn't want to mix the memories though. She banished those images and instead imagined what Jon looked like standing over her. The columns of his thighs pressing against the crown of her head, the heavy testicles brushing her forehead. His intimate, musky smell made her nostrils flare, trying to take in even more of the erotic scent. Her mouth wanted more as well.

For a blissful moment, he obliged, sinking even deeper. She relaxed her throat to accommodate him. As she'd seen in the shower, he was an impressive size and girth, and she sucked on him, wanting more, more and more. When he let out a quiet oath, she moaned against him, and his hands closed over her breasts. Arching up to him when his thumbs flicked over the nipples, she made a plea against his cock, squirming against her restraints.

"You have gorgeous breasts, Rachel, all heavy and ripe. They'd look beautiful in rope bondage and clamps. The curves all swollen, your nipples stiff. When I took off the clamps and ropes, you'd cry out from the surge of blood, the pain. But you'd love it too, and I'd put my mouth on your nipples and soothe them, suckle on them until you'd be begging me to bite them, to give them more pain. But there are so many parts of you I want to pleasure, I might need some help."

She was making helpless noises against his heated shaft. God, he was getting bigger. She wanted him to shoot down her throat, wanted him to pull out and spurt over the nipples he was taunting now. But he had other ways he wanted to torment her.

"Peter loves breasts. While I took care of other things, he'd suckle away all the pain, yet make them even stiffer, needier. Your cunt would get even wetter, but Lucas would take care of that. He's spent a great deal of time studying the way to pleasure a woman with his mouth. He'd thrust his tongue deep into your pussy, do things that would make you mindless. My slave in every way, lost in every desire you've ever had."

Whether or not he was merely painting pictures for her fantasies, her body was responding. She remembered their photos, and now she thought of Lucas, the handsome and athletic CFO, with his mouth between her legs. The brawny Peter, that *Don't Tread on Me* tattoo on his biceps rippling as he cupped her breasts in both large hands. Jon, her Master, calling the shots.

What did it say about her, that she was imagining it? She should be appalled. Both of those men were married. *What are you, some kind of slut?* Cole's voice, an unwelcome intrusion. She stiffened under Jon's touch. Was she one of those cautionary tales, the sex addict who got so lost in her pathetic needs that all of a sudden she was servicing total strangers at her boyfriend's behest? Had her experience at Club More taught her nothing? Though Jon knew the right words, was more civilized about it, was it any different?

Yes, yes it is. Her soul wailed at her, begging her not to fuck this up with her head games. *For a moment, pretend it is, because you've never felt anything like this.*

"You're thinking too much again." He withdrew, and the loss of that heat and strain on her mouth was enough to cause a noise of petulant protest. "It's time to take this up a notch. I wanted to make sure you could handle something the size of my cock and fucking hell, but you can. You've got a devil-blessed mouth, Rachel."

Before she could think of what to say to that, since a polite thank you seemed inappropriate, a broad head was nudging at her lips again. Only this time, it wasn't Jon. It was a thick rubber phallus, it had to be, but it felt...real. Like a hard cock with the velvet give of flesh over it. In fact, she could swear the organ was warm. She started in surprise as he took the thick shaft in slow but deep, giving her that tantalizing terror of having the wide head pushed right against the back of her throat. He stopped there and secured it with straps around her skull, cinching it in until they bit against the corners of her mouth.

"When I finally take that off, you'll have strap marks there for about an hour. Whenever you look in the mirror, you'll be reminded of your submission to me."

The gag *was* warm, pulsing like a man's organ, and it had some kind of scent that reminded her of Jon's cock, his pre-cum. It wasn't anything like the lifeless, rigid sex toys she'd tried. Having it strapped in her mouth like this made her feel even more helpless...and wetter.

He slid his hip on the bed, and from the prop of his thigh against hers, he was facing toward her spread legs. She wished she could see him there, his tempting ass pressed into her covers, the curve of his back and flex of muscle as he braced a hand on the opposite side of her hip and laid a palm high on the inside of one of her thighs.

"If you're wondering, yes, that gag is designed to be as much like a cock as possible. A chamber inside can hold semen, be ejected down your throat when a Master desires to do so. So he can release his seed in more than one orifice at a time. Or it can be programmed to release moisture at the tip periodically. Like my cock did from the tease of that fuckable mouth of yours."

She made a strangled noise of pleasure as, right on cue, it did just that. The taste, while not Jon's semen, had a stimulating similarity to it.

"Tonight it contains an organic mixture that emulates the taste of semen, but with a touch of vanilla, cocoa and sugar on top of it. Dana thinks it's like tasting a man's cock and warm sugar cookies at once. Many women have a sexual response to chocolate or sugar, so it drives your arousal higher. That, and I also included a chemical composition similar to pheromones that's teasing your nose even now."

God, it was turning her on beyond belief, to be spread open for his pleasure, having him calmly explaining these things to her, holding all the control, the reins on her pleasure. K&A's boy genius...who in no way reminded her of a boy in this moment. God, to imagine that he was creating such things...her brain couldn't process it, but her mouth didn't need it. She was licking and sucking at the cock now as if it was his, unable to stop herself, wanting to show him how she could pull that secretion from it, the way she wanted to pull it from his cock. Though he was turned toward her legs, she was sure his body was twisted enough to watch her face as well. The near-bruising hold of his hand on her upper thigh told her she was delivering her message, loud and strong.

"You're making me sorry I didn't load that chamber. If I'd decided to do that, a little while before I came here, I would have lain on my bed, gripped my cock and thought of you. I'd imagine you above me, held in a rope suspension system. You'd be completely restrained, but cradled without discomfort. Like a constellation floating over my bed, or one of those mobiles that babies play with." A touch of amusement entered his voice, but then a raw note of lust pushed that aside.

"I'd be able to see every part of you. The arch of your throat, those needy eyes, the way the rope bit into that soft, round ass of yours. I'd be imagining all that as I jerked off. You'd be begging me to take you down, fuck you. As you begged, your cream would drip from your cunt and splash onto my stomach. I'd bring you down eventually, fuck you at my leisure. But I'd keep you tied and suspended, helpless to however I wanted to move you on my cock. Hard and fast, slow and deep, while I suckled your tits and stroked every inch of your beautiful body."

Rachel made another incoherent plea in the darkness. *Please touch me. God, touch me.* Her body under the shelter of his was quaking, near convulsions, and she knew there had to be perspiration gleaming on her skin. His fingers whispered over her abdomen, but she wanted so much more than that. Yet still he kept talking.

"Tonight I only brought that gag and the restraints, but I have another device. It's small, but very powerful. It looks like a thumb and a forefinger joined closely together. The finger part goes into your pussy, positioned at that elusive G-spot, so I have to adjust it for each woman's unique shape. The thumb portion lies on the clit. There's a joining hinge that clamps down on the labia, holding them in place with a pinch, but the right kind. Usually running my tongue around it eases that, gets the mind in a different place."

She was sure of that. Her mind was going in forty different directions now. In a moment, it was going to shatter into forty million. Her body couldn't take this overload, and so far he was merely talking to her. Since she couldn't have a climax, she'd die from the despair of containing this much pleasure with nowhere to release it.

"When I set the control right, the finger moves inside you, a sweep, a curl." His forefinger moved on her thigh now, a random, small series of movements, no more than an inch in any direction, up and back, side to side, then in semicircular curls. "The thumb strokes your clit, pushes up under the hood, because I don't put it on until you're wildly excited. Almost where you are now."

His fingers slid back to the juncture of her thigh, traced the labia, not touching the clit. Her body bucked against the restraints. She had no control of it, and she made a guttural noise against the gag, squeezing down on it, suckling fiercely. That provocative sugar-and-semen taste awakened her taste buds again.

"I didn't bring that piece with me, because this first time you're going to come from my touch, nothing else."

She couldn't. She'd tried to tell him. Then she arched against his touch, crying out against the gag as two of his fingers slid inside her, his thumb sliding into place over her clit.

"Fuck, you're hot and wet, Rachel. You're making my cock ache for you."

She wanted him there too, but he'd gagged her, tied her down, told her all the choices were his. As if underscoring it, he spoke again. "You prove to me you can obey your Master this time, next time it will be my cock. But you have to work for that. You have to trust me, surrender to me. Let go of the fears, the worries. Your body is made for pleasure. It's begging for it. Don't let your fear deny it."

She couldn't help it. How many nights had she gotten herself so worked up, imagining a faceless Master? Then, once he'd joined her class, that masturbation fantasy had been replaced by Jon. Even with that arousing image, she'd get to a certain point, and then rubbing her clit or her pussy was like scrubbing a floor. No response, just abrasion.

He wasn't rubbing as if he was intent on a goal, however. Instead he was exploring her as if he had hours to indulge himself, his fingers gliding over places that made her tremble, cry out again. Then he'd retreat, his thumb making idle passes over her clit, a light pressure before he moved away. She writhed, lifting her hips for more.

"No. None of that. You lie still and let me explore this pussy. My pussy. All mine." He leaned over and she squealed, rigid, as he blew on her clit, his tongue taking a brief swipe, then a lazy, slow circle over the labia. "You feel how slick you are, Rachel? I'm watching your arousal slide out of you, like a melting ice cream cone. And God, your nipples are so hard and tight, your breasts swollen and ripe. Your body is a feast for a man's lust. You're like a dam, and I can see the pressure building behind those thick walls you've built. We're going to take this slow, relieve it slow so you have room to feel, to experience."

"Fuck...please...fuck me..." She was not a woman who used foul language. And yet she couldn't help crying out against the gag as he did exactly what he said he would. Taking it slow, arousing her further with those fingers, his mouth, then stroking her thighs, her hips, his palms sliding up her abdomen and along the crease beneath her breasts, then following the outer curve, leaving her nipples begging for attention.

Even muffled, it was clear what she was saying. He made soft admonishments, but let her have that outlet. When his hand settled on her throat, constricting her there, her pussy convulsed, a short gush of fluid running down the seam of her buttocks, teasing the perineum. She shuddered. *Please...I can't take anymore...*

But she had to. Because as the long minutes passed, he continued to simply enjoy himself, taking pleasure in her body. He didn't even appear to be trying to make her climax. She felt no bated sense of expectation, a pressure to make her do something she'd said she couldn't. Yet she passed a line where that didn't matter anymore. She abandoned all she knew about her body and begged him with everything she could — her squirming, the tension in her thighs, the arch of her throat against his hold — to try.

Please...try.

She quivered as he tapped her carotid artery, then settled his fingers on her throat again. "Oh yeah, you're tremendously responsive here. You've wanted a collar for a long time. And you don't want some dainty piece of jewelry. You want something steel and thick that holds you close, presses on your throat and reminds you your very life is in a Master's hand. It would have a lock that can only be opened by him. I'd make it smooth, so smooth on the edges, you'd feel the weight, but no discomfort. Somewhere on it I'd stamp a message in Sanskrit, one of the oldest languages known, because this is one of the oldest impulses. To claim, to exert dominance and demand submission."

Please stop... He was giving sharp, painful details to her nebulous fantasies. Her body was rippling, undulating like a heaving sea, emulating the rhythm of sex, of fucking, no shame anymore.

"That's it, girl..." He said it in a throaty whisper. "Show me how wanton you are, how much you want it. Show me how you'd take my cock. Squeeze down on it, squeeze down hard." When he slid his fingers back in, she shrieked at that overload of sensation. His thumb flicked her clit, hard then light, then a stroke. Moving his smallest finger to tease the rim of her anus, he added to the abundance of stimulus she was experiencing. How much more could she take?

"Ben would love to fuck your ass. He's our legal counsel, and it's his favorite orifice to explore on a woman. Imagine it, imagine him taking you there while I take your cunt. Tighten the muscles in your ass, imagine his thick cock is pumping into you there, punishing you for doubting me." And then one finger, wet from her juices, slid into that tight passage, while the other two stayed in her pussy. She strangled on a scream.

"Don't you come, Rachel. Not until I give you permission. But squeeze down on me. I want to feel those muscles clamp around my fingers."

She was terrified. A pressure like a volcano's eruption was sweeping over her. Her body didn't belong to her anymore. It was heaving, bucking, squirming, so stimulated it couldn't choose one distinct pattern of movement. Her neck arched under his hand, tilting her head farther over the edge of the bed, making her dizzy. When he squeezed her throat one more time, reminding her that all her senses, her body, everything, was under his command, that shattering into forty million pieces began.

"Come for me, Rachel. Come now."

Her cunt rippled, contracted, her rectum clenching around his finger there. Her clit hardened and suddenly it was upon her. This wasn't like a volcano eruption after all. She was hit mid-body by a percussion wave that blew her senses out. Her mind exploded in that black night, her head arching back even farther over the side of the mattress, all the blood rushing to her head and her sex, leaving everything in between twitching and seizing.

Now the lava did flow, delicious heat pouring through her. It spilled onto his fingers like the gush of a man's come, she felt it. So thick and primal, her legs jerking, heels beating against the mattress. She whipped her head back and forth, lashing herself with her hair, such that some of it caught in her mouth and she bit down on it. She was gorgeous, wanton, a sex Goddess incarnate, no thought but the pleasure she could give her Master as the climax rolled her over and over in the midst of a dark universe. A universe full of nothing but sensual cries and sweaty, slick flesh sliding against his hold, the one fixed point in that wildly spinning firmament.

It went on and on, until she was at last merely floating and twitching, making soft, wondering cries, a lone dove in a black-as-night galaxy. She might have passed out from the dizziness. If decades had passed when she surfaced from that mind-blowing experience, she wouldn't be the least bit surprised. For one thing, she didn't have the energy for surprise, for anything but raw emotion.

At length, she came back to him, brought out of the fog when he released the gag. Even with her blindfold still on, she felt embarrassed at the saliva collected around her mouth. But he replaced that self-conscious moment with a paralyzing aftershock of pleasure as he kissed her, licking it away from her lips with his clever tongue. She moaned against him, every nerve so sensitive under his contact.

One by one, he released her bonds, stroking the pulse points in her wrists, the arch of her feet and then at last he gathered her in his arms, his lap. His erection was enormous, pressing against her ass, but he seemed in no hurry about that. Instead, he slid the blindfold away, tilting her face up to him.

It was like looking into the sun after being locked in solitary for years. She couldn't do it, was far too vulnerable, but he gave her no choice, holding her chin and throat, reminding her of a Master's binding, that steel collar he'd described so vividly. However, in this moment, she only wanted the collar of his hand, that promise of pleasure he could deliver through the touch of his fingers.

His blue gaze was filled with pleasure and lust, but she noticed the way he examined her face and body, his touch soothing the strap marks along her cheeks. His attention was so obviously on her breath and mobility, she realized he was making sure she didn't require any physical aftercare. It made unvoiced sobs ache in her chest. They were too painful and unwieldy, so they'd have to stay there. She'd remain still now — still and limp in his arms, wanting it all to stay like this forever.

✳ ✳ ✳ ✳ ✳

He wouldn't permit her to do anything for him. "Not this time," he said in that sexy voice that brooked no argument from her. Not that she really had the strength. After such an earth-shattering discovery, that she was in fact more than capable of a climax that could launch her higher and further than she'd thought it possible for any woman to go, she was a boneless creature. No energy to rise off the bed or do anything other than lie quiet amid the glorious wreckage of her bed as he went back into the bathroom.

When he came back, she blinked. He was dressed again. Shirt tucked into belted slacks, socks and shoes back in place, though he hung his jacket on a chair, draping his tie over it. A mix of emotions went through her, but the uneasy portion of them died back some as he slid a hip on the bed. Arranging the pillows behind himself, he gathered her in, sliding her naked body over his thighs so she was sprawled between them, her upper body resting on his chest. She burrowed her fingers into the cloth, her nostrils taking in that dry-cleaned scent, his aftershave.

"I want…" When she closed her eyes, he stroked the tousled hair away from her cheek and jaw, giving the strands a tug as he did.

"What do you want?"

"Please...would you open the shirt?"

He flicked open the buttons with easy dexterity, then lifted her off him enough to pull the cloth out of the belt, open it fully. She melted back against the curves and planes of him. His solid pectoral under her cheek, his ridged abdomen under the small, stroking circles of her fingers. His cock was a hard presence against her stomach.

"Are you sure I can't..." She cleared her throat, her voice abraded from the unfamiliar act of screaming out her pleasure against the broad head of that phallic gag. "I can tell you need something."

"You'll take care of that another time. Right now, you'll lie here and let me hold you. That's what I want. The shirt's the only thing you get for now. No more talking until I give you permission. Just lie here."

How was it he could sound so in control, so calm, and yet he wasn't the least detached? She could feel his passion, and not only through his cock. It was a wondrous discovery, realizing she was intuitively recognizing a Master's point of view. Her surrender had been what he'd sought from her, and obtaining it had given him something as pleasurable as what he'd given her. She wasn't imagining it. The energy coursing through him was a relentless current of desire, pulling at her loose and not-quite-exhausted body. It held a delicious threat, to sweep her away at a future time of his choosing.

So she obeyed, lying still upon him, willing to tread in that current. For so long, she'd been denied the precious gift of a man's desire for her. Sensing it, knowing it was real and true, she savored it, the pleasure of his heart beating, a little fast, under her cheek. Her eyes resting on the proof of his arousal, thick and tempting under the hold of his slacks. The way his fingers stroked her, not a light, absent touch, but with some pressure behind his fingertips, following the contours of her jaw, her throat, the line of her shoulder, tangling in her hair, making it clear that he wanted more from her body, from her.

This was actually perfect, this eye of the storm, feeling all that passion and pleasure circling around her, but letting her just...be. She was included, in the center of it, and yet didn't need to do anything but be quietly amazed at how she'd fared in the thick of it, overcome by what he'd done to her.

She wanted to ask him how he'd known what she hadn't, what had eluded her, but she couldn't. Not now. She sank into the silence. His silence, a silence that stilled mind, body and soul. Though his hands moved over her, keeping her quivering, that stillness was in him as well. It held her to him as much as a dozen commands would do.

Throughout the past few years, there'd always been so much going on in her head, a cacophony capable of driving her mad. A constant litany of expectations, failures, deprecations, wishes... Together they became desperation and desolation. Perhaps because she was casting her own life's reflection on the world, so much of what she saw, heard and experienced seemed pointless, vapid...hopeless. Both the physical and mental forms of yoga had been a saving grace, because in the peace of exertion, the stillness of meditation, the focus on breathing, she'd been able to leave it behind for short periods, hide from it.

This wasn't hiding from it. Jon's tranquility had a power to it, a strength that could transform the world around her. For the first time in a long time, she looked at her surroundings and saw what had once made them appealing to her. There was a whimsical stone cat, carved in a lotus position, sitting beside her bed. She'd found it at a consignment shop and placed it on the secondhand night table she'd repainted in lavender and stressed with silver gray paint.

On the wall, caddy corner to her bed, was a Victorian print. It showed a young governess escorting a child in a park. The governess was looking wistfully over her shoulder, for she'd discovered a couple having a tryst in the shadows of the wood. The man was stealing a kiss from his lover. All of them wore such beautiful clothes, a beautiful picture, but Rachel had connected to the underlying message. A yearning need for love and desire beneath societal constraints.

As Jon had recognized, her bedspread was one of the famous Monet flower scenes, all those soothing melded pinks, greens and lavenders. Jon had said her arousal would dampen and deepen those colors, and she saw that wet patch now, the lighter pink turned dark. *The way your cunt looks now.* She shivered, remembering those words, thinking of the singular intensity of Jon's expression as he'd gazed between her legs.

When Cole had left her, it had been a slow process, but everything of that life had gradually been replaced by her choices in this apartment. She'd surrounded herself with wonder, passion and beauty, but her pleasure in it had been a fleeting thing, overwhelmed by her daily loneliness. One afternoon in this man's arms, and she was re-experiencing the stirring delight she'd felt when she'd found these things, brought them home, made them articulations of herself. It was terrifying. But as long as she was lying inside his silence, not her own, it was all right. She was safe.

While she expected nothing more than this moment, she again wished it could go on forever. But only a child believed something like that could really happen. Listening to his heartbeat, she closed her eyes and gave herself to sleep.

In some sad way, she hoped he'd be gone when she woke, for when that silence broke, so too would this spell. She'd prefer to be alone to figure out how to reassemble the pieces again. To figure out where exactly inside her empty heart to put this once-in-a-lifetime treasured memory.

Chapter Six

ഔ

He *was* gone when she woke, but he'd left an indelible, unsettling imprint at every level of her existence. The first she noticed was on her body. Between yoga and the requirements of being a good physical therapist, she kept herself very limber and flexible, but all the stretching in the world could not prevent the delicious soreness, the result of the prolonged isometric rigor of a universe-altering climax. If he'd plunged inside of her, wrapping her legs around his hips, she would have used those inner thigh muscles in ways she hadn't in far too long, strained to the limit as he pressed them back with his thrusting, again and again.

She could smell the pungent scent of her climax. Putting her hand down there, she found herself still sticky. Touching herself reminded her of his touch, his much larger fingers inside her, the way he'd cupped her breasts in those masculine palms.

There was another scent. It was from his shirt, the one she was now wearing. Vaguely, she remembered him sliding her arms into it when he'd had to leave the bed. He'd murmured something about not wanting her to get cold, but still wanting to see her. He'd buttoned only the two middle buttons, so he'd been able to tease and fondle wherever he wished. Now she brought the open collar to her nose and inhaled the smell that was Jon's neck, that lingering aftershave and male heat.

It took awhile to get her feet on the floor, and when she did, she blinked. Her room was clean. The clothes she'd left on the floor were gone, the dirty dishes removed from the dresser and the coverlet for her bed was neatly folded at the foot. She'd slept like an exhausted, trusting child, so deep he'd apparently been able to call in someone like Molly Maid and they'd worked around her.

The alternative was too outlandish to contemplate. If he'd given her an orgasm *and* cleaned the apartment, he wasn't a mere mortal. The man was a god.

She tottered to her bathroom. Also too amazing to face was the fact that what they'd done last night was technically only foreplay. If he truly had fucked her, she would have needed a crash cart. It made her lips twist in a wry smile, though that same feeling twisted something tight around her heart. Daylight and reality. It was coming. She could feel it like the Four Horsemen of the Apocalypse, ready to trample her under their thundering hooves.

Rachel, stop it. Savor it for a few moments, will you?

In her bathroom mirror she saw the usual features. A forty-something woman whose face was creased with sleep, crow's feet etched at the corners of her eyes, worry lines visible at her brow. But today she saw other things as well. Lips that seemed fuller, bruised by kissing. A look of dazed wonder in her eyes. Her long blonde hair tousled around her face in what she dared to call sexy dishevelment. She was clearly delusional, but the kaleidoscope of images from last night were rotating through her mind, shivering over her mostly exposed skin.

Glancing down, she saw her water glass by the sink contained a casual arrangement of lavender wildflowers and Black-eyed Susans. They grew in the back lot of the apartment building. Paperclipped to a sealed envelope leaning against the glass was a note.

You're braver than you believe you are, Rachel. Follow the instructions in the envelope.

The note had the Kensington & Associates letterhead, the address and phone number in bold script at the top. Jon's handwriting was precise print, reflecting the compressed, dense energy of the man who'd written it.

She stared at herself in the mirror again, the way her breasts were provocatively exposed in the open shirt, how the tails of it caressed her thighs. She thought of that fabric tucked into his trousers, having the oblivious pleasure of molding over his muscular buttocks, the tails folded in near his cock, the curve of his testicles.

Picking up the envelope, she opened it. The words made her sink down on the commode top, her breath shortening, stomach doing a flip-flop.

I wish I could be there with you this morning, but I had an early meeting at the office, and I wanted you to sleep as long as you needed. But you're not alone, sweet girl. My mind is even now on you, and what you must look like, still wearing my shirt, your body well-used by your Master.

She swallowed, a quick spasm in her fingers rippling the paper.

Now that you're up, eat the breakfast I left for you. Take a bath, not a shower. Use those bath beads you've probably had forever and don't use because you don't take time for a bath. Shave your pussy smooth. Wear my shirt belted over the short black skirt in the rear section of your closet and the red heels that are pushed behind the other shoes. No panties or bra. Leave your hair down. In the back of your vanity drawer is a lipstick called Wet Cherry that almost matches the shoes. Wear it. I'll be imagining that color marking my cock when you get down on your knees in my office and relieve the hard-on I've had since seeing you come all over my hand last night.

No preliminaries. No dancing around it. He was taking control. How many times had she fantasized about it? A Master taking over her life, orchestrating her every movement for her pleasure and his own. But her reality had become something so far from that, this was a fairy tale, and a tremendously dangerous one. What did she know about him, except he'd been able to bring her to climax for the first time in years? What did he expect from her?

All things a rational, reasonable woman would ask. But the fear came from another part of her, the part he understood far too well. Her gaze dropped to the postscript.

You're already trying to compartmentalize, box me up as a momentary fluke, something best left as a one-night fantasy. I wouldn't advise that. Trust me, Rachel. I know how to care for you.

It was a cryptic comment, one that could have many meanings. But it didn't matter. Even if he meant it the way she envisioned or desired, he couldn't take care of her like that. It was too late. She lay the letter aside, but this time she didn't look back into the mirror, feeling too exposed. She couldn't do this.

If she was a different kind of person, maybe she could convince herself to throw caution to the wind, let herself have this. Earlier in the week, she'd re-checked the article about K&A's "boy genius" and found out his age. He was thirteen years her junior, any older woman's fantasy. All that stamina and beauty, his feet a decade away from the first threshold of middle age and its painful truths. For him, it was merely intense games. He was a Dom likely used to taking on a submissive for certain periods of time, no commitment. If she let it stop right here, she could say she'd experienced a taste of what she'd always wanted to experience, and that was more than she'd ever anticipated getting. If she walked away now, her heart would be no more battered than before.

Whereas if she let herself have the protracted fantasy, it would destroy her.

The midnight chime had rung for her. This Cinderella had hot flashes and a limited budget. A monthly gym membership and a weakness for sappy movies and dark chocolate. She'd learned to live within the confines of that safe orbit of things that defined her world. So that was it. But he'd given her a gift, and she at least owed it to him to tell him that, face-to-face.

Her two days of self-pity and hiding were up. It had ended with a glorious fireworks show, but it was time to face Day Three and its harsh reality, and get on with her life.

* * * * *

Jon studied the slow-moving Mississippi River from the window of the K&A Baton Rouge office. Jon had liked New Orleans' dark mystery, its unique culture, but since they'd moved to the Baton Rouge location, he'd found he liked the tranquility of this view. The Mississippi's deep, eternal flow was an echo of what he felt flowed in everyone. A sense of truth, of the way life was supposed to go.

Which was why people got so fucked up when they were tossed out of that flow, left on the banks to gasp and dry up, lost to themselves. He ran a hand over his neck, clenched the fingers then loosened them, trying to shake out tension. Trying to get rid of the troubled knot in his lower belly.

Married. For over a year, he'd thought she was married. He should have known something was off, since he'd kept coming back to her class as if she were a damn siren. But he'd never thought to look under the surface, respecting that unbreakable code that another man's woman was off limits. He'd ached for her, for the pain and loneliness that came off her in waves. That he could have tried to assuage months ago.

It wasn't ego, though he wouldn't deny some of that had been involved last night. She pulled things from him. Those expressive hazel eyes, her baby doll lashes framing a mixture of gray, gold and green color as fascinating as a forest's depths. The way her white-blonde hair fell around her face in that wispy, vulnerable way. Her killer ripe hourglass body and how she was so earnest and serious. She needed to smile more. From the first time he attended her class, he'd found he could make her smile, and the hopeful light to it, a candle in a soul shrouded in darkness, had haunted his dreams.

Now his blood burned with the knowledge he could make her do far more than smile.

Knowing she'd thrown him off like that had riled the Master in him. So much for his purported calm. Eastern warriors of ancient times had written that a man should accept the warlike as well as the peaceful elements of his nature. They should be allowed to flow through him unfettered, so that he could take the best aspects of both of them.

Instead, he'd unleashed his Master side like a rabid dog. He'd been goaded, challenged and he'd jumped in with both feet last night. Then he'd left her that note this morning. It was too much, too soon, and he damn well knew it. She'd spent God knew how many years burying it in herself. Just because he could see the gleam of that treasure clear as sunlight didn't mean that she could. And as Leland had clearly pointed out, there was too much he didn't know about why that treasure had been buried.

K&A had considerable resources to protect what was theirs. Jon had assigned Shelley, one of their trusted security personnel, to discreetly watch Rachel's place in his absence, and she'd follow his troubled submissive if she left on any errands. While Rachel slept, he'd also planted the tiny cameras he'd brought in his case last night. Shelley was monitoring the feed from them as well. Yeah, it might be way the hell over the line, but he didn't really give a damn. He'd seen the scar on Rachel's neck from that close gunshot. It had been faint, but the impression was still there. It had branded itself on his mind.

He might have uncovered the treasure inside her, but there were too many demons guarding it. He wasn't going to make the same mistake he'd made at the yoga studio, leaving her vulnerable to them. Shelley was only supposed to call him if something started happening that caused her concern for Rachel's safety, and only she had access to what was coming through those planted cameras. He didn't want to learn about Rachel through an invasion of her privacy. He wanted to unfold the truth of her face-to-face, savoring every bit of it, the good and the bad, learning her soul so that he could wrap his own around it, bring them together as he was sure they were meant to be.

"And then Ben thought we'd hire a stripper to do a lap dance on Nelson's limp dick to prove he actually doesn't have balls."

Jon blinked, turned from the window. "What?"

Matt Kensington arched a brow. The CEO of Kensington & Associates was on Jon's office couch. As he referenced the open laptop next to him, he had a long arm stretched along the top cushions, the sole of one polished shoe braced under the coffee table. Matt preferred the sofa for their office meetings, as it accommodated his tall, powerful frame better, the legacy of a Texas oilman father who'd once been a professional football player. While his patriarch had given him the strong, determined features and broad shoulders, Matt's beautiful Italian mother showed in the aristocratic sculpting of cheekbones, the dark hair he wore cropped short and the intense, deep brown eyes focused on Jon now. "Trying out astral projection?" he asked.

"Sorry." Jon pushed it aside. "I think Nelson's stats on the start-up—"

"Cut the bull. What's going on?"

Jon gave him a tight smile. "I was going to ask you the same. You already know everything we've been discussing, backward and forward. You're babysitting me. Why?"

"I watch your back. Same as you watch mine. It's what we do." Matt kept that gaze pinned on him. "Jon."

He was the leader of their unique alpha pack for a reason. Jon lifted a shoulder. "She's divorced. Has been for years."

"I know. Dana filled us in last night when we all met for dinner. All of us but you. Peter said he figured you were going after her, from the look he saw in your eyes when Dana told you."

"Has he spilled yet?"

Jon glanced toward the new voice. Lucas had appeared in his doorway, one shoulder against the doorjamb. Matt's right hand and CFO was also an amateur cyclist. It showed in the roped strength of his body. Because he was getting ready for another of his marathons, his sandy brown hair was cropped short. The discipline and focus in his silver-gray gaze said he was ready for the competition.

Jon wasn't surprised at his timing. He was just surprised that Ben and Peter weren't here with him. The almost psychic bond the five of them shared was one he'd stopped questioning a long time ago. He turned back to the window. "Should have known you'd be in on this. I missed it. Missed that she was fooling me."

"Doesn't all that karma and spiritual bullshit you study say that things happen for a reason?" Lucas stepped farther into the room, slid a hip on the top edge of the sofa, close to where Matt's palm rested on it. "Maybe you needed all these months to get to know her a little bit, to make the next step easier. From what Dana said, she's a lady who's been burned badly. A lot like Savannah." He looked at Matt as he referenced their boss's wife, then added, "She wasn't as easy to sweep off her feet as Cassie was."

"I'm going to tell Cass you said that and watch her chew you into little pieces."

Despite the weight of his thoughts, Jon's lips curved in an ironic smile as Peter's voice reached them, heralding his arrival a few steps behind Lucas. It was his first easy feeling of the morning. "You all have a bug in my office too?"

"Nope. We just know when you have one up your ass." As Jon turned, he saw the former National Guard captain, an Afghanistan veteran, cross his massive arms and lean in the doorway Lucas had vacated.

The Knights of the Boardroom. Jon wasn't sure if their armor was as polished as the media's mawkish name for them implied. They were more like a wolf pack, bound by primal instinct and animal intuition. All of them hardcore sexual Dominants, with varying styles. They were his friends, but far more than that. Not exactly brothers, because siblings didn't usually share the types of things they did, but brethren, for certain.

The surface history was that they had built K&A to success together. When they went into business deals together, they were unbeatable. However, what simmered beneath the surface was that their minds were remarkably synchronized. They didn't share the same viewpoints, but their viewpoints often hooked like puzzle pieces. Though he was the youngest next to Ben, he'd identified the inexplicable draw between them first, helping forge that bond years ago. It was more than the sexual Dominance. That was merely the base catalyst that had opened their eyes to other remarkable common traits.

None of them had siblings, and they'd all lost their parents too young. More than once, they'd pulled each other out of the fire of personal tragedies. Like the psychic connections of twins, they could anticipate one another's needs over distances. Or across the space between their corner offices, like now. They knew when one of them might be in trouble, whether or not the stubborn bastard was willing to ask for help.

They shared the same moral code in their professional and personal lives, toward women and each other. When one of them found the woman he wanted to make his permanently—which, no surprise, had happened to three of them within the past couple of years—they came together the same way they did in business. They used every resource they had to close the deal. From the moment the claim was made and accepted, that woman was part of all of them. Theirs to pleasure, when her Master offered the privilege. To protect, even when he didn't. And to love, no matter what. So the pack had expanded. Where they'd each had no immediate family, they now had one that commanded unshakable loyalty from each of them.

Though the other four badgered him mercilessly about what they called his New Age bullshit observations, Jon knew they didn't necessarily disagree with them. They'd been born at different times, places and circumstances, but now it seemed inevitable that they'd found each other. The universe was like that.

"So what's the main problem?" Matt took the natural lead as Jon settled on the edge of his desk, trying to settle his mind in the same way.

"My dick."

It surprised them, he could tell. Of all of them, he was the one least likely to resort to crudity. "I went there worked up, because she'd kept me off her scent all that time. But once I was there...I wasn't sure how far I'd get with her. I was trying to establish how deep her submission ran."

He paused, met Peter's gaze. "Unlike Savannah and Cass, who really didn't recognize their submission for what it was, I think Rachel's even more hardcore than Dana. She's gone for years knowing it, playing it out in her head without doing anything about it. It's pretty obvious her husband wasn't a Dom, and all signs suggest he didn't handle it well. Though that can happen, no fault to him, he abused her trust, left her damaged. Her confidence is for shit and she's way too fragile. Whatever happened in her marriage, he did a real number on her."

Matt and Ben already knew about the Club More incident, because he'd filled them in as he told Leland he would. But as he related the bare bones of it, and some of his other general impressions, he saw the same hardness enter Peter's and Lucas' expressions that had entered theirs. No man in this room would tolerate a woman being mistreated, emotionally or physically. Dana had picked on them the most about it, called them a bunch of overprotective sexist Neanderthals. But there it was.

"I know her, but I know nothing about her. She's that closed off. I wasn't a complete idiot this time. I cleared it with Matt to have Shelley keep an eye on her, and she'll do a discreet tail if she leaves to make sure she's okay until I can go see her today." He scowled, shook his head. "I told Rachel to come here, but I don't know if she will. After I left, it probably took all of thirty minutes for her shields to go up again."

"So burn them down next time. Ashes are a lot harder to reassemble."

Jon flashed a grim smile at Matt's flat comment. "That worked for Savannah because she's as ruthless as you are. Plus, at a subconscious level, she already trusted you. Rachel's got a lot going on in her head. She doesn't trust anyone, even herself. I won't completely kick the chair out from under her until I'm certain she knows that I'll be there to catch her. I don't want to make what's already damaged worse."

The men exchanged a significant look, then Lucas grinned. "The universe has aligned. Scorpio is in Pisces, or however the hell he'd say it. This is the one for him."

Jon's brow rose. "What are you talking about?"

"You know exactly what he's talking about." Peter shook his head. "You probably knew it the second you found out she wasn't married."

Matt nodded despite Jon's bland expression. "I've seen that look twice before. The first time was the night Lucas threw down his poker chips and said Cass would agree to marry him in twenty-four hours."

"Cocky bastard," Peter snorted.

Lucas shrugged but memory gleamed in his eye. "It worked."

"With considerable help. Shock-and-awe tactics, bicycle boy."

Lucas bared his teeth as Matt shifted his focus to Peter. "You were the second time. When you came back from Afghanistan and found out Dana was hurt and alone, you didn't even put down your duffle bag before you were back out the door."

"Three times," Jon amended, conceding with a smile. "The night you told us you were tired of dicking around, that you were going after Savannah with the whole fucking arsenal, quote, unquote."

Matt inclined his head again, mouth set in a determined line. "Each of us may not know her name, but the moment she sets foot on our stage, we recognize her right off. Your whole life—every skill you've learned, as a Dom and as a member of this company—has prepared you to go after her. And you know exactly what kind of assets you have at your disposal."

"A whole fucking arsenal," Jon muttered. "Speaking of which, we're one short."

"I'm here." Ben's voice drifted around the corner. "Too much ball-and-chain testosterone in that room. I'm staying clear so I don't get caught in the epidemic. But if you need the kind of help I'm better equipped to provide than any of the rest, you know where to find me."

"He means his ego, which is the size of Texas," Lucas put in.

"Not only my ego," Ben rebounded. Jon heard the snick of a laptop closing and then Ben appeared, flanking Peter. His emerald green eyes, impeccably tailored suit and sharply styled black hair made him every inch the legal pit bull Matt paid him to be.

The surge of reassurance was something Jon could admit—at least to himself—he needed. He had the head of the pack, the calculations wizard, the operations genius and the cutthroat lawyer on his side. And, from a woman's point of view, that was the least of their combined gifts. As Matt had pointed out, he had a unique set of backup resources, ones he had a feeling would mesh well with Rachel's as-yet-untapped gifts. Her sweet pussy had responded with a surge of cream when he'd painted those images in her mind last night.

Always before, he'd embraced something like this as a challenging puzzle, something he could patiently wait for the universe to reveal. He'd enjoy the journey, seeing a clear beginning and end. But they were right. This was different.

Before last night, he might have said the beginning was learning she wasn't married. But that wasn't true. All that spiritual discipline they teased him about, he'd applied with agonizing rigor over the past year. He'd meditated, immersed himself in late night inventing marathons, gone to their favored club and worked out sexual pressure in scenes with various submissives.

All tactics to handle the ache in his groin and the even more painful ache in his heart when they grew to be too much, like when he caught a glimpse of her smile, or the yearning behind her eyes. There'd been moments, such as when she touched him during the yoga *nidra*, that his Master's instincts had shot forth so hard and strong, it had taken everything he had not to reach out with both hands and seize what she was subconsciously offering. Plunder that mouth, wrap his hands in her hair and take, take, take.

More than once, he'd considered not attending anymore, but something had kept him going back. So yesterday sure as hell hadn't been the beginning. It had merely been the drill bit that had plunged into that vein of contained feelings. Emotions were exploding inside him like a full blown, out-of-control gusher.

Matt had called it with pinpoint accuracy. She'd stepped square onto his stage, and everything else was in darkness. In a matter of two days, she'd become the only purpose. Every step was vital. He needed to be careful, plan things out. Unfortunately, his instinct wanted to run her down like a mastiff breathing down the neck of a fleeing rabbit. He wasn't used to being in that kind of mindset. He was the thinker, the fix-it guy. The big-picture guru.

His uneasiness must have shown in his face, for Ben sobered, a rare occurrence. "Seriously, man. You won't fail."

Matt flashed his trademark dangerous smile. "We never do."

"Mr. Forte." Janet, their supremely efficient admin, spoke through Jon's speaker phone. "I know you're in conference, but Rachel Madison is here to see you."

She'd come, and much earlier than he expected. Every part of him reacted, muscles tensing like an eager predator at the end of a chain. He saw it reflected in their knowing glances. Still, trying for calm, Jon lifted a brow, glanced at Matt. "How does she do that? I never have to tell her anything. Not only did she know I wanted to see Rachel right away, she knew she should interrupt me, even if I was in a meeting with you all."

"Probably *particularly* if you were in meeting with us," Lucas said dryly. "Janet is a scary woman. We all know she's a demon Matt hired straight from the bowels of hell. She knows everything."

"Actually, I'm an angel, sent by God to keep you from drowning in all your depravations and sins."

Matt chuckled as Lucas winced. Jon glanced toward the speaker phone. "Point taken, Janet. Show her back here and then you can go back to preening your feathers and shining your halo."

"Please. Haloes are so last millennium. We prefer the aura of light that drives men to their knees in awe and wonder."

"Seems to me they could do a lot better things for you in that position than—" Ben grinned as the phone disconnected sharply enough to cause a static pop on the speaker phone. When Matt gave him a quelling look, the lawyer raised both hands in surrender. "Clearing out."

Peter followed him as Matt rose, gave Jon a nod. "You know where we'll be."

The unspoken message being— *Yes, we never fail, but if you stumble, we're here.* Jon made a Herculean attempt to clear his mind, relax his shoulders.

Lucas lingered last. "You need backup in here?"

"No, I've got this one. But thanks, to all of you. I just hope I haven't fucked it up."

"Well, she's here. That's got to be a foot in the door, even if she's here to put it up your ass."

Before Jon could reply to that, Janet appeared in the doorway. The attractive forty-something in a form-fitting pale yellow suit and pearls offered her cool smile. Her warm voice and professional mien gave nothing of their previous volley away. "Mr. Forte, are you ready for Ms. Madison?"

That's a good question, Jon thought. *Now or never.* He'd said he knew her, but knew nothing about her. He would make the connection, though, because as Matt had said, his whole life had been about this moment. Even if he'd never realized it until now.

Chapter Seven

∞

When Rachel parked in the well-lit K&A deck, she noted they had guards who patrolled each of the four levels. No visitor had to be concerned about the potential hazards of a dimly lit parking garage. Further, the one on her level gave her helpful instructions on how to get to Jon Forte's office from the garage elevators. She was on the approved visitor list, an unexpected and somewhat unsettling courtesy.

She'd been questioning her sanity for the entire drive, but as she stepped into the elevator, she reminded herself again that she owed him a face-to-face explanation. She wasn't here...to be what he wanted. She'd worn her most conservative slacks and blouse combination, the one she used for PT department presentations to the hospital board. She'd pulled her hair up in a neat bun, taming all those feminine strands around her face with pins and a black ribbon.

She'd fought with herself on that, because pulling her hair back so severely only emphasized the stress and age lines. She'd compromised with a light application of makeup—even when making a point, a woman needed some vanity, and the bruise, though much better, needed some coverage—but the color on her lips was a subdued burgundy. While she wore heels, they were sensible black pumps.

Her nerves felt like a wheat field churned up by the passage of a tornado, leaving an uneven impression of the devastation. She vacillated between shivers of pleasure, remembering every millisecond of the night he'd spent with her, and shame at what she'd revealed about herself, how much she'd surrendered. She was frightened, scared of what he'd pulled from her. Nearly a dozen times, she'd almost reversed course to do exactly everything he'd ordered in that note.

To counter that, she'd retreated into anger more than once. He'd sabotaged her on her home ground. She had a world of poison boiling in her gut, and it didn't much matter to her that it was old poison. He'd uncapped the bottle. Maybe if he got a full dose of it, he'd realize how pointless this was. They'd politely say their goodbyes. Oh God, what if he kept coming to yoga class? What if he didn't?

Getting off at the top floor and seeing all the signs of wealth and success—a mahogany desk in the admin area, Persian rugs and priceless original artwork on the walls—gave her pause. Home ground advantage meant something entirely different here. Her home ground had whimsical cat figurines and romantic Waterhouse prints bought at warehouse discount. It was as much a home court advantage as a rabbit's hole was to a terrier. This...this was definitely not that. As she approached the desk, the only thing that eased a smidgen of her growing tension was the plaque the very efficient-looking woman had on her desk.

Secretary is not a derogatory term. Otherwise the government position would be Administrative Assistant of State.

She gave her name, but the secretary was already rising. "Hello, Ms. Madison. I'm Janet. Martin said you were coming up to see Mr. Forte. Follow me, please."

She was taken down a hall designed with open spaces, more exceptional artwork and skylights letting in sunlight. One threw a colored design on the cream carpet and she looked up to see a stained-glass depiction of St. George and the Dragon. A medieval-looking script had been stamped in the decorative frame.

Some days, the dragon wins.

"The Kensington men have an unusual sense of humor," Janet noted. The woman had stopped, giving her a moment to look. Was Rachel losing her mind, or did it feel like the woman knew exactly why she was here, and how this would go? A scary idea because, despite everything Rachel had told herself she was going to say, now that she was a breath from seeing him, she wasn't sure anymore.

This had been a mistake.

"I think I left something in my car. I should…"

Janet had taken a step away from her, and now stood in an open doorway. "Mr. Forte, are you ready for Ms. Madison?"

He must have nodded, because Janet turned then, gesturing her forward. Rachel managed a polite thanks, hoping she sounded far calmer than she was. As Janet passed her, the woman touched her arm.

"You know, knights slay all kinds of dragons. If you give them the chance."

The whispered observation left Rachel staring after her. At least until she heard a quiet throat clearing. Telling her heart to settle back in its proper place in her chest, she turned her attention to who awaited her over that threshold.

Last night, she hadn't had much time to consider him in his working clothes. He often changed into his suit before he left the studio, but she'd only seen him in it at a distance, when he was getting into his car. According to one of her more inquisitive students who'd quizzed him, his silver sports car was a hydrogen-fueled prototype. It probably cost a small fortune.

Now she saw him standing by his desk in his gray slacks and silk tie, his white shirt sleeves rolled up. He had a pencil tucked behind his ear, probably working on the drawing she saw in progress on the large drafting table in the corner. She found it intriguing he was using that instead of a computer screen. He had lead smudges on his fingertips.

She captured all that detail in one hungry moment before she met his blue eyes. They locked with hers, and then his gaze slid over her face, her hair, down over her body. It was a slow, deliberate appraisal, every inch underscoring that she'd not done as he'd commanded. It made something quiver low in her belly. Surely, he'd known she wouldn't. But in his presence she suddenly, fervently wished she had, that she'd obeyed him, given him what would please him.

God and Goddess, she'd known she couldn't handle this. She couldn't make any more stupid choices based on cravings she couldn't afford to have. She'd taught herself that the only thing she could do to protect herself was act opposite from the way she desperately wanted to act. It was her only chance of staying out of trouble, no matter that every part of her felt she was doing the wrong thing. But when she couldn't trust herself, that was the whole point, right?

So though it was exponentially more difficult, she looked straight at him and spoke. As she did, her fingers closed into tight, cold balls and her voice shook. "I came to thank you for last night," she said. "And t-to bring you the name of another yoga instructor. You're...at a more advanced level than I offer...can offer."

She sounded harsh and abrasive, even to herself, but his expression didn't change. She had to imagine her practical heels embedded into the floor to keep herself still.

Jon glanced to his left. "Lucas, can we continue this later this afternoon?"

Her stomach gave a precipitous lurch. Now she thought about jumping out of her shoes and running. She hadn't even noticed the other man. Thank God she hadn't said anything less circumspect. But then she latched onto the name.

Lucas. *He's spent a great deal of time studying the way to pleasure a woman with his mouth. He'd thrust his tongue deep into your pussy, do things that would make you mindless...*

"Sure." The masculine voice was as confident and commanding as Jon's, though not as velvet-toned. It still was capable of running a shiver up her spine. Now that she'd been proven right at least three times, she couldn't deny her ability to detect a Master from a straightforward alpha male. She could modify The Weather Girls' one-hit wonder. *It's raining*

Doms... She was a safari tourist, come to glimpse a lion, and had instead walked into a full, ravenous pride of them.

The anxious humor didn't help her as much as she'd hoped. Having seen the photos, she nevertheless wasn't surprised they didn't minimize his impact on her senses. Lucas Adler moved with the grace and controlled power of an athlete, and the sculpted lines of his handsome face could have graced an Egyptian prince in a previous life.

Though she tried not to look, she couldn't help focusing on his mouth. She'd worn a trim bolero jacket over her blouse, and she was glad for it. His direct, steady glance, combined with the memory of Jon's words, the idea that he might let Lucas put his clever mouth on her, had her nipples drawing tight. She shifted her attention back to Jon before she made a fool of herself by lowering her eyes in automatic deference before both of them. The speculative look, the hint of a feral, humorless smile on Jon's sensual lips, told her he knew exactly where her thoughts had gone.

Lucas was headed toward the door, where she was standing. She should step out of the way, but she couldn't move. Literally couldn't, because panic had frozen her in place. A brush of Lucas' jacket was followed by the touch of his strong hand on her lower back, gently but firmly moving her farther into the office so that he could not only get past her but close the door after him.

She was alone with Jon, and an acre of glass windows overlooking the river.

He was still looking at her, but instead of meeting his gaze again, she moved to those windows. Ten feet of carpet and weighted silence lay between them, but in reality, there was so much more than that. Just like that, all the false constructs she'd used to get herself here, the anger and rationalizations, all the games she played with herself, were beyond her grasp. There was only the sad truth. Too much truth to give to him.

"You shouldn't have done that this morning," she said. "It means nothing. Can mean nothing."

He didn't say anything. No interruption, no argument. She didn't know if that made her feel desolate beyond measure or apprehensive. She didn't want to feel anything. She should turn around and leave. She'd delivered her message. But of course she kept talking.

"When my husband left me, he said, 'The way to your heart is through your...cunt.'" She swallowed, hating how ugly that word sounded now. It had been much different when Jon said it last night. "And he said he couldn't read the road signs anymore."

Jon shifted. His proximity was a heat against her back, like the sun coming in on her front, but she crossed her arms over herself. A reflex, a sign she didn't want to be touched, even though he hadn't moved toward her, hadn't closed that distance. She kept her back straight, chin up, eyes on the moving water, the skyline. "I was so hurt and angry, I lashed out, something I rarely did in our marriage. I told him he couldn't read them because he wasn't brave enough. He said no. It was because he wasn't interested. Not anymore."

She drew a shaky breath, remembering the lancing pain of that final strike. "People are cruel when they're hurting, and somewhere inside him was the man I married, who didn't really mean those words. But it doesn't mean it wasn't true. It wasn't in his nature. I could have lived with that, even been happy, if we were friends, or he loved me for whoever I was, even though he couldn't understand it. When true love exists in a relationship, it can overcome pretty much anything. Isn't that what we tell ourselves? It's what we have to believe to stay sane."

She gave a faint smile, though it hurt her face. "But whether it was girlish fantasy or not, the reality was that I mistook selfish, lazy and overbearing for protective and alpha. And what I was looking for...I couldn't even define it in the first years of my married life. As the world became so sophisticated, I understood it more, but it was already too late, even then. I just didn't know it." She shook her head, looked down at her hands. "Nowadays women are strong, outspoken. They bristle with outrage at the idea of a man looking at them as a possession. Those kind of women would consider me a freak...weak, stupid. Maybe mentally unbalanced."

The chuckle she attempted now came out sounding like a strangled sob. "They'd call me a coward too, but it wasn't fear that kept me from leaving him, telling him off. All I wanted was to take care of him, and be loved for it. Even if I couldn't have anything more, I could have accepted that. The submission is...it's far more than sex. I know you know that. I see it in your eyes."

Her voice quavered again, and she had to pause, compose herself. She was a mature, single woman. She would get through this. But the truth was it destroyed her, knowing she'd finally found someone in the world who understood, and not just intellectually. His Dominance was as innate to his blood as her submission was to hers. Though it was too late for anything else, there had to be comfort in that validation, right? "Sometimes I tried to pretend he was the man I needed him to be. I had this picture of him in my head, and everything he did, I interpreted it as something else. If I tried harder, if I just loved him enough, it would be okay... The worse he treated me, the harder I tried. Until even he was so disgusted with me, he left." She pressed her lips together. "They say life is a journey, and you should savor every moment. I was always a submissive, initially with no words to describe it, or a husband who could understand it. The frustration and confusion of it nearly drove me mad. There was a time...I didn't want...I couldn't see any reason to go on."

She couldn't stop at that marker, because if she did, she would truly fall to pieces. She put her mental weight against that door, before she could hear the report of the gun, see the flash of fire, feel the wet blood on her neck... Or think about the most important reason for it, the straw that had brought her to that terrible moment. She didn't want to share that now, not here. Couldn't do it.

"That was when I started taking yoga." Sensing somehow that he'd shifted closer to her, she blurted it out, pressing her palms against the glass to steady herself. "Something about it...it told me I could find peace there. I immersed myself in it, became an instructor. It helped me find the balance I needed."

She turned then, faced him, and it was so hard, for so many reasons, to meet that steady gaze. "I can't have what you're offering, Jon. You're too young, too late and I'm too fragile. It took me too long to pull myself back off the cliff edge and..." Her voice trembled once more. Closing her eyes, she steadied herself, spoke the desolate truth to that black space. "I won't survive going there again."

"I'm not offering anything."

He moved then, closing the space between them. She wanted to shrink back against the glass, but managed to keep herself still. He had such a smooth way of moving, gathering an energy around him that would always turn a woman's head. Her gaze latched onto the tie. His tie tack was a Japanese *kanji* symbol, one she recognized, because it was on a tapestry in her yoga studio. *Perseverance.*

Her palms tingled, wanting to reach out, touch it, flatten against his chest, feel his heat and heartbeat. When he laid his hands on her tense shoulders, she had another brief spurt of panic, but before she could wrench away, he'd pushed her against that panel of glass. It had absorbed a considerable amount of the sun's heat, such that it burned through the fabric of her bolero and the thin blouse beneath.

"Let me go," she whispered.

"No." The resolve beneath the deceptive mildness was terrifying to her. Gentle, thoughtful Jon, so interested in the philosophy and spirituality behind yoga, yet he also understood the strength of it as well. A mountain could be placid, but it didn't make it less immovable, less capable of demonstrations of utter power. However, while he could easily overcome her physically, he didn't need that. His voice and manner alone arrested her.

"What I left you this morning wasn't an offer, a suggestion or a proposal, Rachel. It was a command. I'm not going to give you a choice. Not right now. Because you've been given far too many. That isn't what you need, is it?"

The ache low in her belly was becoming that spinning wheel she knew too well, a wheel with blades that were going to cut her insides to pieces. "Please...don't."

"Keep your eyes down, Rachel. You'll meet my gaze when I give you permission. You understand?" The implacable tone shut that wheel down, made her knees weak. He leaned in, until his lips were at her temple, trailing down her skin in a highly distracting way until he reached her ear. "Tell me you understand."

Squeezing her eyes shut, she realized she'd latched onto his shirt at the waist, digging her fingers into the cloth as an anchor. A hard shudder ran through her body.

"Ssshh, girl. At the end of the third class I took with you, you told me you saw an old soul in my eyes. We talked about how we both believe in reincarnation, the idea that the physical body isn't the sum total of a human being. You remember?"

She nodded. He tightened his grip. "Well, when I look in your eyes, I see a young soul, one who had her wings clipped too soon. She doesn't realize they've grown back, that she can spread them out and fly, finally realize the potential that's been there all along."

"Jon—"

Shifting, he closed his hand over one of hers at his waist. When he detached her fingers, he gave them a quick squeeze and then turned, taking her across the room to the drafting table, the stool there. He slid a hip onto it, then perused her with that lingering, appraising look. "Take off the shoes."

He'd tolerate no disobedience, no discussion. She didn't know what that would mean if she resisted, but her pulse thudded hard against her throat. Her shoes. If that was all he was asking, she could do that, right? And truth, they were pinching her feet. As she slid out of them, giving up the two-inch height they'd offered, she immediately realized why slaves were made to go barefoot. There was a distinct difference in status, looking down at her feet clad only in thin stockings, positioned between his polished dress shoes. Her toes curled into the deep carpet.

"Now the hair. Take it down and hand me the pins."

He'd told her to leave her hair down in the note. He'd told her a lot of other things in that note as well. Would she strip down here if he ordered her to do so, no matter who might come in? She realized then that Lucas hadn't closed the door fully. It was pulled to the doorjamb, a small sliver of hallway visible. She needed to—

"Do as I tell you, Rachel. Trust your Master to take care of you."

It made her stomach jump. Coincidence, or had he read her thoughts that clearly? No matter what it was, she'd already raised her arms, and was pulling out the pins, letting down the uneven wisps in front that fell like feathers against her face, caressing her cheeks and lips. Then, finally, the clip and ribbon that held the bun, the twisted tail falling against her neck in a serpentine curve that teased the modest open neckline of the blouse.

"Don't straighten it. Hand me everything."

She extended her hand, but he didn't take them, not right away. He gripped her wrist, drew her between his spread thighs. Then he plucked the hair fasteners from her, set them aside.

"Put your hands on my knees and leave them there."

That at least was easy enough. She relished even that limited touch, though she knew she shouldn't. She shouldn't be doing any of this. She felt the muscle layers that ran from his thigh into the kneecap area, a hint of the bone beneath. She remembered his execution of Sleeping Thunderbolt once again, the strain of those thigh muscles, the flex of the calves. The arch of his beautiful body. Her gaze drifted. The way his thin cotton trousers had molded his groin area, drawing her eyes there...

Slacks of course were cut loosely, but with his thighs spread, she could discern the curve of testicles and more than a hint of what else was there, giving her the gratifying torment of knowing he was also aroused.

"Rachel, did I give you permission to look at my cock?"

"No." She dropped her gaze to her feet quickly.

"Good girl."

When he cupped both strong palms around her throat, a moan caught there, beneath his touch. She'd never had such a startlingly intense reaction to such a simple contact, but he'd recognized it for what it was last night. *You've wanted a collar for a long time...* Untwisting the tail of her hair, he spread it over her shoulders. Then he moved up to her face, burying his fingers into the thick strands there, combing it all out with his fingers in slow, firm strokes that had her eyes closing, her body swaying toward him.

His touch dropped to her jaw next, cradling it, his thumbs sweeping along her throat again to send those ripples of reaction across her body, like a sudden breeze flitting over still water. When he pushed the jacket off her shoulders, she didn't resist, might have even shrugged to help. It dropped to the floor behind her. Her heart thudded harder when he flicked open two additional buttons of her blouse, revealing her bra. It wasn't overly sexy, a serviceable undergarment with a touch of pretty lace at the cups and enough padding that her nipples wouldn't disrupt the way the shirt smoothed over her bosom. His arm slid around her waist, his fingers plucking the shirt free of her belted slacks.

121

The pressure of his hold brought her in another step, her hips pressed against the inside of his thighs. She wasn't breathing. He'd touched her last night, but denied her the ability to touch him all that much, except for lying on his chest at the end. Now her body burned with the need to touch and taste, but he hadn't given her permission. She embraced this state of longing, satisfaction held out of reach by his will. It was painful, pleasurable—a rhythmic seesaw between both, almost like the slow drag of a tongue along the clitoris, from the base to the ultrasensitive top, intensity building and receding, building and receding.

That was entirely the wrong kind of thought to be having right now, because her breath had caught in her throat, fingers twitching, thighs tensing. Everywhere he was touching her was coming alive, taking away her ability to think.

Reaching up under the shirt, he slid along her spine, making her arch into him. When he breathed against her jaw, it was flavored with a satisfied, very male half-chuckle. With no hesitation, he unclipped the bra so it loosened beneath the blouse.

"Unbutton your cuffs and take it off through the sleeves. Leave the shirt on."

He left his hands resting low on her hips as she did it, but leaned against the stool's backrest, watching the arch and stretch of her body as she complied. Opening the cuffs, she slid one strap down over her wrist, then the other, then pulled the whole thing through. He took it from her hand, lifted it to inhale the inside of one soft cup. Watching him do it made her breasts ache for the mere stroke of his breath. His gaze dropped to them and another of those tiny moans caught in her throat at the flare of desire in his eyes. He didn't seem to mind her watching him now, but when his gaze shifted back to her face, she lowered her lashes on instinct.

"I like seeing a woman's nipples through a thin blouse. Particularly yours. Kneel for me, Rachel."

She remembered what he'd said about the lipstick, about how he wanted it marking his cock when she sucked him off. Her pussy was already wet, she could feel it, but now those internal muscles clenched, wanting him, wanting to service him that way.

She should have learned from last night he wasn't predictable. Instead, once she was on her knees, he began to stroke her hair again, applying pressure so that she slid to one hip on the Berber carpet. Now leaning against the outside of his left leg, she dropped her head to his thigh as he petted her, slid his knuckles along her cheek, played his fingers through her hair, fondled and massaged.

"The drawing I'm working on has to be done in the next hour. You'll stay right where you are until I'm done. No matter who comes in, or what occurs, you stay where you are. Tell me you understand."

"I understand." Her voice was barely a whisper, but she got it out, and thankfully, he didn't ask her to repeat herself.

"If the position gets uncomfortable, you tell me, and I'll give you permission to shift. Until then, all you have to do is kneel at your Master's feet, Rachel. That's the only responsibility you have."

She couldn't bring herself to call him that, but every time he did, her reaction to it was obvious, in the way her pussy clenched on too much empty space and her skin tingled, from the tips of her breasts to the sensitive pulse points of her wrists. It was like the mere word cast a net over her, the rope of it caressing her everywhere, holding her to him.

The surface part of her mind was resisting, screaming that she couldn't possibly do this, that she knew this wasn't going to work, that she'd come here to bring an end to it and she was impossibly weak. But there was another part of her, quieter yet somehow stronger, that made her close her eyes and press her cheek into his thigh, enough that her lips could graze the stretch of his slacks over it. His hand continued to stroke her neck, his fingers tangling in her hair. When she did that, the grip tightened briefly, but he didn't stop her from doing it.

She heard the scratch of his pencil, felt the minute shifts of his body and knew he'd begun to work on the drawing. She couldn't help stealing glances at him, at once amazed and incredibly aroused by how focused he was on what he was doing, the set of his mouth, the quick shifts of his eyes over the drawing elements. Occasionally, he rumbled something, a calculation or other thought he was voicing aloud to himself, and he might erase or move to another part of the paper.

She made a discovery of her own, that her body could be in an astounding state of lassitude and intense awareness simultaneously. Her body literally throbbed, blood pounding against pulse points, everything in her so physically needy that it was like running out of oxygen. But she was also so incredibly still under his touch, content to stay this way until the end of time if needed. Because it pleased him.

Kneel at your Master's feet. The only responsibility you have.

She knew humans had an incredible ability to rationalize bad decisions. If it had been an athletic event, she would have won a medal for sheer quantity long ago. However, so what if she chose to savor this one moment of her life? If she had to turn her back on it in the next few moments—

No, not *if*. She knew it was a foregone conclusion that she ultimately had to reject all this. But then, that was a few minutes from now, wasn't it?

Even knowing how pathetic and flimsy that was, she couldn't resist the chance to be here, quiet under his will, so aroused at how he was doing his work while at the same time exerting his Mastery over her... She wanted him to take her here, on his office carpet. She wanted him to open his slacks and let her suck him to climax. She wanted to fall asleep this way, tied up in all these delicious unrealized imaginings.

Though the way his hand was stroking through her hair suggested an absent-minded gesture, she could sense how attentive he was to her presence, to everything she was feeling.

Those who thought men couldn't multitask had never met Jon Forte. She had no doubt he could design the answer to free energy for the world while making her so aroused she might die from the feeling.

"Jon."

At the familiar male voice, she came out of her reverie, her pulse jumping at the quick rap of knuckles on the door. Out of the corner of her eye, she saw it push open.

It was Peter.

Chapter Eight

Jon flexed his hand on her nape, a reminder as she began to push herself away from his knee. A flutter of embarrassment and uncertainty went through her, the muscles under his touch going tense as wire. "I'm on the phone with Brad in Costa Rica," Peter said without preamble. "They have an error code on the CNC. Brad's thinking it may have been damaged by a power surge. His guys have traced the ladder logic to a certain point, but now they're thinking we need to send over a factory expert to look at it. I was thinking I'd let him tell you what's up first, just in case you have a different take on it."

"Okay, put him on speaker."

If there had been any discernible pause, anything she could call a surprised hesitation or shock at finding her here, she didn't detect it in Peter's voice. He also didn't greet her, didn't address her, didn't acknowledge her separately. He was treating her as a slave doing her Master's bidding.

She might not have been in any BDSM clubs until her ill-advised visit to Club More, but when she was at the peak of her crazed fever to integrate this in her life, she'd delved into hundreds of Internet scenarios that stoked her own desires. However, it wasn't even that which told her Peter's behavior was appropriate, expected. She just *knew*.

The realization sent a hard jolt through her, a combined physical and emotional reaction she couldn't control. Peter touched her shoulder, an intimate slide of his fingers over the line to her collarbone. Through that casual touch, he would recognize there was no bra beneath, even if the stretch of the nearly transparent silk over her erect nipples didn't. He pulled her hair, a mild tease, before he moved toward Jon's desk and punched the button on the phone on the desk. "Brad, I've got Jon here. Go."

Last night had been a shock to her system, the details of which she'd begun to deny and avoid almost before she let herself revisit them. So in all her years of picturing the first true Master-sub experience of her life, she never would have imagined this. Or how overwhelming and stimulating it was, such that the shaking was getting worse. She had to lock her jaw so her teeth wouldn't chatter. She kept her eyes down, fastened on Jon's polished shoe. She wondered who did that for him. Probably a dry cleaner. The laces were precisely double-knotted. The thin dark sock etched out the bones of his ankle. She couldn't help herself. She made a track along the curve of that ball joint with her fingertip, a whisper of a touch, then followed the slope of the shoe's mouth.

He was asking questions of the invisible Brad. The questions were involved, technical issues regarding machine programming and gears, engine parts. Listening to him talk like that, all while having her at his knee like this, was quite possibly the most erotic thing she'd ever experienced. He hadn't stopped that absent stroke of her hair, but as she slipped a finger inside his shoe, trying to trace his insole, he gave a lock of hair a quick tug, a reproof. She stopped, but kept her hand on his foot. He didn't tug again, so she was glad the contact was okay. Her cheek was against his thigh after all, lips near the outside of his knee.

From the position of his legs, Peter was apparently leaning against Jon's desk, his ankles crossed. Unlike Jon and Lucas, he wore jeans, Nikes. He probably had his arms crossed over his broad chest, biceps contracted in a way sure to catch a woman's eye.

Until this moment, she realized she hadn't even thought about her blouse being open several buttons. In this position, Peter definitely could see the bare curves. Instead of being appalled, she was excited. She was safe with Jon. A Master who would take care of her, like he said.

"Call us if that doesn't work," Peter said at last. "We can always send someone down, and I'll be back there next week."

"Hey, bring Dana with you again. She scalped me last time and I want to win my money back."

"You're an embarrassment, Brad. You should know better than to play Blind Man's Bluff with a blind *woman*. I'll tell her you're ready to lose more of your money though."

Peter cut the connection after a few more comments back and forth. "Thanks, Jon. I knew you were on a tight timeline on that drawing, but this was holding up production."

"No problem. I'm pretty much ready to send this down to scanning. Just need to put the revision number on it. Rachel's good for the concentration."

"I'll bet she is." Peter pushed off the desk and moved to stand beside Jon, studying the drawing in progress. As he did, he gave her shoulder that teasing caress again, and then he caught the collar of her shirt, eased it off her shoulder. Rachel held her breath, every nerve ending conscious of Jon's fingers as he adjusted his sensual, slow massage so Peter could trace her bare collarbone. When he dropped to the upper curve of her breast, it made her jerk, sent a jolt through her nipple like electric shock, even though Peter didn't touch it. "Beautiful," he murmured.

It wasn't trepidation making her quake like that, not by a long shot. She was burning up with desire, two men's hands touching her at one Master's behest.

...let my friends gang rape you in an alley...

No. It wasn't like that. It wasn't. She thrust it from her mind, her hand tightening on Jon's foot. Whatever this was, she wanted it clean and pure, a treasure she could lock away from all that, because she was smart enough to know it was going to end soon enough. The fact Peter was so comfortable with her here had to mean that there'd been others. Jon was a young, single man, and they'd obviously shared subs before. It was as she'd realized earlier. Whatever this might mean to her, and what it was for Jon, could never be the same thing.

"Hey." She didn't even realize her aroused trembling had become something else, or that Peter had left, until Jon bent and put both arms around her, pulling her deeper into the vee of his legs. Her back was against the stool between them. She was twitching with an emotional reaction that felt too close to a panic attack for comfort. "Easy. Breathe. You're amazing, Rachel."

"You like your women edgy and neurotic?" She gave a harsh chuckle, but she was holding onto his arm that stretched over her breasts. "God, Jon, that was...I didn't even...it didn't bother me. I wanted...more."

"I know."

"This is the way it starts." She needed to get up, needed to put space away from him. "I can't get lost in this."

He kept her captured inside his arms easily. "Rachel, if you'd been here alone, and Peter had done that, what would you have done? No, stop squirming. Close your eyes, imagine it. I'm not here. He is. You're sitting on the sofa, and he leans down, unbuttons your blouse, pulls it off your shoulder to admire your breasts. How does that feel?"

She set her jaw. "Wrong. He's engaged." At his silence, she knew there was more to it, but she couldn't say that, any more than she could call Jon...what everything in her wanted to call him. She settled for a whisper of the truth. "You aren't there."

He cupped her jaw, tilted her head up and back to his mouth and claimed her lips. Hot, strong, forceful, so she continued to quiver in his grip, submitting to the demand. When he lifted his head, she was nearly limp. "You're damn right I'm not." She saw that flash of steel, his lips set in a serious line. "You're teaching tonight, right? But tomorrow your schedule is clear?"

She should wonder how he knew that, but all she could think about was the picture they made, her on her knees, pulled back against him, her body arched up to him this way, breasts straining against the partially open shirt, every part of her hungering for him. His long legs caging her on either side. Those blue eyes filling every corner of her vision. She nodded.

"All right then. Tomorrow night, I'm going to come to your place at seven o'clock. It better be spotless, the way you normally keep it. I'm particular to eggplant parmesan and a good red wine, and from what I saw of your kitchen, you like to cook. You'll put out one place setting. Mine. Any food you eat or wine you drink that night will come from my hands, my mouth."

It would never happen. Between now and then, the enchantment of this moment would disappear and her fears would return. The spell only existed in his presence. She'd be calling him frantically, hoping to get his voice mail, telling him she'd had something unexpected come up. She'd run away to check into a hotel for the night. She'd —

"I'll be on time, so five minutes before I get there, you unlock the door. Then you kneel by my chair. Submissive position. Hands behind your back, back straight, knees parted to shoulder width. You leave your hair down. You don't do that too often, do you? Because you think you're too old to wear it down like a girl, but you can't bear to cut it." Before she could respond, he continued. "Turn up your heat to keep warm, because other than this beautiful hair, you'll wear only that pair of cherry-red heels. What's your favorite flower?"

She couldn't keep up with him, let alone voice her reservations. "Wildflowers," she whispered. "No particular kind."

"What grows wild on the roadsides, hmm?" His lips brushed the sensitive skin behind her ear. "Perfect." Sliding his hand down the curve of her spine to her ass, he weighed one buttock in his hand. As he smoothed his fingers over the fabric of her slacks, then tightened his grip, a needy sound came from her lips.

"I know you're worrying that by tomorrow night you'll have shut down or be running from this again. And you will be. But I'm going to give you a leash, something to keep you tethered to my will, even when I'm not with you to enforce it. Come with me."

He rose then, bringing her to her feet. They were standing so close together that the curve of her bottom slid over his erection. She froze, the urge to rub against him so overwhelming she didn't think she could stop herself. Holding her hips to keep her still, he bent his knees enough to slide his hard length along that indentation between her legs and up the crease between her buttocks. She gasped, needing his strength to keep from swaying forward.

"Yeah, you're hot for it." His voice was husky, rough with his own lust, and she would have sold her soul in that moment to be fucked by him. Straightforward, raw, no embellishment. "Hot and ready, and that's how I want to keep you."

He guided her over to his desk. "Lean over and put your palms on the wood." His hand was pressing into her back even as he gave her the order, and she had no will to resist. Her fingers curled, uncertain, as he slid her belt free, then unhooked her slacks, opening up the zipper so the fabric fell loose and lower on her hips.

"Stay right in this position." He was moving away, and now she was staring out the windows at the river, realizing how many scenarios like this might be playing out behind tinted glass. She heard his door close, the lock slide into place.

"Peter was a brief hint of possibilities, but this is between you and me."

He caught both the slacks and panties beneath and slid them down to her thighs, leaving her bottom naked to the touch of the air. She swallowed, fears and worries rising again.

"Easy, girl. Stay like that and be quiet." He'd moved to a closet, was rummaging. She heard drawers opening and closing, and then, interestingly, the sound of metal tools clinking together. "This adjustment will do...I think. Yeah, that'll do the trick. I need to custom fit one of these for you, but in the interim, this will work."

He returned then. "Close your eyes. I want you to feel what I'm putting on you before you see it."

She obeyed, that amazing little jump going through all her limbs as he fitted something around her throat, a strap of some sort that buckled. Then a slim chain drifted along the line of her spine as he threaded it down the back of the shirt. It apparently divided into two pieces, because it went around her waist and he hooked it together again below her navel.

His hand slid over her mound, and something cool and metal pressed against her clit. When it pinched, she gasped, a choked sound of arousal as the nerves he'd been stoking the past hour caught fire. It took everything she had not to writhe against him, push into his hand.

"Steady there. Be still." His other hand gripped her buttock again, squeezed hard enough to hold her motionless as he pressed here and there. Suddenly that metal piece seemed affixed to her clitoris, a slightly alarming feeling. Then another, smaller piece was being eased into her pussy, just inside the entrance. It gave her a curious and dizzying sense her labia had been spread and opened, only a bit past its normal resting place, but the sensation made it feel much more vulnerable. Another slim chain ran from there between her buttocks, hooking to the waist chain and then continuing to the back of her neck, attaching to the collar piece.

"All right, open your eyes. You can use your fingers to feel."

When she obeyed, she saw there was in fact something that looked like a metal molded shield fitting snugly over her clit, making the throbbing beneath all the more excruciating.

132

Below that, the piece that dipped into her pussy worked like an additional clamp to hold the clitoral piece.

Jon closed his hands on either wrist, brought her arms up and her hands to where she could feel the buckle of the collar. There was a pendant there...no, not a pendant. She swallowed.

"It's a lock," he confirmed. "It holds the collar and the end of the chain, Rachel. You can't take any of it off. Only I can do that. Now, it's not unbreakable. You could probably tear all of it off if you were pretty determined. A really sharp knife would cut through the collar. But I'm betting you won't do that, because this will keep your mind on everything I've told you to do, not on the many reasons you think you shouldn't."

As he turned her to face him, she knew she had to be wild and wide-eyed, her body in a roiling state. He hadn't put a vibrator inside her, turned it on high speed. It hadn't been necessary. Like having her on her knees next to him, it was what it all meant that stimulated every nerve ending, captured every thought. He tipped up her chin, held her gaze with an unwavering stare.

"One of our drivers will take you to your class tonight. The driver will wait for you, and take you home afterward. Tomorrow, if you need to go to the grocery store, he'll take you. You're not driving while you're wearing this. I hate that I won't be able to watch you teach a class, knowing all this is beneath your clothes, that you're wet and needy." He flashed a wicked grin. "I'd wear loose-fitting yoga clothes and stay away from headstands, unless you want to explain some things."

She wasn't sure if she wanted to strangle him or tell him not to do this to her. Or beg him to come home with her. There was no room for shame or inhibition with this feeling, and she expected that was the point. "I don't expect cleaning and cooking will take up your whole day," he continued. "There's a book by your bed. You have about fifty pages left of it. You'll finish that, so you can tell me how it ends. I also want you to meditate for an hour sometime before our date tomorrow."

133

Sure, and she'd figure out the answer to Middle East peace while she was at it. He was insane, but even worse, he was now quite serious.

"You'll bathe and shave the way I instructed you to do this morning. Now, two very important things." He lifted two fingers, taking one down as he made the first point. "One. No release without my permission. Two." He slid that one finger along her nose, to her mouth, spreading moisture from her tongue onto her lips. It made her acutely aware her lower body was naked to him, her bare pussy inches away from his body. "You will wear that lipstick tomorrow night, because I *am* going to see those moist, painted lips wrapped around my cock, watch your tongue lick my come from them."

"Jon…" No question, his name a whimper, her knees buckling with all of it. He had her around the waist now, though, and he pushed her back down, face forward, until her upper torso was flat against his desk, her sensitive nipples registering the cool wood through the thin cloth. The position constricted the collar and chains at her throat, between her buttocks and against that clit piece. When he put his hand on the back of her neck, it was as effective as if he'd clamped her to the wood. He crowded her, the hard evidence of his arousal between her legs, increasing the pressure on that clit piece. It took everything she had not to move.

"I let you get away with defiance this morning, but it will be the last time." He slid his finger along her spine, briefly tangling the chain. "Come to think of it, this isn't enough of a reminder. You need one more."

"A reminder of…what?"

Instead of answering, he slid his arms underneath her, lifting her at the bend of her hips, forearms pressing into her lower abdomen and above her breasts. Turning, he carried her without any awkwardness the three strides to the drafting stool. Before she could react to the unorthodox transport, he had her bent over it. The slacks around her thighs inhibited her movement. She had one thrilling moment of dazed comprehension as he picked up a flexible 18-inch metal ruler, and then he slapped it down on her bare buttocks.

She gripped the edge of the stool, a cry breaking from her lips. It hurt so badly the sting was just the beginning of it. It radiated out, every nerve ending screaming. But then he brought it down again.

He was holding on to her forearm, his own stretched out in front of her, and she bit down on him, trying to hold in the next shriek. He didn't flinch, didn't remove his arm. Even as she was biting she had to taste him, like some crazed animal. Oh God, this hurt. But her covered clit was against the stool, and a spasm racked her, an insane, unexpected surge from the depths of her womb.

"J-Jon..."

She came during his fifth, sixth and seventh stroke, and she was sure she had welts, possibly even broken flesh. But the climax racked her convulsing body, undeniable proof of her gut-level reaction to the pain, the punishment.

He didn't touch her otherwise, though, so it was hard, intense and then done, leaving her gasping, her mouth still open on his skin. She was making those little whimpers again, and as he lifted her to her feet, she had to sag against him. He held her with one arm, sliding her panties and slacks back in place with the other. The climax immediately soaked the panel. He took his time with her clothes, as was necessary one-handed, but seemed to take great pleasure in it.

"Let me..." She was struggling to breathe, wanting him to let her go so her knees *could* buckle. "Let me suck you now. Please."

Was that her voice, that rough, uncontrolled plea?

Instead, he tucked in her shirt, pushed her back against the drafting table as he curved his fingers over her clit, bound inside that metal mold under the fabric. She pushed into his touch, a wave of aftershocks making her moan again. He let her ride it, his unrelenting gaze on her face, not letting her hide from him.

"Not right now." He buckled her belt back in place, then cupped her buttocks, bringing her off the table. She flinched at the firm contact, the agony and yet the remembered ecstasy of it making her lick her lips. "This, along with the rest, should keep your mind occupied until I see you tomorrow night. It's also a reminder you obey your Master, or you accept the consequences. Now look at my eyes."

He had to guide her there, a hand to her chin again. "For the next twenty-four hours, you think only of your Master's will. You've waited a long time to prove how devoted a slave you can be. Don't deny yourself what you truly want."

* * * * *

After he saw her out to the lobby, Jon turned her over to Max, the trusted head driver of the K&A limo fleet. Max had a variety of talents. He'd once been a Navy Seal, so understood Jon's instructions completely. If Rachel got discomfited by having a driver at her disposal and tried to do her own driving, he would make sure, with tact but firm insistence, that wasn't going to happen.

Jon realized his instincts had taken him further down Matt's suggested track than he'd expected. He wished they didn't have that damn meeting in New Orleans tomorrow morning. If they hadn't been planning it for the past month, he would have played the friend card with Matt to the nth degree and gotten out of it. He could have chosen a more gentle strategy, been more romantic than Dominant, but his gut had told him wooing was the wrong tact with her, particularly when she'd shown up with that tremulous jut to her chin and deliberate brush-off of his instructions. But there was no doubt that he was backing all those unresolved feelings into a corner. Before too long, she'd lash out at him, a cornered, injured lioness.

After tomorrow, he'd ask Matt for a few days off.

He was only in his office a few moments before Peter came in, Lucas and Ben right behind him. Jon knew Matt had left for an early lunch with Savannah. They tried to catch a sandwich together to hear the Wednesday jazz-in-the-park series once a month. Before they'd become a couple, it was one of the things Matt had worked into his schedule to get Savannah to stop living, eating and breathing her job. It had helped amp up her trust in him, so he'd had a more secure foothold to win her surrender, as Jon had pointed out earlier.

Jon was glad he was sitting behind his desk, because he was wound up pretty tight and didn't need Ben making jabs at his obvious, unrelieved erection. For all that his measures were going to give *her* a pretty agitated yoga class, let alone a restless night, he didn't anticipate sleeping at all. The mere memory of her responses had him jacked up even harder, and he fully intended to observe the same restriction he'd inflicted on her. Next time he came, it was going to be in her mouth or her lovely, needy pussy.

He should have known the K&A team didn't need to see it to know. Ben raised a brow. "You should have let her ease some of your pain, brother. You look like you could go off if one of us whistled Dixie at your dick."

"You've really got to get over your crush on him," Lucas advised. "It's embarrassing to the rest of us."

"It's those come-hither blue eyes and that pale vampire skin. Can't resist."

"Last month, it was me in my stretchy bike shorts. Come out of the closet and be done with it, man. You know there's a reason you're so into ass-fucking."

"For sweet, soft asses that come with a pussy, thank you. None of you qualify. Though your dick is so small I might…"

Peter was studying Jon's face. He gave Ben a thwack upside his head and Lucas a shove. "Shut up," he said. "Our boy's not in the mood."

Jon drummed his fingers on the desk. "I feel like a fucking Viking raider pillaging a convent of novices barely out of puberty."

"You're on the right track," Peter said quietly. "I saw her face, Jon. She needs what you're offering."

"But at this pace?" Jon templed his fingers and stared moodily at his desk. "I normally don't come at it like this."

"You're fine." Lucas sat down on his desk as Peter took the couch and Ben propped on the drafting table stool. "I've seen you go into a dungeon, pick out a woman who's never even met you and by the end of the night, you've sent her to Nirvana and back. You trust your instincts more than anyone I know. There's only one reason you're not doing it now."

"And why's that?" Jon flicked his glance at the CFO, envying his relaxed posture, foot propped against the desk panel, arms crossed over his chest.

"Matt told you earlier, same as he told me with Cass. She's the one. The one who matters more than any woman you've ever had. It's fucking with your radar, making you scared shitless you're going to screw it up."

When Jon shifted his attention to Ben, the only unattached male in the room, the lawyer shrugged, spread out his hands. "Happy as I am not to be among the ranks, I'm not going to argue with him. I've watched it happen to each one of you, and it's too fucking the same every time. You go from being completely content to enjoy a woman for as long as it's mutually beneficial, to zeroing in on one like a stag in rut."

"Nice image." Lucas beaned one of Jon's stress balls at him. Ben caught it, but he didn't turn his gaze from Jon. "It's the real deal, boy-genius. And from the little I saw, she's worth it."

Jon rolled his eyes at the nickname Ben used to goad him. "I swear to God, if I ever get that gossip columnist over a spanking bench...what the hell was her made-up name? Celeste De Mille?"

"Don't worry, took care of it. Remember? You lost money to me on it. She's a little spitfire." Ben grinned, threw the ball to Peter. "Not your type though. Best stick with Rachel."

"I will." Jon shifted his attention to Peter. "You want to weigh in on this?"

"Your girl was fucking irresistible," Peter said bluntly. Sending the ball back to Ben, he added, with another wicked grin, "Gorgeous tits. If she's as hardcore as you think, Dana would love to play with her."

Jon straightened in his chair. "What's Dana doing tomorrow?"

Peter's grin became a sexy, feral smile. "Whatever I tell her to do. After she checks her calendar, that is. And tells me what I can do with my high-handed attitude."

"Pussy-whipped." Ben rolled his eyes, fired the ball back at him. When Peter rose and instigated an impromptu game of office football, sending Lucas out for the pass, Jon leaned back in the chair. He still had that tight feeling in his gut, but they'd helped ease it considerably. Peter knew he wouldn't ask if it wasn't important. Dana would know that too, which meant if there was any way she could help tomorrow, she would.

At the deepest level of his mind, Jon knew they were right. About everything. The moment he'd learned that Rachel wasn't married, something primitive yet undeniable had broken loose inside him. That was another trait each man in this room shared—when he set his sights on something he couldn't do without, failure was not an option.

Chapter Nine

ɚↄ

He was the devil. A devil blessed with irresistible hands, a sorcerer's voice and magical tools that took away her sanity. The evening class was beginner level, thank all the gods and goddesses, because if it had been advanced, she wouldn't have survived it without making a complete fool of herself. She had no attention span.

No, that wasn't correct. She was *entirely* focused—on what her body was feeling, on every movement of that serpentine chain along her spine, around her waist, trailing her hip bones, the friction of it between her buttocks. Sitting down tightened the chain along her back and pulled at the collar. Not in a way that blocked her air, but made her acutely aware of the petite padlock on her nape. She'd discovered there was another in the small of her back, where the chain that ran between her buttocks rejoined the one at her waist. Together, the two locks kept her bound in that harness.

She'd worn loose yoga clothes as he suggested, but tucked in her shirt so only the collar with the padlock showed. Since no one asked about it, it had apparently passed as some trendy Goth charm jewelry.

She really didn't have any energy to spare toward that type of self-consciousness, anyway. Her clit pulsed and pounded inside that pliable metal piece, and she was acutely aware of the pressure of the clamps that held it in place and spread her pussy open enough to drive her to distraction.

Surprisingly though, the item that captivated her the most was the temporary collar. Her fingers kept coming back to it, trailing along the edge, remembering how it felt when he'd buckled it, then snapped that lock in place so she couldn't remove it unless she chose a destructive method like a knife. She wouldn't do that. He'd known her too well. Though she might resist a note left on her bathroom counter, she wasn't capable of removing a Master's collar. Not one he'd placed on her.

When she got home, taken there by a polite driver she'd been too distracted to really notice, except that he was handsome and physically intimidating, in a very female-reassuring way, she fixed herself a large mug of chamomile tea. She tried to read the book he'd told her to finish. It was a romantic suspense with a few mild sex scenes, hardly graphic, yet every brush of contact between the two protagonists registered on her own skin. No part of Jon's device impeded any bodily functions or her natural range of movement, but there was no way to sit, lie down, stand or move that didn't increase the agony of want.

When she finally fell asleep, it was way past midnight. She woke with her hands between her legs, pressing on that clitoral hood piece, massaging it, her body within a breath of climax. She snatched her hands away as her body rocked, her pussy spasming, still caught up in her dream. Jon thrusting into her with his hard, thick cock, his hands clamped onto her hips, her body arched up to him in total surrender, legs locked high on his back over those tight, pumping buttocks...

"No, no..." She tried to thrash free of the sheets, of any type of contact against her flesh, and ended up standing in the center of her bedroom, swaying as the blood rushed alarmingly from her head. Her freestanding full-length mirror was in front of her. She'd worn a nightgown to bed, a flannel one, as if wearing something totally sexless and thick could help. Unable to bear the cloth sticking to her sweaty body, she couldn't get it off fast enough. She stripped it off, along with her cotton panties, kicked it all away from her, breath still coming fast and hard.

She was afraid to look at the mirror, but she couldn't help herself. The image shocked and mesmerized at once. She saw an exotic, feral creature whose lips were parted and wet, eyes wide and pupils dark with lust. The slender chain clung to her damp flesh, falling between breasts tipped by large, erect nipples. Her thighs were wet from far more than perspiration, her continuous arousal now no longer stifled by the cotton panties and the liner she'd had to put there to keep her from embarrassing herself during the class.

A far cry from a mere day ago, when she'd worried about whether or not she could get excited enough to produce her own lubrication. As she watched a bead of it roll down her thigh, she couldn't sort out her feelings at all. She felt so incredibly desirable, as if any man near her right now would smell how ripe and ready she was to be taken. And yet, he'd also see that collar. Her hand went to it now, curved over it, felt the restraint. She belonged to a Master. So they could smell how slick she was, how entirely...fuckable, yet she was off limits. Until he came to her.

Goddess, she was losing her mind. Was this why he'd done it? She couldn't seem to have a rational thought. How was she going to make it through the hours until their dinner?

Turning toward the bathroom, she turned on the cold spigot in the tub full blast. He'd told her she better follow his instructions, and one of them was taking a bath. She'd take another tomorrow—or rather, later today—but right now she'd immerse herself in the cold, turn herself blue and chattering if she had to do it, but she had to relieve this ache somehow. Her mind was still trying to tell her she was making the biggest mistake of her life, sliding down a hill toward misery and humiliation, disappointment. But that weak voice couldn't outshout her body, what it wanted, what it would have.

He'd known it. Damn him and bless him both.

* * * * *

In the morning, she made an unexpected decision. He'd told her when he arrived that night, he wanted her in only the lipstick and red heels. She arranged both out on the bathroom counter, so she'd see them while she was cleaning and cooking, but she decided not to wear any clothes at all today. Somehow, it felt right, as if he himself might have pushed it that far, if he'd thought she could handle it. She could imagine the way he'd say it.

You won't wear clothes in your apartment unless I command it. She also found it was easier to bear the friction of that harness he'd put on her, though not by much.

He'd told her to meditate for an hour. When she dutifully stretched out on the floor of her workout room, she chose the position she preferred when she was under great stress, Da Vinci's Vitruvian Man pose. Since it was a symbol of proportion and balance, it had helped her in the past. Legs spread out to form a roughly equilateral triangle, arms stretched out to either side and pointing up so that a straight line could be drawn from one to the other through the center of the head.

Assuming the pose, she scoffed inwardly at the idea that she was going to be able to calm and center her mind, knowing how difficult the meditation portion of her previous night's class had been, and the restless night she'd had. However, while she lay there, trying to focus on the breathing, things took an unexpected turn.

As she brought herself to mindlessness, spiraling down, breathing slow and deep, she became aware of every movement that such breaths made across her body, as if she'd become a pond with a flirty breeze dancing over it. And she wondered what would happen if she stopped trying to fight it.

She didn't mean give in to her body's desire to climax, flout his will. Not that. However, instead of struggling to stay so far from that climactic edge she made herself crazy over it, she wondered what would happen if she instead played near it. What if, instead of keeping herself so far out of range she was out in the cold, miserable and envious, she enjoyed the heat of that fire without immolating herself?

So as she lay in her somewhat meditative state, she let her hand drift first to her throat, then down, trailing over her sternum. When she cupped her breast, her lips parted on a tiny sigh at the feel of it. She had soft skin, and tonight it would be even softer. She'd already put out those bath beads, the moisturizers she'd add to the bath water tonight. She had a honeysuckle scent she thought he'd like.

She also had a honeysuckle vine growing on her back balcony. Maybe she'd don a robe briefly to bring in some of the blossoms, scatter them in the water. Draw out the center stem to touch that one bead of sweetness to her tongue, imagine it as a bead of fluid on the tip of Jon's cock. She'd hungered to taste him yesterday, enough that she'd begged for it. If he had let her leave his office the way she came to him, she would have been mortified remembering that now. Instead, locked in the erotic restraint he'd given her, she licked her dry lips, recalling the way he'd looked, the thick root of him hard against his slacks.

When her fingers grazed her nipples, her hips pressed deep into the carpet, her pussy making that ripple. She kept traveling down, her palm against her stomach, tracing the edge of her pubic area. She didn't touch the clit piece, but she played along the creases of her thighs, wiggling and smiling a little at the sensations that chased themselves up and down her body. God, she was alive, and on fire. Yet she was also a mixture of other things. She was all sensation, every element known and unknown.

Lifting her arm, she blew along her skin, watching the fine hairs rise. As she dropped the limb back beside her head, she arched up, readjusting her stance to that Sleeping Thunderbolt pose, remembering Jon in it, but now imagining he'd ordered her to hold this *asana* while his palms molded her breasts, while he inserted a vibrator in her pussy so she came in this restricted position, all muscles straining, a scream bursting from her throat like a war cry. A cry of freedom...the freedom to chain herself to him, accept his collar with no guilt or worries. The muscles strummed in her thighs, her lower belly.

You're fooling yourself. You're visiting Disneyland, and when you come back out the gates, you're going to be the same middle-aged, tired woman who went in there. You've just been dazzled by pixie dust.

Fine. She'd let herself be dazzled. The collar on her throat gave her permission, right?

The knock on the door was unexpected, but she wouldn't be surprised if Jon had sent his driver back with bagels this morning, an excuse to make sure she wasn't trying to run errands by herself. No worries there. She'd been so worked up last night, she'd had the driver take her to the grocery store after yoga, certain that she wasn't going to leave the house at all today. Having to pretend she wasn't on the cusp of a knee-buckling orgasm around normal people had been too difficult to contemplate.

If it was the driver, she'd have to apologize. Beyond hardly noticing him in his position in the shadowed front seat, she wasn't sure if she was supposed to have tipped him. He'd been considerate, not engaging her in any superfluous conversation, though he'd escorted her to her fourth-floor apartment, carrying up her groceries and making sure she locked her door after him. She'd remembered a large man who reminded her a little of Peter. He'd had serious eyes and a steady hand at her elbow, but beyond that the details were a little hazy.

Rising from the floor, she slid into the terrycloth robe, the only robe she had. She wished she had something silky and provocative, but then, it wouldn't matter tonight, would it? Jon didn't want her to wear a robe. For one heart-jumping moment she wondered if it could be him at the door, his plans changed so that he could come early and end her torment, but Janet had told her they were definitely traveling.

Therefore, she was mildly disappointed but not surprised to see the driver through the peephole. She *was* surprised to see who was with him. Unlatching the door, she pulled it open. "Dana. Good morning."

The slim black woman smiled and tapped her cane against the driver's calf. "I told Max I could figure out how to get up three flights of stairs and count down to your door, but he's like a big, goofy guard dog."

Max lifted a brow. Now that she saw him in the light of day, she realized he was in fact a great deal like Peter. Not as in family resemblance, but in build and coloring. Dark blond hair, gray-eyed, large boned and lots of trained muscles that she'd bet had been used in military service. He towered over both women, and had shoulders perhaps even wider than Dana's fiancé. Rachel decided Max could be quite a lethal guard dog when he wanted to be. However, his gaze was laced with fondness for his charge.

"Maybe I wanted to see a sweet-natured woman for a change, so I thought I'd come up here with you and see Ms. Madison."

"Nice." Dana punched him in the side. With approval, Rachel noticed she packed some strength behind it.

"The shoulder's doing well."

Dana cocked a brow. "I'm not here to visit my physical therapist, thank you very much. You try to bend me into a pretzel today, I'll leg sweep you and pound you like a sandbag."

Rachel laughed. "Come on in then. I'll offer you some tea. Max, would you like some coffee?"

"No, but thanks." He guided Dana over the threshold, met Rachel's gaze. "I'll come back for her when she gets out of line. Which will probably be about the time I get to the car."

"Go away, Cujo." Dana waved her cane in his direction. "Go maul a few preschoolers. I'll call you when I'm ready to leave."

Max gave Rachel another smile. His gaze drifted briefly over the loose fit of the robe, the collar it revealed. Was it her imagination, or did he linger on her cleavage, tracking that tempting silver chain until it disappeared into unseen regions? He didn't make it overt or inappropriate. Two days ago she might not even have registered such a quick flash, but her ramped-up hormones were honed to any evidence of male awareness.

On her side of things, now she couldn't help but notice the way his shoulders filled out his chauffeur's uniform or wonder what his lower torso might look like without the drape of the coat hiding it. Her cheeks flushed as he caught her gaze on its downward sweep, but he simply gave her a nod and turned back toward the stairwell. "Lock the door," he called over his shoulder.

After Rachel drew Dana in and closed the door, the black woman made a face. "He's such a worrywart. Believe me, he's standing on the stairwell listening. And he's like one of those trick ponies that can count. If you slide the deadbolt in and out really fast, like twenty times, he'll still know if you stopped on locked or unlocked. He'll come back if it's not locked."

Rachel gave her a glance as she shot the deadbolt in place with a definitive thud. "That sounds like the voice of experience."

Dana grinned. "A girl has to get her fun where she can. The blindness gig comes with exceptional hearing, so sometimes I wait until he's almost walked back up to the door to turn it into the locked position that last time. Then, when he's turned around and gone about five steps away, I might slide it back out again, to keep him on his toes."

"Poor Max." Rachel shook her head. Then she couldn't help but laugh. "Oh Dana, I think I really needed you today." She hugged the other woman, a suitable gesture for the occasion, but as the woman's body made contact with hers, Rachel realized body contact might have been a mistake. Dana wore a form-fitting stylish tee over her snug jeans, and even through the terrycloth, Rachel was hyper aware of the curve of her small breasts, the slope of the spine beneath her palms, the scent of her skin. She found herself holding on a little longer, a little closer, than what was expected for a friendly hug.

She wasn't into women, but with her erotic awareness stoked to simmering, the ability to touch was a genderless craving. Though the man she wanted with every ounce of her aroused body was Jon, it was the same reason she'd noticed every single one of Max's pleasing features.

It was kind of scary to realize the only thing keeping her lust contained was that collar, not social constraints. Otherwise she might have given Max an equally enthusiastic hug, with far more wandering hands. She was on the verge of embarrassing herself and couldn't seem to care.

Dana seemed to pick up on it, because she ran her own palms over Rachel's back, dropped them down to catch her fingers in the robe's front tie and tugged on it a little, letting the ends slip through her fingers before she at last stepped back. "They get you pretty wound up, don't they?"

"Is it that obvious?" Rachel thought about Peter yesterday, the way he'd touched her. The way Lucas had, as he eased her farther into the office. A remarkable bond seemed to exist between the K&A men. And that would likely include the women. How much did Dana know? Rachel wasn't sure if it would bother her on a normal day. All she knew right now was it didn't.

"Not too obvious." Dana flashed a grin, underscoring the obvious lie. Then she sobered. "Jon's protective. They all are. He wanted me to come here, spend the day with you, if you'd like that. He hates that he has to be away from you right now."

"Well, that's just silly. I mean, we… It's not that we're strangers, but we have just started…whatever this is. Right?"

"Hmm." Dana set aside the cane. When she reached up toward Rachel's face with both hands, Rachel stilled, not sure what she was about. The woman laid her palms on Rachel's cheeks, slim fingers stroking to her jaw, then down farther. Rachel drew in a breath, her heart thudding as Dana investigated the collar, stepping closer to feel the lock on the back of it. Her breasts, clad in the soft T-shirt, brushed Rachel's. Even through terrycloth, the contact made her pulse thud. What made it worse or better, depending on her perspective, was that as Dana investigated, Rachel felt the black woman's nipples tighten. It aroused Dana, knowing Rachel was collared. Then she cupped Rachel's skull, lifted onto her toes and put her mouth on Rachel's parted lips.

Blessed God *and* Goddess. Again—*not into women*—but it didn't matter. It was sexual contact, and her body was ravenous for any kind of touch that wasn't her own. In some way too primeval to explain in civilized company, it gave them a provocative bond, that this woman also called her man Master, submitted to his ownership. Rachel had imagined Peter carrying out his threats, Dana bent over his knee, that large hand smacking her bare buttocks, giving them a deep rose tinge under the brown pigment. And of course from there it wasn't much of a leap to remember Jon's use of that ruler on her own still-sore ass. Dana's kiss was like an initiation, a welcome. A reassurance that Rachel wasn't alone on this path.

Rachel dove hard and deep into that kiss, making a whimper in her throat as she gripped Dana's waist. Dana brushed her hands aside, though, and slipped the robe tie. Rachel breathed a sigh of relief as the garment was pushed off her shoulders, freeing her body once more. Then Dana explored, following the chain down from Rachel's throat, between her breasts and over her abdomen. She stopped short of her clit, following the chain around to the back and then smoothing her graceful hands over Rachel's buttocks, her knuckles trailing across skin. Interestingly, though Rachel quivered and jerked from the near misses around cunt and nipples, Dana was obviously careful to offer no direct touches there. Eventually, her hands came back to claim Rachel's, fingers tangled and holding together.

When the other woman at last broke the kiss, stepped back, Rachel stared at her in amazement. Dana's mouth was wet with hers, her brown eyes considering, a secretive but rueful smile playing around her lips. "That *bastard*. No wonder he wanted me to come spend time with you. You'd jump a teenage Boy Scout selling popcorn tins right now. It would serve Jon right if I let you do it. Or called Max back up here and let him take full advantage of it, though he probably values his job *and* his life more than that."

Rachel imagined the slimmer, less physically imposing Jon against Max, but then she remembered that look he'd had when his gaze fell on the bruise on her cheek. No, it was probably best not to make any assumptions about the unpredictable, fascinating man who'd invaded her life over the past couple days.

"I was thinking I could have checked out his ass more without that coat he was wearing," she managed weakly. "It covers a lot."

"Trust me, you could bounce a quarter off Max's ass. The advantage of being blind." Dana affected an exaggerated Southern belle accent. "Sometimes I can't help stumblin', now can I? I just *have* t' grab onto the person next to me before I fall. And I can't see where I'm grabbin', darlin', now can I?" She gave Rachel a broad wink and a grin. "Peter gave me a real walloping for that one, because Max was such a tattletale. But I wasn't sorry."

Something unexpected came behind Rachel's laugh. A tiny sob. Ever intuitive, Dana made a reassuring sound in her throat, her hands squeezing Rachel's hard. "C'mon, girl. Let's sit down and have that tea. You keep the robe off. I can't see you anyhow, and I know you're more comfortable without it."

* * * * *

"Not just more comfortable," Rachel admitted as they sat at her cheerful bistro set by the window, mid-morning sun streaming in. "It felt...like what he'd want. You were the one who told him I wasn't married, weren't you?"

Dana had her now bare feet drawn up and curled on the chair edge, one arm linked loosely over her shins, the other hand holding her coffee mug, since she preferred that to tea. When they sat down, Rachel had noticed Dana also wore a set of dog tags, embellished with a solid silver frame. They were strung on a chain along with a handful of jasper beads that picked up the mixed rusts and earth tones of the T-shirt. It was a short chain, the tags falling below her collarbone, making them easy to read. *Winston, Peter R.* It might as well say "Property of", Rachel thought with a longing pang beneath her breast. She noticed Dana toyed with them often as she spoke, as she was doing now.

"Yes, it was me. I hope that's okay. Jon has an unbreakable code, they all do. But he kept coming back to your classes. He's thought about you a long time, Rachel."

"I'm older than he is."

"You're older than two thousand years? Really? Because I'm pretty sure Jon's soul dates back to the Druids. I see him standing on top of some temple platform, gazing into a forest, and when he turns his head, he has this mystic charisma that tells you he's some kind of conduit for the gods."

"Wow. You get all that without sight?" Because it was all too accurate.

Dana grinned. "Some things you see better when you don't look with your eyes."

Rachel sighed. "Thirteen years between us, Dana. And it's not only the years. He did all this to keep my mind spinning with lust, and believe me, it's working, but at some point I have to come down from that. From his standpoint, I know that will be okay. He's probably had plenty of relationships like this, and I guess I should be glad that for the first time in my life I get to experience a Master's touch. It's better than I ever imagined, because of him. I should just let that happen, enjoy it while it lasts, but I don't know if I can. I don't know if..."

Dana put a hand over hers on the table, traced the fingers with the same sensual touch she'd used when she'd explored the chains on Rachel's body. "No ring. You took it off."

"Jon did. I couldn't...couldn't bring myself to put it back on."

"Hmm." Peter's fiancée cocked her head. "People make their own decisions. It's obvious you have a lot of hurt stored up in you, a lot of disappointments. Now you're figuring out how to deal with those against a force of nature like Jon, and I think that's good. He needs to see that, know what obstacles he faces. You're right—pretty much up until two days ago, Jon could walk into a BDSM club, or hook up with someone in his business or social set, and thoroughly enjoy a short-term relationship. He's very good at seeing them to their natural end and making that end go down smooth as silk."

She was supposed to be glad to be hearing this, instead of wanting Dana to stop putting images in her head of Jon with other women. Dana's fingers flexed on hers, as if sensing the direction of her thoughts.

"I think you need to know a little bit more about the K&A men. Would you like to?"

A sensible person would say no, would resist being drawn deeper into a world where she couldn't stay. Instead she already had her mouth open to give her answer. "After yesterday, I'm overflowing with curiosity."

"What happened yesterday?"

Rachel hesitated. What if what Peter had done wasn't acceptable to Dana? How would she handle that?

"I expect my fiancé was somehow part of whatever happened." Dana reached out with a foot, nudged her with a toe. "That's part of what those five are about. Don't worry, just spill it."

She did, briefly, aware now that Dana picked up a lot from what wasn't said. The woman kept her head in that listening tilt, her eyes thoughtful. When she pressed her lips together, her fingers curling around her knees, Rachel reached out, touched her.

"Please tell me that was all okay, or expected. I couldn't forgive myself if somehow I let something happen that would hurt you in any way."

"Oh hon, nothing to forgive." Dana closed her hand over Rachel's fingers on her knee. "I'm here to tell you, when the K&A men decide on something, a woman's got a snowball's chance in hell of having any say in it at all. She's just got to hang on for the ride of her life." Now her smile was back. "The reason I reacted the way I did was because of how much I like you. And how glad I am that Jon chose you this way. It's happy sadness, like at a wedding."

"I don't understand."

"You won't, not until it comes from inside, so I'm not going to say a lot about it, but whatever Jon's relationships with women have been in the past, trust me when I say you're different. You want to know about the K&A men? They're a pack, a pack that's connected on some visceral male level that's scary as hell to experience, while at the same time you never want that experience to end. You belong to one of them, but in a peripheral way, you belong to all of them. Like a family, only you have a lot of feelings and experiences with this family that would be highly frowned upon if you truly were blood-related."

She flashed a grin. "They each have a specialty, if you can believe it. If there was a Cordon Bleu for pussy-eating, Lucas would be their valedictorian." At Rachel's startled reaction, a choked laugh, Dana nodded, a sage look on her pixie face. "Peter... My man is tit-obsessed. He can do things to your breasts with a touch, a flick of the tongue, the removal of a nipple clamp at the right moment, that can make you come in a heartbeat, without touching any other part of your body." A little shiver ran over her skin and echoed in a reaction over Rachel's.

"All of them have... They're all...?"

"Yes, and it does make the tongue trip up and the heart ricochet with the thought of it. All five of them are sexual Dominants. They're so different, and yet there's this incredibly similar core to them. Ben..." Dana snorted. "I can't wait to see the woman who will finally catch his attention. Poor girl. You don't see it at first, because of the slick, charming lawyer thing, but he's probably the toughest, most hardcore Master of all of them. And his thing is...well, no way to put it delicately. He's a master at ass-fucking. Cass and Savannah haven't experienced it directly, because, as I said, each of the guys are somewhat different in how their Dominance works."

She paused, apparently mulling the best choice of words. "When a K&A man finds the woman he wants to make his permanently, they share to a certain level, but there are certain lines not crossed, depending on both the Master and the woman, what he knows her needs are. Like Matt. Savannah, his wife...the lines are more clearly drawn with her than me or Cass. They'll do soft play with her on occasion, but it's Matt who holds the reins, always. Lucas will sometimes allow a little more with Cass, but it still stays along the lines of voyeurism, heavy petting, things like that."

Dana shrugged. "I'm all Peter's, and yet he knows I like being shared at times, as long as it's only with them, and as long as he's a part of it." Putting a hand on her heart, she patted it dramatically. "That's how I know about Ben firsthand. I think it's possible to die from having both inside me at once, because I pretty much blacked out during the orgasm."

Rachel's mind was whirling. "Wow. I don't think I could..." But she was lying. The idea was already whirling in her head, frightening herself. That darkness loomed again, how deep she was willing to go, how much of herself she could lose.

"Easy." Dana reached out again, only this time her fingers slid over Rachel's knee, along the inside of her thigh. A few scant inches, but it was enough to have Rachel's mind centering again, remarkably. As her legs trembled, Dana pushed on them, spreading her knees out so they touched the chair arms. The black woman slid out of her chair, taking the same bent knee position on the floor as she'd had in the chair, only this time she braced her back against one of Rachel's calves, her toes against the arch of Rachel's opposite foot. "It's easier that way, keeping your legs apart, isn't it? Sometimes, when things start to spin in the wrong direction, taking the position you might take if your Master is with you helps you to kind of balance."

With a shock, Rachel realized that was probably why she preferred the Da Vinci position for meditation whenever she was unsettled. Even without a lover in her life, the spread legs, the arms over her head, was a position of submission.

"W-what's Jon's specialty?"

"You have to ask?" Dana chuckled. Reaching up, she tweaked the chain at Rachel's hip, sending a jolt right down to her pussy at the friction to the clit piece. "The man's a mechanical and chemical genius. Ben thinks Jon's contribution to history will be the Pearly Gate Detonator, a vibrator that allows a woman to die from orgasms, no matter her age or physical condition. That way she can have the best possible end when she's terminal or too ancient to carry on anymore. Ben says it would be like a rocket launcher, shooting her straight up and over Heaven's gate, no passport needed."

When her hand slipped from the chain back to Rachel's thigh, caressing the pale flesh there, Rachel closed her eyes, not wanting the contact to stop. This was crazy, amazing…perfect. And as Dana herself had said, scary as hell. "What about the head of K&A? Matt Kensington?"

"He's the king," Dana said simply. "As corny as that sounds, it's his energy that sort of pervades all of it, connects them. He's Machiavellian when it comes to erotic strategy, and though I think he has a lot of his own skills in the orgasm-to-die-for category, he's also more exclusive than any of them. Savannah is his queen, his everything. He can touch your shoulder, and you know he's totally in command, but you don't mess with what's between him and Savannah."

"I'm not sure if hearing all this is making it better or worse." Because it was making her want what she couldn't have even more intensely. "You know this is giving me a hundred more questions."

"It's hard to explain it until you experience it." Dana rubbed her cheek against Rachel's leg, then pressed her lips there. Rachel stroked a hand over her close-cropped hair and Dana immediately turned to tease her pulse with lips and tongue. Her elegant fingers closed over Rachel's wrist as she lifted her head, dropped it back against Rachel's leg to smile up at her.

"Don't freak out, hon, but what happened yesterday was like the first act of a master play, being written straight off the cuff by Jon, with sheer Master's intuition. He didn't tell Peter, 'Hey, come in here after she's on her knees and play with her a little bit'. They pick up cues from each other. It's fascinating, a little terrifying, but after you get used to it, it works in all the right ways."

Rachel noticed Dana hesitated, as if she wasn't sure if she should say what was in her mind next. "What?" she asked. "I want you to tell me, even if you think it's something I can't handle." Which was entirely stupid, but there it was. She wanted to know everything.

"What I was trying to say earlier... Before they found their wives, when they went to a club, they'd do their thing with the casual subs they hooked up with now and then. However, when it matters...it's more like what you experienced yesterday, and that was an introductory taste. The very fact they brought you to that gate means Jon wants to take you fully through it. He wants to shut the door behind you, lock it permanently. You're his choice for forever. I'd bet my life on it."

Rachel drew her hand away, suddenly cold. "You think..."

"Doesn't matter what I think." Dana grimaced good-naturedly, giving her a light pinch, though it didn't lighten Rachel's mood. "Changing your mind about a future with him is Jon's job, and believe me, these guys are good at convincing a woman of the most unlikely things. I was a club hopper until I met Peter, and I've enjoyed a variety of Masters, in a lukewarm sort of way. However, he was it, everything, the second I met him. Savannah and Cass will tell you the same thing. We all had that in common."

"He couldn't be thinking that. It's not possible."

"Why not?" Dana's brow creased. "Why can't you believe that you can have something like Jon?"

"Because I couldn't, not for so many years. And...the wanting it destroyed so much of what I had." Rachel rose then, awkwardly stepped over Dana and retreated to the living room, wanting that robe. After she shrugged it on and belted it, she found Dana had returned to her own chair. The woman was waiting for her, listening for the sound of her footsteps, and probably to a lot more. The scuttling sound of Rachel's mind skittering away from this absurdness, like a rat seeking an escape from a sinking ship.

"Rachel." Dana spoke softly. Though it brought Rachel to the kitchen doorway, she leaned in it, shying away from coming back to the table. "I'm telling you what I know about the K&A men. You wanted me to be honest, and I'm telling you I believe that history is about to repeat itself, for the fourth time. It's why I reacted the way I did to what happened to you yesterday, because I'd love nothing better than to have you as part of our family." Dana gave her a small smile. "You don't have to argue with me about it. I'll wait to see what you have to say on the other side of it."

"You're wrong. I can't... For me to handle this, to do this, I have to accept it as a temporary thing." Then she could enjoy it awhile, and wouldn't have to face all this unresolved pain she'd had to bury. "I don't...it's not that way. I respect and understand what you say, but that's not what I want. And I'm sure it's not what Jon wants. He couldn't possibly."

Suddenly, Rachel wanted Dana to go. She couldn't bear to see the confidence the other woman had, so smug and sure that things would work out. She didn't understand, didn't know...

"Rachel." Dana's tone held the firmness of the minister she was training to be. Rachel already knew Dana's lack of sight gave her a unique ability to pick up distress, and her compassion now reflected that she could feel Rachel's grief, welling up so deep and strong it couldn't escape notice from a well-attuned heart. "Will you come back and sit?"

Rachel shook her head, wrapped her arms tighter around herself. Though Dana couldn't see the gesture, of course the fact she didn't move was an answer itself. The blind woman cocked her head, considering, her eyes appearing to focus on the wall above Rachel's head.

"All of us can get trapped in our pain and loss," she said quietly. "It's worse if there's no one there to help when it happens. We learn to cope, and we cope by building walls. So nothing terrifies us more than having those walls brought down. It becomes your skin, and nobody wants to be skinned and left raw and bleeding. We believe, to the depths of our soul, no one will protect us, give us warmth and healing. We don't think we deserve it."

"I need you to go." Rachel picked up the cane, brought it to Dana's hand. "We'll call Max. I'm sorry, but I need you to go."

"First, let me say this." Dana tapped Rachel's chair, a quiet command to sit. With that preacher's tone, Rachel found herself obeying, though she tugged the robe even closer around herself. For all that they were sightless, the dark eyes became more intent, more focused. "I do understand, Rachel. Not the exact nature of your pain, but the depth of it."

She gestured to her eyes, the scarring that was still visible on her left arm. "After this happened, I walled myself up like I was in a grave."

The change of subject, the gravity of it, stilled Rachel the way the reassurances couldn't. Though from her medical records she of course knew the kind of injuries Dana had sustained, the woman herself had never spoken directly of it, or the aftermath.

"I was in this silent hell, scarred, hideous," Dana continued. "I hated bathing because I had to touch my face, my body. I lacked the will to take my own life, but I'd died, just the same."

A faint, bittersweet smile touched her mauve lips. "In a few moments, like one of those hypnosis sessions, I'm going to snap my fingers and take us back to a different reality, the playful, sexy one that existed when I walked into your door. If you change your mind and want me to stay, we'll start working on this dinner you're supposed to make. I'll talk to you while you're taking your bath. We'll gossip about celebrity hairstyles—you can describe them to me and I'll laugh. We'll talk about the state of the world, and what your favorite color is. In other words, we'll be girls and talk about whatever fun, frivolous crap we want to talk about."

She shifted, her hand closing on Rachel's again. "And that collar he's put on you, all the delicious feelings that go with it, that are stirring up your body and making you want him so hard? They'll come rushing back, and then you really will need me to leave, because the closer we get to dinner, the more everything in you will become attuned to wanting him, to wanting to be ready for your Master in the way he commanded. You feel it now, hearing me say it, right?"

Rachel nodded, then voiced the word, reluctantly. "Yes."

"Good. So I'm going to tell you one thing now, before we go back to girl talk or you decide to toss me out on my ass. Peter Winston reached through that darkness, blasted those walls, brought me back to life. He gave me back myself, the person I thought I'd lost, as well as something new, something I'd never thought possible. Give yourself a chance at that, Rachel. I know it's terrifying. However, I can promise you this. When one of these men sets his sights upon you, as crazy as you think he's making you, you'd be *really* crazy not to make that leap of faith. I promise."

Chapter Ten

ဩ

She did end up letting Dana stay. It was an interminable afternoon, but it would have been far worse without her there. As Dana predicted, once they started focusing on dinner and straightening up the house, which required a wide range of physical movement, Rachel's focus returned to the stimulation of her body by Jon's diabolical device. She'd never think of vacuuming the same way again.

Describe an eggplant in very purple, very sexual terms... Imagine rabbits fornicating, then substitute the faces of your least favorite high school teachers... She became very grateful for Dana and her quick wit, the firm press of her palm on her back, a reassurance rather than a provocation, helping her breathe and smile.

That help had continued while she bathed herself, a precarious idea in her state. Dana had sat on her vanity stool, distracted her from the strong reaction of her body as Rachel soaped places that begged to be rubbed and stroked even more. Peter's fiancée had quizzed her on the book Jon had insisted she read. Rachel managed coherent sentences more or less...and ended up laughing a lot.

At some point, hearing herself, she realized she sounded like an excited, much younger version of herself, keyed up and flustered by a date with the boy she most wanted to be with. That thought brought a yearning so sharp and deep it rippled outward from the heart and through every artery and vein, making her shake in the tub, one hard convulsion. She held Dana's cool hand against her forehead, let Dana stroke her hair, reassure her. "It's going to be okay. It's going to be more wonderful than you can imagine."

That was what was scaring her so much.

Several times during their preparations, she'd had to simply stop, her legs planted apart, body quivering as she tried to get the yearning to die back enough that she didn't end up writhing on the floor like a person possessed by spirits, squeezing and touching herself everywhere she longed for Jon's hands to be.

Of course all that stimulation was the delicate harness's design and intent, and she couldn't say she wasn't glad for it, because it took her mind from the emotional debris and uneasiness that Dana's fantastic theories had stirred. Besides that, she could hardly deny that she'd wanted this night, no matter what happened afterward. Jon had said it, a sorcerer who knew the right words to cast the irreversible spell. *You've waited a long time to prove how devoted a slave you can be. Don't deny yourself what you truly want.*

Just one night to unleash this part of herself...or rather, hand that leash to a man she trusted. A man she accepted was a Master, even if she couldn't dare the temptation of calling him her Master.

She'd always thought it was an overused metaphor, comparing sexual tension to a volcano about to blow, but as the clock ticked onerously toward seven, she understood why it had earned the status of a common cliché. Every movement of the minute hand took her desire a degree higher. When she was standing over the stove watching pasta boil, even the sheen of perspiration she experienced on her face and throat made the nerve endings tingle. The mist from the pot tickled the delicate pocket of her collarbones, the tips of her breasts.

At six-thirty, the food was ready, sitting in the oven to stay fresh and warm, the bread wrapped in foil. They'd put candles and flowers on the table, along with one place setting. The significance of that, witnessed by Dana's quizzical fingers, underscored and made it all the more real. Her nerves had twisted into double knots that made her even more aware of every inch of her exposed skin, Dana's casual brushes against her, the way her own thighs touched as she walked, stimulating her further.

However, by the time Max rapped at the door, something else was happening as well. Rachel was shimmering with anticipation and something she wanted to call happiness. She ignored the dour voice inside that suggested it was hysterical euphoria.

She still had her hair pinned back, but that had only been to keep it out of the food as they re-checked everything. As of a few moments ago, she'd stepped into those cherry red stilettos and put on the lipstick. Looking at herself in the mirror, with the collar and dainty silver chains running across her body, she felt like a sensuous descendant of Lilith. And that didn't feel like a bad thing at all.

Still, propriety lurched back to the forefront when Dana took her hand, began to drag her toward the door. Rachel balked. "Dana, I'm not wearing the robe," she hissed.

"Trust me." When the woman reached the door, her hand outstretched to find it, she called through the panel. "Max, you need to close your eyes, okay? Promise you won't open them."

"I don't even want to know." His sigh was audible. "All right, they're closed. But I will need to open them to get you down the stairs."

"Don't worry, I won't let you fall. I'm specially trained to navigate in the dark. You'll have to trust me for a change."

A snort. "Yeah, like that's going to happen."

Dana gave Rachel a wink, then turned the knob.

She was the corner apartment, at the end of a hallway and around a slight bend, so her door was nested in a sheltered arch, not immediately visible to her other neighbors. Even so, panic did a quick skitter through her when Dana yanked the door open.

Max stood there, arms crossed over his broad chest. He'd apparently gone home after normal business hours, so instead of the suit, he was wearing a form-fitting T-shirt and jeans, his dark blond hair tousled over the high forehead. There was the beginning of a faint five o'clock shadow on his Superman square jaw.

He is so *hot*, Dana mouthed. Rachel had to stifle an astonishingly girlish giggle, but even as she did, she had to wonder again at the man's likeness to Peter. She assumed Dana had never actually seen Max, since she'd told Rachel she hadn't come to Baton Rouge until after being wounded. But given Dana's heightened senses and intuition, it was logical, the blind woman bonding in such an affectionate way with a man who had many of the characteristics of the one she obviously loved with all her soul.

Rising high on her toes, Dana put her hand over Max's closed eyes, bracing her other hand, the one holding her cane, against his chest. He automatically put his own over her wrist and on her waist to steady her. "Rachel is wearing nothing but a pair of cherry red fuck-me heels. That, and a matching lipstick so wet and luscious-looking it's probably called Carnal Sin." Dana grinned impishly and poked his chest. "See, I knew I'd have to put my hand over your eyes. You couldn't help it. Your eyes popped right open. Your lashes brushed my hand like feathers."

"I'm going to strangle you," he promised, but there was a resigned smile on his firm lips. However, at Dana's provocative description, Rachel noted his fingers had flexed on Dana's waist. That Lilith feeling increased inside her. He wanted to look. She was worth looking at. She looked like every male's fantasy. At least for this second, she was aroused enough to believe it.

"Oops, forgot. She is wearing one other thing. Something Jon put on her to keep her hot and bothered, but I won't describe that. There's only so much a big, manly guy like yourself can take. I'm going to say goodbye to her now and then we'll go. You need to keep your eyes closed, or Jon will be really mad."

Max sighed again. "The eggplant smells very good, Ms. Madison," he said politely.

"Thank you," Rachel replied, at a loss. Dana smirked at both of them, then her hand slid away from Max's eyes. He had beautiful, thick lashes, Rachel noted. Then Dana turned toward her, that devilish look still in her gaze.

"Thanks for letting me visit this afternoon. We should do it again. I like spending time with you when you don't have me stretched out on a mattress, torturing me."

"I'll leave that job to Peter tonight." That made Max chuckle and gave Rachel a smile herself. When Dana came to her, she had a pretty good idea what she was about. With her body already humming, it was no hardship to let those slender brown hands slide up and along the outside of her breasts, again avoiding her nipples, but settling on her collar before Dana leaned full into Rachel, bringing their lips together for a playful tongue-tangling kiss. Rachel couldn't help it. She was too close to seeing Jon, and a moan rose in her throat. Her hands convulsed on Dana's hips, fingers curling over the pockets of the snug jeans she wore, feeling the toned female ass beneath.

Max swore softly. "Goddamn it, Dana." But when Dana at last slid back, Rachel saw his eyes were still closed. She also saw his cock was a thick line against his jeans. It drew Rachel's fascinated gaze, made her moisten her lips.

Dana brushed her finger over her own mouth, collecting some of the wet color Rachel had transferred there, and then brushed it over Max's, giving a yelp and a short squeak of laughter as he bit the finger, caught her wrist and gave it a light shake.

"Peter shouldn't let you out of the house without a leash."

"I think that's what you are, big guy." Dana impulsively gave him a hard hug, a gesture of true affection, though Rachel expected Max got the reward she had, of feeling Dana's tight, aroused nipples through his T-shirt. "You're a treasure."

She turned back to Rachel, gave her a hug too, this one with no sexual tease to it, though Rachel still had to absorb the shock of physical contact to her overly alert body. "Good luck," Dana said, then her voice lowered, underscoring the new intimacy and understanding between them. "Tonight, keep in mind what I told you, without thinking too hard about it, okay? It'll be all right, all of it. Trust him. And trust that part of yourself you maybe haven't trusted in way too long, if ever."

"Okay," Rachel said, though she wasn't sure about any of it.

"Better freshen up that lipstick." Dana lifted up on her toes then, balancing herself by holding Rachel's bare waist, fingers tangling with the chain at her hip. She whispered in her ear. "I'll bet Max peeked. You're too damn irresistible. I don't have to see to know you look absolutely beautiful — it's coming off you in waves. Whatever your heart truly desires, you can have it tonight. I know it."

* * * * *

Max remained where he was, eyes closed, until Rachel closed the door. Leaning against it, she listened to him and Dana move back down her hallway. She was starting to feel the way Dorothy might have if, instead of being whirled away to Oz, that glittering place had set up camp *inside* her gray farmhouse.

Her gaze went to the clock. Fifteen minutes. He'd be on his way here already, and she knew he'd be prompt. He'd have called otherwise. Her gaze slid over the room. She'd turned on Kitaro's *Silk Road* composition and the exotic yet soothing melody filled the apartment. When she'd played part of it for Dana, the woman had given her a thumbs up.

"Peter and I are pretty much heavy metal junkies, though he's also given me a new appreciation for country songs about shirtless boys on tractors." That quick grin. "I'd never buy the stuff Jon plays, but when I'm there at his place, it fits the mood, the man, everything. This is like that. It's perfect. For both of you."

Thinking of the past few minutes with Max, Rachel remembered what Dana had said about her night with Peter *and* Ben. Had Jon done things for Dana, under Peter's direction? Did she want to know? Did she want to experience such a thing for herself? If any part of those unsettling things Dana had said earlier about the K&A men were true—and certainly she'd experienced something of the sort in Jon's office—it was a very likely possibility.

It was pointless to speculate. She'd already told herself things were going no further than tonight. Tonight was her fantasy. Tomorrow she'd have to grip reality, no matter what.

Not for the first time, that weak litany reminded her of buying a whole chocolate cake on impulse, having a piece, then going to bed with the firm self-admonition that she'd throw the rest away in the morning and never have another fattening, decadent bite. She was old enough to be smarter than this. But here she was anyway.

At five to seven, she put his salad bowl on his dinner plate, scooped the blackberries, goat cheese and shredded greens into it, ladling a light drizzle of vinaigrette over it. She'd wrapped the bread in a towel and put it in a basket to his left, including a small dish of olive oil with herbs. The eggplant parmesan was on a trivet, the casserole dish sealed to hold in heat. She poured half a glass of the red, setting the bottle in a pewter wine holder to breathe.

Unpinning her hair, she let it cascade onto her bare shoulders. Though she'd been naked most of the day, now she felt truly vulnerable and bare. Kissing Dana, teasing Max, it had been...adventurous, playful. But this...the trembling in her lower belly told her this was something else entirely, if her mind wasn't already telling her that. It was consumed with him. He'd be parking in the lot, walking up to her building. If her neighbors were out, walking their dogs or doing their evening jog, they'd see him. They'd wonder about that handsome, charismatic man, wonder whom he was going to visit.

Would they believe it was her, the middle-aged tenant of 401D, the one they usually saw leaving in exercise clothes or her practical therapy wear? Could they imagine her now, kneeling like this, waiting by his chair, waiting to serve his every desire? Could they imagine all the things he might do to her tonight?

She'd had to dry herself between her legs more than once over the course of the day, her arousal an ebb and flow, depending on the direction of her thoughts, or Dana's provocation. Now her thoughts made a heated drop trickle over her calf, where her legs were folded beneath her. It was too close to time, so she didn't move. She had the titillating thought that he would want to see her arousal, wouldn't want her to wipe it away. Collecting it on his fingers, his tongue, his cock…that was his right, not hers. When the clock chimed seven, all rights were his.

He'd be walking up her stairs. He wasn't the elevator type, not for a mere three floors. The shaking was back, sweeping out from her lower belly, through her thighs, her breath shortening. She'd left the door unlocked, as he'd commanded. Her only responsibility now was to wait.

Her gaze lifted to the clock. One minute. Her eyes closed. The building had excellent insulation. Even the McPhersons, who lived directly below and who had two young boys who didn't do anything at a walk or low decibel, rarely penetrated the quiet of her corner apartment. It was something she'd always appreciated, but now she wasn't as pleased by the solid weatherproofing on her door that muffled approaching footsteps. But she could envision it. His walk, the way his body moved, the intensity of the blue eyes.

For hours he'd filled her mind, but now she hungered for the real man. His scent, his heat, his *presence*. Even if it was just the sound of his shoes rasping along the concrete walkway, she couldn't wait another second to grasp some tangible evidence of him. Her clit was back to throbbing beneath that metal sheath, a tiny heartbeat.

The door latch turned, and she had to make her fists relax. Just in time, she remembered the position he required. Straightening her spine, she laced her fingers at the small of her back, which thrust out her breasts. As she spread her knees to shoulder width, her hair whispered over her left shoulder, falling forward over the breast. She was staring down at her pussy, seeing the tracks of her arousal on her thighs, the flush of her erect nipples. The satiny finish of her red heels pressed into her buttocks.

The time for panic, the "what the hell am I doing?" was past. She was committed to this path now, for tonight. There was a freedom in that, such that one anxiety went away, leaving an entirely different kind in its place.

Her breath slipped out in a sigh as she caught his scent. She literally felt his energy enter her apartment, spread out, touch her. The bolt turned, the doorknob locked and the chain slid into place. Each metallic click twisted her tension even further. Suddenly, the throbbing in her clit was a fire. With one touch, he could set her off, all that banked sexual need recognizing that release was so close...but if it was his desire, he could also prolong it for hours.

He'd stopped at the archway to her dining nook. She could feel him assessing everything, how she'd followed his instructions. If she was braver, if she could believe in a future, she might have said, no matter how her voice shook, "Good evening, Master." But she didn't. She just waited.

When he moved, stopped behind her, her fingers flexed in their tangle at her lower back. He touched her hair, and she gasped, trying hard not to lean into his hand, but wanting to, more than she'd wanted to do anything her whole life. Her calves were now so slick with her juices she had to tense her thighs so she wouldn't slide to one hip.

Above her knotted hands, something ticklish, soft, slid up her spine. Flowers. He let them spill over her shoulder so she could turn her face into that spray of wildflowers, a plethora of colors, textures, fragrances.

"Thank you," she whispered.

The flowers slipped away, and she heard the whisper of them being laid on the tablecloth. Then his fingers slid over her spine. It was such a dizzying rush to feel that contact, it took her a moment to realize he'd unlocked the padlock to the waist chain.

"Lift your chin, keep your eyes down."

That firm, even voice. Her pussy spasmed, hard, and she made a small whimper, even more desperate than what Max had heard. When he touched the collar, she spoke before she could stop herself.

"Please don't."

He stilled. "Please don't what, Rachel?"

"Don't take the collar off. Please."

"I won't. I'm taking everything else away though. No talking again until I give you permission."

He unhooked the chain in front with a set of pliers, and it dropped into the vee of her lap. It glanced off the clit hood, making her jolt.

"Lean forward on your hands. Calf pose. Knees spread the same width."

The *asana* required a concave position for the back, like a sway-backed cow, but it also lifted the ass pertly in the air. With her knees spread out that way, he was seeing everything. He removed the chain from her waist and from between her buttocks, and then his fingers slid between her legs, cupped the clit piece and the clamp inside her labia that had held it in place, as well as kept her pussy open. She shuddered, but managed to hold her position. When he pulled it all away from her, leaving her in nothing but the collar, she moaned at the friction, her arms quivering.

What was he thinking? What had he thought, seeing her waiting for him as he'd commanded? Did he think she was beautiful and irresistible, as Dana had said? Was she going to really take herself into that insecure territory?

"Child's pose. Frog modification."

He'd straightened up now, and she dropped her ass down on her heels, spreading her knees so her upper body, her abdomen and breasts, pressed to the carpet along with her forehead. Her arms stretched forward, fingertips reaching.

"Grip the table leg, at the foot."

As she did, he stroked the line of her spine. "That metal piece was so wet. Your clit was slippery as the inside of an oyster shell. You've been aroused all day, haven't you?"

"Yes."

"I've been hard all day, thinking about it. I want my dinner, but I want this first."

He slid his hand beneath her then, thumb pressing against her anus, his other fingers sliding through the slick lips of her pussy and settling over her clit. He stroked her with all five digits, sending an explosion of sensation through her.

"Oh..." She cried out, and yet he continued that methodical stroke as her body convulsed, trying so hard to hold the pose he'd demanded.

"This is my pussy, isn't it, Rachel? I can demand anything I want from it. And I want it to come. Right now."

Child's pose was aptly named, because for this it made her as vulnerable and unprotected as a babe. In the folded position, she couldn't move her lower body, except for those tiny, involuntary rocks of motion, and it made the power of that long-withheld climax all the more explosive. Her gaze inadvertently flitted to the clock. Seven-oh-two. Two minutes since he'd arrived and she was...

Her mind lost the script, lost all sense of place and time as the climax detonated, exploded, literally ripped through her. The power of it was terrifying, overwhelming, eternal. Even

171

the well-insulated walls couldn't possibly muffle harsh screams like this, but she was beyond such things. She was a creature of pure flame, of gushing release.

His other hand was against her bare back, holding her down while those fingers worked her. When he shoved three of his fingers into her at the pinnacle of her climax, she wailed, thrown onto another crest, particularly when the fourth finger stayed at her clit and added a vibration of sensation at the right moment, when she thought she couldn't take any more. She was wrong. She dropped her hips even lower between her spread and folded legs, grateful for the flexibility that let her push her clit even more eagerly into his touch. She let go of everything but the feeling, every part of her subsumed by what he was doing to her, unable to control the waves of incoherent cries, moans, whimpers and pleas that broke from her lips. He whispered to her, a rough male growl.

"That's it, sweet girl. Come hard for me. Keep coming for me, keep screaming for me."

She might not have blacked out as decisively as Dana had, but she was pretty sure she phased through three or four different planes of existence before she began spiraling down to earth. What had Ben said? Jon could catapult a woman straight over the Pearly Gates, right into Heaven. She was pretty sure she believed it, with every ounce of her soul. But she didn't want to go to Heaven. Not if he wasn't with her.

He had his arm around her waist, lifting her. She made an uncertain noise, not sure if she was capable of such a wide range of movement so soon, but he was relentless, straightening her up onto her knees, bringing her back against his body. He had her hips pulled into the vee of his thighs as he squatted behind her. She opened her eyes in time to see him lift his fingers to his mouth, suck her fluids from them.

Before she knew it, she'd twisted around and was straining up, had her mouth on his, those fingers between them, so she was tasting him and herself at the same time, licking him frenetically, licking his lips, tasting his tongue, wild and disoriented. Cupping the back of her head, he took over, turning her all the way around on her knees and cinching her in to his hard body, kissing her senseless, taking away everything but pure, blissful compliance.

"That's only the first time you'll come for me tonight." He lifted his head at last. As he shifted to a sitting position on the floor, holding her in his lap, he caught a finger beneath her collar, a sensual tug holding her in place now, reminding her of her manners when she would have strained toward him again.

She stared up at him. "I missed you."

The serious mouth softened, though the fierce light in his eyes only grew brighter. That sodalite color, so many versions of blue when lit by everything happening behind the intelligent, concentrated gaze. "Not anywhere near as much as I missed you. Matt said he thought I'd be willing to give Consolidated Electronics our whole damn company if it meant I could leave one second sooner. You're gorgeous, Rachel Madison. The picture you made when I came in...on your knees, waiting for your Master. My cock may have been hard all day thinking of you, but seeing you like that has made it ache so much it hurts. Can you feel it?"

It was under her ass, and it was taking all she had not to squirm and rub herself against it. It was thick steel, making her rapidly beating heart stay that way.

"I could help with that." Swallowing, she swept her lashes down, her fingers curled in his shirt. She loved him in his suits, his tailored shirts and silk ties. It made her want to devour him. "You said you wanted me to wear the lipstick, so I could...mark you with it."

"You'd like that, wouldn't you?"

She nodded, barely able to contain her eagerness. "I'd be happy to do it for you now...before anything else."

"Look at me then, and ask properly."

He knew how to make things more difficult and intense at once. As she complied, her throat clogged at the sheer impact of meeting his gaze, so close and penetrating. Her fingers burrowed in his shirt front, and she was glad he hadn't told her to remove her touch. "Please…let me suck you. Let me give you pleasure."

"You do that, just by breathing. There's a word missing though."

She lowered her gaze again. "I'm sorry… It's difficult." But she wanted to say it, so much…

"You'll get your wish, but because of that omission, you only get to use your mouth."

He stood, shifting her back to the floor onto folded knees. As he rose, she saw the line of his slacks stretched taut on his thighs, because of the strain his cock was putting on the fabric above. She swallowed. He held her hand for an additional moment, then gave it a squeeze and released it. Taking a seat at his place setting, he turned the chair so he was facing toward her. "Stand up, put your hands behind your back."

She did, conscious of how his gaze coursed over her legs, the tendons elongated in those high heels, the way they tilted her ass. "Now turn away from me and bend over. Half-fold position. Keep your feet close together and put your hands on your calves."

When she did, he leaned forward, set his hands to her hips. A mewl of need broke from her lips as he fastened his mouth over her framed pussy, lapping away her climax, swirling deep into her channel, tasting her. The nerves were still vibrating, overstimulated, and it made her legs tremble on those teetering heels. He had to hold her fast. When he finally sat back, she was gasping.

"I wanted to clean your come away so I can see you get wet for me all over again. Kneel."

As she did, she kept her gaze lowered, though she got another good view of that engorged cock. He picked up his wineglass, tasted. "Good choice."

The simple praise made her glow, silly as that sounded. But then her attention snapped elsewhere as he unhooked the slacks, opened them. She knew she was supposed to keep her eyes down, but she couldn't help peeking through her lashes as he adjusted the slacks and the briefs beneath to bring his thick cock into view, the end glistening as she'd imagined when she'd plucked that honeydew blossom. Only there was far more collected at the tip than a tiny drop.

"Come here and put your mouth on me. Go down as far as you can and then stop."

As she leaned forward, her hands knotting behind her back, she inhaled his scent, the primitive, animal odor of an aroused male. When she put her mouth on him, she thought about that lipstick leaving wet red marks. The way it had on Dana's mouth, on Max's. Her body was wrung out from the climax of a moment ago, limbs still unsteady, yet she didn't care. She wanted more of him. She literally wanted to be fucked to death by him, however he wanted her. His touch, his cock inside her mouth, her pussy...everywhere. She was his, and she wanted him to use her hard, thoroughly, until every ounce of his lust was sated, three times over.

She slid down, down. Halfway there, he was at the back of her throat, stretching her lips with his size and length. She relaxed her muscles, took him deeper, felt his broad head test her gag reflex, but she was determined to hold him there.

He'd taken another sip of the wine, but then he put it down and used both hands to gather up her hair. He transferred the thick mass of it to one hand, held it in a twisted grip as he began to push her down even farther.

"Center your mind, Rachel. Mind over matter. I know you know how to do it."

If he hadn't given her that release, she couldn't have done it. But every part of her was compliant now. Not just her mind, but her relaxed muscles as well, nothing holding her back or harboring reservations. So her throat softened, and he slid deeper, until she was holding him to the root, her breath coming through her nose in shallow draughts.

"That's my good girl," he murmured. "My beautiful slave. We go at my pace."

She followed his hold on her hair, the pressure of his knuckles against her nape. Sliding up his length, she drew in her cheeks to create suction and used her tongue to trace that vein pulsing under the flare of the head. His hand tightened, a convulsive jerk. The power of giving him pleasure surged through her. As he pushed her back down, she pleased herself, exploring the breadth of him with the tip of her tongue, stroking him further with the flat of it. Up again, down again. He had control of her pace, but she seduced him with her mouth until she could tell he was setting the pace his body dictated. She was making involuntary little animal noises that vibrated against his head when he shoved himself into her throat. God, he was beautiful, so hard and thick, virile as she'd expected him to be.

As erect as he was, she anticipated him being closer to release, but she underestimated his stamina. He made her work for it, give him everything her mouth could offer, making those pleading noises. He was breathing hard as well, and he hadn't reached for the wine again, all his attention on her. The pumping rhythm in her mouth was the rhythm of sex, and she wanted him pounding inside her, thrusting into her so hard he'd ram her bed against the wall, drive her into the mattress. Make her earth move.

Unexpectedly, he pulled her off him, and fisted his cock, hard, holding the base. She could see that vein throbbing beneath, knew how close he was. "No," she whispered. "Please..."

"Ask properly." His jaw was set with rigid concentration. "Or I come in this napkin and you only get to watch. Don't think, Rachel, just say it."

"Please let me finish you, Master. Please...Master."

It made her gasp in pain, but the look in his face was a balm against the wound the word tore open inside her. He nodded, his face set in implacable lines. "Use your hands then. I want to feel those pretty fingers against me."

She didn't need to be told twice. She wrapped both around his base, treasuring the feel of the velvet skin over hot steel, the heavy testicles she stroked with reverent fingertips. He made an ominous rumble in his throat, a warning to get down to business.

She set her mouth back over him, not thinking of anything. Not what she'd unwisely said in the heat of the moment, not tomorrow or how impossible this all was. She just focused on sucking her Master to climax.

He exploded in her mouth, his hand clamped on the back of her neck, digging in as she moaned her pleasure and encouragement and took him all in, swallowing him down. He rammed up into her mouth, and she had the titillating impression of his hard thighs, partially revealed by the open slacks. His ass was flexing against the wooden seat, taut muscle obvious even under the fabric. She wished he was naked, even as she also couldn't deny how arousing it was, to be stripped bare for him when he allowed her only short glimpses of the body under his clothes.

As the powerful climax spent itself to the last drop in her throat, he pumped a few more times, slowing his pace but keeping it going, letting her savor long drags of her mouth along his length, feeling him twitch at the increased sensitivity. His hand on her hair convulsed in tandem with the reaction of his cock. She sucked the ridge along his head, traced the slit where his semen had shot into her throat. He was still semi-erect, and she thought she could do this all night, keep servicing him with her mouth.

Her Master had other plans.

Chapter Eleven

ഔ

Drawing her away from him at last, he set her on her heels as he tucked himself back in, refastened the slacks. He pulled the belt free, set it aside and then he leaned forward. Lifting her by the elbows, he drew her up into his lap, letting her curl there like a child.

She closed her eyes as he cradled her, adjusted her body so her legs draped over one chair arm. When he slid his relaxed hand between them, his knuckles pressing against her inner thigh, it reminded her of his right to touch her wherever he wished. But with that demand was this cosseting tenderness that overwhelmed her after such blinding passion. "Oh Jon. I can't...I don't know what to say."

"Last time I checked, you don't have permission to say anything. Not unless you ask first." But there was humor in the quiet reminder. She relaxed further in his arms, noted she was still quivering. It was then she also noticed the ring on his middle finger, and remembered that vibrating sensation. It appeared to be a simple band, but on the palm side, there was a tiny, thick disk. It had to be the source of the vibration that had taken her fading climax up to a whole new level. She was beginning to realize Jon wasn't content with a woman's "normal" orgasm or even the typical intensity of the aftershocks. He wanted to stretch the limits of her endurance, every time. It was a daunting—and terribly thrilling—prospect.

He pressed his mouth to her forehead, dipped to kiss her lips, tease his taste from them, from her tongue. "Talk about torture. I'll never leave you like that again. Thinking about you, knowing how hot and needy you were feeling...it's a wonder I got anything done today. Did you come by yourself?"

The question was weighted, his hands stilling upon her. She swallowed. "Almost. Once. I was sleeping, though, and couldn't help it. I woke up and sort of stopped it."

"Sort of." He squeezed her hip in mild reproof. "Well, we'll add that to the tally, won't we?"

Tally? She wasn't sure she wanted to know what that meant, but there was something she really did want to know. "May I...ask something?"

"You may. Sweet girl."

The sensual caress of that voice spread heat through her, as if being held and surrounded by that strong male body weren't already making her feel safer than she'd felt in...maybe ever.

"Why..." She paused, struggling with things she'd stopped talking about years ago, such that it was hard to speak of them even now. But he was waiting. "For so long, I couldn't climax. But you...you acted like that didn't worry you at all. How did you know? How *do* you know?"

He stroked silk flesh high on her thigh, his gaze dropping there with that intent focus that could get her aroused again in no time. She held her breath as he went higher, made a circle, stroked her outer labia. "Your breath gets short, the closer I get to your pussy, waiting for that one...bare...touch." She made a noise as he brushed his finger over her clit, then returned to making circles on her thigh. "I've met very few women who can't climax, Rachel." He met her gaze. "Whereas I've met plenty who've never had lovers who took the time or had the confidence to seek the key that would unleash that part of them. I've met even more who, through that history and their own lack of confidence and other emotional issues, built the walls that reinforce the problem."

He saw things she really didn't want anyone to see, but with him she didn't seem to have a choice. She laid her head back against his shoulder, considering this remarkable and amazing male creature who'd come into her life like an irresistible storm. It wouldn't last. Couldn't last. Her heart cracked a little, and her hands closed in her lap, fighting the desire to trace his brow, slide her finger over his lips, see if he'd nip or lick at them, like Max.

"Will you tell me about yourself? Things I don't already know."

He tipped her chin up, holding it so he could keep her captured in his regard. "There are twenty-five thousand, six hundred and twelve things you don't know about me. I'll tell you one each day."

She managed a smile, but thought the gesture was attached to her heart, the way it pulled painful strings there. "Jon." Her voice was a whisper.

"That means it will take you seventy-plus years to know everything about me. When I turn one hundred, that will be the last one. Though I expect by then you'll know the very first and very last thing you need to know about me, the only one that matters."

"Don't do this." She tried to fold her arms against herself, hugging them up under her ribs, drawing in. "Jon, I can't..."

"Can't what?" Closing his hand on one of her arms, he pulled it away from her body. His touch slid down to her wrist and then he put her hand between her legs, his fingers pressing over hers on her pussy, so she felt the wetness his mouth and the climax had left there. It effectively pulled her attention back to him, made her feel out of control. He had the control.

"You just want one night, Rachel? Is that it?"

"No..." How could she deny wanting more of this? It wasn't about what she wanted, but what she could handle. "But I don't expect...promises or commitments. We can't...you can't... When you're done with it, I'm not going to expect anything, but in order for that to happen I can't...there's no need to act like we have a future together."

She stumbled to a halt as his expression cooled. *Don't ruin this, Rachel. For God's sake, shut up.*

"Hmm." He cocked his head. "I understand. Spread your legs for me."

Uncertain, she shifted, and then sucked in a breath as he moved her hand to the side and slid his fingers back into her, pushing in deep.

"Now cup your breasts and offer them to me."

She had to brace her elbows on the chair arm, but she managed it, sliding her hands under her bosom and then tilting back against his hold so the pink-tipped breasts tilted up toward his unfathomable gaze.

"Stay like that."

Keeping his hand inside her, he reached over his plate, to the casserole dish with the eggplant. Removing the lid, he dipped his finger into the sauce. Steam was coming from it, but he was able to collect enough to bring it to his mouth, taste. Approval laced his expression, but she was still uneasy about that hardness around his mouth, the stillness of his gaze on her. Picking up the ladle, he scooped up more of the sauce and brought it over her breasts.

"This is going to burn some, but it won't be unbearable. Don't move."

She had a second to brace herself, then the hot marinara hit the upper curve, making her jump as it slid down and over her nipple. His mouth descended upon it, licking the sauce away, tasting her beneath it, scoring her with sharp teeth that made her gasp. Then he did it again to the other nipple. As he did, his fingers played inside her, sliding, scissoring, stroking. Her neck strained, and she wanted to drop her head back and thrash at the feeling, but she stayed utterly still at his command, the emotions of the past few moments swirling around them. While it made her nervous, it couldn't repel what he was building around her again, walling her up in sensation, taking rational thought away.

When she was shuddering in that self-imposed stasis, he removed his fingers, put the top back on the casserole dish, took another swallow of wine. Pushing back from the table, he lifted her in his arms and moved away from the dining nook. He took her down the hall, to her bedroom.

"Jon, I'm sorry. I didn't mean to—"

"Sshh."

The almost absent command reassured her, because there was a thoughtful note to it. As if he wasn't mad now but...thinking. Then he put her down on her stomach on her bed, but he guided her feet to the floor. "Brace yourself up on your arms and raise your ass. I believe you need another spanking, because the one I gave you at the office hasn't sunk in. And I think it's best to get that out of the way before you rack up more than you can handle at one go."

She was powerless to resist his commands, even as things were gathering inside her she didn't know how to handle. How to release. She'd angered him, she was sure, but she didn't know how to fix it, and she was taking a one-way slide toward misery, her mind starting to pull her away from this moment, this wonderful adventure she'd had to screw up by opening her mouth...

Laying his hand on the back of her neck, he pushed her face down to the mattress, but left her ass canted high in the air. "I'm not going to stop until I'm done, and I'm not going to tell you the number of strokes. I want you to give yourself to the pain, and wherever else your body or soul takes you."

"Maybe we should—" She got out the three desperate words, but that was all she managed.

He had a strong hand. The palm smacked her bottom with force, sending a sting throughout all the nerve endings and ricocheting right into her pussy, her nipples, reminding her of all the hours they'd been stimulated by that chain upon her, those metal pieces. Another slap, and her ass wobbled in reverberation, her knees having to lock to hold her in place.

"On your toes," he ordered, his voice stern. "I want that ass reaching for my punishment."

Her emotions fought a pitched battle among themselves, but she obeyed, straining up another inch, even in the tipped heels. The next strike startled her, because it wasn't his hand. It was the back of a brush, the carved oak hairbrush he'd taken from the dresser. The wood stung fiercely against her already tender buttock. As she internalized that shock, he did it to the other cheek, and then he set about alternating, side to side, hand to brush, never letting it get into a rhythm. Stinging heat became painful fire, but she kept lifting up to him, until she realized she had tears on her cheeks and sobs were catching in her throat. That emotional knot she'd resurrected loosened, unraveled. She was begging him now, but she wasn't sure for what. It was just his name... No, it wasn't...

"Master...please..."

She was too far gone for the shock of it to stop the words, but as she cried out in real pain at the last strike, he dropped the brush to the side. She let out a small shriek as his hands closed hard over the abused buttocks, and then she choked on her latest sob as his tongue thrust into her pussy, his mouth sealing over that and the perineum, then moving upward, teasing the rim of her anus, making her moan further. He was turning her over. Before she could blink or move to dash her tears away, he had her stretched out on her back, and he was lying full on top of her, his body insinuated between her legs. His arms were around her, pulling her in to his chest, but the open vulnerability of it, the fact she could only curl around him, her legs and body spread open to him, kept the tears coming.

He framed her face then, making her look at him. "Tell me one thing about you, Rachel. Something I don't know."

I think you may know everything. Because I feel like you're standing right inside my soul. Because she was trembling, and because he'd laid her wide open, he'd made the one thing she could barely handle thinking about, let alone saying, come out of her lips. The thing she hadn't been able to bring herself to voice in his office.

"My son died in Afghanistan. He was nineteen years old. I held him when he was born, and a roadside bomb blew away those perfect legs and arms, that beautiful face. He had my nose and my smile. His father's eyes."

Jon nodded. He stroked away the tears, traced her lips. She was going to shatter. "I need to move. Please."

"You'll lie like this, spread beneath me, and trust me to hold you together."

But it was too late. That pain had already shattered her soul. What was once resilient had proven itself too fragile, and there was no putting a porcelain doll back together after it had been broken. Though she was glued together, there was no hiding the cracks. "I don't know what this is for you, Jon, but I'm not strong enough. I thought I could do at least tonight, have this, but I made the wrong choice. Seems I'm always making the wrong choices. I'm too old to make one that's this wrong."

Propping himself on one elbow, he swept his thumb along her cheek bone, teasing the corner of her mouth, wet with the tears. "Close your eyes."

When she hesitated, he sharpened his voice, repeated it, though there was something in the tone that made it reassuring, even with the note of reproof and command. She closed her eyes, her throat aching with those tears.

He held the pause a long moment, stroking her, letting her still, focus on what might be coming next. Occasionally a soft noise came from his throat as she hiccupped on a sob, but when she had settled down, he spoke again. "Most of us, even as we grow up, continue to look at the world through the subconscious of the age we were before we hit the reality and disappointments that we discover as adults. So, when you look at yourself in the mirror of your mind, you're looking through the eyes of a certain age. How old are those eyes, Rachel?"

It made her even more uncomfortable, but as long as he had her spread-eagled and pinned like this she couldn't be less than honest. "I guess...nineteen or twenty. Right before I had Kyle."

With her eyes still closed, she leaned her cheek into the hand that was sliding down her cheek, curving around her chin. Jon's voice was a rumble in her anxious mind.

"The therapist I had to see when I was twelve said that I had the outlook of a forty-year-old. I told him I was the reincarnation of Galileo, or possibly the ancient bard Taliesin. Never could decide. Maybe both. So see, under either interpretation, I'm far older than *you*."

A weak smile tugged at her lips, despite herself. She opened her eyes then to see him trace that smile, caressing her dimple. His eyes were full of so many mesmerizing things. Compassion, desire, knowledge. A complete and utter absorption in her that unbalanced her reality, the way she'd always told herself life had to be. A lock of his dark hair had fallen over his brow, and when she reached up to stroke through it, his palm followed the line of her upper arm, then came down to cup her breast, weigh it thoughtfully.

"You have nice, heavy breasts. You looked to me like a woman who's nursed a child, your breasts lower than a woman your age who hasn't." Before that observation could discomfit her, he bent his head, licked the nipple with casual pleasure, spoke against it. "I can see you nursing your baby with these beautiful, ripe breasts, swollen with milk, your nipples so large. You'd both be in my lap, and I'd watch him suck, equally fascinated and envious, hoping I might get a turn soon. Babies are little tyrants who trump even a Master's demands."

It startled a half-chuckle out of her, winning an answering glint from his gaze. Then he sobered. "Why are there no pictures of him, Rachel? There are no photographs in your home at all. Only paintings, most of them about tranquility, serenity." His glance went to the picture on the wall, the governess yearning toward that clandestine kiss. "Except for this, a window into your soul. You've made this your refuge, because every time you go out, reality is pretty hard for you, isn't it?"

"You know, I'm beginning to understand why dating a clueless male isn't such a bad thing."

"Too late," he commented. "The pictures?"

She molded her hand behind his on her breast, liking the dusting of hair on the knuckles, the long, strong fingers. So different from hers, the times she'd tried, futilely, to pleasure herself in this bed, imagining her far-too-feminine hands as a man's. Her throat was clogged with memories, but she found the answer for him. "I couldn't handle the questions. The, 'oh who is this handsome young man?'"

She looked left, toward the closet. "I keep the album tucked in between my sweaters. Most nights, I look at it before I go to bed." She'd done it so often the slick page corners were permanently worn from her fingertips. "I keep it in there because when people see a photo album, they figure it's okay to look, like it's public property. I couldn't bear someone visiting, picking it up on a whim and having to talk about it, answer questions…"

"You don't have a lot of those either. Visitors." As relentless as those blue eyes were, it was the press of his body on hers, the firmness of his groin against her pussy, everything that intimate connection could mean, that kept all of her soul spread open to him. She felt like nothing was hidden, yet in the dim light of her bedroom, she was also warm beneath him. Sheltered. The things she was in the privacy of this room, she could be with him. It was unsettling. She wasn't sure she could deny him anything.

"Everyone likes you, Rachel," he continued. "You could have a great many good friends, but you don't. You give the impression that you lead separate personal and professional lives to keep people at a distance. But the most I've ever heard you mention is having drinks with the other PT people. Was that true, or a deception?"

"No, I do go occasionally. They drink, act silly. Talk about younger men at the club. Like you. I join in."

"To blend." He touched her face as a new rivulet of tears started down her cheek. "Oh Rachel. You've isolated yourself so much."

"No. It was a choice, Jon." She struggled for composure. "I do better when I don't get close to people. Things don't spill out that they can't handle, that they don't want to handle."

He bent, closed his mouth over those tears. Her trembling hands gripped his biceps, his strength. Then he lifted his head an inch or two, giving her a curious look. "Do you have any childhood scars?"

It took her a moment to orient herself to the change in subject. "Um...I fell over a wooden bench at the ice skating rink when I was ten and cut my knee pretty badly. You can still see the discoloration there."

"Left knee," he said, without glancing down.

"Yes."

"Hmm. I wondered about that." Sliding down her body, but continuing to stay between her legs, he settled his hand on her upper abdomen, fingers spread out over that wide point beneath the spread of her ribs. It was the solar plexus chakra point. When unbalanced, it was the one most likely to project fear, lack of confidence...the one that would allow the intellect too much sway. She knew enough about Jon to know his positioning of that hand was deliberate, the soothing stroke of it. Leaning down, he put his mouth on that childhood mark on her knee. She stared at his silhouette cast from the dim hallway light and wondered at him. "Scars anywhere else?" he asked, his mouth still on her.

"I'd love to think of about a hundred places, if you're going to do that..." But her attempt at humor was swept away as he made his way up her thigh, his mouth cruising past her hip bone, and then pressed his lips with unerring instinct somewhere else. Something trembled low in her stomach, and those tears threatened again. "Jon..."

"Stretch mark, right? So very faint...you have great muscle tone through here, but you can still see the impression. It must have been a hard labor."

He devastated her. But he didn't leave it at that. When he came back up her body, lay back down upon her, she swallowed a surprised breath as he reached between them, opened his slacks. She caught her breath in the back of his throat as he fitted his quite obviously revitalized cock into her opening. She trembled again, harder, inside and out, hovering on this moment that was painful and everything she wanted at once. His eyes held hers, seeing all of it. "Mine, Rachel," he murmured, those blue eyes vibrant, fierce, at odds with his gentle tone of only a second before.

"Please..." The word whispered out of her lips. He shifted, sinking inside her, pushing through those muscles that had not had the pleasure of welcoming a man's cock for so long. And never a man who held her heart and soul the way this one did.

His progress was slow but inexorable, seating him deep, filling her. When he was all the way in, she was overcome, her arms wrapping around his back. Holding him tightly, she pressed her face to his chest as he cupped the back of her head with both hands, whispering to her as she shook, as she worried that she might break right then.

He stayed so still inside of her, letting her feel that connection, the lock between their bodies. It took a long time for her to pull herself together, but he waited her out, waited until she spoke against his chest, her voice muffled.

"You... You didn't show me any of your scars."

He eased her head back to the mattress, pressed his mouth to her jaw, a touch of his tongue on the carotid pulse.

Propping himself on one elbow again, he gave her a long look, then whispered a knuckle over her cheek, directing her gaze to a small mark on his forearm.

"I got this when I learned how to pop a wheelie on my bike. I was so excited I fell off it right afterward." Rewarding her tentative smile, he lifted up, moving to his knees. As he did, he held her hips, taking her with him so they remained joined as he shifted her ass onto his thighs and kept her on her back, body sloped down to the bed, head on the pillow. It pushed his cock up high inside her. His eyes flickered, registering the ripple of reaction over her skin, the arch of her back, the swallow that moved her throat.

"You know, when we're young, and we fall or cut ourselves, we take pride in those marks, after they happen." Though he had her impaled, that velvet voice was the most persistent restraint of all. He was opening his shirt, and now he pulled it to the side, showing her a longer scar that ran along his left side. Her fingers fluttered to settle on his bare skin, savoring the chance. "I was trying to create a Fortress of Solitude out of long window glass shards I took from a construction site bin. I tripped and fell into a pile of them."

"Ouch." Automatically, her fingers smoothed over the line, but he caught her wrist, brought her attention back up to him. Now he touched her face, traced the lines that fanned out from her eye.

"Every crease here is a smile, a tear, laughter. They're layers over that nineteen-year-old girl who didn't know then what it was to lose a child, or to have your husband hurt you so deeply."

"I didn't divorce him." It was hard to push the words out. The truth was taking the air out of the room. But he stroked her throat, eased the lump there.

"I know you didn't. He divorced you."

"H-how do you know that?"

Increasing his grip on her hips now, he slid partway out, then came back in at the precarious angle. Her pussy quivered around him, her nipples tightening under his gaze. Though he was beautiful, tempting as a god like this, she wanted him completely naked, lying down upon her. She wanted to feel the muscles of his bare thighs pressing against the soft flesh inside of hers.

"A submissive of a certain nature will never leave the person she considers her Dom, even if he isn't one. Or doesn't deserve the title." His mouth became a hard line now, his eyes delving back into her in that way that stripped her raw, yet sheltered her from the wind at the same time. "She refuses to give up on the relationship. She'll kill herself, her soul, trying to please, to figure out what the answer is. She can't walk away, demand something else. Certain submissives can, but you can't."

She was turning into a wreck, a tangled mess of heartbreak and arousal, old emotions warring with the new. He leaned down, whispered into her hair, and she held onto his voice, the feel of his body joining with hers.

"I saw that nineteen-year-old the first time I met you. That's why I call you a girl at times. I see that sweetness and hope and fragility, all of it beneath those life experiences that made you the strong woman you are."

She'd never seen herself as strong. Not until now, looking into the eyes of a man who believed it. Who believed in her.

"You remember earlier, what you said to me about not needing promises or commitments?"

She nodded, a quick jerk. "It made you mad. I'm sorry, I just—"

"I'm talking now." The tone was mild, but the look in his eyes wasn't. She closed her mouth. "One of the reasons I wanted to get the spanking out of the way was because I was about to lose my temper. And that doesn't happen too often. Lie still."

Though she couldn't help a sound of anguish, he shushed her as he withdrew from her body. When he tucked himself back into his slacks, he gave her a brief glimpse of her juices glistening on the full length of his cock. He left the shirt open, though, and pulled her up. She was back in his lap, his feet on the floor as he sat on the edge of the bed. Taking hold of her jaw, he caressed her throat, holding her attention.

"I'm only going to say this once. You're not going to talk about this being a one-night deal or a temporary situation any more. I won't tolerate it."

Over the past couple days, as well as tonight, she'd had a couple glimpses of this side of Jon, a man she'd always before associated only with a firm quietude and gentleness. What had surprised her was she responded to him as a Master, whether he was being merciful or ruthless. But this side of him had the ability to keep her completely still, as if his gaze was a lock as unshakable as restraints he'd put on her. It also sent a quaking feeling through the deepest parts of her, the same way such physical restraints would have.

"You're the type of woman who needs commitment," he said. "Love. If I wasn't prepared to bring those to the table as part of what I can offer you, I never would have started this. So if you try to run from me, run from that, you'll find I don't shake that easily."

Lifting a brow, he raked his glance over her. "When I'm inventing, I focus on what I know will fix a problem. I'm not a heavy-handed Master, but if I think that's what you need, that's what you'll get. You ever try spouting that bullshit again, you won't sit down for a week. You got through a marriage by lying to him about what you needed, when he didn't have the balls or depth of soul to handle the truth. You won't need to do that with me and, what's more, you won't get away with it. You got it?"

She stared up at him, those words tingling through all her extremities, and swirling thick and heavy in her core. "Yes," she managed.

"Yes, what?"

He was going to insist, no matter how many times it pulled at the fears inside of her. "Jon..."

He slid his hand fully around her throat, squeezing above the collar, making her pussy react. He knew total possession was the key to her pleasure. "When you were sitting by my chair, waiting for me to come to you, what did you want? What was it you wanted more than anything?"

"To please you."

"Any Master who walked through that door? Like Peter or Lucas? Or Max?"

She flushed. "I didn't—"

"Just answer the question."

"No." She was sure on that. "Just you. With them, it was because of you... I haven't felt like this...for anyone. Ever."

Those stern eyes went vibrant, like pools of deep Caribbean waters. Daring, she reached up, traced his lips. When he allowed it, pressing a kiss into her palm, relief and terror warred inside her. "I'm so afraid."

"I know. I'm here, Rachel. I'm not going anywhere."

He nipped a finger, gave her a sweet, lingering kiss on her lips that changed the mood, took her away from those paths into a different part of the garden he was offering to her. When he moved his lips to her erratic wrist pulse, she slid several silken feathers of his hair between her knuckles. The dark paths were still there, still calling to her, but at least for this moment he'd made her believe it was okay.

"You wanted to know one thing about me," he murmured against her skin. "'I'll give you one of those twenty-five-thousand things now."

It worried her, what he was going to say. That darkness still felt too close, and she was sure he'd overestimated her courage, what she could handle right now. She even closed her eyes as he spoke, too afraid to see it happen.

"That is some of the best damn marinara I've ever tasted."

* * * * *

When her eyes opened, startled, he had a faint smile on his face, though his eyes remained on hers, far too shrewd, watching her every reaction, every emotion that flickered over her face. "That's not really something about you," she said at last.

"It is if I tell you that your marinara is now my absolute favorite, because of the way it tastes when I suck it off your nipples."

Then his mouth was on hers, giving her the remnants of that flavor, as well as the musk from when he'd plunged his tongue into her pussy. He made the kiss lazy, tantalizing, nipping at her mouth. She clung to him, her body loose and liquid beneath his as he at last pushed her back onto the bed. She wondered at his unpredictability, how it kept her emotions from setting into one track. He might do it deliberately, though so much about him seemed intuitive, as if he was in her head, anticipating her even before she knew what she wanted.

He shrugged off the shirt, the rounded curves of his shoulders gleaming in the dim light thrown by her bedside lamp. "Lay your arms above your head, beautiful girl," he ordered, his hand at his slacks again. "Hold onto the rails of the headboard."

She obeyed. The tracks of her tears were drying, and while the sadness that had caused them lingered, it had competition with the coil in her lower belly that responded to the command, to what might be about to happen.

"Open your legs, bend them at the knee. Show me your pussy, how much it wants my touch."

Limbs quaking, she did it. That trembling seemed to be a permanent state around him, as if everything he did rocked the foundation of who and what she was.

Bless all the gods, he discarded the slacks and boxers beneath, coming to her lean and gorgeous and naked at last, a thin foil packet in his hand. His cock was brushing his belly again, just as her cunt was slick and needy once more. As she watched, he slid the condom over himself. She realized then he hadn't done so before, and the only reason she could determine in her desire-fogged mind was he'd had no intention of finishing at that point. That he'd known how it would affect her, the first time, and he'd given her time to experience that wave of overwhelming emotion, shuddering in his arms from the mere act of penetration. And he'd made it skin to skin, underscoring the intimacy in a safe way.

He'd shown both enviable control and overwhelming sensitivity at once. While she loved the latter, she had room for the physical now, and she wanted to see him lose control, feel it. And she wanted to lose control with him.

As he rolled on the latex, her hands curled on the spindles of the headboard, a poor substitute for his heated, thick length. One part of her wanted to do that for him. Another wanted to beg him to leave it off. She had no fear of disease, not from Jon. He would never expose a woman to any kind of danger from himself. As for the other...she couldn't articulate it, too many vulnerable emotions involved. She wished she had the bravery to follow her heart, to ask him to leave it off. But that wouldn't be fair. Jon would never leave a child without a father.

"Rachel." His palm settled once more on her upper abdomen, connecting her to his energy, drawing her gaze back up to his face. "Focus only on me. On this. Feel."

Kneeling between her knees, he guided himself to her, pausing at the ring of tight muscle. "Relax for me. Just like class, we're moving together. We fit together."

Her lips parted, throat working at the promise of that connection, and her muscles eased, pulling him in. As before, he kept his eyes on her face, studying every change in her expression, her parted lips. He'd made her leave the heels on, and they stabbed into the mattress pillowtop, for he kept the other hand on one of her knees, telling her he wanted her to maintain the bent-legged position until he was fully seated again. At this angle, she felt the pressure of that glide into her body even more acutely, such that she was making those noises in her throat as he sank in to the hilt.

He lowered himself onto her body then, sliding one strong arm behind her shoulders. "Put your legs around me. High on my back. I want those sexy stilettos brushing my shoulder blades."

She complied, loving the way it felt, him so closely joined to her, his face so close, hands touching her, commanding her body. He held her still then, one palm closing on her thigh. "By the end of tonight, I'm going to have tasted every inch of you, Rachel Madison. Taken you so many times you'll have trouble walking. I'd love to come to your Monday class and enjoy the hell out of seeing you explain to your class why you're not as limber as you usually are. And the whole time you'd go through the practice, I'd be thinking about fucking you in the showers right afterward."

"That will make it hard to...reach a medita-meditative state."

"Having trouble talking, sweet girl?" The look he sent her was pure male satisfaction, and she tried to steady her voice, give him a spirited volley in return.

"It's only Friday. I'd heal by Monday."

"You assume I'm going to let you out of this bed this weekend." He adjusted himself even more deeply then, a tiny pain. When she made a noise of helpless pleasure, all teasing left his expression.

"From this night on, I consider it all mine. Every beautiful blonde lock of hair, that tender spot on your knee, the pretty line of your ankle. Your pussy, your breasts, your gorgeous round ass. It's all mine. Say it."

"Y-yours."

He put his forehead to hers, touched her lips, barely a breath. "Say it without the fear, Rachel. Feel it deep inside. Say it."

"Yours." A whisper, like a breeze sliding through her, sure and quiet. Incontrovertible.

"Good. And being mine means I'll make sure you know what pleasure feels like, not just in your body but in your heart, mind and soul. I'll dedicate myself to it. I'll satisfy your every desire, every fantasy, and in return, you'll give me all of it, every deep part of yourself, because I meant what I said earlier. I'll take care of you. You can't trust any of it yet, but you will. For now, I'll keep saying it so you can keep remembering it."

She couldn't have found words to answer such incredible things, but she didn't have the chance. He pulled out, then thrust back in, and she arched up to him, crying out at the power and determination behind it. All the restraint he'd shown up until now, the finesse, the lingering torment, were left behind. He did in fact know what she needed, when she needed it. Now he gave her a Master's lust, his animal possession, made her feel like she would be pushed to serve him to the last ounce of energy, with every straining muscle.

Despite the recent climax, the punishing, excruciating rhythm had her body climbing that steep roller coaster again. She clung to him with legs and arms, burying her face into his neck, the strands of his hair against her forehead.

He'd teased her about the marinara, letting her have some breathing room. But these earth-shattering words were a reminder that there was an invisible leash attached to that collar she still wore, and he would only let her back away a certain amount. It was thrilling and terrifying at once, a duality she was beginning to accept went hand in hand with her first-in-a-lifetime feelings for Jon.

How many times had she told herself that, after tonight, after this point or that point, she'd back away, push him to arms' length? She'd been fooling herself. One didn't push a

Master at all. Not unless one was willing to deal with the consequences.

She wouldn't survive it. To do that, she'd have to accept the improbable was possible, and that she could trust him. That she could believe the things he said about her, things she couldn't believe herself.

So, ultimately, it wasn't about not trusting him. It was about not trusting herself, the courage of her own heart. She'd doubted that part of herself from the first time she'd seen her failure in Cole's eyes. Now the organ beating so frantically in her chest had so many cracks, there was no way it was strong enough for this. The problem was, she didn't think Jon was going to give her any other choice.

That too was a thrilling and terrifying possibility.

Chapter Twelve

❧

Jon had enjoyed the company of many submissives, as Rachel had accurately guessed. He'd never had one like her. Though he always cared for the women he bedded, he didn't have the emotional investment he had with this one. Still, it amazed the man and roused the Master to fever pitch, the way she anticipated his demands as if she knelt obediently in his brain, watching every flicker of activity beneath her silky lashes.

He'd depleted her emotionally and expected that to affect her physical endurance. As such, he anticipated outlasting her tonight, driving her over the edge of exhaustion and beyond, and he did. He'd intended to do so. As he'd said, he wasn't a heavy-handed Dom, but he knew when it was needed. She needed his ruthless demands, because they fed a soul too long starved of the chance to serve a Master.

Every time he took her body, or put her on her knees to suck him off again, or placed her back in Child's pose to eat her pussy to climax, she gave him every ounce of energy she had. Her voice became hoarse from screaming, and her legs trembled if she tried to stand, such that he had to help her to the bathroom when it was needed. She didn't want him to go in with her, and he let her have that, understanding a woman's vanity, but he was at the door to take her back to the bed. Seeing how much she wanted to give him, beyond the last reservoir of strength she possessed, made his heart fill with feelings he knew exactly what to call, feelings she was too afraid yet to hear.

He'd seen the look in her eyes when he'd first put on the condom, and he'd read the emotions clearly enough that the Dominant in him had wanted to toss aside the irrelevant thing and take her the way he should, nothing between them. But the feelings that kept her silent, still thinking this would end, had stopped him. Just as she was afraid of binding him to her unwillingly, he wouldn't ever let her believe that a life they created was what made this permanent. There would be time for all that, once he had her heart nestled trustingly in his hand.

The last time, when he slid inside her—rough enough to make her moan with a slave's deep desire to feel the pain with the pleasure, gently enough not to abuse sore tissues too much—she managed to wrap her arms and legs around him, but she was clinging like a leaf not sure of its grip. He'd depleted her to the point she thought she wasn't capable of another orgasm, and he suspected she was right—at least in this position. He gave her his once more though, because he knew she needed that, needed to know she'd served her Master well.

Then he showed her that serving her Master well also meant giving him *her* pleasure when he demanded it. Once again gagging her with the cock plug he'd brought, he slid down her body and spent long, leisurely minutes arousing her with his mouth. Thanks to Lucas' tutelage in how to re-awaken a woman who'd been stimulated repeatedly, he was able to bring her back to a short but intense climax that had a small amount of her cream spurting on his tongue one last time. It drove him crazy seeing the way she was sucking on that gag frenetically at the end, her hungry eyes wanting his cock. But he wanted to give her tenderness now. She'd earned it.

So instead, he removed the gag and rolled her over onto her stomach to give her a thorough Tantric massage. He started at her feet, pressing his thumbs into the soles, working his way up her legs. He took his time on her shoulders, an even-handed, rolling and caressing of the muscles. The chakra clearing was trickier, because as he passed his hands six inches over her body, he had to flick his wrists repeatedly to get rid of the more destructive energies. It was like sloughing a snake's skin even as he saw a new one forming. He put aside his ego, knowing years of pain and denial weren't going to be obliterated in one night. He'd have to be satisfied that he'd stirred those chakra energies up quite a bit tonight, knocked a lot of things loose.

He'd been telling her the truth. However long it took, he was here. She wasn't going to shake him or shut him out.

When he was done and brought her food and drink, he had to lift her to a seated position. She blinked blearily at him. He'd brought some eggplant and bread, the wine for him and water for her. She'd put a pitcher of ice water and a glass on the table if he wanted it with his food. She'd thought of things like that, and he knew anticipating his needs, both domestic and sexual, were an integral part of her nature. He wondered and cursed at the ex-husband, a man he didn't know but who had so obviously not appreciated the gift she was. Worse — instead of appreciating it, he'd abused it.

Setting those negative thoughts aside, he lifted her, moved them to a roomy easy chair in her bedroom. Adjusting her in his lap, both of them naked, skin to skin, he shared a plate of eggplant parmesan and a glass of water with her, occasionally sipping at the wineglass he left on the floor to his left. True to what he'd promised, he didn't let her touch a fork or glass with her fingers. He fed her himself and satisfied her thirst by holding the glass to her lips and watching the movement of her graceful throat as she swallowed.

When at last she slept, he held her close. There was a quivering undercurrent to her repose, one that made her press herself to him, slide her arms around his shoulders, hold on tight. In the unconscious state of her dreams she sought the comfort of male companionship, the Master she'd lacked for far too long.

He kept his arms banded around her, rocked her, all without waking her, soothing her in those dreams. He was here, she wasn't alone.

His gaze moved over the room, lingered on the closet where the photo album was hidden. Her life with her husband had made her brittle, fragile, and the death of her son was the tragedy that shattered her completely, turned her into this shell. But Jon had known she was still there, burrowed deep in its spiraling tunnels. The truth had been in between the lines of what she'd told him at his office.

If her husband had simply been a vanilla guy who didn't understand the D/s compulsions of his wife but who truly, deeply loved her nevertheless, they could have figured something out. As Jon had recognized, she wasn't the kind of submissive who would have left her husband because he wasn't a Dom. All she truly needed was to be loved. If he could have accepted what she was, and how that could manifest itself in a vanilla relationship, they would have had a chance. Instead, Rachel Madison was beaten down and plain terrified of trusting another man with her heart.

All of which might suggest he should move slow, take the relationship on a lazy ride before he pushed her where he intended to take her. However, his intuition told him differently. While he didn't always abandon common sense in the face of eerie coincidence, he couldn't deny the similarities. The two married and one almost-married K&A men had all known their chosen women for a certain number of months beforehand, as he had with Rachel. But because of their unique circumstances, once each man set his sights on her and fired the first shot, so to speak, he'd had to close the deal within an extremely short time frame. Savannah, in the course of one night. Cassie, twenty-four hours. For Dana, it had been three days.

While his and Rachel's circumstances didn't define the timeline quite so precisely, he knew Rachel wasn't at a point she could endure the usual seesaw of a relationship's development. And if he was being honest, maybe that was why the urgency had as much to do with his feelings as hers. He wouldn't tolerate the stress that could cause her, the doubt and fears, based on her past history. Jon knew what he wanted, and he was willing to use the "shock and awe" tactics Peter had referenced to help her believe it. He wanted her to make that leap toward him, away from what had been and into what he could offer her now. What he *would* offer her. So instead of hiding from the truth, he'd convince her she could take shaky steps down that road, her hand firmly in his every step of the way.

He already had a plan in mind, but it would take some coordination. Luckily, he knew where he could find help. Sliding out of bed near dawn's light, he tucked the covers around her exhausted body and went out onto her balcony. Opening his phone, Jon pressed Peter's number. The obsessive bastard was the only one he knew for certain would be up and doing his morning workout by sunrise. At one time, Lucas would have been up and biking ten miles before work, a mild workout for him, but since Cass was legal guardian of her younger siblings, his mornings were usually a bit more chaotic these days.

"Yeah." Peter's voice was pitched low, and Jon's brow rose.

"What? Dana isn't doing a triathlon with you before breakfast?"

"She had an exhausting evening."

Despite his other concerns, Jon had to smile at the tone of a sated predator in Peter's voice. "Is your fiancée acting out again?"

"When is she not? I think she likes doing that."

"Only because you punish her for it. Have you ever considered getting her a driver who doesn't remind her so much of you?"

"Why do you think I have him drive her?" Peter's wolfish smile was as audible as the devotion in his voice. "She likes to keep me on my toes."

"I'll say. You better give Max a good bonus, though Lucas will make you take it straight out of your check." Jon leaned a hip against the rail, grinned. "I shudder to think of her idea of a bachelorette party."

"Thanks for that terrifying reminder." But Peter's manner changed then, became more sober. Jon was sure he was now gazing at his sleeping fiancée. He was probably sitting in his roomy recliner, still in his boxers but with his laptop balanced on the arm while he reviewed the overnight reports from their Central American plants.

"It's her way of telling me she won't be considered helpless, no matter how much I try to take care of her."

"Is she doing okay?" Jon knew that in addition to physical therapy, Dana was also in psychotherapy to deal with the PTSD and other emotional issues that dogged a soldier who'd experienced such a traumatic injury. His question was twofold, for that journey had affected Peter as well, who understood it both from the perspective of a fellow veteran but also as the significant other who helped her through the night terrors, depression and other challenges.

"Yeah. Lots better in fact. She's come a long way, Jon." There was pride now, and it reassured Jon to hear it enter his friend's voice. "She's tough as nails, but don't tell her I said so. She's much feistier when she thinks I consider her a porcelain doll."

"You do consider her a porcelain doll. She knows you'd wrap her up in cotton if you did what you wanted, instead of what's best for her. She's a smart lady."

"She's that and much more. But Jesus, I hadn't even thought about a fucking bachelorette party…"

Jon chuckled, but before he could say anything further, Peter changed the subject. "This isn't why you called. Dana filled me in on some other things. Pisses me off and breaks my heart that someone messed Rachel up that way. She deserves a lot better. You know she refuses to put down her physical therapy fee for billing when she treats a vet, even though the VA covers it? I know she doesn't have a lot of money. I gave her grief about it and she was stubborn as a rock. Says it's her personal way of giving back."

"I'm not surprised." Though it made Jon's heart swell even more toward the woman sleeping two rooms away from him. So strong and so fragile at once.

"Tell me you're calling because you want some help." Peter's voice, nudging him back to the here and now. "Because we're there, whatever you need."

"Yeah, read my mind."

"As usual. What are you thinking?"

Jon spent the next few moments laying it out with Peter, planning for a few contingencies. When they were done, Peter had promised to handle the coordination with Ben, Lucas and Matt. It freed up Jon's morning so that he could focus wholly on Rachel.

His anticipation of that was another reminder that the timetable in his head might be driven by his own feelings as much as her needs. He'd told Shelley to shut off the feed the moment Dana and Max had arrived at her door, and once she'd fallen asleep tonight, he'd removed the cameras, tucked them back in his overnight. Looking at her sleeping in his arms, he'd known he wouldn't be leaving her side again, not until she'd recognized he was her Master now.

Rachel might have to battle fears and doubts for some time, as Peter had indicated Dana still did, but unlike Dana, Rachel didn't yet truly understand and accept she'd never have to fight them alone again. Until she did, he'd resolved he wasn't abandoning her to the demons in her soul, even if he had to take her to work and keep her chained to his desk.

His mouth tugged in a wry smile at himself. It didn't take long to rouse the Neanderthal in a so-called enlightened man. All it took was the right woman.

After he laid his phone on the glass-topped patio table, he braced his hands on the balcony rail, enjoying the sunrise. She had a tranquil corner here. When he'd commanded her to clean up her place as well as make him dinner, she'd understood there were two layers to his order, that he wasn't being a horse's ass about tidiness. As soon as he'd stepped into the apartment, he'd noted the difference in the space from his first visit here. Despite her sensual agitation, he'd felt the core of who Rachel really was, evident in the atmosphere. Yes, she hid here, probably far too often, but she drew strength from this place as well. If he did what he should, balanced his own needs with his Master's understanding of hers, he'd make that fulcrum shift to him.

So first things first. Calm the inner Neanderthal. Offering the universe another rueful smile, he stepped to the middle of the balcony and started to center his mind, focusing on his breathing. Once in the proper mindset, he started a set of sun salutation repetitions. He had his palms in a prayer *mudra* over his head, his body grounded firmly through the soles of his feet, when he knew he wasn't alone.

"I do that every morning," she said, her sleep-husky voice stroking him. "Right where you're standing."

"Come join me then," he invited. Adjusting his position so she could step out next to him, he was pleased to see she wore his shirt. Though she'd buttoned it so it modestly covered her thighs, the couple open buttons at the neckline showed a pleasing line of cleavage. She'd rolled up the sleeves.

"Hope you don't mind," she said with a shy smile he found altogether appealing. More so than the shadows and worries lingering behind it. In answer, he brought his lifted arms down around her, drew her close so she leaned into his body for the deep, sun-soaked morning kiss. Then he held her for a few minutes, asking nothing, demanding nothing, but that she hold him back.

"When I first woke up, I thought you were a dream. The best dream ever." Her lips moved against his bare chest. "Then

I got up, and my body told me I'd been dragged behind a truck."

He chuckled. "Complaining?"

"Hardly." Lifting her head, she gazed up at him. "Though I'm completely out of my element here."

"On the contrary. Everything I saw last night said you've been out of your natural element for far too long."

She slid her fingers up to her bare throat, worried at it. "You took it off. The collar."

"Yes, I did. While you were sleeping." He touched her there. Her tremble, the desire behind it, sent a spike of hard need through his chest, his groin. He kept his voice mild, however. "You remember how I invited you to join me for that Tantric Yoga seminar?"

At her nod, he continued, "The chain, the clit piece, all of it was designed to give you a prolonged sexual build, so that by the time I got here, it wouldn't cross your mind that you couldn't climax. You were focused on pleasing me, on containing your release until I gave you permission to climax. And when you did climax, where did you experience it?"

"Everywhere." It came to her lips without thought or analysis. She closed her hands fully on his waist, fingers sliding along his hips. Her most innocent touch could stir his cock, and he knew her body needed a rest, no matter that she would serve him until she dropped. He settled his hands on her wrists, stilling her.

"Though the sexual component is only a part of Tantra, the belief is that an orgasm should come from all parts of the body, not merely the sex organs. However, if I had to do it over again, knowing what I know now about you," he slid his fingers into the spaces between hers, twining them together as he brought her closer, enjoying the press of her breasts through his shirt, the brush of her bare thighs against his in his snug boxers, "I wouldn't be so heavy-handed. All I needed to achieve the same result was that collar."

Releasing her hands, he slid his arms under hers, hooking his hands on her shoulders so he arched her away from him. Her pelvis pushed against his groin as he settled his mouth on her throat, and he savored the soft gasp of air from her parted lips, the loose way she gave herself over to his support of her body. "Even that might have been overkill. You're such a responsive slave, I could have collared you with the brush of my lips here. And when I left you in the morning, I'd put one drop of my aftershave there as well, so you'd be captured by that scented mark."

All of that was true, but he also knew she craved a physical collar, something exactly like what he'd described to her in his office. That Neanderthal part of him wanted her wearing one, just as much. However, like the removal of the condom, all of that would have its time and place.

"That touch of aftershave, the way you're reacting to how I'm kissing you now… You already understand the way of it. Most people focus on cunt, cock, the same singular way they focus on the sex itself. The goal isn't physical, though that's a pleasurable side effect. Divine intimacy is the true ecstasy. A divine intimacy with each other and the energy that brings us together."

Sliding his hands into her hair then, he let it spill over his hands. She'd caught on now and remained utterly motionless, her eyes closed, her expression concentrated on every contact point he was giving her. "You know all that though. You know that I could press a chain of those same kisses around your wrists and ankles, and you would consider yourself as restrained as if I used steel. If we're at a restaurant, and I slide your blouse off your shoulder and make you leave it that way so I can toy with your bra strap, I'm exercising my right as your Master. That's a caress you feel in your soul. Your orgasm comes all the way from there, if I'm doing it right."

"You did it perfectly right last night." Her voice thick, she lifted her lashes to gaze into his face. "Jon. I want to touch you. I want to give you that experience as well."

"You have. You do. And you will again. Practice with me here first." He stroked his knuckles along her cheek. "Do some sun salutation cycles with me. And then I want you to practice a Tantric position of my choice."

A tentative sparkle passed through her beautiful gray-green irises. "But remember my flexibility is impaired this morning. Your fault."

"I accept the blame. Now and in the immediate future." Giving her a wicked smile, he lifted his arms, planting his feet once again.

He saw her gaze travel over the stretch of his body, linger on every part. True to their discussion, though she noted his cock, firm and prominent under the boxers, her attention was a covetous slide of sensation along his arms, his throat, down over his abdomen, the angle of muscles at his waist, his thighs, all the way down to his feet. Standing with only a foot between them, the energy between them was heavy, languorous, as if they were rays of the sun that had simply spilled on this porch, ready to twine together as common elements. He wanted her badly, but the wanting was a pleasure of its own, one to prolong.

Raising her arms, she took a matching position. Shoulder to shoulder, they folded forward together, moved into the Down Dog *asana*, to Plank, to Alligator, then Cobra, then Swan, back up into the starting position, palms folded together overhead. Some gurus practiced the sequence or one like it hundreds of times a day, but after about twenty sets, she was perspiring, and her body was quivering, which was what he wanted.

"Last rep."

She nodded, eyes closed, deep in that zone. As they came back up, his arm brushed hers as they did the Swan movement. Sliding his arm under hers, he clasped her forearm to turn her so they faced one another.

"Now for that Tantra position you promised me. Follow my lead, and use my strength."

Centering his weight on his left foot, he raised his right knee. He extended his foot past her hip, then bent his leg, sliding his calf across her buttocks, forming a triangular brace support around her, his ankle resting against her opposite hip.

When he nodded, Rachel lifted her right leg, mirroring the position by sliding her bent leg behind him, her heel pressing into the side of his buttock, twining them together. Guiding her arms around his neck, he gripped her thigh with one hand, and slid his other arm around her back, pressing her breasts into his chest and lifting her up enough to align them properly. At a brush of hardness, she realized if he was naked, he could fit the head of his cock into her pussy at this angle. But that awareness was a small part of the intimacy of the position.

"This presses the sacral chakras together and, as a bonus, the solar plexus and heart chakras." He smiled down at her, his eyes warm and intent. She focused on her balance, but she didn't need to devote much energy to it. He was so well-grounded on the sole of one foot, he was able to steady her with both his strength and confidence. They were two parallel currents, but in this moment the energy snaked together, brought even closer by all they'd shared last night.

But the general meaning of Tantra *was* weaving, wasn't it? The idea that two energies could intertwine. Of course she was sure the spiritual aspect of it was man intertwining with divine energy, but she couldn't think of any better way to do that than this.

Oh Goddess. She loved him. Deeply, fiercely, a journey that had been going on for well over a year, but it was undeniable in this moment.

"It's all right," he said quietly. "I won't let you fall, Rachel."

Too late.

* * * * *

After they'd finished up their practice, he shared her small shower with her, and finally gave her leave to touch him as she wished. Every fine line of muscle, length of limb. The man's ass was sheer artistry, worth lingering over, exploring with every one of her ten fingertips. When she made the shy request, he gave her a tender look, turned his back and put his palms on the shower wall so she could slide her hands unimpeded down his back, down to trace that tight seam. Then she molded her palms over his hip bones so that she could press her back to his. His buttocks fit into the curve of her stomach as she ran her hands over his chest, exploring the ridges of his abdomen, then down, to find him more than ready for her to slide her hands along his cock, over his heavy testicles.

When he turned, so fully aroused it seemed daunting because of how sore she was, he lifted her up against the wall, coaxed her to relax for him. "Will you refuse your Master, Rachel?" The sensual threat against her temple was met with a vehement shake of her head, her nails biting into his back. He sheathed himself so carefully, building her climax like a spring rain, a slow but thorough soaking of the ground so it was ready to be seeded. The initial ripple of feeling expanded into a breath-stealing climax with shuddering intensity. He came right after her but kept himself still, every muscle like iron under the wrap of her hands, her legs.

She clung to him like a child as he moved them both out of the shower, slid her feet to the floor so they could dry. Taking the towel from her, he rubbed it between her legs, dried that area himself, then knelt, holding her hips as he licked and nuzzled her there, making her body sway like a willow over him, her wet locks of hair brushing his head, his shoulders. He stopped when she was breathing deep, shuddering, and rose, threading his hands in her hair to stroke it from her face. "Cats like to mark humans by rubbing their faces against them after they shower. It restores their smell upon them, so other cats know that's their human." He kissed her, so she tasted herself on his mouth. "I have a similar ritual. Bagels and tea, or a full breakfast?"

Not sure she could contemplate a full breakfast with an army of happy frogs doing pirouettes in her stomach, she chose bagels and tea.

He chose what she would wear, going through her closet and picking out a gauzy thin cotton dress that followed the curves of hip and breast as well as the line of her thighs as she walked. It was a very feminine dress, the hem flaring out to swirl around her calves. In the long-forgotten back of her lingerie drawer, he found a lacy ice blue thong with the tag still on it. But he refused to let her wear a bra, no matter how much she hedged. It bothered her, not so much that the dress would reveal the shape of her nipples, but knowing that her breasts didn't sit as attractively high and rounded as they did in a bra.

When he made her admit that worry to him, he gave her a look from the chair where he'd been sliding on his hiking shoes. Max had left him an overnight bag outside the door, and he now wore jeans and a faded blue T-shirt with an earth-colored representation of the Mandala *mudra* on it, a pair of hands joined in the circular symbol of wholeness.

"Come here."

When she came close, he took her hand, pulling her between his knees, and then made her gasp as he put his mouth over the nipple, right on top of the dress fabric. The moist heat dampened it as he suckled leisurely. It didn't take her long to be whimpering, writhing against him. He kept her still with his hand spread across her ass and gripping her firmly, reminding her of the still uncomfortable places where he'd spanked her with the brush as well as his ruler. After long moments, when she was gasping, he moved to the other, gave it equal treatment until she was making pleading noises in her throat, her pussy soaking the lace thong so that the wetness dampened her twitching thighs.

As he lifted his mouth at last, he nuzzled her jutting nipple one more time before considering them both. "I should have brought clamps for these," he noted. "But I won't mind devising more organic ways to keep them erect through the day." Now his gaze rose, and that Master's expression stilled her. "This is the way I want you, Rachel. I want to see what's mine, have it soft and ready to handle, whenever I want to touch it. When we sit down at breakfast, you'll keep your knees parted beneath the table. I won't embarrass you in public, but your body will always be accessible to my demands. All right?"

She nodded, put her fingers up to her throat unconsciously, before she realized she'd done it.

"Is it easier with the collar?"

"In a way, though I don't really understand why."

He took that hand as he rose and kissed it, a touch of his tongue between two fingers. "I think you do. But today, you do it without the collar. Until I give you the one I really want you to wear."

On that unsettling note, he took her out of her apartment and out into the world. The bagel place was a short walk from her place, but she found herself conscious of everyone they passed. Early morning dogwalkers and joggers, people emerging from other buildings in the apartment complex to get in their cars. People who might know her by sight as she knew them, going about their normal business. But today she felt as if a spotlight was on her, because nothing felt usual at all. As always, Jon seemed to read her mind.

"I'm not sure they'd recognize you. You're always so tidily put together, and this morning you're like a gypsy woman. Your long hair flowing about your shoulders, your body moving like a woman who's been thoroughly taken, all night long. Those beautiful breasts of yours, quivering under that thin fabric, your nipples drawing every man's eyes. The way you're walking, your hips swaying as if you're dancing. Trying to tease me, get me hard."

She flushed, digging her nails into his palm a little, since he was firmly holding her hand. "I am not."

"Yes, you are, because you're aroused and you want me to notice. You're a good girl, my sweet submissive, and you won't force the issue, but with every movement, you're begging for attention. And it's nothing that should mortify you. It's a signal that rivets men. Some of the women too."

She remembered how she'd imagined herself naked but collared, so men would look but not touch, not without Jon's permission. Her palm was moist with a pleasurable anxiety, but she was noticing things as well. A lot of women were looking at Jon, before their speculative gazes shifted to her. She could almost hear the scream of their thoughts. *How the hell did someone like him end up with something like her?*

From the frown that creased his brow, she was afraid her face had revealed the thought. Fortunately, they'd arrived at the coffee house. It had an outdoor seating arrangement among a maze of potted flowers, and he chose one of the bistro tables, pulling out her chair and guiding her into it. He helped her scoot inward, but then he flicked his gaze down. When she recognized what he was communicating, the spike of reaction went straight through her pussy, made even stronger when she parted her thighs, aligning her knees with the front legs of the chair. The skirt fell past her knees even seated, so she wasn't revealing anything, but she was acutely aware she was now open to him, and the position pushed her pussy down against the rough texture of the warm iron mesh seat, increasing the stimulation.

He nodded in approval, stroked back a strand of her hair. "What do you want? Stay here in the sun and relax while I go get our order."

She offered to do it, but he shook his head, leaned in and spoke against her ear, taking a moist nip there that shivered down her spine. "You will serve me when I demand it, sweet slave, but right now I want the pleasure of caring for the woman who belongs me."

She managed to stammer out a preference, then met his mouth in another teasing kiss. Pulling away at last, he squeezed her hand before he moved to the door of the coffee house. When he reached it, he held it open for a woman and her daughter. The mother smiled at something he said, blushing a little as any woman would, faced with the full blast of Jon's charm and handsome face, that mouthwatering body.

"Go, *cougar*."

When Jon had pulled out her chair, she'd noted a nearby female foursome sharing their morning latte. Twenty-somethings with perfect bodies and smooth complexions with no lines. The muted comment had come from them, as did the titters that followed.

Of course, she should have expected it. The first thing a group of women did after noting an exceptionally handsome man was to measure his companion with critical eyes, assess her worthiness of such a prize. But why should she care what they thought? She didn't. The problem was what *she* thought gave their mockery power, making her shoulders stiffen, her body hunch defensively. Their reaction only amplified her own insecurities. She wished they'd had breakfast in the apartment. This worked better there, when it was just the two of them.

The girls left as Jon was coming back out. They moved past her, not making much of an attempt to avoid hitting her with their oversized designer handbags and laptop cases. As they offered saccharine apologies, their gazes were straight ahead, on Jon. They brushed by him, giving him flirtatious feline smirks, though he courteously stepped back, offering them more room to pass than they took. Rachel tried to shrug off the feeling it left her, but of course when he reached her, put their purchases on the table, he reached for her hand. "What is it, Rachel?"

She shook her head, folded her hands in her lap instead. "I wish you'd let this just be a fantasy. It's not going to survive reality."

"Really? And what's reality? A group of catty girls who don't know shit about life yet?"

She flinched. "You don't even know how old I really am, do you?"

"You're forty-three," he said.

"Great. You can tell I'm forty-three." She gave a miserable half-laugh. "Guess I'm glad I at least look my age, and not older."

Jon slid his chair closer, his knee flanking hers, and touched her chin, bringing her eyes up to his face. "I know how old you are because Dana told me," he said, a touch of impatience in his voice. "I don't know what a forty-three-year-old is supposed to look like, but to me you look like a deeply sexy, sensual, kissable, fuckable forty-three-year-old woman. A woman with a heart so deep and generous it's an honor to know her. A woman who's everything I want, the submissive I've been waiting a lifetime to meet. I want you, Rachel."

She wanted the words to penetrate the armor that seemed to be coating her soul. When a man like Jon said something like that, he meant it. But she couldn't believe it. He didn't know, couldn't see...no matter his intuition, it just wasn't possible. When he dropped his hand to her arm, making it clear he was going to follow it down to her forearm and make her take his hand, bring them up to the table together, she went rigid.

"Please don't."

"You're getting into some serious trouble." His fingers tightened on her upper arm. "I want the woman who teaches yoga classes to eighty-year-olds as well as eight-year-olds, who helps people struggle through difficult physical therapy regimens. The woman who's lost a son and tried her best to honor her marriage oath. That woman would tell those girls to go to hell. She knows that love doesn't apply a measuring tape between ages before it measures between two hearts. You're better than this."

Capturing her wrist, he won the physical contest between them, bringing her hand back to the table with that distracting sense of restraint. Now his jaw was set, his eyes cool. "This has nothing to do with the difference in our ages, because you know that doesn't mean a damn. This has to do with your fear of loving and trusting someone. You think you're too fragile, and if you get hurt, you won't survive again."

Of course he understood what the problem was. But right now that intuition she admired merely made her feel resentful and angry, as well as more frightened. She couldn't handle feeling frightened anymore. She wanted to go home.

"Yes." She yanked her hand away, hitting the tray with her elbow so the cups vibrated from the impact. The old, festering poison boiled up inside her, scaring her even more. It would shove him away, make him go, and she needed him more than anything. But the poison didn't care, and she couldn't let the poison touch him. "I won't. I can't deal with it. I can't love someone with my entire soul again and have them throw it back in my face like it's worthless garbage. Like I'm worthless garbage..."

If someone like Cole, an average guy with a nine-to-five job and a thinning spot on the back of his head, had thought her worthless, what about someone like Jon? It was only a matter of time.

"Excuse me...I have to...I'll be right back." She shoved back from the table, the chair scraping, and the bistro tables were so close together it formed a momentary barricade between her and Jon. Fortunately, there was a back way out of the seating area. An open gate took her down a side alley toward the restrooms. As she hurried through that gate and around the corner, she discovered a shade garden there, statuary and a small bench. The sanctity of the women's room was where she was headed, but she only made it to the bench. Her anxiety and her long night made her knees buckle. She fell to one hip onto the bench, bracing her hand on the rough wooden edge, trying to breathe, to get hold of herself.

This was the dark underside of last night, the side she kept trying to ignore. Along with feeling more alive than she'd felt in a long time, she was stripped bare, having to stare at parts of herself that had been kept carefully and tightly bandaged for a long time.

When the rustle of paper alerted her to another presence, she saw his hand as he placed the bag in that open spot between her braced arm and body. Then he stepped past her folded legs. Straddling the bench behind her, he slid both arms around her, one across her chest above her breasts, the other at her waist. He didn't say anything as he eased her back into the shelter of his body, holding her.

She hadn't expected him to follow her. No man had ever chased after her when she was in pain, when she ran from it. No man had ever sent her the message that Jon was sending now, that he wasn't going to let her be alone with it.

Her jaw set against the surge of emotions that thought brought. She clutched his forearm as she pressed her forehead to his shoulder. It helped even more when his other hand curved against her temple, holding her there.

Only what mattered should be said. And what she felt now was determined to come out, even in such humiliating and inappropriate circumstances.

"I've been alone for a long time, Jon. Even when I was married, I was alone." Her voice broke, but when he held her closer, she found the ability to continue. "For years and years, it seemed. I deal better with the pain of that, the sheer agony of it, when I can keep people at arms' length. And someone like you..."

She gave a near-hysterical snort of laughter. "I cut coupons. I have a budget. I scrub my toilets on weekends. I worry about age lines and middle-age stomach fat. You're offering me what every girl dreams about. You're right, it's not exactly the age difference, but I'm not a girl anymore, no matter what you say. You're like the prince, coming for Cinderella when she's already..."

"Too old to dream? To believe in happily-ever-afters?"

"I'm not bitter," she said. She stroked his arm in nervous movements, wondering at how strong it felt, so capable of bearing anything. "I don't want you to think that. And I'm not one of those women artificially closed off, still secretly hoping the right man will pry open those doors."

"I know that. I almost wish you were, because that would make this easier. But you wouldn't be the woman I want if there was anything artificial about your feelings." Gently, he pushed her head back so she could look up, meet his gaze. "You've walled up so many wonderful things about yourself, things you think no one wants. To me they're treasure, Rachel. And I plan on opening every one of those things."

How could she believe that? How could any woman, especially one who'd seen enough of life to know that such things didn't exist?

"I don't believe in happily-ever-afters either," he continued, giving her a mild look of reproof. "That suggests the story has an end. Life is always going to have ups and downs, challenges and bad moments. That's what life is. What I do believe in is finding the person to share it with. All of it."

He shifted, bringing her even closer. With his arm wrapped around her waist and her turned into his body like this, one leg now over his thigh, the other foot braced on top of his, she couldn't imagine anything that would look more intimate to passersby. "Now," he said quietly, holding her in his gaze in that way that made it impossible for her to look away. "You've as much as said it. The age stuff is bullshit, so we won't go there again. Instead, you tell me what's really happening here."

She swallowed. Like last night, when he'd pulled her deepest possible pain from her, Kyle's loss, she couldn't not tell him. He was like a priest and lover at once...but only one label truly fit, didn't it? That one word that said why he could open up so much in her, the word she had so much trouble saying. So she told him this instead.

"I married my husband at nineteen and had Kyle shortly after. I believed Cole was my prince. That's not a slur against him. I'm sure he thought I was his princess, the way we all do in the beginning. There were a lot of things that went wrong with our relationship. Though my son never knew the underlying...issues, he eventually viewed me with a similar impatience, because a boy learns how to treat his mother from watching his father."

She swallowed. "Kyle's death came after our divorce. I could have stood next to a stranger at his funeral and felt more connection. He brought his new wife. Stood with her. I stood alone, but I told myself to take strength from that. I *stood* alone."

Right now, she was taking strength from Jon's arms around her, and that seemed far more real and substantial. "Later, that thought mocked me. What does it mean? That you're strong enough to stand alone...against what? Being alone means you're alone. No more, no less. We attach significance because it makes us feel justified, important. And it means nothing."

She shook her head, frustrated with herself. "I have no idea what I'm trying to say, Jon. I should be saying it better, but... I look at you and all I do is feel, not think. And my feelings are taking over everything. I don't want to be alone, but I've done it for so long, I don't know how to handle *not* being alone. I had to box all of it up in my heart, and I'm afraid of what will happen when you open it up, because I know you will. And I don't think I'll survive you turning your back on it, once it's all pulled out and turned upside down."

"Then believe that I won't. Because it's not going to happen."

His expression was compassionate but also measuring, intent. As his knee pressed into the give of her buttock, her foot slid further over his, twining ankles.

"When a submissive like you loves, Rachel, she puts everything into that love. Every scrap of pride, every bit of who and what she is and wants, and as such, her identity becomes that love. She's lost when it turns out to be not what she expected, or even worse, it's betrayed or rejected. So the best way to deal with it is to pretend it wasn't, to go on as long as you can until there's no denying that it no longer exists, and then something gets broken inside of you."

He framed her face, taking away the tears his words were evoking. She cried so much around him. When she hitched over a silent sob, his mouth tightened, reacting to her anguish, though his hands remained soothing. "You can go with all the therapy mumbo-jumbo bullshit that says you're merely a woman who needs to stand alone, who needs to learn self-esteem or self-confidence, but when you're the type of person you are, that's not where the problem lies. The truth of it is, you had a gift to give, and you gave it to the wrong guy. End of story. The gift is still there, if you're brave enough to give it again. And I think you're exceedingly brave."

She tried for a wry smile, hurting still. "Is bravery the reason I bolted from perfectly good bagels and tea?"

He answered the smile, though his eyes remained serious, heartbreakingly tender as he stroked her face. "They caught up with you. They're right here."

"I didn't expect you to give chase."

"One day you'll know when you're hurting like this, the first thing you should do is run to me, not away from me. Until then, you won't ever outrun me, Rachel. I'll never permit that."

Her hand fell on his thigh and she put her forehead on his cheek, closing her eyes as he slid his hand under her hair, a slow stroke of movement along her neck. He kept doing it, waiting her out, letting her think about what he said, letting other things rise to the top, slip from her lips.

"You're right," she whispered. "As much as it hurts, it *was* really simple, when all was said and done. Almost tedious. My husband and I were one thing when we got married and time changed us both. Maybe the seeds of those differences were there in the beginning and we didn't see it, didn't anticipate those changes. He was... overbearing and I...mistook it, subconsciously, for something else. In hindsight, I also think we brought out the worst parts of each other. I baffled him, and the unhappier I seemed, the more frustrated and angry he got. I don't blame him...and I guess I don't blame me, but it happened, and it hurt... He'd already left me when our son was killed, but if anything, that drove us further apart."

She closed her eyes then. He remained silent, breathing with her, being with her as that turmoil settled, as she got her breath back. He didn't offer her platitudes. He didn't say he understood, because of course he couldn't, not really. It didn't mean she couldn't lean on his strength, feel his sympathy and care. His heart and arms were open. That was the message she heard in his silence, and it helped deepen her calm. She might be feeling more foolish as she composed herself, but his silence wasn't condemning or judging. It was support, pure and simple.

"The bagels smell good," she said at length.

"You smell better." He nudged her hair aside, dipped his head to nuzzle her throat, his hair brushing her face. "Or it could be the two together. Fresh baked bread and female. My female."

"You're relentless."

"Exactly. You might as well give in now." Reaching past her to the bag, he kept holding her, such that he pushed her backward in his arm span. The stretch made her chuckle and hold tighter to him for balance as he pulled out the blueberry bagel she'd wanted.

When he straightened, he released her to pull off a piece of the bagel. The heat steaming out of it brought her the yeast smell, awakening taste buds. Before she thought to reach for it, he held it up to her mouth. "From my fingers, Rachel."

Those blue eyes had so many ranges of expression. Compassion was now replaced by that steady expectation that put everything inside her on high alert, all of her senses focused on what he might demand.

As she took the bite, closing her lips briefly on those digits, she did it without a single self-conscious look around her.

"Good." He handed her the rest, then took out his own bagel and passed her the organic green tea she'd wanted, though he laid an arm over her thigh, crossed over his, keeping them in the intimate position of lovers.

"Will you...tell me more about yourself?" She was honestly sick of thinking about herself and the fears a relationship with him could provoke. She was ready for a break, no matter how hazardous that might be. "What kind of kid were you?"

"Gawky limbs and thick glasses, a hundred percent science geek. Even had a stutter for a while. Don't let the boyish good looks and charm fool you."

"I actually don't find you boyish at all," she admitted. "I've never met a man who made me feel so safe...and cared for. I doubt myself, Jon. Not you."

"It comes out to one and the same, because it affects both of us." He put the bagel aside and slid both arms around her again, only this time he brought her up tight against him, her hip pressed against his groin, both legs hooked tight over his thigh as he kissed her, long and deep, until she was leaning into him again. His hand dropped down to her hip, gave her ass a squeeze that made her flinch.

"Still tender," he noted against her lips, a sexy gleam in his eye.

"Inside and out." Daring, she added, "And all I want is more."

"That's good. Because you're going to get plenty more, sweet slave. You already earned a punishment for not taking my hand at the table and an even worse one for trying to run away."

The fingers she threaded through his dark hair trembled a bit in response. "Do you have to work today?"

"Not this Saturday. I plan on spending the morning with you. This afternoon, we'll go to my place for a few hours, and tonight, I'm taking you out to a proper club."

She stopped in mid-motion, gaze darting up to him. "Oh Jon. I don't know."

"I do. After breakfast, we'll go pick out something you'd like to wear. With my approval, of course." He put his hand over hers, already anticipating her next thought. "You won't be hedging about money. I have plenty of it, and what I spend on you is my business, not yours. Understood?"

That was clearly his Master's voice, stern and uncompromising. She nodded, a little uncertain, but trying to take things in stride better than she had when they were at the table.

"I'm a little freaked out," she confessed. "Can we talk about something else for a little bit, so I can process? Something that helps me...I don't know, feel more balanced. What's the worst thing that happened to you as a child?"

He curled his hand over hers now on his shoulder, slid his thumb into the cup of her palm to rub, then tugged her hair with the other hand. "My job is not always to make you feel more comfortable, Rachel. Especially when I know you need to be off-balance. But I'll answer your question, if you ask me with the proper address."

That was exactly what she'd been attempting to do, she realized. Assert some kind of control with the personal information, and he'd recognized it in a heartbeat. She was starting to think his flat statement that she wouldn't get away with lying to him meant lying at any level, even when she wasn't immediately aware she was doing it.

She moistened her lips. "Master, would you please tell me the worst thing that happened to you as a child?"

"Well done." He nodded, and the hold on her hair eased. He stroked instead, following the strands down her back, a more soothing gesture, one that lingered at her waist then dropped lower. Sensitive nerves responded as he idly traced the depression at the base of her tailbone.

"My parents were killed when I was ten. That's why I had the stutter for a while."

"Oh Jon. I'm sorry." It was instinct to comfort, to lay her hand over his forearm. He joined hands with her, bringing both to his lips for a nuzzling kiss. As he caressed her knuckles, he studied them, his expression caught between past and present.

"He was a middle school teacher, English lit, and she was the school nurse. A student brought a gun and, well...the usual thing." His grip increased on hers, reflecting the weight of those memories. He'd obviously learned to deal with them, but it didn't mean they didn't still have the power to overcome him. Just like she knew she'd never really "get over" Kyle's death, that horrible, ridiculous expression.

"He killed several students, wounded others. My father was shot when he tried to talk him down. The shooter got my mother when she tried to help the wounded. She was actually a trained midwife, but also served as the school nurse. You would have really liked her. And my father knew everything about every book that had been written before the twentieth century, and nothing about any written after. That's what I told him, a precocious kid's scorn for a parent's talents. I inherited his library. I think I read all of it during my junior high years." A smile touched his lips. "Everything from *Paradise Lost* to Pliny."

She tried to match his light tone. "*The Kama Sutra*?"

"Cover to cover, baby. The original text, geared toward wealthy young males in that society. And I dog-eared more than a few pages of that one."

It made her laugh, but she also impulsively hugged him. He accepted the embrace, and she felt something different from him then, taking comfort for a deep wound that never healed. Now it wasn't about getting into his vulnerabilities to balance her own. This was about understanding more about the Master and lover who absorbed her, on so many levels. And the more she knew about him, the better she could serve him—if she dared to believe this would last. "Dana said that there were things that connected you to the other…to the K&A management. Is that one of them?"

"Oh go ahead and say 'Knights'. That damn article has infected everyone's brain."

"Well, it wouldn't if it wasn't so darn appropriate." She gave his knee a light pinch and won retribution as he returned the favor. However, he pinched much higher up, sliding his hand beneath her skirt. She stilled as he left it there, tracing a line on the inside of her thigh, all the way up to where it met her hip. Looking down at the thin cloth, she saw the shape of his hand move there, so close to the seam between her legs.

"What did I tell you, Rachel?"

Her brow furrowed, then she remembered. "Oh…" She parted her knees, but before she could look around, he touched her chin.

"Your eyes stay on my hand. I won't embarrass you. This is a small exercise in trust, taking steps toward the bigger ones."

"I trust you more than I've trusted anyone, ever."

"I'm glad to hear it." He caressed the crease between thigh and hip, sending electric tingles to her pussy that urged her to squirm on the rough, sun-warmed wood of the bench. When he slid his finger beneath the lace band of the thong at her hip bone, she was acutely aware of the way the fabric

226

burrowed deep between her buttocks, teasing the rim of that sensitive area. "Back straight. Let me see those nipples hardening."

It made her cheeks flush, because of course they were, stressing the dress fabric. He shifted, his shoulders blocking the immediate view from anyone who might step into the alley. Then he stretched the elastic of the gathered neckline so it caught beneath her breasts, exposing and framing them fully to his gaze. His incidental touches to her bare curves as he made the adjustment had her fingers clutching the bench edge. When he was satisfied with the view, he bent, picked up his tea, sipped it as he studied her exposed, quivering curves in pregnant silence. She held her back straight. Held totally still, though it felt so wicked to be sitting like this, near one of her favorite coffee shops, exposed purely for the sexual enjoyment of her Master.

"Yes, things like that connect us." It took her lust-saturated mind a moment to realize he was answering her earlier question about the other men. "All of us lost our parents young. Ben was actually in foster care from the time he was five years old. Ran away from bad situations a couple times, lived on the street. At age nine, he tried to pick Jonas Kensington's pocket. Matt's father. When Jonas asked him why he should let him go instead of calling the police, Ben argued that he was doing him a public service, making him conscious of the value of his money, so he wouldn't take it for granted. And, in point of fact, if the lesson had value, then Jonas should really give Ben a percentage of what was in his wallet."

Despite her current aroused state, she couldn't help the breathy laugh. Seeing Jon's gaze flicker at the way it made her breasts move caught it in her throat.

"You are so damn beautiful," he murmured. She trembled at a deeper level then, responding to the sudden fervency in his tone. He didn't touch her, but she'd never felt so...enveloped, in a man's attention.

He lifted his eyes back to her face, a wry quirk now at the corner of his mouth. "That was the abridged version of Ben's argument. Mr. Kensington described it as worthy of a closing at a capital trial. Needless to say, he didn't let Ben go. He worked to find him a better foster home placement and committed to financing his education. When Jonas was killed by a Mexican drug runner on the border, Matt was seventeen. But he was born for business, had been part of his father's industry practically since he could walk. He took over his father's interests, even his philanthropic ones." Jon lifted a shoulder. "And in this particular case, I say philanthropy with a grain of salt. Matt's no fool. He saw the advantage of training up a sharp lawyer, particularly when he decided to refocus his father's business toward manufacturing acquisitions."

"I'll bet." She let out a gasp as he cupped her right breast, his hand warmed from holding his cup. He thumbed her nipple, flicked it. As he did, he slid his other hand beneath the skirt again, but now there was no teasing. His knuckles slid firmly over her clit, then down, finding the opening of her pussy under the lace panel of the thong.

"Already slick for me again, aren't you?"

"Yes." *Yes, Master.* God, she wanted to say it so badly, without prompting, but instead she bit her lips, feeling the heat in her cheeks increase as his fingers pushed into that opening, enough to have her heart rate rabbiting.

"All right then," he said, his penetrating gaze reading every reaction flickering over her face. "Let's go shopping and see if we can keep that river flowing. I intend to dip into it pretty damn often today." He slid her dress back into place, a heartbeat before a couple came around the corner, headed for the restrooms. "Keep your back straight," he reminded her, picking up his tea again. "Don't you hide those gorgeous nipples. They're mine. Every part of you is mine to display as I wish."

She was beginning to believe he could make her come with his velvet commands alone, the things they did to her body. She obeyed, though she felt a little self-conscious as the male stranger's gaze slid over her and then screeched to a halt on that part of her. She detected it in her peripheral vision but kept her gaze on Jon, her Master. This was for him, and no one else. Nothing else mattered.

God, she was losing her mind. Hopefully she'd find it again before she made a complete fool of herself.

Chapter Thirteen

∞

As a woman on a limited budget, Rachel had learned to appreciate the pleasure of window shopping, the occasional indulgence of walking in and buying something modest on impulse. She'd never experienced shopping with a handsome, wealthy and attentive man who was adamant about paying for everything. She suspected it might ruin her for window shopping ever again.

Though she tried to be conservative, she quickly learned his caveat—that he had the power to approve or disapprove a purchase—didn't mean he would deny her the things she liked. On the contrary, it meant he would refuse her something she'd chosen for self-critical or price reasons, hand it back to the solicitous salesperson and then choose the item she'd really wanted all along. He hadn't allowed her to bring her purse, had pocketed the key to her apartment, so she had nothing to carry, no responsibility beyond anticipating his desires.

It was overwhelming, flustering. It swept her off her feet, made the sun brighter, the breeze softer and everything about the world seem better, more hopeful. And her mood warily became more hopeful with it.

"So, exactly how rich are you?" she teased him, stopping at a jewelry store window to point out a garish collar of diamonds on a velvet display. He eyed the piece with lifted brow, gave her a sidelong glance.

"If you promise to wear that tacky, overstated thing to the next K&A board meeting, I'll get it for you. But it's the only thing you can wear."

She laughed. "I don't think it's my style. The necklace, that is. I won't say a word about the other."

"But it excites you, doesn't it?" He bent to brush her ear with his lips. "The idea of that."

She cleared her throat. "I'm surprised you didn't take me to a place with...toys."

"I don't care for most of those places. I don't think you do either. And you're avoiding my question, Rachel." He touched her chin, a gesture she'd noticed he did whenever she most wanted to avoid eye contact. But when she most wanted to look at him, like last night, he increased her pleasure with denial. A balance of her needs against her wants.

"Jon, you've already made me feel better about things I didn't expect to feel better about, ever. I know you need me to trust you, but..." She went silent, the old pain stirring.

"But he made you feel ashamed of those cravings. As if it somehow made you faithless or..." Though Jon spoke softly, it didn't make the truth any less harsh.

"Wrong." She got the word out. "He made me feel it was dirty, immoral, twisted. That I was...a perverted freak."

He'd used a lot of other, worse words than that, but she couldn't bring them to her lips. She didn't need to do so. The frost in Jon's gaze said he understood. He turned her fully toward him, resting his hands on her shoulders.

"All right then. Let's deal with that. Here's another thing you need to know about me."

When it came to Jon's far-less-gentle side, she was fast learning that he gave no warning. The frost vanished, replaced by fire. Gripping her hair with both hands, he yanked her head back and set his teeth to her throat, an open-mouthed demand that had her swaying into him. One arm dropped, cinched around her waist, anticipating her jerk of surprise when he bit, suckling her hard. She closed her eyes, not wanting to think about passersby and their reaction, not wanting anything to interfere with the incredible surge of heat he sent through her body.

As he lifted his head, he pressed his lips together, obviously savoring her taste. Raising her hand without thought, she touched them, slid her fingers over the moist, firm heat. At his pointed glance, she lifted the other hand to her throat, felt the mark he'd left there.

"Despite all sorts of spiritual perspectives I have that might make you think otherwise, I *am* possessive." The flame in his eyes matched the fervor of that marking. "But I think you already understand that. I want to be the Master of your pleasure, of your protection, of your happiness. If I determine that controlled situations where you receive pleasure from others is part of that equation, if I know that would excite and please you, then you'll likely find yourself having that experience. But whether or not I ever agree or disagree with a fantasy you have, it will be guided by those tenets. There is nothing you can imagine that I will ever condemn or make you feel is wrong. All right?"

"All right." She knew it would take time to believe him, because Cole's repelled countenance was branded in her head. But hearing Jon say the words was something she'd never experienced before, so she'd accept that as a first step. She cleared her throat. "Okay. Then I admit to a deeply personal fantasy about writhing in pig entrails under a full moon."

"You perverted freak."

It made her laugh out loud, swat at him. She was happy to be gathered back under his arm, have him press a lingering kiss to her temple, even as he squeezed her ass, a quick admonishment. "Brat. Now tell me why *you* don't like sex toy shops."

She shrugged. "Even the ones that are supposedly welcoming to women still have a cheesy, wrong-vibe feel to them. Like they still don't quite get it, you know?"

"That's part of why I don't go to them. That, and I'd rather create the toys myself."

"You should open your own store. You could call it The Toymaker." She grinned up at him. Putting a hand on his chest, she trailed her fingertips under the neckline of the worn T-shirt, such a relaxed movement she'd done it before she thought about it. His eyes warmed on her at the intimacy. "Though you'd probably have to have a foyer area with candy," she added. "You know, to give to the kids who wander in, thinking it's their kind of toy store."

"A good idea, but unfortunately, I can't pursue such an entrepreneurial opportunity. We've all pledged our eternal souls to Matt. If we try to leave K&A, we'll explode in flames the moment we step out the revolving door in the lobby."

He kept her laughing at things like that as they continued to stroll down the sidewalk in the merchants' district, her leaning into his side, her skirt occasionally fluttering across his legs. The sun was on her hair and back, the wind ruffling through her hair, and Rachel thought she'd never felt so content in her life.

"I'll take you to a place in Florida that's a true women's erotica boutique," he said at length. "Not a storefront with fluorescent lighting and the feeling that you need a shower. The owner is a Wiccan priest."

"Seriously?"

"You'd really enjoy him. Maybe too much. So you'd probably need to keep in mind his wife is the town sheriff." He bumped her hip. "Justin doesn't call it a sex shop, and that's not pretentious semantics. It isn't a sex shop. Eroticism is a state of being, a sacred one, that pervades the entire relationship, and he gets that, in a way you feel all the way through when you visit his place."

She'd love to visit it with him. Travel with him. She'd also love to walk on this sidewalk with him throughout eternity, his arm around her. He stopped then, fishing in one of their bags. "Here, close your eyes. Since you've denied my offer to buy you tacky diamonds, I'll give you a truffle from the shop we just visited. Part your lips, just a little."

When she obediently closed her eyes, he teased her with it, smearing the slightly melted coating over her lip, letting her have a small bit of sweetness on her tongue.

"This is like first love," she said, keeping her eyes closed. "Everything so vibrant and amazing, everything sensual..."

"That's all you, sweet girl." Putting his mouth on hers, he tasted her and the chocolate. His hand on her jaw kept her still, merely experiencing the way he did it, and when he broke the contact, she knew from the touch of his breath he was studying her face at close range, his thumb slowly moving over her cheek.

"You're more than a dream come true," she whispered. "I'm not sure if I was ever ambitious enough, even in my dreams, to believe in something like this."

"Well, that makes two of us." She heard a thickness to his voice that tightened his hold around her heart, even as his words gave her a jolt of shock. Apparently he registered that, for he gave her that reproving squeeze again, leaving his hand on her ass to stroke the most rounded part of the curve. The intimacy in such a public place, indecent enough to invite tsks but not interference, took the simmering of her blood up a notch. He was testing her, she realized. Figuring out what kind of cravings she had in small, subtle ways. Voyeurism, exhibitionism...being shared. And while he was doing that, he was engaging her emotions, like now.

"Why are you surprised by that, Rachel? You think I ever expected to find a woman with so many of the things I wanted in a relationship? Your sexual nature, your spiritual outlook, your beauty, inside and out. And some things I didn't even realize I wanted until I started taking your class. Every week was the opportunity to learn something new about you, to see if it fit the mold. But most weeks what I learned broke it, and created an even better one."

"You're going to take my breath away."

"That's all right. You can have mine." He slid the rest of the chocolate in her mouth, but before he could withdraw, she dared to catch his thumb in her teeth, suck the chocolate left on it, a tease from her own tongue that won her a heated glance...and another kiss.

Though last night had been all about denial, today he was so generous with his touch and kisses, gentle or demanding, or ones like now, where he coaxed her mouth open with sexy lassitude. She didn't care who saw, didn't even know there was anyone to see as she leaned into his body, let his arms come around her so sure and steady, so strong and right.

When at last he lifted his head and she opened her eyes again, he gave her that quirk of a smile that sent striations of light through the multi-hued blue of his eyes. "So, now that we have everything you need for tonight, are you ready for me to take you to my roach-infested house and let my dirty socks and unwashed dishes change your mind about me?"

"If you'll show me your workshop. Geppetto." The taunt won her an even deeper, more sexy smile. "But at some point I need to get my makeup and a few other things."

"We'll stop on our way to my place. I don't want to be away from you. You'll spend the afternoon with me and get ready at my house. All right?"

She took a deep breath, trying not to think about what she was getting ready for. "As long as you haven't been fooling me all along and you're really a serial killer."

"Don't judge. I've only taken out competitors who annoyed Matt."

"*Rachel, Jon.* Wait up."

As Jon turned, he recognized Sarah and Ellen from the Wednesday morning class. The women were headed toward them, both loaded with shopping bags.

He registered Rachel's instant tension, how she was warring with herself about whether or not to pull away from him. Of course, as smart as she was, she had to realize the women had seen them walking together like lovers. He ran a reassuring hand down her back, satisfied despite her apprehension. As much as his reluctance to share her amused and surprised him, he wanted her to be seen by those she knew, to help her get over this hurdle.

"Have you gone over to the dress shop on the corner? They are having a to-die-for sale on gorgeous shrugs. And the shoes..."

She blinked, visibly amazed as the women rattled on for several moments, the same way they would if she'd met them by herself. Sarah put a hand on Jon's arm, closing their affectionate circle, a way of acknowledging him, even though the subject was of female significance. But after several moments, Ellen beamed at them both.

"We've been hoping the two of you would get together for the *longest* time. Every time you use Jon to demonstrate poses in class, the way you work together..." Ellen sighed. "I've told Sarah a hundred times, haven't I? They are just perfect together. It's as clear as a children's picture book."

Sarah jumped in then. "And my husband, Bob—you remember Bob, he came to the class that one time with me—I told him what Ellen said, and Bob said 'well, isn't she married?' I told him then I'd bet my best pair of shoes that she's not, that she just wears that ring to keep men from hitting on her, because she's so beautiful."

Rachel flushed, shrugging her shoulders. "I don't know about all that, but yes, I'm not married. Not anymore."

"Oh I always knew it, no doubt at all." Ellen nodded. "You never talked about him. Your husband. Whenever you talk to a wife, at some point the husband comes up in the conversation. He's such a part of you, it's like you're talking about yourself."

Sarah made a noise of agreement and glanced at Jon, giving him a conspiratorial elbow. "She never did that, not in the three years I've been taking her class."

"Apparently, some things are more obvious to women." He gave both women a fond smile before he turned a much more intent look toward Rachel. "Otherwise I would have gone after her much, much sooner. I'm making up for lost time, trying to sweep her off her feet."

Ellen laughed. "Well, any woman who doesn't go for that offer is crazy. You let me know if she turns you down. We'll help console you."

While the women were obviously pleased with him and the whole situation, Rachel was struggling to keep up, to figure out how to feel about this. Unlike those twenty-somethings, these two women, who had a regard for her, a long-term acquaintance, obviously felt this was a good match. A *perfect* match. It left her thoughts on all of it topsy-turvy again.

As if he'd picked up on it, and of course he would, Jon bantered with them, a few easy and complimentary exchanges, and then he had her moving down the sidewalk again, though not before Sarah gave her a hug, putting a quick whisper in Rachel's ear.

"You look *so* good together. You let yourself have that one, you hear me? You deserve something that nice." She met Rachel's eyes, and though she didn't say it, Rachel heard it echo in her heart.

Someone so much a part of you, it's like talking about yourself.

* * * * *

When they arrived at Jon's house, she was given even more to think about. And to despair about. His home was not only perfectly suited to him, it was the type of place she'd love to call home. Cedar siding, and a custom architecture that blended into a forested twenty-acre lot. The house had lots of screened-in outdoor porch area on all three levels, with a carport under the pilings where he parked the silver car. As they drove up, she noted a widow's peak that would give an even more vast view of the surrounding woods.

"I have an infrared scope up there. At night, you can watch all sorts of wildlife. Deer, fox, raccoons. I do my yoga in the mornings on the top porch. The bird calls and swamp frogs are so loud, sometimes I feel like I'm in the middle of a symphony. There are nature trails, and several of them lead to a manmade pond with a little boat. I've got a mooring buoy in the middle of the pond, so I can tie the boat to it on a long line and then lie down in it, float and think. Sometimes I'll even go to sleep, and occasionally the alligator that lives in the pond will bump against it, wake me up."

Delighted by his enthusiasm for his home, the rapid-fire list of things he thought would attract her, and did, she laughed. "That would wake me up, for sure. I'd paddle back to shore so fast, I'd set records."

"I think he's saying howdy, being neighborly. He's only about six feet long, so he's still a junior."

"Oh well, six feet. I feel much better."

He shepherded her up the stairs to the second level. She could tell from the variety of things on the first-level porch, as well as the dust on the windows, that must be where his workshop was located. In contrast, the front door on the second level was flanked by clean diamond-paned glass that had a single *om* etched into either side, the powerful yoga symbol that represented everything, the unfolding or expanding of the experience of life. Seeing that somehow underscored the significance of crossing his threshold, such that she hesitated, needing a moment before taking that step.

"Did you have this built after the K&A offices moved from New Orleans?"

"You've been doing your research." His quick look made her cheeks flush. "No, I've had this house awhile. Since it's a short trip from New Orleans, it was my weekend getaway." Jon shrugged. "My parents were from here, so I wanted some roots in this area. Fortunately, that meant I had great contacts to help us switch our main office after Katrina. Matt liked it so much, we've stayed longer than expected. It helped that Savannah also had a satellite office here she could transition into her base." He opened the front door from a keypad, and then swept his arm forward. "Don't say I didn't warn you."

He'd been teasing her about the dirty dishes of course, but it was unexpected all the same, in an amazing way. He had a potted forest of delicate, spidery Japanese maples that accented the dark wood futons and comfortable floor pillows. Several stone table fountains and a large sculpture fashioned of various curved metals blended into the environment. It gave the open area a tropical, misty feel. To the left, she saw a spacious silver kitchen, and to the right, a stairwell led up to a loft bedroom.

Skylights and tall rectangular windows allowed light and forest views at all angles. On either side of the bed upstairs were two tall plates of dark blue textured glass, over which water poured, lit from the bottom to make the drops sparkle. The bed was a canopy, but like nothing she'd ever seen before. The head posts were two smooth and twisted branches that arced over the mattress, crossed and then dove down to form the foot posts as well. She suppressed a smile, noting a couple of silk ties carelessly thrown over the lower arc of one of them.

"Couldn't decide yesterday?"

"Well, I had a very important date. I wanted to impress her with my fashion sense." He set her bags on an entryway table. "Want something to drink before we head down to the lower level, where I cut the bodies into little pieces? I have wine, beer, water, soda…pretty much whatever you want."

"A lemonade?"

He smiled, that gesture that made his breathtaking features even more so. She expected she could sigh like a girl over them all day long. "I sure do."

As she watched him cross the room to the kitchen, she could tell this was where he was comfortable. This was *home*. It made him, and the place, all the more appealing. When he came back to her, she wanted to touch, but she wasn't sure what the rules were here. As usual, he anticipated her. Wiping the top of the bottle with a napkin, he offered it to her. "What do you want, sweet girl?"

"I want to touch you. I want..." Her gaze went upstairs, to that bed. She wanted to be straddling him, wanted to feel his hands on her hips, driving her down onto his cock. She wanted him to tie her wrists to those curved posts with his silk ties and make her crazy with those clever lips and even more clever hands.

Sliding a hand around her nape, he drew her to his mouth. Right before the distance closed, he spoke. "Show me what you want."

The words broke it all open inside of her. The blatant though affable envy she'd seen in Sarah and Ellen's eyes. Hours of shopping, filled with conversation as well as casual or far more intimate touches, keeping her body alert to his. The way he'd gazed at her selections with serious eyes and firm mouth, evaluating her choice not just as her companion, but as her Master.

She slipped her arms over his shoulders, digging into muscle, and gave him every bit of what she was wanting, conscious or unconscious. Pressing her breasts against him, the aroused tips, she ground her stomach hard against his groin, her leg sliding to the inside of his as his other arm banded around her waist and closed that nonexistent distance even further. It took him less than a second to take over the kiss, cupping her head to take it deeper, make it even rougher, more demanding. She moaned in her throat as his other hand dropped to her skirt, closed over her buttock, that tender area she was ready to have him make even more so, if he felt she needed it.

He broke the spell first, lifting his head to stare down at her flushed features. While he was obviously aroused, a look entered his gaze she didn't expect. It worried her a little bit, the considering speculation in it. "I want you to test something for me."

* * * * *

His workshop was a stark contrast to the simplicity and open space above. It was a conglomeration of parts, electronic gizmos, computer screens and open testing areas that had shards of what alarmingly looked like charred, blasted metal and shattered wood pieces swept into corners.

In one section, however, there was a cleared platform. On it was a straight chair and an adjustable podium, the height set proportionate to the chair. A copy of the *Kama Sutra* was on the podium. She lifted an eyebrow at that, but he opened a utility closet, fished around an array of clothes to pull out a thin body suit in black. "This is something I've been working on. There've already been a couple prototypes at different adult trade shows, but I wanted to take the idea a little further." He straightened, his tone changing. "Take off all your clothes, Rachel. Here, in front of me."

Her hands were nervous, curling in the fabric of her dress. When she hesitated, he added, "You want to be the type of submissive who's always ready to obey her Master. You're not used to the way of it, but it's there in you. Give yourself over to that. A small test for tonight."

Tonight. That nebulous concept was back, flitting around in her stomach while all sorts of provocative imaginings darted through her mind.

She slid the dress off her shoulders, pushing it down to her waist. His gaze followed it, down the slope of her bare breasts, lingering on their heavy weight, the jutting nipples. She stepped out of her shoes before she hooked the waistband of the dress and shimmied out of it, letting it pool around her ankles.

"Turn around as you take off the panties. Bend over, show me your pussy as you do it. Make me hard, Rachel. Stay in that position."

She pivoted on her foot, her hair brushing her shoulders as she complied, easing the cotton lace down her thighs, bending forward and balancing on one foot as she took the undergarment off, adjusting her stance so he could see what he demanded. When he approached, she shivered in anticipation as he parted the folds of her cunt, and his fingers slid inside of her. Along with something else. It felt like two quarter-sized pieces of fabric being pressed against her labia, and then they were inside of her, as he pushed them against the walls of her vagina. When he slid free, he did the same thing to her anus, using the lubrication of her aroused pussy to slide the small pieces inside.

He stepped back. "Now straighten, only do it in a way your Master would like."

She came up slowly, keeping the arch in her back as long as possible, then tossed her hair back so it slithered in waves over her shoulder blades. Lifting her arm, she gathered the silken strands and looked over her shoulder at him.

Any worries she had that her wanton display was comical at best were dissipated by his reaction. He had his head tilted, and she saw that intriguing combination in his gaze again, the man appreciating her display with blatant lust, the engineer making some type of calculation based on what he was seeing. Then he came forward with the garment in his hand. "All right, step into this. Hold into my shoulder if you need to do so. It's tight."

It certainly was, such that he helped stretch the fabric over every curve. It outlined her pubic mound, her breasts and nipples, the cleft of her ass, as if she was wearing paint instead of clothing. She felt a little self-conscious about the unavoidable mid-section thickness that came with being a mother in her forties, but he brushed her concerns away as he adjusted the body suit here and there, indulging himself with a far less functional caress or squeeze, a stroke or pinch that had her arching into his touch and drawing erratic breaths.

Distributed inside the fabric of the suit were more thin wafers. They had some type of metal component though, because he was adjusting their placement with a magnet, moving them here and there, so that when he finished they were centered at her nipples, her clit and her throat, for the suit came up high under her chin. More were at her wrists, ankles, the base of her spine...over two dozen places, including chakra energy points, she noted.

He'd commanded her to remain utterly still while he made the alterations, but after he finished, he wanted her to move. A full forward fold, where that magnet and the brush of his fingers moved along her spine, to the impression at the top of her buttocks, then lower. Then a twist of her upper body, a lift of her arms, showing the full range of movement. He did something else with the device she'd assumed was only a magnet, and suddenly it felt as if all those points, and the fabric itself, had melded to her, the wafers moving with those erogenous points. It was a little claustrophobic, like getting an unexpected second skin, but as he encouraged her to keep moving about, it became more comfortable.

"All right, how's that?"

"Good. May I ask...what does this do?"

His expression reflected his approval at her deference. "The easiest explanation is it simulates sexual stimulation and intercourse through a combination of direct contact and acupressure."

Rachel blinked. "What?"

He gave her an absent half smile, studying something on his handheld and scanning her body with the magnet sensor at the same time. "I was going to use Dana or Cassandra for the first test, but a much better option presented herself."

She glanced over at the props. "And the podium and book, what are those for?"

"Take a seat and I'll show you."

She sat in the wooden chair as he adjusted the podium so that she could view the book at eye level. When he opened it to the middle, she saw the pages were blank, the *Kama Sutra* cover a façade. Before she could ask about that, he'd moved to a monitor on a workbench nearby. When he hit several keys, she heard a beep. "There you are. As we do this, it will record data on your reactions. I can use that to make the suit even better."

"Have you named your invention?" She tried to ask it casually, though she was feeling more than a little unsettled, thinking about what he said it could do.

His lips twisted. "They call the one at the conferences 'the sex suit'. Pretty unimaginative. I'd like to come up with something far more aesthetically pleasing to a woman's ear. If I have Justin market it in his store, maybe he can help me come up with a proper name."

His attention went back to the monitor, fingers tapping, hair tousled over his brow. A man in T-shirt and jeans who nevertheless looked as in control of his environment as he did when in a suit. "Keep your hands on the chair arms and put your heels outside the legs, so your knees are spread. Don't be alarmed by this next step."

"What—" She gave a short yelp as her wrists and ankles were suddenly immobilized.

"I used that technology first at a board meeting where Lucas was winning over Cassandra. The suit doesn't require bracelets on the wrists and ankles though. It uses highly sensitized magnets to hold the arms and legs to the chair. Don't worry about tipping it. It's anchored to the floor."

"Okay, the serial killer thing is coming to mind now. Only it's an elaborate Hollywood movie where he chooses diabolical, complicated ways to immobilize his victim."

Hearing the note of panic beneath the desperate humor, he glanced up at her, those blue eyes blinking through a few strands of dark hair. The silken brows drew down and he came to her then, moving with his lithe grace to take a knee between her restrained feet. Cupping her face with his strong fingers, he brought her attention to that commanding touch, his serious features, the firm, sensual mouth. "Unless it's for your pleasure, like a spanking, I will never hurt you, Rachel. I promise."

"You scare me. On so many levels. You're...so much at once, you know?"

"You've been imagining me in your mind well over a year. And I've been imagining you. So it's not at once. It's just we're finally making it real." He gave her that look that scared her most of all. "In a few moments, I'm going to make you mindless and crazy with desire in a way you've never felt before. And that will be far bigger than any fear or worry. All right?"

"Okay." She swallowed. His smile didn't quite reach his eyes.

"Because I've got you restrained where you can't run, you're going to hear me say this for the first time, but it sure as hell isn't going to be the last. As much as you deny it, you know exactly what kind of Master I am. I don't say something important unless I've given it a great deal of thought, from every angle. You're what I want, not just until I find the next pretty face. I love you, and you better get used to that, and everything it means."

He'd been so absorbed in his invention, she hadn't been expecting such a declaration, though even if she'd had some type of warning, she didn't think it would have prepared her. As she stared at him, stunned, he leaned forward, dropped a provocative kiss on the rise of her breast before he raised his head, his face inches from hers. His intense gaze registered her gasp, the widening of her eyes as he slid his hand down over her pussy, a firm, possessive grasp rather than a caress, holding the pressure there as her heartbeat quickened, the pulse of her clit fluttering wildly against his touch. "You don't believe me now," he said quietly. "But I'll have plenty of time to punish that doubt out of your head. A lifetime."

Did he understand how knocking her off her axis like this could dredge up the debris of her life? Maybe he did, because he'd chosen to tell her now when, as he'd pointed out, he'd restrained her so she couldn't run. Before she could find words, he rose, returning to his monitor. "Now, focus on the book. Let that take your mind wherever it will. Instead of getting bogged down in thoughts and emotions you don't want to deal with right now, that you don't have to deal with right now, start imagining something else."

He'd given her an out she was more than willing to take, dangerous as she knew that could be. But the lights were dimming, putting the platform in the spotlight and Jon in the shadows. As that happened, the white pages of the book shimmered, an electronic tablet. It had a similar theme to the *Kama Sutra*, however, because the first image was a sketch of two people in coitus. The female was on her hands and knees, the male entering her from behind, his fingers pressed into the generous curve of her buttock. Rachel could see his cock partially entered into her, and her hair was thrown forward, her breasts hanging loose, begging to be squeezed and touched.

On the edges of the platform, vertical streams of air started up, wavering with light that formed images, making the workshop disappear entirely. Deer, bounding through a field of lavender flowers on one side... A rainbow delving into a valley... Clouds slipping away directly before her, as if she were flying.

She let out an amazed sound, watching the holographic images dance around her, but there was more. A ripple of sensation passed along her throat, her wrists, as if she was being caressed there. She tipped back her chin, feeling the sensation of it drift down her sternum, past her breasts and along her rib cage. A stroke along her hips and upper thighs, behind her knees, like a lover's scattering of kisses, awakened her body without touching any of the more typical erogenous zones, thereby heightening their need to be touched further. As always, for her, Jon knew denial was the most powerful aphrodisiac.

Remembering his command, she returned her gaze to that tablet. Another page, this time a man on his knees, eating a woman's pussy. Both beautiful, sexy and sensual figures, absorbed in what they were doing. While she lay on her back, her legs were pointed straight up and crossed at the ankles, a rope attached to a ceiling hook holding them in that position. It reminded Rachel of the Legs-Up-The-Wall pose, or *viparita karani*. Her arms were stretched out to either side of her, each wrist held by another man, both naked. All three were fully erect, implying that each would have his turn with her.

Her pussy contracted, and then she gasped, because it wasn't coming from her, not exactly. The picture helped her easily identify what she was feeling. It felt as if a man was stroking her with his tongue, teasing her clit, then sliding down from there to push his tongue inside of her, lap and lick, thrust, getting her ready for his cock. Arching up into the feeling, she found the restriction was not limited to her ankles or wrists, but included her back and thighs as well. She was totally immobilized, except for her head and neck, her tightly curling fingers and toes.

Now it felt like a man's hands were caressing her lower back, another's sliding along her throat. The soles of her feet were being teased by nibbling lips, though the body suit only came to her ankles. The pressure points being stimulated were awakening other parts of her, things that had no sensors on them all. It increased the sense of helplessness, the feel of being totally, deliciously out of control. He could do anything to her. She could die of pleasure here. Her body was making tiny jerks, her mind spiraling among all the different sensations, her pussy throbbing hard. She felt like *kundalini* energy from the strong sacral chakra was dancing through her body in a swirl of deep ginger color. It coated her skin, engaged her mind and deeper.

He'd told her he loved her, had known how deeply that would disturb her, and yet now he was wrapping it up in this, something impossible, magical, a near out-of-body experience that was happening *in* her body, because the last thing she wanted to do was leave her body at the moment. It made the impossible possible, and she realized how clever he was. She didn't have the brain cells to resist it, or him.

Her nipples began to tingle and then respond as if being pinched by unseen fingers, stroked, plucked. "Oh…" she cried out as the sensors he'd put in her anus came to life as well. It was as if a man's thick finger, lubricated and ready, had slid into her there while his mouth was so busy at her pussy, more hands and mouths on her nipples. Suckling, teasing, as other places were stroked, gripped and pulled. She snapped her head back on her shoulders, then rocked it forward, her hair tangling around her face. The book had changed to match the image she was feeling. Two men, taking a woman from the front and behind, as others closed in, pressing a kiss along her thigh, sucking her fingers, biting her throat.

This time it was a scream she wrested from her, as those sensations descended upon her in full force, engaging her imagination and taking it even further. The tongue was replaced by a definite penetration, a sense of a man's cock stretching her, his testicles pushing down on the outside, his cock stretching her enough her clit felt the pressure, the friction. At that same moment, the finger now deep inside her rectum withdrew…she *felt* it withdraw, and then it was replaced. Burning, as if a thick cock had pushed into her from behind, taking her ass at the same time another man took her pussy.

The suckling feeling on her nipples increased, as did the sense that a hand was closed on her throat, holding her, reminding her she was her Master's slave, all of this done by his will. The stimulation was incredible, overpowering, overwhelming. She was vibrating in the chair, responding to the thrusts, even if she couldn't move much.

The holographic images around her had changed, no longer gentle, sensual nature scenes. It was a crowd of men, rough-looking, raw, alpha men, men with lust in their eyes, watching, waiting, because they would take her like this, over and over again, at her Master's behest, bringing her to climax until she was overcome from too many brain-shattering orgasms. She could feel their hot breath, the heat of their lust, sense the arousals pressing against constricted jeans, visualize the flex of muscles under their T-shirts. Many were shirtless, an outright display of virility. She imagined those muscles rippling, firm buttocks pumping as they shoved into her, took her to ecstasy, again and again. They would take, because her Master had decreed they could, because he fed off her pleasure like a drug.

Where was he in all of this? She needed to see him...she knew his hands were on the controls, but things were so crazy now, had become so fantastic, she needed to see him, needed the reality of him.

"Master..." she cried out for him, again and again, until suddenly the hologram shimmered to darkness, the tablet gone. She let out a glad cry, tears inexplicably springing to her eyes as his very real hands closed over her throat, his lips on her open mouth. His tongue tangled against hers and she shattered in that red and dark womb of pure lust and need, sheer feeling. Though the hologram was gone, the thrusting, licking, pinching, stroking never stopped, and she screamed out the orgasm, so harshly she felt the pain to her vocal chords, still raw from last night, but she couldn't stop. Right now there was no conscious thought of that, of anything but how his hands, that flesh and blood collar, and the demand of his lips, made it *all* his demand, his desire...

It took her past orgasm and into an even more intense realm, like a trip to the fairy world where time passed so differently. She wasn't sure if she ever finished. Her body simply reached the limit of its endurance. She continued to weakly jerk and whimper, emitting sudden long and plaintive cries as she was hit by short, intense aftershocks. It was as if the cocks were still fucking her, the mouths suckling her nipples, the hands elsewhere on her skin, but now they all moved in unhurried, deep rhythms, the suckling and caresses a soft squeezing instead of harder pinches. Those hands on her back, arms, legs, were kneading, like when Jon gave her the massage. She was limp again, waiting for the next onslaught with no ability to resist it. If he was going to cut her into pieces now, she had no objection.

At long, long last, everything came to a slow, teasing halt. She lay against the chair, her head back as Jon's mouth cruised over her brow, her lips, her nose. She was released from the chair, but she had no ability to do anything. He stripped the suit off her, leaving her naked, and lifted her in his arms. Guided by dim wall lights, he carried her back up the stairs. Her eyes were half shut, her body hanging in his grip, but she realized he'd ascended the stairs to the loft when she was laid in his bed. Looking up, she saw the natural twists of the canopy, the crossed arms of a tree. Those two tall plates of dark blue glass shimmered with the fall of water, a soothing whisper of sound.

Her arms fell out to either side when he laid her down, because she didn't have any strength, but she tried to part her legs, knowing she needed to be in that position. He'd told her so, right? Always accessible.

"Good girl," he said. His expression and voice were as raw and rough as any of those fantasy holographic images. Then he was lying down upon her, and he was as bare as she was. She made a yearning noise as his cock, enormous, hard steel, pushed into her soaked pussy. The inner tissues were so stimulated she kept making the cry. His size was because of watching her reaction. Because of her.

"Just lie there," he said. "Take your Master."

She wanted nothing else, nothing but to feel him inside of her, the way his cock's head pushed through those tight walls, then dragged back, then forward again. She couldn't possibly orgasm again so soon, but sensations almost as deep and intense as those aftershocks rippled through her. Having him inside her, taking her like this...there was something as fulfilling and satisfying about it as even the strongest orgasm she'd ever experienced. This was the one thing the marvelous device he'd created couldn't provide, the most important thing. Intimacy.

"Jon...Master. Please...my arms..."

He understood. He slid his arms around her waist, up under her shoulders, giving her the support she needed to lift her heavy, quivering arms and wrap them around his neck. She gazed up at him as he held her eyes in his, that midnight blue, the pupils dilated in determined lust.

"Call me that again."

"Master." She had no hesitation about it right now, not with everything open to him. And he hadn't torn her open, as she'd feared would happen. He'd simply opened her like sunlight opened a flower, an inexorable compulsion toward life and growth, something no living thing could truly resist. The way he reacted to her calling him that—the flex of his jaw, the concentration in his eyes, the way his thrusts became more demanding, asking more of her body than she thought possible but wasn't—made it all so worth it.

When he came, seed jetting deep inside of her, she realized he hadn't worn a condom. But there was no need. Whatever came from this union, she would want with every ounce of her being.

Only a fool protected herself from something sacred.

Chapter Fourteen

೮೦

Euphoria lingered, a sense that she was caught in a dream and happily content to stay there without questioning anything. Once they'd both recovered enough, he'd bundled her in a thick robe, sat her at the bar in his kitchen and cooked her a light early supper—crepes with strawberries and whipped cream. He fed it to her as well, sitting so her knees pressed against the inside of his thighs as he faced her on a matching stool.

He'd only pulled on a pair of jeans, leaving the top unbuttoned, and he indulged her desire to touch. She'd dipped her fingers in the whipped cream, painted them along one pectoral, then leaned in to kiss, lick. Every move lazy, erotic but not driven to sex, not right now. Now was all about feeling every small moment of pleasure, and when he caught her wrist at last, lifted her hand to suck the stickiness off her fingers, she gazed at him, quietly amazed to see her hand being held in the grasp of his with such casual possession.

When he took her on a more thorough tour of his workshop, he explained some of his work-related projects. She noted he kept her drawn close to his side, making sure she didn't trip over anything in the clutter. After that, he helped her back into her dress and comfortable sneakers to take her on a short walk of the property, strolling through the woods as he pointed out different features. He was a patron of local artisans, she saw, having installed a variety of natural sculptures off the paths, interesting shapes and forms that blended into the landscape. When they got to the alligator's pond, she saw he had a screened gazebo there with a hammock inside. They took a nap, her lying in his arms, both of them rocking with the wind that passed through the gray and green forest, the calls of nature all around them.

As they'd walked through the woods, her arm had been around his waist, thumb hooked in the belt loop of his jeans, his arm draped over her shoulder. They walked well together, the slide and bump of their bodies as natural a rhythm as they'd found during their coupling. She didn't know what she'd been expecting as an aftermath, but like his device that took into account all the many erogenous points of a woman's body, a way to nurture the full range of her emotional needs as well. Jon had chosen to spend the rest of the afternoon letting her see his world, ask questions and simply be with him, feel how easy that was. How right.

The uneasiness didn't start to return until night drew in and she knew they would soon be going to the club. He laid out the clothes he'd bought for her, enjoyed watching her don them, so much that her body, in a pleasurable languor most of the afternoon, began to stir again. He was already dressed when he told her to finish her makeup and left her for a few minutes, saying he needed to check on something in his workshop.

Nervous enough already, she didn't dare speculate on what he needed from there, but she finished her makeup and hair, straightened up the bathroom, folded his jeans and T-shirt and left them on the dresser before coming downstairs to the main room. She'd only wandered among the Japanese maples for a few minutes, enjoying the artwork on the walls, when he returned. While she didn't see him carrying anything, she noted he hadn't yet tied his tie, the strips of silk lying on his starched shirt front. For all that he looked handsome in anything he wore, she found his suit was like a knight's armor in truth, reinforcing and underscoring his authority, that sexy confidence.

It made her smile, thinking of his earlier exasperation with the Knights of the Board Room moniker. When she came to him, her pulse elevated again as she noted the approving way he took in her appearance, the way her body moved in what he'd bought her.

She'd loved the dress she was wearing at first sight, but of course she'd tried to choose something more conservative, a moderately sexy black cocktail dress. Jon had simply taken the black dress out of her hands, pointed to the one on the display that Rachel had truly liked. He'd had her try it on, but had forbidden her to look at herself in the mirror in the dressing room. It had been difficult to obey the directive, enough that she'd closed her eyes and turned her back to the mirror as she was dressing. When she stepped out, it had been worth it. One look at his face had been a hundred times better than any mirror. That, and the fact that the young assistant manager, doing inventory at the blouse rack, had almost dropped his jaw on the ground.

It was the color that had caught her eye. Midnight blue and black, a swirling pattern that looked like brushstrokes and splatters of paint across the extremely snug fabric. All those toned yoga muscles were clear to see under the mini dress that stopped so high on her thighs that bending over would reveal she wore absolutely nothing under it. The top was a straight neckline barely above the line of her nipples, with a long two-part sash. One pulled up from the outside of her right breast, framing it, the other coming from behind, both threaded into a ring on her shoulder. The tail draped down her bare back all the way to her thigh, a floating, dream-patterned scarf.

Her hair was piled high on her head, held with a pair of polished sticks that had whimsical onyx gemstones shaped like cat heads. She'd loved them, not surprised that Jon bought them, but surprised that he wanted them as part of the outfit. It seemed to be a message, that this night was about her, who she was, both as a woman and submissive, as much as it was about his desires as her Master.

She'd dusted powder blue glitter over her arms and back. Her skin beneath it emanated scents of lavender and vanilla, from a new lotion Jon had picked out for her specifically, tasting it on her flesh right there in the store. She was pretty sure that the salesgirls' toes had curled, watching him. She knew hers had, feeling it.

More than a little self-conscious at the memory, what it did to her body and mind, she took the two silk ends of his tie and began to knot it for him. Doing the domestic task shifted her focus, but not so much in a good way. She remembered how much she'd anticipated being a wife, taking care of a loving husband. Believing in so many things that had turned out not to be true, she'd clung to the fantasy so desperately, for so long. That jagged feeling in her stomach bloomed, but then Jon bent his head, gripping her wrist as she finished the knot.

He spent a good five minutes teasing, nibbling and suckling her wrist until her knees were weak and her thighs were damp. The seesaw of her emotions slammed her back down into the dream she never wanted to end.

He glanced out the window as the limo pulled into view. "I figured we'd have Max drive us. I assume you have no objections?" He gave her a look. "You're blushing a little bit, sweet girl. I think from now on, I better keep you and Dana apart. She's a bad influence."

"Terribly bad," she agreed, with a shy smile. "She's wonderful. I'll have to invite her over more often."

Jon affected a resigned sigh, but caressed her lower back, giving her ass an unexpected but thrilling smack before he guided her to the front door, held it for her. Max let out a wolf whistle as she came down the steps, and she blushed even harder. Her legs trembled, somewhat because of nerves and residual weakness from her earlier shattering experience, but Jon's hand was on her elbow, the other around her waist, guiding her down the steep wooden stairs in her dark blue stiletto heels. She also noted Max moved to the bottom and held out a hand as she took the last step. It made her remember something else Dana had said during her visit, while they were busy making the salad for that memorable dinner.

I think they got dubbed the Knights by that columnist for a whole different reason. You spend any time around these guys, you'll find they act like you read about in old poems. If a woman comes into a room, they all stand up. Every one of them is solicitous of her needs, her comfort, her safety. Dominating a woman isn't just about sex for them. It's about protection, cherishing, guiding. If they think something's bad for you, you may win the point, but you'll have to fight tooth and nail over it. It's way deep into sexist territory, but they don't apologize a bit for it.

And truth, it really overwhelms you. The whole time you're trying to stand your ground and tell them you're not going to be treated like an egg, it's like struggling out of a Godiva chocolate fudge bath.

"Come on, Max," Jon drawled. "You've seen me in a suit plenty of times. No need to get all hot and bothered over it."

It made her laugh, helped ease that tension in her lower belly, especially when she saw Max grin. She felt included in something, content, excited... Dare she say it? Happy?

Max led her to the open door of the limo, offering her a warm, reassuring smile that told her she still looked a little keyed up. Jon underscored it when he got in, drawing her close to his side. A slight tap on her knee and meaningful glance from those steady blue eyes reminded her, and she parted them, the gesture helping to draw her mind to other things, though things no less capable of putting butterflies in her stomach. Especially when he curved his warm palm high on her bare thigh.

This dress was far shorter than the one she'd wore to the coffee shop. If Max adjusted his mirror, it was entirely possible he could see there were no panties beneath that scant covering. He didn't, but the idea that he could, that she'd parted her knees specifically to give Jon access to that part of her, whenever he desired it, made her restless in a primal way. It all swamped her senses—her appearance, where they were going, everything they'd done so far leading up to this moment. Trying to calm herself, she took her mind back to the balcony, when she and he had done the sun salutations, side by side, everything synchronized.

As they drove to the club, Max and Jon spoke, not excluding her but not requiring her participation, and she was grateful for that. She couldn't help getting a little more nervous, remembering Club More, but from the moment they pulled up to Surreal, the club the K&A men preferred, the worry ended. The club was a large, attractive structure of white stucco, clean blue and silver lights bathing a front awning that showed doormen who looked like Secret Service professionals, in suits cut well over their broad shoulders. They wore hands-free radios and watched the arrivals and departures through the valet parking area with careful eyes.

Unlike Club More's seedy surroundings, the nearby businesses were respectable establishments. She recognized the name of the steakhouse that Cole liked for his beers and nachos after playing eighteen holes, though he'd never taken her there. She pushed that out of her mind. Tonight wasn't about any of that. Though it did give her a twinge to realize that he'd been close to a place like this so often, known of her longings, and yet never tried to take her there. Like Club More, she hadn't known much about Surreal except that it was far more exclusive, an expensive membership or hefty guest fee needed to grace its doors. Still, that hefty guest fee could have been a nice anniversary present or birthday or...

Stop it, Rachel. What's the matter with you?

Jon's hand closed on hers again, rubbing her palm, obviously picking up the distress that had appeared in her body language. She made herself relax. This was another once-in-a-lifetime experience. She wasn't going to lose a minute of it because of old resentments or hurts. Instead, she focused on their destination as they pulled into the parking lot.

Those who chose to park their own vehicles and walk up to the club entrance were mostly couples or groups. While some sported sexy fashions she might see outside any nightclub, she noted some were likely wearing more blatant fetish wear, evidenced by the fact they approached the door in velvet cloaks or light wraps. No blatant BDSM attire outside the club walls. Others were carrying travel bags, suggesting there was a changing area.

"Lucas, Peter and Ben will be here tonight," Jon said as Max pulled into the lane opposite the main entrance. "I'm looking forward to introducing you."

He squeezed her thigh, an unspoken message that could mean a variety of things. She wondered if Dana would be there as well, but she simply nodded, trying to hold onto that earlier euphoria with both hands.

As he helped her out of the car and gave Max some instructions, she studied the people passing her in the parking lot. This was a world on whose outskirts she'd stood for a long time, looking in, so she admitted the curiosity was competing with nerves. It was easy to pick out Masters or Mistresses, because those were the ones that, when their direct gazes turned to her, she automatically shifted hers, an instinct that she supposed told them clearly what she was.

The submissives gazed back at her with as much interest, most of it openly friendly, sometimes downright appraising. As if they knew they might come into intimate contact within the walls of the club, suggesting such shared play was part of their relationship with their Master or Mistress. She still wasn't entirely sure where Jon stood on such boundaries, though he was obviously okay with hints of it to drive her to distraction. But the actuality of it? She wasn't even sure how she felt about that tonight.

However, when she'd looked up at him from the cushioned sanctuary of his bed, felt him release inside of her, it had formed a bond. Right now, despite her excited nervousness in this wholly new but achingly familiar environment, she felt safe with Jon, able and willing to explore or be curious about anything without fear of misstep. She hoped she could hold onto that feeling, because she really, really wanted to do so.

Gripping her elbow, Jon turned her toward him then, pressing her back against the side of the limo. "I told you not to wear a necklace for a reason tonight. Lift your chin."

She did, her eyes glued on him as he produced a collar in a midnight blue velvet that matched her dress. She wondered how he'd gotten it so quickly, but she was starting to accept that Jon had amazing resources at his fingertips. Like her earlier chains, the collar had a heart-shaped padlock in the back as a fastener. It also had a dainty silver D-link embedded at the front, with a translucent blue crystal pendant dangling from it. A word etched in silver floated inside the teardrop shape.

Owned.

In feminine brushscript, that one significant word was all lowercase, because of course, capital emphasis wasn't needed. It was in the eyes of the Master watching her reaction, how she closed her fingers on it, her own form of possessiveness, as he fastened the collar. The strap was over two inches wide, brushing her collar bone and putting pressure on her throat almost up to her chin. The width accentuated the length of her neck and gave her an even more owned feeling than the pendant, though she loved the way it dangled and teased, a patter of reminder through the collar's thin but stiff material.

"This isn't your permanent collar. It's not quite ready yet." He gave the strap a little tug, his fingers whispering over her hold on the pendant, the flicker in his eyes saying he'd registered the heat that it had created in hers. "But this will tell anyone that you have a Master."

He slid the wrap off her shoulders then, dropping it back through the open window of the limo. Then he gave her that meticulous, appraising look.

"There's no way I'd let you in there without that collar," he said, a growl entering his voice. "I want to make it clear that you're hands off...unless I give anyone permission to touch you. How would you feel about that, Rachel?"

It was hard to articulate it, with his gaze so very close, but she'd thought about it quite a bit over the past couple days, stimulated by what had happened in his office, with Max, and the way those holographic images had made her feel. As if her body had been recharging all afternoon, it was suddenly revved and ready for this, eager. But her mind felt thick and clumsy over the question. She was better with intuitive, physical responses than answering such a thing, but she knew he wouldn't let her get out of it.

"I would feel... If it was for your pleasure...it would be okay."

"No." He caught her chin, his finger linking into that D-ring. "Tell your Master."

"If it's someone...who belongs to you. Not that, exactly. A part of who you are, what you are...like..." She was going to say Max, but her gaze in that direction was enough. "Or the others...you work with." She remembered Peter and Lucas again, those intimate touches that were so casual. "Touching. I think I find that...exciting. If you're part of it. And if it's not..." It seemed way too demanding to say she wasn't sure she wanted anyone but Jon inside her, between her legs. "If it's...some stranger, someone you don't know...or you're not really there, I don't think I'd like that as much. But I'd do...whatever you want me to do. If it made you happy."

"You know what makes me extremely unhappy, Rachel?"

He pushed her back flat against the limo, caging her with his arms. The sudden aggression, his uncompromising tone, demanded her full attention. "You, deciding to do something that truly frightened or hurt you, out of some misguided idea that my happiness is different from your well-being. They are one and the same."

* * * * *

As her face began to reflect the struggle and misery Jon understood too well, he wanted to curse the past that had done this to her. She was so excited, fresh and beautiful, she had no idea how captivating she was. He refused to let anything mar that tonight. So he touched her chin, her lips, adding gentleness to bring her wary gaze back up to his. "I know what kind of submissive you are, that you *would* do anything I wanted. That's what caused things to go in such a wrong direction with your husband. You're not with him, you're with me. I will stay attuned to your emotions and needs, Rachel, but part of what I absolutely require as your Master is that you stay honest with me, at all levels. Your pleasure drives mine, do you understand?"

He knew his eyes had cooled, conveying the current of dangerous steel he carried beneath his usual calm, because he saw it in the nervous press of her lips, the quiver of excitement it also caused. "If you *ever* do something that frightens or causes you the wrong kind of emotional or physical pain, just because you thought it would please me, I will punish you in ways that will drive in the lesson so hard, you'll never do it again. You understand? Say it."

"I-I understand. I'm sorry."

"I didn't demand your apology, sweet girl." He pressed a kiss to her mouth then, teasing her lips open and making her moan as his hand slipped between them, dipped below that very short, snug skirt. With unerring accuracy, he slid two fingers directly into her pussy, all the way to the base knuckle. As she caught his arm, fingers digging in, her eyes lifting to him in aroused shock, he spoke through taut lips. "Repeat the lesson."

"I...my pleasure...drives yours. Oh God..." Rachel swallowed as he rubbed her inside, withdrew and drove back in. In another moment she was going to wrap her legs around his hips, let him finger fuck her to climax, to hell with anyone watching. "Jon...please. I understand."

He twisted his touch, stroking his knuckles on that sensitive spot inside. "Not what you call me, Rachel. Not without my permission."

"Master," she managed, and let out a throaty sound that caught the attention of several passersby. She saw several knowing glances thrown their way as they continued to move toward the door, recognizing a Master handling his submissive. It turned her on even more.

"I don't...I don't want anyone inside me but you. But other things...might be okay. But no matter what...what you want...I trust you." After so many years of having to guard her words, it was so difficult to say what she really wanted. It could make her chest tight, as if she were going to cry. However, his expression was patient as well as expectant. Though he was doing his best to drive her past her inhibitions with one hand, it was the other one, stroking wisps of her hair away from her temple, lingering on her cheek, that gave her courage. When it got right down to it, for better or worse, she trusted him to know her better than she knew herself.

"I...don't want to *not* try something that you know I might want, just because I'm afraid. But the actual sex..." Jon's cock sliding into her cunt, that connection, the energy that met there... "I don't think I want to share that with anyone else."

"Good girl." He eased out of her, brought his hand to her lips. "Clean your Master's fingers."

She did, and as she did, she was quietly amazed at how all her senses targeted him rather than their surroundings. He was in complete command of everything.

When she was done, he used a handkerchief to finish the job, then slid the cloth back into his coat pocket before taking her arm and guiding her to the club doors.

There was a member check-in area, but Jon was waved through with a quick glance from the maître d'. While that made her think of who else he might have brought here, she remembered his earlier words. He hadn't been required to say what he'd said to her—after all, she'd made it clear she hadn't expected commitment or monogamy—so it underscored the possible truthfulness of it, that bringing her here was special, not just another casual submissive. Now, whether or not she would be in an emotional position to believe that later, when she was in her right mind...

But right now, her body was singing, and her heart and not-right mind were willing to join in the chorus. Particularly in such a magical environment. She felt like sex-on-stilettos. She enjoyed the way it felt, walking in the shoes, letting the snug hold of the dress dictate her pendulum-hip movements as they headed into the public play area. The dance floor levels lay beyond, but it was this immediate area that grabbed her by the throat.

Surreal had a lot of mist, lights and silver props, as well as view screens of different areas that those sitting in booths or at the bar could enjoy without crowding up to the place where the action was actually occurring. Right now it was a male sub in a stock being fucked by another large male. The sub sucked frantically on the strap-on cock of a Domme in front of him, her black-gloved hand gripping his hair to make him suck her faster, bumping the clit stimulator against her with a more pleasing pressure and rhythm.

On another screen, a female submissive was suspended in an elaborate rope bondage harness that included tight cinching around her breasts. They were swollen and flushed, nipples almost blue and enormous from the constriction. She was being spanked with a paddle that had holes, leaving circular red marks on her pale flesh. She was crying as she came, her body shuddering, face flushed with ecstasy.

Watching that on the screen stopped Rachel in her tracks. Jon's hand slid from the small of her back to her buttock. As she watched, he gathered the hem of her micro-dress, inching it up until he was fondling her ass, fully revealing it as he did so, watching the screen with her. Though it was a shadowed, dim environment, it still aroused her intensely, him enjoying her as he wished, where his ownership and her place as his property was completely accepted. She'd taken the step from submissive to slave, and liked the idea of him considering her all his in that way.

Further, it had only taken her a matter of seconds to feel right about it. She'd waited her whole life to feel like this, to be in a moment like this, surrounded by others who were immersed in the feelings and needs she had... People who *understood*. It was like being a child and coming to Disneyland for the first time, seeing all the things that embraced the soul of a child. Having those things confirmed, reinforced. Celebrated.

* * * * *

Ben leaned back on the bar, one foot braced on the bottom rail of his stool as he took a swallow of his drink. Like the other two sitting with him, he watched Jon's progress through the public play area, letting Rachel see the sights.

"Most of the closet ones are shy and tentative the first time, looking for reassurance. Look at her." The lawyer gestured, a faint smile on his face, though his green eyes were serious, tracking her almost as closely as Jon. "The only reason she's hesitating is the same reason a kid in a candy store does. There's so much here she wants, she's not sure where to start. Good for her. God, I love an older woman. Even when they've been busted up inside, they'll reach for what they want with both hands, if you clear the road enough."

Lucas dipped his head, but a frown was creasing his brow. "No argument, but she's too unstable yet. She's still running from that pain, not facing it head-on. She doesn't believe down to her soul that she can trust him."

"And it's been what? Not quite forty-eight hours? Our boy's losing his touch." Peter gave Lucas a wry look, and the CFO shrugged.

"We all know it doesn't have anything to do with time, not when there's already a relationship in play. It has to do with the type of catalyst you bring to the table." Lucas considered Rachel as she stopped in front of one of the view screens, every line of her curvy body shimmering, as if there was an electric current causing her to vibrate. "Jon's picking up on it though. Notice how close he's staying? She could get knocked off balance and pushed under pretty quickly."

"Yes, Obi-wan. You afraid she'll eat more candy than is good for her? Isn't that Dana's problem?" Ben grinned and winked at Lucas behind Peter's broad shoulders.

Lucas snorted. "Dana was already well immersed in the club scene when Peter met her. She has an endless capacity for sweets."

"That's for damn sure." Ben tossed Peter a smirk and Peter shoved at his stool with a booted foot. Neatly surging to his feet, the lawyer caught the stool, keeping his whiskey steady in the other hand. "Easy there. Just making sure the almost-married bear still knows how to growl."

"He'll be happy to put his big furry foot up your ass. With claws extended."

"Don't tempt me with foreplay, soldier boy."

"Hmm." As unofficial point man tonight, and used to their byplay, Lucas brought his attention back to Jon, watching how the man gauged her reaction to each display. The CFO lifted his brow when he let Rachel drift back to one, like letting a compass choose north.

"Look sharp, gentlemen. Surreal's going to get a rare public performance from us tonight. Jon's made his choice."

Chapter Fifteen

ଛେ

Though the biggest crowd was in front of the girl in rope suspension, Rachel's curiosity drew her to where a woman was pilloried between two posts, her legs spread out wide enough that her cuffed ankles could be hooked to the eyebolts there. The same had been done to her arms, held straight out from the shoulder. The pillars were carved in the shape of elongated male and female nudes, rough, simple outlines in the wood so that it kept its functional post shape. The images reminded her of Shakti and Shiva, the male and female deities that symbolized the *kundalini* energy exchange in Tantra. She noticed worn places on the posts, where she imagined countless fingers like this woman's had clung, the grain smoothed by the friction and perspiration of nervousness, desire, pain.

She jumped when the whip hit, a cat-o'-nine that fanned out over the woman's shoulders, her back, then lower, across her naked buttocks. She had on a simple collar, a silver cuff. However, it appeared to be custom made, suggesting the man whipping her was her dedicated Master. More than that, Rachel's gaze strayed to the only other jewelry they wore...matching wedding rings.

The woman's back was already red with the stripes, her ass pink and inflamed with heat. He came to her then, yanking her head back by her hair and kissing her while she moaned, obviously close to climax. She was begging in a harsh whisper, words easy to read. "Please let me come." The Master caressed her throat, her jaw, shook his head. Clamped a hand on her tender backside and pinched hard, making her cry out and writhe more.

Jon shifted Rachel in front of him so she could see better. It also allowed her to lean back against him, gave her his protection on all sides, and in front by the one arm he had around her waist. He slid the other hand under the clinging fabric, over her hip bone and then down, down, two fingers surrounding and pressing on her clit, idly tormenting her there. If the Master on the platform turned around, he could easily see what Jon was doing. The dual stimulation, mental and physical, had her leaning more fully into her escort. "Keep your hands at your sides, palms open," Jon said in her ear. He'd anticipated how difficult it was to do that rather than reach up, hold his neck, or even grip a small fold of his slacks to hang on as an anchor.

Her breasts had ached in reaction to the girl in breast bondage, nipples of course drawing up hard, and now they burned for attention. All of her did, every inch of flesh. She wanted to be the woman in front of her. She wanted all the clothing stripped away, wanted Jon to touch and mark every inch of her overheated, needy skin. The music from the dance floor was pumping through the soles of her feet, and the energy of this place was like that, surging through her, matching her increasing heartbeat, her increasing wild need to let out some of the desire she was feeling. She wanted this, this form of painful release she'd never experienced directly, but wanted to, so badly.

The Master had uncuffed his wife, helping her straighten from the spread-legged position. He massaged her hips and her wobbly knees, suggesting she'd been there awhile. Then he recuffed her wrists to one another and did the same to her ankles, holding onto her to keep her steady. Bending, he lifted her over his shoulder, her cuffed hands falling down his back as he put his hand squarely on her abused backside, his fingers settling over the glistening and flushed cunt they could see through the almond-shaped opening between her thighs. Holding her like that, he slid two fingers in, then used his thumb to massage her clit. So highly aroused, he'd known he'd finish her in such a vulnerable position. She cried out, begging him for permission.

"Please, Master...let me come. Let me come."

"Come. Gush for them. Please your Master."

Her body writhed on his shoulder, and Rachel appreciated the man's brawny strength, because it would take some power to hold a climaxing woman so still, though having the ankles and wrists bound to one another as they were certainly helped, she was sure. The woman squirmed, screamed, shuddering, convulsing, and Rachel couldn't look away to see if the audience was as riveted as she was, though she gave a little cry of her own as Jon's fingers rasped over her clit. A hard stroke, his mouth opening on her throat to set his teeth there, as the woman came.

In that position, they all saw the creamy fluid spill from her cunt in several generous offerings. As Rachel watched, the Master beckoned to a man in the crowd. Intrigued, she watched a handsome blond with vivid green eyes come to the platform. He placed a familiar hand on the Master's chest.

The brawny man covered the other man's hand with sensual affection, making it clear the three were intimate. The blond said something that had the other man smiling, then he leaned in and licked away her release, running his other hand over her buttocks around the Master's hand, caressing, enjoying and reassuring her at once. She made those bleating noises and shudders that came with aftershocks, and Rachel realized she was matching some of those movements with tiny jerks of her own as Jon continued to work her clit with such slow and maddening movements.

As the three moved off, he lifted his mouth from her throat. She felt the throb of where he'd bitten her, knew from the ache he'd left another mark over the first.

"Your turn," he said.

She wasn't sure she'd heard him right, but then he smoothed her dress and stepped up the short step to that platform. As he tugged her with him, the heat of the spotlights was suddenly closer and brighter. In her tour of the public play area, he'd recognized the one scene that fascinated, disturbed and scared her the most. Pilloried, stretched between two demands, helpless to them.

Short and snug as the dress was, the coverage was somewhat of an illusion. But she noted how he'd smoothed it back in place before he brought her up here. He could strip and bind her, but he'd obviously wanted the crowd to see her at the beginning, put together, sexy, beautiful. She saw all of that in his eyes.

When was the last time she'd thought of herself that way without prompting? Laying her hand against the Shakti side, he guided the other one so her palm pressed to Shiva. Now that she was up here, she could see the posts could be adjusted, that they were fixed onto curved tracks that would allow them to be closer, wider, or even at diagonal angles.

He'd chosen two sets of cuffs from an attendant, and now he brought them to her. She stared up at him, barely breathing as he kept his attention on her wrists, wrapping the cuff snugly on her right wrist, then hooking it to that eyebolt. She couldn't speak. She didn't know how right now. She felt held there by what he wanted, what he seemed to know she wanted, and that want was growing large, capable of crushing her with its weight.

"Sshh..." he murmured, though she'd said not a word. He threaded a hand through her hair, a gentle stroke that became firmer as he tilted her head back. He was so close, but he didn't kiss her. Instead, his gaze roved over her face, her lips, making them part, making her wet them, wanting his kiss. He smelled so good, that male aftershave smell. The jacket etched the line of his shoulders, drawing her attention to the tie around his corded throat, the tie she'd tied for him. The silken, ebony strands of his hair brushed his collar, and she followed that to the smooth line of his shirt, how it delineated his chest. As he shifted, her attention went to the belted slacks, the muscular waist she knew was under that buckled strap, and even lower, to the cock she knew was already straining the fit of the tailored slacks. Her fingers curled in the cuffs, registering the unmovable force of the posts.

He stepped back then. An attendant had brought something else to him, the briefcase he'd carried into her apartment that first night. Though her back was now to the crowd, she had a sense that it was growing in size. Given the deference Jon was shown here, and the artistry and skills he'd shown her in a short time, she realized he could be a popular performer. It gave her a sinking feeling, but he'd said she was special. Different. Could she believe that? Was she hopelessly deluded and naive? And could she really resent how he'd obtained his skills, skills that had so far brought her to some of the most intense sexual experiences she'd ever had?

She started as a familiar hand slid over her lower back. She looked up into Peter's eyes, and he nodded toward her opposite side. "I don't think you've met Ben yet."

She shifted her attention to another impossibly handsome man, one perhaps a year or so younger than Jon, with black hair and brilliant green eyes. Though not as broad as Peter, his shoulders were certainly broad enough, his fit body enough to command a woman's attention. He wore a charcoal gray suit, an emerald tie over a black dress shirt.

"And you remember Lucas."

Lucas stepped up behind her, so she had to turn her head, then drop it back. With a smile, he cupped her skull in his hand, let her fall all the way into his palm, a dizzying sensation as she looked up at him. "Hello," he said.

She may have mouthed *Hi*. She wasn't sure. The men were flanking her on three sides, Jon in front. When she straightened to look at him again, the serious set to his mouth heralded a shift as distinctive as if he'd barked an order, only this was a command that hummed through her blood, not needing anything as overt as sound. On instinct, she nodded to each man again, only this time she lowered her eyes, acknowledging she wasn't surrounded merely by Jon and his friends, but four different Masters.

Remembering Jon's questions earlier, and her own thoughts about where her boundaries were, who could touch her at his behest, she knew these had been at the top of that short list.

"Gentlemen, strip her for punishment, please. Leave the heels on."

Punishment? It was a word capable of making her even more off center and short of breath, but she tried to calm herself with the three-point breathing, not wanting to miss a single second, even as she harbored a dark fear of the things all of it might release in her. When she'd looked into Jon's face, seen the mesmerizing power in the blue depths, the thought of what he might be capable of unleashing inside her made her tremble.

Peter was the one who untied the sash, his fingers moving along her powdered skin, bringing her the smell of lavender. He didn't hesitate or fumble, a man familiar with the curves and vulnerabilities of a woman. Since he lifted the fabric away from her skin as he freed her breasts, he didn't brush her nipples, though they were erect and begging for friction. Then down to her waist, over her hips, his knuckles sliding along her skin as he brought the dress to her ankles.

When he touched her calf, she lifted her feet clear of it, one at a time. Lucas' steadying grip was on her waist. Then Peter nudged her to a wider stance, until her heels were placed outside the range of her shoulders, putting her off balance. The pillars were adjusted, aligned with her ankles, and then they were cuffed firmly so there was no range of movement, even if she wavered like a reed in a monsoon.

Ben and Lucas pulled the top of the pillars out to form a vee angle, so her arms were stretched out as far as they could go. They adjusted them so her shoulders were pulled back, her breasts thrust out, her bound ankles creating an angle that arched her back and tilted her ass upward as well. It was an extremely sexual and open position, entirely vulnerable and arousing at once, the pillars locked in place to hold her fast.

Ben had stepped off to the side with Jon, his hand on the side of Jon's neck. It was the affectionate gesture of a brother, similar to the way Jon dipped his head to speak back in his ear, so they could have a private moment yet hear one another over the crowd noise. Ben nodded, glanced toward her. When he'd first stepped onto the platform, Rachel hadn't seen it in the affable body language and genial expression, but now she saw clearly what Dana had said about him. *He's probably the toughest, most hardcore Master of all of them.*

It was in the intent way his gaze passed over her body, stripped except for her collar and high heels. Perhaps because of how open she was right now, in many ways, she saw a glimpse of exactly what kind of Master he was. He could judge exactly how much a woman could endure, but he'd then bring her to such an overwhelming subspace she'd leap off that edge, merely if he commanded her to do it. That was his thing. He demanded utter devotion, proof of a woman's unconditional surrender. Oddly, she sensed he wanted a woman's soul, but not her heart.

It was a little frightening to recognize such a thing in this defenseless moment, but Jon was here. He was her Master. He knew her heart. She was standing naked in a crowded club, cuffed to two posts. She was trembling, but any trepidation was of herself, of the sheer power of what was inside of her, responding to all this. Craving more, harder. A pressure was growing inside that needed pain, stimulation, something to release it.

Lucas stepped in front of her, blocking her view of Jon. What was the cologne he wore? It was such a male exotic scent, it made her think of Egyptian pharaohs again, as did the precise cut of his cheekbones, those intense eyes.

"Open up for me," he said. She saw he had a gag like the one Jon had used the first night, the one shaped like a man's cock. This one was shorter, but thicker.

Obediently, she parted her lips. As the shape of it passed between them, knowing a man's eyes was on her, watching her take it, she curled her tongue around it instinctively. It was flavored with honey and sugar, stirring her saliva glands and making her suck a little harder. Rather than fastening it in place right away, Lucas played with her a few moments, sliding it back and then forward, watching her work the length of it. The muscle flexing in his jaw made it clear she was doing a good job of affecting him. Her body rocked toward him, even as her gaze strained to look around his shoulder. Where was Jon? And what did he mean by punishment?

She didn't have long to find out.

Lucas at last strapped it to her head, smoothing the fasteners beneath her hair line at the nape, though he made them snug, so the gag pushed down on her tongue when fully seated, rendering her silent and keeping her from teasing the gag, or him, further. There was a glint in his gaze, a light smile on his lips as he caressed her still working jaw. Leaning forward, he brushed her temple with his lips. "You get over your fears, sweetheart, you're going to be damn irresistible. Jon's going to lose his mind over you."

He stepped away then, letting her see Jon again with her hungry eyes. He moved forward, circling her as Lucas and Peter drew back to two chairs placed at the rear corner of the platform where she could see them, making it clear she was on display for them. She wasn't sure how she would have felt about facing the unknown crowd, but knowing they were there, at her back, and these Doms were at her front... Oh God and Goddess, the heat of it was making her dizzy.

Jon passed behind her, his fingers trailing down her back, but he stopped short of her ass. He shifted, and she could tell from the corner of her eye that he'd faced the crowd. At the same moment, the attendant to whom Ben had been talking pulled a curtain cord. The black drape behind Peter's and Lucas' chairs drew back, revealing a mirror that allowed the crowd to see her face, her gagged mouth and needy expression. Worse, she could see all of them staring at her.

Jon's hand settled on her back, a reassurance. However, when he addressed the crowd, she learned his velvet voice translated well into the ringing tones of a Master addressing a crowd. It even brought the noise from other nearby demonstrations down to more hushed tones.

"The submissive you see before you has been in need of a Master's punishment for a long, long time. She believes she's not beautiful, not worthy of a Master's love and attention. Of my love and attention. I'm very disappointed by this."

The overpowering physical arousal she was experiencing hadn't anticipated an emotional assault. It hit her below her heart, a sharp blow. Her lips pressed down on the gag, her nostrils flaring with the need for air, fingers clutching at the posts. When her gaze flickered to Peter, Lucas and Ben, who'd now taken a seat with them, she was startled to see Jon's tone reflected in their faces. Reproof, stern admonition and something else that stirred that pain higher up, made her heart beat faster. This wasn't roleplaying or playacting. The things Dana had hinted at, their cohesion as a solid, Dominant unit, was clear here. Jon's intent was fully reflected in their body language. They didn't like what they were hearing, and they would all make her accountable for it.

"If I wanted to use her like a cheap whore, hand her out to anyone who wanted her, she believes that would be my right. Even if it destroyed everything fragile and amazing that has only recently begun to stretch its wings inside of her. She doesn't believe she deserves anything more, believes she can't hope for anything more than that."

Okay, that ache was ascending into her throat. She looked toward the foot of the mirror, so she could cast her gaze down, stare at the row of polished shoes and well-cut slacks. She couldn't look at any of the men. She wanted free. This push-pull between the emotional and the physical was putting the taste of panic in her mouth.

"She doesn't realize what a gift she is, what a treasure I've discovered in her." He settled his hand on her shoulder now, that tender juncture with her neck. The pointed caress stilled her. "But I think a little well-placed punishment will help her discover her value, help her strengthen her realization of what being a slave to a Master truly means. In the past, when someone committed a crime, the authorities punished them in public like this, so that they remembered the lesson and never repeated it. That's our intent tonight, but for her ultimate pleasure and yours. As most of you know, we don't often play this deeply in public, but when one who belongs to us needs the lesson, we don't hesitate to do what needs to be done."

You belong to one of them, but in a peripheral way, you belong to all of them.

Jon moved back to her front now, his firm touch moving over her tense fingers in the cuff. He loosened their curl so they lay flat on the wood again, then let his hand drift over her arm. She gazed up at him, suffering, communicating myriad things she didn't know how to express, so maybe the gag was a good thing. She didn't know if this was where she wanted to be anymore, though some part of her knew she did, that she couldn't back away from this. He'd brought her to the starting line, and he was challenging her to have the courage to run toward something instead of away from it.

"I'm here," he said, meeting her gaze. Touching her chin, stroking over her stretched lips, he tightened his grip on her jaw, underscoring his words. "I'm always going to be here."

* * * * *

He shifted then, so blissfully all she could see right now was him, not the mirror or the others. "Rachel, did you ever have a male teacher when you were in school? One who attracted you in a particular way?" He spoke in that raised voice that carried through the crowd, but the way he kept his focus on her, it was all about the two of them.

275

An answer to his question sprang right into her mind. Mr. Montgomery. Mixed with his energetic and creative teaching style, there'd been a natural authority to him. It gave him control over every person in his class with little more than a direct look or a slight lift to his deep voice. He hadn't been extraordinarily handsome, but had the look of a rugged, middle-aged Viking warrior, broad shouldered and strong.

She nodded. Jon's lips twitched, though his gaze remained serious. "And did you ever imagine him punishing you for passing notes?"

That twitch at his mouth reminded her he could be more than one thing, elicit more than one emotion from her at the same time. So he'd remarkably intertwined a sliver of humor among her spiked emotions, cushioning her. It helped. She held his gaze, glad now he offered her that lifeline, and gave him a slight nod. It had been a quiet, shameful fantasy, one she hadn't thought about for a long, long time. She'd remembered it on occasion in her marriage, realizing it was early evidence of those inexplicable needs that Cole had made her feel were appalling.

The humor died away, probably because he saw her emotional shift. He caressed her face, holding her attention. "Never again, Rachel," he said, low. "I'm going to punish you, not for passing the notes but for being ashamed of wanting that fantasy."

Ben now rose. He had two things in hand. One was a nylon flogger. The other was a switch.

"In the one-room schools of our past, they used hickory switches as a very effective way to maintain a student's attention." Jon addressed the crowd again, though his gaze held Ben's an extra moment, a significant exchange that sent a capricious wave of panic through her, understanding what might be about to happen. Her Master settled his gaze back on her face, and that expression confirmed it even before he began to speak.

"My friend here knows more about the female bottom than any man I know, how every individual nerve ending can be stimulated to maximum response. He's devoted a great deal of time and study to it." He cocked his head, and his voice modulated, addressing her specifically, though the audience could still hear him. "I know you've already recognized exactly what type of Master he is, sweet girl, and you can probably well imagine him as your stern teacher, can't you? He's going to punish you, and like the other night, I'm not going to give you a number. He's going to keep going until I tell him to stop. I'll know when you've had enough."

Her breath had speeded up, such that she was making small, helpless noises against the gag. It only fueled the fire in his eyes. "Give yourself to my desires. Believe that I know what it is you truly need and want. In time, you'll be brave enough to tell me, and then we'll go to even deeper levels. But tonight I'm going to prove how far down that path I can take you, merely from what I know of you now."

Ben had disappeared, and she knew he was behind her. Jon stayed in front, laying a hand on either side of her throat, his thumbs teasing that sensitive pocket of her collar bone beneath the midnight blue strap. Then his gaze rose. "Begin."

She hadn't expected Ben's hands first, so she jumped at that initial contact. He'd set aside the tools, because his large fingers slid fully over her buttocks, molding their shape and weight, the depth of the valley where they met her thighs, then slid back up the crevice between. Those fingers parted her cheeks wide, so wide she felt the stretch on her anal opening. She'd played in that area privately of course, and though she was tied here naked, she hadn't realized the startling defenselessness of having one of her most private openings displayed to a crowd. Then, all that disappeared, because his fingers were tracing that rim. His knee pushed against the inside of hers as he knelt. A second later, his mouth was right upon that intimate area.

Holy Goddess… He didn't waste time on preliminaries. He already knew she was well aroused, but of course there'd been no direct stimulation to that part of her. When the wet heat of his mouth touched that sensitive nerve circle, everything in her body arrowed toward that point of contact. The fingers holding her buttocks dug in, conveying how strong his hands were as he kneaded and pinched, sensitizing all of it in an unpredictable pattern of discomfort and fondling.

She strained forward against Jon's hands as he saw every reaction, the way her lips strained around the gag, making her lips slick with her saliva. She was sure her expression was wild and uncertain, but she couldn't look away from him, not now. It was as clear as a spoken command that he expected her to look at him, let him see all of it.

The rest of her life, past and future, dropped away. This moment was like finding herself at the gates of Heaven and Hell, not sure which way to go, but knowing the decision didn't rest with her. That decision was out of her hands, and she could only surrender to judgment.

Ben's hands and mouth at last drew away, but hellfire was quick to arrive. The first slap of that switch came so quickly on the heels of the stimulation, she wasn't expecting it. Her body was still shuddering from the pleasure when she received the pain. Because she hadn't tensed against it, fire sang unimpeded through her flesh. He'd cracked it square over both buttocks, at the most cushioned point, her response arrowing straight into her pussy. She made a plaintive scream against the gag, her lashes fluttering against eyes wet with stress and more. Jon's hold shifted over the collar, reinforcing the reminder of it as he caressed her chin. His to protect, cherish. Punish.

A second strike, and she cried out. It really hurt. But then there was the flogger, layering over that. Her nerves were in chaos, still burning in pain, her body shaking and flinching. A firm, brief smack against her buttocks, the nylon cords wrapping around her hips, between her legs, was followed by a lick and sting of sensation as he hit her pussy square. Then back to the buttocks. Just as she was sinking into that feeling, the switch was back.

And so it went. Her nerves gave up anticipation, and abandoned her to full, jittering reaction, taking pain and pleasure the same way. Perspiration broke out on her face and body. Ben never paused, but once Jon took a towel from the attendant, stroking it over her brow, the place between nose and lip, the indentation of her chin. He leaned forward, nibbling on her lips around the gag, his breath caressing her skin. She screamed as the next strike with the hickory switch felt like it cut through skin. Her hands convulsed in the cuffs. Then Ben spread her buttocks, his mouth once again busy on her rim.

She screamed again at the sensation, until she was making a repetitive shrieking response in her throat, her tongue hampered by the phallic gag. Jon kept up that erotic play over her quivering lips with his own skillful mouth, touches of his tongue. She wasn't climaxing, but it was like she was being overcome by sensation, and sound was the only way to release some of the enormous pressure building inside her. But that wasn't enough for Jon. God help her...

Lucas and Peter rose from their seats now. Jon drew back, clearing the path to her. Since Peter and Lucas were both large men, if her brains weren't so scrambled and she wasn't clinging to Jon with her gaze, terrified he'd disappear, she might have appreciated the grace with which Lucas dropped to one knee between her legs, putting his hands on her hips. Peter stood to his left, bracing his hand over hers on the post as he leaned in, cupped one of her breasts and bent his head to take the nipple in his mouth, at the same moment that Lucas' tongue found her clit and started to lick.

She was choking on her passion, so close to climax, yet the fiery pain of the hickory held it out of reach. That, and what Jon was holding in his hands now. It was a phallus, so thick that surely it was bigger than a woman was meant to

279

take, even well-greased as it was by the attendant. Jon had another that seemed only slightly smaller, and he handed that to Lucas, who passed it without conversation between her legs. His forearm brushed against her calf, Ben bracing himself on the small of her back as he bent to take it.

Lucas slid his tongue around inside of her in a way that had her swiveling her hips with the motion, begging for a thrust that would emulate the fucking she needed so badly. She couldn't take this. She couldn't. And yet she had no choice.

When Lucas straightened, her body pleaded for him not to stop, that it was far too soon. He licked her off his lips, taking an additional taste, and she saw his gray eyes were fierce silver with appreciation. He glanced at Jon. "She's dripping wet. She's got a shameless, hot little cunt. She can take whatever you want her to take."

Her husband had said crude things to her, in a terrible, hurtful way. But they seemed to know when to say things crudely, to drive her even crazier.

Peter took Lucas' position to better stimulate her nipples with clever hands, his devil-blessed tongue. She mewled, her body twisting and writhing in the restraints. Her gaze clung to Jon's face. If she could speak, maybe she'd protest, make her fear or trepidation known, but now her fate was his to determine. Peter's hands settled on her thighs now, increasing the sense of being widened. She felt the brush of the dildo as Jon guided it down there. Ben's tongue stabbed deep inside of her ass and she arched forward, right onto it. The broad head pushed between her labia.

"Relax for me, sweet girl," Jon murmured. "You can take this. I know you can. Just relax..."

She was being split open. It wasn't comfortable, but it wasn't unbearable either. At that moment, Ben started to work the other one inside of her. He moved through the outer ring of muscles easily enough, and began to manipulate it through the second ring as Jon got the head of the large phallus through and started moving up her channel.

Now those short screams were long, strangled cries. Her ass was on fire, her pussy and anus being stretched so hard by the thick phalluses. All while her nipples were being suckled, squeezed and stimulated, to the point her attention was divided everywhere, no one thing able to take precedence over another.

When at last they had them as far as they were going to take them, an attendant stepped forward with a harness, and Jon strapped them in place. She thought she'd been trembling hard before, but now she was like a woman in the midst of a seizure, her body racked with convulsions.

"Thank you, gentlemen." Jon nodded to them. "I'll take it from here. Rachel, meet each of their eyes directly and say thank you."

It was harder than anything else, surprisingly enough, because she was stripped so raw. But she managed it with Peter first, mumbling the words incoherently against the gag. Her nipples were as stiff and aching with arousal as they'd ever been. She thought of Dana, being the beneficiary of that adept mouth whenever Peter wanted to torment and pleasure her both.

Then Lucas. He'd given her a taste of the cleverness of his mouth, but she believed without question that he could drive a woman to complete insanity with it—and she'd embrace it. Her pussy contracted, just from passing her gaze over those firm lips that would still have her scent on them.

They were both well aroused, two powerful men who reminded her of the holograph, each man waiting his turn with intent, hot gazes, but after she completed the etiquette, they nodded, acknowledging her, and moved back to the chairs. The hickory switch slid over her shoulder, curved around her throat, lifting her chin as Ben bent over her shoulder, pressing his body against her ass so that thick plug seated even more deeply.

"I didn't hear my thank you, darlin'."

She said it one more time, and when his hand descended, gripping her ass, she wondered at how it stimulated both the lingering pain and the pleasured nerve endings. It surprised her when his lips brushed her neck with far more gentleness. "Jon's right," he purred. "You're a pure treasure. Unlike Jon, I'm going to hope you forget this lesson, so one day I have to help him repeat it. Harder."

Jon exchanged an unfathomable look with his friend that she wasn't sure was accord or warning. Her mind couldn't wrap itself around anything that complex. Two plus two was far beyond her right now, though she was sure that the answer being four wasn't a coincidence, given what had been happening for the past…however long it had been.

It wasn't over yet. The section of the platform that held the pillars was marked by a circle on the carpet, but it wasn't merely a design. It was a dais that could be rotated. As Jon moved to the control and flipped it, engaging the motor, alarm flooded her chest. Instead of a mirror reflection, with his shoulders mostly blocking the view, she was about to come face-to-face with the wall of strangers witnessing her punishment.

Chapter Sixteen

ဆ

May all the gods help her, she wondered if the entire population of the club had moved to this spot. It was a sea of attentive faces, the measuring eyes of Masters and Mistresses, the rapt, intent faces of submissives and every range of flavor in between. She now understood, in every quaking, aroused nerve, the significance of administering this kind of punishment in front of an audience. The stares, the energy of the dense half circle of bodies around her, underscored how exposed she was, displayed for them this way.

In the mirror, she'd seen that the men had aroused her so her nipples were large and hard, her cunt dark, flushed and dripping profusely. Not only did her thighs glisten with the wet tracks, but a tiny, embarrassing puddle marked the platform between her legs. Her pussy was stretched by that dildo, the other deep in her ass, both of them harnessed there so that Jon could keep her impaled as long as he felt necessary. The way she was restrained, her arms stretched out and back, she looked like a bird pinned in the position of flight, her breasts thrust forward like tempting fruit to be handled, her ass pertly in the air as if inviting animal coupling.

Aroused, terrified at every level, there was still another component to it. Every part of her was attuned to the fact this was Jon's will. Jon had done this to her, she'd surrendered to whatever Jon desired, because his desire was in fact the same as her own, impossible to tell where one began and the other ended. He'd given her a full-flavored taste of what he'd indicated earlier. When it was like this, it was the way it was meant to be, both what the Master and slave wanted, needed, craved. Demanded and begged for at once. Though she was in a state she'd never before experienced, her emotions a mix too complicated to track, fear warring with desire, she felt like she'd come home at last.

When he turned her, she was staring into the crowd, but that was far too much, so her eyes flickered over their heads. Since she was on a raised platform, it put her in line of sight with the elevated mezzanine and the bar, all the additional faces there. She would have retreated swiftly to the safety of a lowered gaze and the hope Jon wouldn't make her raise it again, but one of the people at the bar caught her attention and held it like a polar magnet.

Dana.

The blind woman was not alone. From the second her gaze landed upon them, Rachel had no doubt who the women with her were.

Apparently, with the exception of Dana, blondes were favored by the Kensington men. Dana sat to the left of two exceptionally beautiful females. Both wore tailored skirts, thin blouses and tasteful, expensive jewelry that suggested they'd come straight from work. However, something about the way they were worn suggested what was beneath them was far less office-etiquette. Or that the women were simply responding to their environment.

The blonde next to Dana gripped her hand. Her lips moved, perhaps describing everything to the blind woman. While the crowd before them were voyeurs, that wasn't what Rachel felt from the unwavering regard of the three women. They were witnesses, bound to her in…solidarity.

That blonde had to be Cassandra Adler, Lucas' wife. Her reasoning skills were not at their best at the moment—she gave another moan as Jon made an adjustment to the plug in her backside, stroking the rim—but other levels of perception were on high volume. She expected if she could see her chakras, they'd be like disco strobe lights, open and vibrant, receptors on maximum sensitivity.

She identified the blonde next to Dana as Cass because the third woman was intimately flanked by a man leaning against the bar, a relaxed but obvious escort to all three. He was standing, not on a barstool, since she didn't imagine he was the type of man who'd ever take up a seat when a woman might need one.

Just as she'd recognized the two women, she knew who he was. The Italian-Texas parentage showed in the dark eyes and close-cropped hair, the handsome yet rugged features. The mantle of power he wore on his shoulders didn't need the enhancement of the business suit he wore. He'd shed his tie, the shirt open at the throat, but if he'd stood there naked, it wouldn't make him any less intimidating, or mesmerizing. This had to be Matt Kensington.

So therefore, the woman to his immediate left was Savannah. She was everything Rachel had read about. Cool, breathtaking, intimidating in her own right. Yet when Rachel's gaze tripped over the still, porcelain features, she found herself unexpectedly trapped there...in recognition.

Maybe everyone else would see reserve, but Rachel saw a history in those eyes, a history that mirrored her own. This woman knew what it was to live for *years* thinking she was falling short, that she'd never be good enough. Feeling like a failure inside, even as everyone told her she was successful.

It resonated inside her, squeezed her heart hard. Seeing that made Rachel see other little things. The way Savannah held her jaw, how her fingers were over Matt's on the bar, a little tense and unsettled, as if she'd recognized herself in Rachel as well. Matt was giving all three women his protection, but the way he curved into the side of her body in particular showed he was in sync with her needs and moods. The way a Master would be.

Jon slid his hands over Rachel's shoulders, up to the back of her neck. As he folded his body over her, blanketing her, the gag loosened. Shaken by what that brief bond with the women had given her, she turned her face into his neck, breathing in his scent, burrowing as much as she could, wanting to be subsumed in the stillness of his very soul. He gave her a blissful second, his head pressed down over hers.

"I love you," he said softly, and slid the gag from her mouth, caressing her lips with a cloth to dry the saliva that came with it. "I want them to hear you come, every word you say, every plea you make. Don't hold back. Your Master wants to hear you."

Now he straightened, his hands moving down her back, and she groaned as he worked the larger dildo out of her pussy, though he left the one in her ass. He massaged her labia, teased her cunt until she was making those cries again. The crowd was a heaving sea of shifting bodies, flashing eyes, bared teeth. She careened upon the waves of pure lust. It was stoked by the more intimate and personal scene that unfolded before her at the bar. Not having the mirror where she could watch Jon, as she wanted so desperately to do, she kept her gaze there.

Peter had left the platform to join Dana. As he stepped onto that end of the mezzanine, he slid an arm around his petite submissive, lifting her full off the stool to kiss her with erotic demand that made Rachel gasp, her own body hungering for such intimate contact. As he lowered her back to the seat, still kissing her, he slid his hand between the legs that Dana parted immediately. He rubbed her beneath the latex mini-skirt she wore as she clutched his biceps. Rachel noticed she kept hold of Cass' hand, their fingers tangled and stroking one another unconsciously, caught up in the same wave as Rachel.

Sliding Savannah's hair to the side, Matt bent to touch his mouth to the delicate flesh under her ear. Her long nails cut into his palm as he slipped one of the buttons of that silky blouse. As Rachel watched, panting, he reached in to cup her breast, lifted it free of a lacy bra and stroked a thumb over a prominent nipple, obvious through the sheer fabric. Savannah's head dropped back against his broad shoulder, her face turning away to give him better access.

But even through that, the women's attention came back to Rachel. Though Matt and Peter weren't looking toward her at the moment, she felt a link to them as well. It was her and Jon and them. The mass of humanity drove her arousal even higher from their presence, but what gathered it all together was this intimate circle, the fact they'd pulled her into the center of it. And what would shatter her, take her completely over, was the man behind her now.

Jon put his hands on her hips again, and she cried out, sheer ecstasy, emotional and physical, as his heated, bare cock pushed into her. She wished she could see it, the graceful movement of his body as he opened his slacks and levered the thick organ to her opening. Stretched and abused, she nevertheless welcomed him with tight, slick muscles, holding him as he drove in deep, joining with her there in front of all those eyes.

She was so hot and overcome by all of it, the climax thundered toward her like an unexpected flash flood when he'd done three, blissfully slow strokes. "Master..." She gasped it out on instinct. They'd never talked about rules, she realized. They just knew, she just knew, what she needed...wanted.

"May I... Please let me come!"

He held his silence, pushing in, dragging out, thrusting, working her faster, then slow, and she became desperate, crying out for the permission. "Please...please...Master." The heat was sweeping over her, pussy spasming, and in another second she'd be in breach of the obedience her Master should demand from her, never to release without his permission. "Help...can't..."

"Now, Rachel. Come for your Master. For me alone."

That sense of disorientation, of being lost on a turbulent tide of sensation and the collective desires of those around her took over, swept her up and over, and she was at the hub of it, held by Jon's sure, steady grip. As she was pulled away into sensation, her last coherent thought was that the pillory, the environment, the men, even the presence of the other K&A women, was an ultimate organic device engineered by him, a Master whose will she was helpless to resist. She was lost in a rushing river, dependent on him to guide that narrow boat through the roaring waters.

She was screaming again, this time shrieking like a banshee, lost to all of it, her ass squeezing down on the plug as she lifted to meet his every thrusting stroke, as he began to slam hard into her, mixing the pain that lingered with a pleasure that wouldn't be denied. His hands captured her breasts and squeezed the nipples, and that additional sensation rocketed her higher. She was straining back and forth against her restraints, feeling everywhere his remarkably fully clothed body was touching her, wanting to serve him, devour him, hold him...

It was too much. Something broke inside of her, that concrete dam that had suppressed her emotions, pain and loss, disappointment...crushing loneliness. It rushed over her, driven over the wall by the unstoppable force of that climax and all that it meant, all that she could no longer deny. There would be no rebuilding that wall, no matter what happened. She was naked, shivering and vulnerable, protected from whatever came howling toward her by one man. One Master's love.

That sense of timelessness again, such that on the downward slide, she found herself blinking hazily, as if she'd come out of a long journey into a fantastical place, and reality was hard to comprehend. But on the downward slide of that incredible climax, she met Savannah's gaze. There she once again saw understanding. Comprehension of the panic and ecstasy, all wound together, a restraint even more frightening than physical bonds. Rachel grayed out some then, because the rush of blood, the quivering of nerves and limbs, overcame her. But when she phased forward in that hazy dream state, those three beautiful women had risen from their places at the bar.

With Cass guiding Dana, they were winding their way around the edge of the crowd until they reached the platform. There, Lucas and Ben gave them a hand up, Peter and Matt bringing up the rear. As they did, Jon touched kisses all along the curve of her spine. Some of her hair had come down in the front during her thrashing like a feral creature. It wisped along her cheeks, over her eyes. He'd caressed it to the side when he kissed her neck. But now he was withdrawing, his hands lingering on her hips, giving her a squeeze before his touch disappeared. For a harrowing moment, she was alone with the crowd, no familiar faces before her or in her peripheral vision.

Then female hands stroked the hair, finger-combed it out of her face, helped to re-secure it with the pins and sticks she'd used. Rachel saw it was Cass, her generous bosom smelling like a jasmine fragrance as she leaned over Rachel. Dana had a soft cloth, and wiped her face, the tears and remaining saliva. Pressing her lips to Rachel's temple, she moved behind her, following the line of her spine and hip with her slim fingers until she located the base of the anal plug and eased it out. A third hand, Savannah's, Rachel assumed, pressed on her lower back, a reassurance as it was removed.

She didn't see Jon, but she could *feel* him. He'd stepped back, letting them cosset her, and with all her senses so open and vulnerable, she thought she understood why. This had been a punishment, and he was letting the lesson sink in by giving other submissives the role of her aftercare. They would comfort and soothe, but he would wait to do so until she did what every instinct told her she was supposed to do.

It was hard, so hard, yet every emotionally exhausted fiber of her knew she would do it. However, she truly needed this moment first. As Cass and Dana gently and efficiently cleaned between her legs and buttocks, ran damp, heated cloths down her legs, over her skin, grounding her in this world once again, Savannah came to her front, stroked her face. In her bent position, Rachel's head was at the level of Savannah's breasts, the lace edges of the bra and curves

289

partially revealed by the button Matt had slipped. Still bound, Rachel raised her gaze to the woman's face.

Savannah gave her a nod, then slid her arms around Rachel's shoulders, letting her put her face against that perfumed bosom, take comfort in the softness, the understanding, the calm over the storm. Her hands were cool and strong, everything she needed them to be.

Finally, her arms and legs were uncuffed. She tried to hold her own weight, but of course she was still trembling too badly. As the three women held her, she had one rasping word on her lips.

"Jon."

Savannah turned her toward him, her arm around Rachel's bare waist. He stood a few feet away, studying her with those quiet intent eyes, the way he'd so often studied her during class. She moved one foot forward, but now Cass stopped her. Dana knelt, urging her out of the first stiletto, then the other. Now she stood on bare soles, completely naked, except for the collar he'd put on her. A proper slave.

They wouldn't let her move forward without their help. The pressure of her forward motion told them where she wanted to go, though, so she was leading. When she reached him, her knees let go. They slowed it down, helped her sink in a controlled movement to a kneeling position. Then they stepped back, that space on the stage becoming a silent circle for the two of them alone.

Lifting her attention to his beloved face, Rachel let her eyes dwell briefly on every feature, then she swept her gaze down, bowed her head. "I'm sorry, Master," she said softly. She didn't have the strength to say it louder, but it was only him who needed to hear it. "I'll try...but I need you to remind me I'm worth loving. It's been so long since...I felt loved. T-thank you. Please...forgive me. I need your forgiveness. I'm so sorry."

How could she make sense of the tears that came now, the fact that she was sorry, and happy, and sad and exhilarated, and exhausted? And all his.

She waited, her gaze on his feet. As she did, something else happened. Hands settled on her shoulders, a male leg pressing against her bare hip. Peter bent, tilted her head back and kissed her on the lips, offering a quick stroke of her face with a tender hand. The cool judgment she'd seen when he sat in the chair was gone. What was there now was heat and comfort at once, protective and kind. Then he put pressure on her shoulder and neck, directing her to return her gaze to the floor. As he stepped away it was Lucas taking his place, lifting one of her hands to kiss it, fondle the fingers, teasing her chin up for one brief second to give her a nod, show her the acceptance in his gaze as well before he stepped back.

This time her gaze returned to the floor on its own, understanding what was required. Ben's knuckles slid down her spine, giving her a shiver as he probed between her buttocks, that opening that had burned when he first slid the plug in. Then his mouth touched her nape, a nip and a "Well done", before he too was gone.

She was hungering for some word from Jon, some indication that she'd met his approval, but she couldn't deny how overwhelming this was. As well as a little scary, the ramifications of being accepted in such a way, the responsibility. There was no going back from this, no retreat, because Jon now had enough people to surround her fully. And while none of them could stare into the depths of her soul the way Jon could, they all understood her in a way that was too hard to resist.

Her chin was lifted once more and now Matt Kensington squatted in front of her, studying her with dark, unfathomable eyes, his hand strong and sure on her face. He didn't say anything, just held her in that gaze. With a hard lurch in her chest, she recognized it for what it was, a moment like an ancient tribal ritual. The leader didn't need to say anything. He was making a point of looking at her, of showing the others in the pack that he *saw* her. He accepted her. And she'd never be without family again.

The realization became something so difficult to contain, her fingers tightened on her knees. She needed Jon so badly she didn't think she could breathe another second without him. And then Matt was gone and he was there, her Master.

She stared at his feet, directly in front of her. She wanted to surge up, wrap her arms around him, have him hoist her body up and let her cling to him with arms and legs like a child, but she waited on the knife-edge, the most painful thing she'd done so far. She was lost, uncertain, and only he could save her.

His long-fingered hands came into the scope of her vision first, closing on her hands and lifting them. Then he brought her gaze up to him as he squatted, flanking her with his knees. As he kissed each palm, his gaze dwelled on her. She didn't know what to call what she saw in his face. It was love, yes, she couldn't deny it, but there was more. For this one second she truly believed she was the most important thing in his life. A sense of utter belonging and possession wrapped around her, making her feel more warm, safe and loved than she'd ever felt in her entire life.

"Forgiven," he said. "Completely and forever."

* * * * *

Because she was still so shaky, and the showers and changing rooms were on a lower level, he carried her, the others making a path for him through the crowd. When he reached the shower area, however, he left her with Savannah, Cass and Dana, giving her a quiet smile, caressing her face. The women tugged her floating, dazed self into a private but spacious shower stall. With a lot of strokes and kisses, they helped wash so many things away, leaving only the things that mattered.

Comfort turned in time to playfulness, and it amazed her to touch and be touched with such easy joy. She felt like a member of a harem for a powerful sultan—or in this case, five sultans—glorying in the state of sensuality that belonging to such men could keep at an astonishingly high level. She hadn't believed in a dream like this, had resisted it, and why? Now that she'd experienced it, she knew she'd give almost anything to feel like this. She'd never understood there *was* a line between dangerous addiction and courage. It was both painful and thrilling to realize how close to the positive side of that line she'd perhaps always been. But she believed in cycles, Fate and karma. If she'd learned to have that courage before Jon had come into her life, it wouldn't have been the same. Now was the right time, the way it was meant to be.

They dried her, put her back in her dress, helped her with her hair, and she helped them with theirs, since they'd all gotten equally wet. They talked very little of specific things…it wasn't needed. That would come later. They also seemed to understand she couldn't handle much of anything beyond immediate thoughts, simple needs. Playful touches were mixed once again with comforting caresses, hugs, long moments of simply being held. The reassurance of women speaking in quiet conversation.

When at last they emerged, Jon was waiting at the top of the stairs, hip propped on the rail. He was talking to Ben, who straightened from his panther's slouch against the wall and gave all the ladies a thorough perusal and rakish grin, the charming lawyer back in full force. "What I would have given to be in that shower," he noted, taking in all the wet hair and heated, damp skin.

"No boys were allowed," Dana informed him. "Boys are gross."

She escaped his swat at her backside, stuck out her tongue in his direction, then ran for the direction of Peter's voice. Ben followed in mock pursuit, though Rachel noticed he stayed close enough to grab her if she stumbled. Rolling her eyes,

Cass squeezed Rachel's arm and left her with a smile to join Lucas. Both he and Peter were seated on a velvet divan, Peter's long legs sprawled out while Lucas leaned forward on his elbows with restless energy.

Dana landed on Peter's lap, wriggling there until he gave her thigh a light slap to settle her down and threw a wide grin in Ben's direction. Lucas rose to slip an arm around Cass' waist, his hand settling low on her hip, stroking the line of it under the skirt. From the heated look in his eyes, he was ready to do some of his own playing here, and Rachel realized then that their particular scenario had probably guaranteed all couples would enjoy one another to an even more intense level tonight. Savannah stroked Rachel's brow, gave her a thoughtful nod before she moved down the hallway where Matt was talking to a man who looked like the club manager, and, based on the relaxed body language between them, a friend. As Savannah got closer, he held out his hand without looking in her direction, knowing she was there, and drew her in to his side.

"I'm taking you home."

A sigh shivered out of her as Jon spoke in her ear, his voice husky and a little dangerous. When he turned her to face him, she was graphically reminded that, while she'd been taken over the moon with her climax, he'd withheld his release. The lust pulsed off him in waves, every line of his body taut with desire, the blue eyes intent. The way he gripped her, the sense of aroused urgency in his strong fingers, gave her a delicious fear, knowing her Master would be in the mood to take when he got her home. She wanted him to do so. She wanted to meet his every demand, wanted him to fuck her savagely, with no care for her own needs until he was fully sated.

He closed his hand on her ass. She could feel the heat of his skin, the solid muscle, through the thin layers of clothing that separated them. "I'm going to fuck you for the rest of the night, long and hard, until you can't handle it hard anymore.

Then I'll be gentle, but I'm going to keep doing it until your pussy creams upon demand. And I'm going to do it in your bed, so you'll get used to having my scent there, on everything that's a part of your life."

Her pussy had already dampened at the first sentence. She'd barely gotten her breath back yet, and her body had been sorely, deliciously used. However, she wouldn't tell Jon she might need that gentleness sooner than later. Not because she was avoiding telling him what would hurt her, as he'd warned her against earlier. But because she knew he would know. He was so conscious of how she was feeling, how tired or weak she was. He would know the limits of her endurance and test them the way only a Master could.

"I'd like that." The words were a fervent breath of sound as she looked up at him. He stroked his finger beneath that velvet collar, twisted to increase its hold. "Master."

"Good girl," he said, that blue fire getting hotter.

She realized she hadn't really given him any indication of her feelings about the rest of what had happened tonight. Though she expected he knew that too, she glanced over at the others. "I'd like...I'd like to see them again."

"You will. And not just like this. This is my family. Your family." He spoke the overwhelming truth that would take time for her to handle, but in a good way. "We'll get to spend lots of time with them. Would you like that?"

"Yes, very much."

"Good. Maybe we'll do dinner with them next Friday. You haven't eaten Italian meets Tex-Mex until Matt cooks for you. It's incredible. We'll fly down to his place on the Gulf for the weekend if your schedule allows for it."

Normal things and totally ground-shaking changes in her life, all mixed together. She could only nod, lean in to his body as he moved them into a walk, shifting his arm to her waist. "You're still trembling," he said quietly. "I can carry you."

She shook her head. "As much as I love the way that feels, I want to feel the trembling. I want to know you did this to me."

"All right. I'm going to have Lucas walk out with us so he can be with you while I tip the doorman. Then we'll go home."

The look he gave her said they'd barely make it into her apartment before he'd be inside her again. He might not even take time to open the door. He'd push her into that partially hidden alcove, shove up her skirt and take her against the paneled wood of her door, hitting it with a rhythmic thud. Anyone who came down the hall would recognize the sound, know what they were doing. Then later, when he took her in her bed, the silhouette of his shoulders would be over her in the darkness, the climax a rolling tide that would send her to dreams...

* * * * *

She felt like pure, sparkling water. When they emerged from the club, it was remarkably early, only about ten o'clock. The stars were so bright, even with the lights of the city against the sky. She had Jon's collar on her throat, and with that and her sexy dress, coming out of this kind of club, it was obvious what she was to those coming in. Their knowing glances made her feel...breathtaking. Powerful and submissive at once, so aware of all the male energy around her, but particularly the energy of the one with the doorman. Jon met her gaze, heated, strong, and she was glad for Lucas' brief touch at her back, guiding her. She was besotted, enraptured, completely —

"Rachel?"

It was like hearing an unwelcome voice in the middle of a particularly good dream. It didn't make sense, made things disorienting. Though she really didn't want to, she turned toward it.

Cole had become more avid about golfing during the latter part of their marriage, probably to escape the obvious fact that their marriage was failing. She'd been no better, sometimes actually relieved to have more time alone. She'd learned loneliness was preferable to being in the company of someone who obviously would rather not be with her.

Earlier, she'd recognized the nearby steakhouse as one of Cole's favorite watering holes. But the chance of seeing him had been so remote, too absurd a coincidence, she hadn't considered it. Even though everything in her life, the spirituality she embraced, had proven to her over and over again that random occurrences often weren't. The parent who unexpectedly came home from work at lunchtime to find the teenagers rendezvousing in their bed, the wife running into the mistress at the mall...

Fate had thrown him here at this exact moment, hadn't it? To teach her something, tell her something. But what? The sick fear returned, her stomach already knowing what her mind refused to process.

He stepped over the parking lot markers, crossed the short strip of grass between the two businesses. She struggled to focus over the roar in her head. The last time she'd seen him had been at the funeral. He must be working out, because he'd dropped some weight and looked pretty fit, but the stress lines around his eyes and mouth, the simmering unhappiness he carried with him, had not changed. She ached for that, ached that she'd contributed to it. She'd been yet another disappointment in his life.

He stopped in front of her. Whereas each time Jon's gaze traveled over her, she felt vivid and alive, purely sensual, Cole's raking perusal turned every exposed inch of her flesh into something crawling, putrefied.

A moment ago she'd felt gorgeous, a creature of pure sensation. Her still-damp hair had brushed her bare neck, curling blonde strands a sexy frame for her face. The erotic dress had held her generous breasts firmly, the high ride of the hem and stiletto heels showing off her toned, slim legs. Now her hair was a disheveled mess, the far-too-scanty dress and tottering heels revealing an older woman's inappropriate foolishness. Her nipples were embarrassingly obvious.

As his focus moved over Jon's collar on her throat, she almost cried out at the pain of having the significance of that stripped from her, tossed aside with no chance of grabbing it back. It was no different from a fancy poodle's collar, something ridiculous instead of beautiful, full of personal meaning. Cinderella had been discovered by the stepsisters, and Cole's gaze was their rough, cruel hands, tearing away all the pretty trappings to leave her a worthless cinder maid again.

"So I guess you found what you were looking for." He spoke in a flat tone, and she had enough sense to think he might be in as much shock as she was. She managed to hold her position, but her knees were wobbling, and not from sensual overload. She couldn't find a single word to say.

In the awkward silence, his face got hard, tight. "God, Rachel. I guess there's at least one good thing about Kyle being dead. He never had to see his mother like this."

At one time, she hadn't realized that words, as well as silence, were weapons far more potent than a gun. They could tear open the heart far worse than a mortal wound. She'd known that, the day she'd fitted the gun under her chin. Only a spasm in her nervous hand had turned the weapon, shot the bullet not into her brain, but past her throat. After that, she'd figured out how to live with the horrible pain of spoken and unspoken wounds. But this took her back to all of that, reminded her what had pushed her to that awful, isolated day in her apartment.

Through the roaring pain, she was vaguely aware of Lucas being joined by Peter on the other side of her. She hadn't even realized Peter had followed Jon out, but now she had a fortress of heated male muscle around her, as well as a heady, lethal aura of barely leashed fury. It pushed in on her, held her up like bracing a mannequin, but Lucas and Peter had stabilizing hands at her elbows, reinforcing it. Then Jon stepped squarely in front of her.

Chapter Seventeen

ॐ

There wasn't a lot of space between her and the man Jon knew had to be her ex-husband, but after hearing that last line, Jon moved into it without hesitation, forcing Cole back a step. While he might not have Peter's shoulder breadth, his were wide enough to block Cole's view of Rachel and focus him on the most important thing right now — his own well-being.

"You'll walk away now, without another word."

Like the men behind him, Jon excelled at what he did by correctly assessing others. Through the few guarded things she'd said, and his interpretation of those things, he found he'd had a pretty accurate picture of Cole. Perhaps at one time he'd been a man who'd loved his wife, but time had changed him, made him harder. Jon saw a resentful beta personality. Cole had likely seen himself as an alpha, and taken a wrong turn with it, probably in many aspects of his life. His son's loss would have shut a lot of avenues down, made him even more bitter. Now Jon saw a cauldron of discontent and disappointment, and a bullheaded refusal to look inward to resolve any of it. It was everyone else's fault, not Cole's.

Before ten seconds ago, he could have pitied the man. But he'd heard the missile Cole had fired. The words had hit Rachel dead center, shattering her fragile confidence with bull's-eye accuracy, for it had targeted the things she feared most about herself, as well as the unhealed wounds. Every scrap of joy and pleasure she'd earned tonight had been blasted away. He'd seen it happen right in front of his eyes, the tightening of her face, the anguish in her hazel eyes, the way her body almost crumpled in on itself in front of him, so that she was ashamed of everything about herself, inside and out.

When that transition happened, his pity changed to something else.

The rational nature and pacific tolerance that characterized him was replaced by something Jon had rarely felt in his life. Since the others were so in tune with him, he wondered if Ben had stepped up to his side to support him or to prevent murder.

When Cole's expression got surly, probably fueled by a six-pack or two imbibed at the golf course and over his steak dinner, Jon's lips barely moved. "I mean it. One word, and you will regret ever being born. More than you already do."

The man had the good sense to pale beneath his golfer's tan. Whatever Cole saw in his face, he apparently believed, and of course it was reinforced by the three men at his back. However, frustration and alcohol were overriding good sense, and Cole's hands closed into half fists. Jon could tell he was trying to get one more look at Rachel, and he shifted, engaging the man's gaze again. "You had your shot. She's not for you. She's mine now. You have no rights here. Let it go and walk away."

Cole's jaw was hard as glass and as breakable, but he gave a short nod, turned on his heel and moved away. Jon saw a curious group of three golfers standing by a car, waiting for him. Apparently they'd shared a meal, but they hadn't wanted to get involved in whatever this was, even boozed up as they probably were. Cole wasn't as fortunate in his choice of friends as Jon was, for certain.

Peter alone was intimidating enough to back down most aggressors, but when Jon turned, Lucas' silver eyes were still cold enough to have frozen Cole's dick off. And of course Jon had known from the first the most dangerous of their group stood to his left. Devoid of his deceptively pleasant lawyer façade, Ben had the face of a man who could murder someone in the middle of a crowd, and then talk his way out of it while cleaning the blood off the knife. It was something he didn't appreciate enough about Ben. Jon made a note to mention that to him, send him a Hallmark card that expressed it, if he could find an appropriate one.

But any satisfaction about that disappeared when he focused on what was most important to him right now. Rachel was looking down, her fists locked in a knot under her breasts. He slid his arms over her, brought that curled, wounded body in to his, holding her close. But she reached up between them, fumbled at the fastener of the collar. "Take it off, please." Her voice was hoarse, raw.

"No, Rachel. That's not—"

"Now. *Now!*" She shoved away from him, pulling at it. "Let me go."

She was constricting her breathing, pushing hard against her windpipe by tearing at the velvet strap. As she spun away, the slim heels weren't made for that kind of uncontrolled movement. One broke and she stumbled, but Jon caught her before her knees hit the rough asphalt. He lifted her, screaming and struggling. Peter had already sent an urgent gesture to Max, where he sat in the limo at the entrance area, and he quickly maneuvered over, stopping near the men. Lucas got the door and Jon ducked in, still holding her. They shut the door after him, leaving him in the roomy and private compartment to deal with the hysterical woman in his arms. Max wisely already had the privacy screen rolling up between them.

"Rachel. *Rachel.*" She refused to respond, fighting him like a wild animal. As he held her hands away from her throat, he saw terrible things in her face, desolate things. The woman he knew wasn't in control. This feral, wounded creature didn't understand soothing words, meditation and balancing chakras bullshit. His heart wrenched, a combination of shared anguished and deep fear, as he realized he was seeing the darkness that had likely made her pick up that gun four years ago.

He believed in Fate. Fate had brought them together, and no matter how bad this was, Fate had meant this moment to happen, to give him the chance to go head-to-head with her past, prove that she had someone in her corner who could help her put it to bed, let those wounds heal.

He pinned her, forced to abandon gentility or finesse to unlatch the lock on the collar before she could strangle herself. It tumbled from her neck, but when he had to shift his grip, she scrambled to the far side of the limo, breathing hard. She curled up in the corner, fists clenched, body drawn tight as a bow.

Damn it, he'd told her he'd be whatever kind of Master she most needed, even if he had to set aside rational thought and answer uncontrolled animal instinct with the same. He'd told Cole the truth. He would protect her with everything he was, even the darker side all men carried inside of them. From the lingering effect of the club performance, he had more than enough banked animal lust willing to roar up to the forefront and help.

"Don't touch me. Get away from me. Leave me alone."

To hell with that.

His two instincts flip-flopped, the primordial eagerly surging forward, the protective shoved to the background. But they were one and the same in this instance. And he was a lot fucking stronger and faster. Yanking her out of the corner, he banded an arm around her waist and flipped her to the limo carpet on her hands and knees.

She tried to turn on him with nails and teeth, giving him her rage. He was pleased to see it, even as he controlled her, shoving her back down to her elbows. He held her there grimly, one hand on the back of her neck as he freed himself from his trousers. The skirt was so short that this position fully exposed her ass, the pussy still ripe from their earlier fucking, wet from that and the girls' shower play. As he slammed into her, he heard her snarl, her cry of protest.

He gave himself over completely to that instinct, his cock hard and thick, knowing what was his to take, but he wouldn't leave it at that. He was driving into her like a battering ram, but she was getting hotter and wetter, and when he slapped her ass, a hard spank to command her attention further, she contracted on him, a short gasp breaking up the outrage.

"Stop. Stop it."

As her arousal built, her furious, frantic demand became an anguished plea. A plea that stabbed him in the heart, for she was pleading for his help, to drive all the rest away, to make all the shrieking pain in her heart and head stop. *Stop it. Please stop it.*

There was nothing he wouldn't do for her. So in answer, he let go of her neck and braced his body over her with one arm, reaching beneath with the other to find her clit and rub it with knowledgeable fingers, feeling how swollen it was. Her hand latched onto his braced forearm, her forehead against his elbow. Her teeth sank into his arm, but as an anchor, not an attack.

She was still pleading, incoherent, and the tearful sound of it, the way the nails of her other hand dug helplessly into the carpet, tore something apart inside of him.

He would give her pleasure, but that wasn't the end goal. He was striving for pure possession, the message it sent. What he'd told her. *Mine to protect. Mine to cherish.* And she did deserve to be cherished, god damn her ex-husband to hell, and all the evil in the world that had taken her son from her. She was the only one who didn't see it.

The message might not be getting through, but the elemental force he knew dwelled within her was surging up to balance the madness. He was thrusting hard enough to give her rug burns. *Good.* Her breath was pumping as hard and fast as he was now, punctuated by short, jerky sobs. Her cunt was so slippery it was making provocative sucking noises while he fucked her. She cursed him with a creative viciousness that demanded an answer.

Dropping down over her then, he put his arms on either side of her shoulders, back pressing into hers as he kept working her. When he pulled the dress down, her breast filled his palm, the nipple firm as a new cranberry when he pinched it. She tried to buck him off, but her body was in control now, softening to the claim of his, and her hips were rising to meet him. Ramming home, the deepest thrust yet, he seized her throat, bringing her to a full halt, holding her still with his weight and strength. She shuddered and quaked against him, her pussy rippling against his cock.

"I don't need a collar to know I'm your Master, Rachel. And neither do you. You curse at me like that again, and I'll have my cock down your throat for the entire ride home. I'll pull your wrists back and tie them to your ankles so only my fist in your hair keeps you on your knees while you're sucking me."

Something broke then, something that deflated everything in her...desire, passion, anger. She went limp and shuddering beneath him, the throbbing of her pussy like a tiny ticking clock in an empty room, evidence of the life that was there, but so much space, a space that echoed in the pit of the belly and made the heart ache.

He could have pushed her on to climax, but he knew her body's arousal had balanced her emotional pain. He'd leave the two at odds for now, and give her what he most wanted to give her. When he cautiously eased his hold, she had her head pressed to the carpet, sobs now taking her fully. He slid out of her, rearranged his clothes and then picked her up. Bringing her back up to one of the seats, he cradled her close in his arms, holding her fiercely, her face tucked into his neck as she cried.

"I'm here," he muttered. "I'll never leave you alone. You'll never be lonely again."

But as she cried, her knees drew up against his side, her arms folding over her chest. Those sobs seemed to have the power to break her, no matter how closely he held her. It alarmed him, how it suddenly seemed she was more alone than she'd ever been, more shut away from him than he'd yet experienced.

The Master in him could reach her body, certain parts of her soul, but how did he reach her heart if grief and loss amputated it? What if it was now out of anyone's reach, even her own?

* * * * *

Once the tears stopped, she didn't want him near her. She didn't fight him, didn't draw away, but he felt it in every resisting line of her body. She looked brittle as glass, her face tired and worn, makeup smeared. She sat docile, unresponsive, as he used ice and his handkerchief to clean up her face.

After they reached her place, he told Max they'd get a few things and then be back down. He didn't want her at her apartment tonight, and maybe not ever again. She could bring the things she loved to his place, and turn her back on the isolation, loneliness and escape her home had too often represented.

When they got to the fourth level, one of her neighbors, a sharp-eyed older woman with a small load of laundry topped by a spy novel, was coming from the elevator. As they passed her, Jon nodded courteously, but Rachel stopped, reached out and touched the woman's arm. "Mrs. Lowery, can you hold on a moment?"

Turning on her heel, she faced Jon, extricating her elbow from his grasp. Her hazel gaze was as flat and empty as a swimming pool. "Thank you, Jon. I'm staying here tonight, and I need you to go home and leave me alone."

Mrs. Lowery, in that unfortunate way that women had, intuitively picked up on the vibes of a sister in need of backup. She put down the basket.

"Rachel, don't do this." Jon glanced between them, trying to look genial and concerned, rather than simply hiking her over her shoulder and taking her the rest of the way down the hall, Mrs. Lowery be damned. Rachel quivered, seeing it in him, and though Mrs. Lowery would interpret that quiver as the wrong kind of fear, Jon knew differently. Yes, it was fear, but fear of herself, not of him. Rachel had far more experience shutting people out than letting them in, and she was using that skill now. Her eyes were filled with dull pain that he wanted to soothe, even as he wanted to give her the spanking of her life.

"I need tonight, Jon." She cleared her throat, her fingers pressing into Mrs. Lowery's arm. The woman patted her soothingly, eyeing Jon. Not an ounce of fear in her expression, which clearly said, *I can start screaming and bring the entire complex out here on your ass, bucko.* Any other time he would have been thrilled that Rachel had such a diligent neighbor, but now *nosy, busybody* and *pain-in-the-ass* were a few of the choice words coming to mind.

"I'm not...you don't have to worry about anything, okay? I need to be alone with this. Please respect that."

He wanted to take her hand, make any kind of contact, but Rachel stepped back, anticipating him. She wrapped her arms against her body, everything about her locked down. Mrs. Lowery shifted slightly, coming in between them. Given how he was feeling, the woman had balls.

He knew when it was necessary to fall back and take a different tactic, retreat and regroup, but damn it, this was not a fucking business meeting. This was his heart and soul, and she needed him. But she wouldn't let him help her. He had no choice but to back off, for now. He wasn't going to leave it like this though.

"I'm walking you to your door," he said coolly, and firmly sidestepped Mrs. Lowery to take Rachel's elbow, despite her flinch. Before either woman could say anything, he met the neighbor's mistrustful gaze. "I will not go into the apartment with her. I know you have your hand on the cellphone in your coat pocket. If I don't walk right back past you in five minutes, you can call the police." In the woman's brown eyes, he saw the root of what she needed to know. He could at least offer her that, with full sincerity. "Rachel will come to no harm from me. She knows that. She's just upset."

Mrs. Lowery's gaze shifted to Rachel, who turned her head, stared at the floor, but didn't deny what he'd said. The neighbor studied him again. "Make it three minutes, and if I hear so much as a squeak from her, I'll have my son out here to toss you over the railing and you can take the direct route back to the ground floor."

Despite the frustration roiling in his gut, Jon had to appreciate her. He wondered if Janet had an older sister Matt didn't know about. He nodded, put pressure on Rachel's arm and directed her tense body down the hall until they reached the recessed archway of her door. Taking out her key card, he fitted it into the lock, pushed the door open a crack, then handed it to her. He'd had the key since they'd gone shopping earlier in the day, and he had to shove down the feeling of dreaded finality that came with putting it back in her hand. When their fingers brushed, before she could draw away, he had his hand closed on both of hers.

Knowing Mrs. Lowery was still listening for the tone of the conversation, but wasn't close enough to detect the content, he lowered his voice to a murmur.

"What are you doing, Rachel?"

"I know you won't take no for an answer, Jon, and I really, really need you to." She kept her gaze focused on his chest. Her fingers were cold and tight beneath his, her face pale. His frustration tipped back into fury, but he reined it back viciously, knowing that wouldn't help. However, as if sensing it, she quivered again, her gaze flicking up quickly, then back down. "At least for tonight. Please."

Lifting her chin, he held it in a tight grip even when she would have pulled away. "Do you still have the gun?"

The shock that crossed her gaze was the first emotion she'd displayed since their volatile coupling in the car. He didn't wait for an answer. Instead, he pushed her up against the door, letting her feel every insistent inch of his rigid body, head to toe. "I won't leave you like this, Rachel. You can have a dozen Mrs. Lowerys and her sons in this hallway, and they won't budge me an inch if I don't think you'll be safe."

Her eyes closed, her hands curling against his jacket, cold fingers whispering against his shirtfront. "I didn't think I could be more humiliated tonight, but I guess I was wrong."

"Rachel, for God's sake..."

She shook her head. "I'm going in here, shutting the door, and for the next little bit, I'm going to be by myself. I need that. I truly do. If you have any regard for me at all, you'll respect that. Please." Her lips trembled, and now those thick doll's lashes lifted, swimming hazel eyes locking with his. Her voice was a rasping whisper. "I promise you, on the soul of my son, I will not harm myself. All right?"

He cupped her face and wasn't surprised that the rawness of his own voice was a close match to hers. "Rachel, don't shut me out. Don't close yourself down like this again."

She gave a small laugh, a half sob. "Let me go, Jon. I don't have the strength for what you want. Though I really, really appreciate you offering, my visit to Oz is over. Go find the woman who has that strength. For tonight...I'm so tired. Let me go to sleep. I need that peace. The peace of sleeping alone. I need..." Her voice broke. "I need to be numb. Please go."

The sound of her tears, her broken voice, had footsteps coming swiftly down the hall. Giving him a despairing look, Rachel turned and slid into her apartment, closing the door decisively in his face.

* * * * *

The peace of sleeping alone. He understood what she meant. Inside that peaceful place, there was just enough room for her to fit, without touching the jagged edges of memory that hugged so close to her. If someone shared that space, she'd be forced against those painful and sharp points.

He would have persisted, except for a couple things. Mrs. Lowery had apparently fabricated the story about her son, but she appeared at his back armed with a Pomeranian. Though the armload of yapping dog wouldn't have deterred him, he knew there was some truth to what Rachel said, that she needed time. She'd promised him she wouldn't hurt herself, and though he knew an unstable person would say anything to placate their friends and family, she'd met his eyes, and for that one moment at least, he'd seen a quiet calm. It didn't completely resolve his worries on that score, but he had to live with it, unless he wanted to break down the door.

And while she took the time she felt she needed, damn it all, he'd use that time to think, plan a different strategy. When they were kicked in the balls in a negotiation, they didn't rush the field driven by pain and anger. They put some ice on it, and thought about how best to win the overall game.

So he went home. Sent Max back to the club to pick up the others, then ran the nature trails on his property twice, an eight-mile trek. He'd followed it up with an intense ninety-minute hot yoga session in his downstairs workshop. He'd kept the air off and only now had opened the windows that overlooked the screened porch. Wearing a loose and faded pair of jeans, he turned in slow circles on the revolving stool at his drafting table, the sweat drying on muscles stretched to their limit.

Damn it. God damn double fucking shit on a brick damn it.

Everyone was nicked and dinged to a certain extent by the natural progress of life. He'd understood that Rachel was badly damaged. The pain she'd felt from years of emotional estrangement from her spouse, then from the devastating loss of her son, had resulted in a meticulously constructed life that revolved in a peripheral way around people, passing inspection, but not attracting attention. The yoga and the physical therapy were ways she could offer parts of herself while continuing to protect the wounded center too raw for intimacy of any kind.

He remembered how she kept the photo album in her wardrobe. She had lots of acquaintances, but no real friends. She'd found her way to the center of the merry-go-round of life, where she could be dazzled by the colors and lights, enjoy watching the pretty ponies, but she was never on the ride herself. Because people saw her, most didn't see that she wasn't moving with them—just watching from her still point.

It made him realize that he might know her better than anyone, since the whole purpose of his weekly visits to her yoga class over the past year had been to study her, to analyze why he was increasingly more attracted to her. And she'd still been able to fool him, keep him on the outside all that time.

His fist curled on his thigh, as he again recalled that instant transformation, from the quietly wounded yet strong and outrageously sexy woman, to a cringing, insecure and pathetic creature, a version of herself he sensed she'd once been full time. He wanted to rip Cole to pieces, but it was far easier to destroy a human body than the memories it had inflicted upon her.

That was the key, wasn't it? How to overpower those memories. He'd known from the beginning he needed to close the deal fast, that she would keep erecting shields faster than he knocked them down. As Matt had said, he'd had to break them apart, make it impossible for her to resurrect them.

So sure he would be her shield until she had the faith and confidence in his love to stand without them, he'd taken her to the club. He'd broken them apart, all right. In his arrogance, he'd never anticipated something like this. And now she was defenseless against the pain of her own soul that she'd spent years trying to survive.

Fucking hell. He'd picked up his bolt cutter and was flipping the handle out and back while he rocked on the stool. Now he tossed it back down on the workbench with a resounding clang against the metal frame. He didn't care. He was going back over there. If he had to break down the damn door, he'd do it. She wouldn't call the police. He knew she

311

wouldn't. And if Mrs. Lowery did, Rachel wouldn't let them haul him off to jail. Maybe. Of course, that was why Matt paid Ben the big bucks. He could bail him out.

"You missed our usual post-club midnight dinner. Giuseppe had some outstanding limoncello tonight."

Jon turned toward the open window to the porch and the familiar voice, finding Matt sitting on the sill. His boss was still wearing slacks and dress shirt, but he'd lost the coat, the collar of the shirt open and sleeves rolled up. He dropped the takeout bag on the floor and brought both legs inside, bracing them in a comfortable splayed position as he tossed Jon a cold import from the small cooler he also had with him.

Even immersed in a project, Jon usually detected any visitors pulling into his drive, no matter the hour. But he expected his senses were a bit off tonight. He'd called Peter after leaving her place and filled him in, and had known Peter would pass the current status on to the others, but still he was surprised to see Matt.

"I'm going fucking insane. I can't stay here and do nothing."

"You aren't doing nothing. You're thinking. And from what I know of your mind, that's the energy equivalent of a full army on the march. She's all right for now."

Reaching into his pocket, he produced a small black revolver, and laid it on the nearest worktable. "She keeps it tucked between her towels in her linen closet. From the bluing on the muzzle, Max thinks she probably hasn't pulled it out of there since...since she used it last."

Jon stared at it, then at his boss and mentor. "I saw how she reacted to Savannah at the club," Matt continued. "So when Peter told me what happened, I had Max take Savannah over. Rachel didn't want to talk, but she let Savannah in. She let her tuck her in and sit by her bed until she fell asleep. My baby's spending the night on her couch, keeping an eye on her through an open door." Matt gave him a faint smile. "You'll owe me for that. I don't sleep without her. Once Rachel was asleep, Savannah looked through her things, found the gun. I could have sent Max in to do it, but Savannah knows her way around firearms. Plus, a woman would have a better idea where another woman would keep a gun. Once she found it, she gave it to Max and he brought it to me."

Jon found his voice at last. "How did you know about it? I hadn't told anyone."

Matt lifted an unapologetic shoulder, pulled out a bread stick and pushed the bag toward him with his foot. "I watch after my people, Jon. When you started getting invested in Rachel Madison months ago, I knew the signs. So when you made your move last week, I had her name run through a couple of my contacts."

"Wow." Jon ran a hand over his tired face, digesting that. "Some part of me feels like I should be pissed off. But considering you were able to step in where I fucked up, I guess it would all be ego."

Matt snorted. "Of all of us, you're guided the least by your ego. It's why you excel at diplomacy when things get really heated. But you do have one, Jon." He lifted his beer, quirking his brow. "Despite our teasing, we all know you have as big a dick as the rest of us. And you didn't fuck up, by the way. You couldn't have anticipated what happened tonight."

Jon surged off the stool, moved restlessly around the workshop. "I should have. That's the way these things work, Matt. We both know that. We've seen things crop up during a strategy session that bug us, but because of other priorities we don't cover them the way we should. Then, sure enough, they bite us in the ass when we least expect it. I've been racing against a clock, and the whole time I've had that niggling feeling I was missing something vital by taking things at that speed, and sure enough, there it was." He gave a short, harsh chuckle. "There's a reason for those seemingly contrived coincidences we see in the movies. Fate doesn't like deception or loose ends, and has a way of putting them right in your face."

"So you had a setback, that's all. You fall back, regroup, plan a different strategy. Do you think she loves you?"

"She wants to. And I know I love her." Jon stopped at one of his unfinished projects, a modification to a CNC arm that, if he figured out the right programming, might be able to increase their production rate at the plant in Honduras. He laid his hand on the cool metal, stared at it. "It's been growing in me this whole year, since I met her. As great a life as I have, the hour or two a week I spent in her classes made it all ten times better. I think I've memorized every expression she has, the way she moves, the way she smells...

"That first class, when she laid her hands on my forehead during the *nidra*—a closing ritual for yoga," he added, knowing Matt preferred boxing at a gym for his workout regimen, "I swear everything in me just went still. She works me up, gets me hard and hot with a look, but she can also make everything in me go still and quiet as well, a sense of absolute peace, a balance. She walks the same paths I do. She's the one. But I'm afraid that waiting so long to bring that to fruition has made me push things too fast, and I'm using how it was for all of you to justify my own impatience. And as a result, this has happened."

"Hmm." Matt moved to the stool near his, bringing the ignored takeout bag. Pulling out two containers of food, he sent a pointed look at the other stool until Jon returned to it. Then he slid one container over to him, tossing a set of metal utensils next to it. At Jon's look, Matt grinned. "Rosalie always tells me to bring them back for the next takeout order. She knows how I hate to eat with plastic."

Jon shook his head. "Savannah should worry about the relationship you have with that woman. I'm going to tell her you have a culinary affair going on with a seventy-two-year-old Italian grandmother."

"Savannah has no problem as long as it keeps me from demanding that she cook for me. Not that I'd ever be that brave." Matt flashed his teeth. "My stomach is not iron-clad."

"And pissed-off women who commit murder prefer poison as the weapon of choice." Jon gave a half chuckle, but then he sobered. The food smelled good, and knowing Rachel was safe, that Savannah was with her, did help. Matt would have known that. He knew how to bring out the best in his people, give them the right environment to do their best work, or in this case, their best thinking. As always, Jon wondered if Matt was a reincarnated Machiavelli—with a kinder heart and a Texas drawl.

"Out of all three women," Jon said thoughtfully, "Savannah has the most of what Rachel has, doesn't she? That pain so well contained, it's like a bomb. The night you detonated it for Savannah, you went for a completely controlled environment. I should have done that. She just always wanted to experience a place like Surreal. But I wasn't expecting her ex to show up and set off the charge like that."

"As you said, you can't run from Fate. Plus, you tend to excel at handling the unpredictable. You handled it the right way, even though you don't feel like that now, because she outmaneuvered you at her apartment. Expect some shit from Ben on that, by the way."

"I'm sure. Remind me to pull out my underused ego and gloat like a damn peacock when his heart finally takes a fall."

"I'd like to see that," Matt said, his dark eyes serious. "Ben needs that in his life. The last thing I'd ever accuse Ben of is being maudlin. He's as practical and live-in-the-moment as they come. But…"

When he shrugged, Jon finished it. "He's starting to feel lonely, watching all of us find our other half. It's like he's a foster kid again, watching all the other kids with parents who love them."

"Yeah."

Jon knew when it happened for Ben, he wouldn't gloat. None of them would. They'd do exactly what they were doing for Jon now. They'd give Ben everything they had to make sure he found that inner peace that came when a man found the answer to all of it in one woman's eyes. Everything he was or wanted to be became about her, for her. She was a comfort zone, where everything was possible.

He stopped, a breadstick halfway to his mouth. He'd been focusing on pulling her out of *her* comfort zone. He'd put her into an environment she craved yet was an entirely new world, outside her vivid yet passive fantasy life. He hadn't thought about handling her *in* her comfort zone, opening her mind and letting her see what was possible from that perspective.

The stool rocking stopped. "I got it," he said. "That's it."

Matt's firm lips curved, and he flicked opened Jon's steaming pasta primavera, gesturing to his fork. "Good. Eat, so I can tell Cass I fed you."

"She's such a mom."

"Well, raising five siblings will do that to you. Tell me how you need us."

"I think this will be just the two of us." But as Jon took up his fork, he gave Matt a look. "Still, thanks for all of it. Thanks for being here when I needed it. As usual."

"I will not be hugged," Matt said sternly.

Jon considered the food. "You're awfully nurturing for someone who doesn't hug."

"Eat it and shut up, or you're fired."

Chapter Eighteen

‰

Rachel hung her sweater up on the hook on the back of the studio door and considered the tranquil space, the stray beams of sunlight coming through the rice shades. The adjacent fitness club was quiet this early Sunday morning. It was good that the first thing she was doing in the "real world" since the Club Surreal fiasco was this private with Mrs. Hannenburg. She was in her eighties, and did beginner yoga to keep her joints flexible. Because of how slowly she moved, she preferred a private, and any conversation she offered were easy, automatic response topics, like the current weather or whether her grandchildren would visit soon. Calming, more aligned with Rachel's reality. So different from last Sunday, her private session with Jon.

Savannah had been calming, though in a different way. In the morning, she'd embarrassed and yet comforted Rachel by making her a simple breakfast of organic scrambled eggs and fruit. She'd asked her about her schedule for the next day or so, but said nothing about what had happened in the parking lot or anything about Jon. Rachel couldn't talk about Jon yet. Just thinking about him set her body to yearning, remembering every single, explosive second they'd shared at the club, and the way he'd taken her down in the limo. She'd never anticipated such sexual ruthlessness from Jon, but she'd welcomed it, embraced it, even as it had drained and destroyed her at once.

She needed him desperately, enough that when she'd taken a shower this morning she'd felt the shakiness of it in her lower belly, in the empty clutch of her hands. But she was too afraid. That was her whole problem, wasn't it? Jon thought she had courage, but he was wrong.

She closed her eyes, her throat aching. Savannah had left her this morning with a warm hug, a long look and the press of her elegant hand. It was odd how the woman had probably said less than twenty words to her, yet Rachel felt as if Savannah had understood all of it. But she still didn't know how to interpret the woman's parting long look. Simple compassion? Or like Savannah was looking into a mirror of her past, wishing she could tell that image something that it wasn't ready to hear?

Well, she'd have plenty of time to think about it alone, wouldn't she? She'd walked into this eyes open, knowing this would happen. She wouldn't lean on anyone to help, particularly Jon, because it wouldn't be fair to drag someone like him down into that. He deserved so much more than a woman who was already past the best moments of her life, who was mired in a history she didn't have the strength to overcome.

She went to a full lotus position on her mat, stared at the emptiness around her. When she couldn't bear that anymore, she closed her eyes, began her breathing, hoped for Mrs. Hannenburg to get here soon.

In one nostril, out the other, clearing the sinuses. Back straight...she remembered how Jon required her to keep her back straight as she sat by his chair. The cool touch of the studio air slid over her breasts and she recalled his touch there, the way his hand slid between her legs, parted for his pleasure...

She squeezed her eyes shut more tightly. See? Just sex. The spurts of arousal were a virus, a malady she'd contracted. Jon had given it to her. His absence was the cure. In time, her libido would shut back down, with all its unattainable desires.

But it was more than her libido. She remembered how he'd curved his body protectively behind hers here, sharing the same mat. How he'd talked to her at the coffee shop. The way he'd draped his arm loosely over her shoulders, holding her close as they strolled past the shops. The crease in his brow and his intent absorption among all his workshop dust and tools as he created a new marvel that drove a woman insane.

For the past year, he'd been a constant presence in her life, whether in her mind or physically in her class. A presence she anticipated like buried treasure, rediscovered every week for an hour or two. She remembered everything. The way he laughed when the other women teased one another or him. The intent way he looked as he did the postures. The way he focused on her.

She slowed that thought down, replayed it. Every moment he'd been in her class, he'd had his attention on her in some way, big or small. It had made her feel better about...everything. Now that she'd seen the way he looked at her when his desire was completely unleashed, she couldn't help but recognize traces of it earlier. That desire, that total attention, had been simmering in his gaze from the first class. It had been given wings the moment she asked him if she could touch him, and he'd given her permission.

He hadn't come back weekly because of his desire to join a yoga class. He'd come for her. Only for her. And she'd grown addicted to him long before he'd found out she wasn't married.

"Oh Jon." Her hands, pressed in prayer *mudra* in front of her sternum, turned and curled against her aching heart. "I can't give you what you want. Though I want to. I really, really want to. It's too late."

"No, it's not. Because you already have given me what I want."

She opened her eyes, somehow not at all surprised to see him leaning in her doorway, wearing the familiar tank and cotton trousers for his practice. The sight of the leanly muscled body, the serious set of his mouth, those silken dark strands of hair that fell over his high forehead, were all capable of making her breath hitch, but it was the look in his blue eyes that took it away entirely.

"Did you kidnap Mrs. Hannenburg?" Though she wanted to sound calm, her voice was barely a whisper. His eyes dwelled on her face, the gemstone color so deep and still she could feel it reach out to her, draw her in, so that she didn't really want to speak. Or move. Or do anything but gaze at him avidly.

"Ben is taking her out for coffee and homemade pastries even as we speak. She seemed willing to be kidnapped, particularly when we told her we were surprising you for your birthday."

"My birthday isn't for some time." She tried to remember she couldn't have him, and all the reasons why. "And I try not to notice it anyhow."

"Well, that's going to change. Because I intend to celebrate every year you're a part of my life. It also depends on how you define birthday. For some people, it can be the day they decide to embrace something new, take their life in a whole new direction."

"Jon." She looked down at her hands, despairing. She wanted him so badly the need ached in her joints like a flu.

"You really pissed me off the other night. And you scared me." When she lifted her gaze, she saw he was masking nothing. His expression reflected those volatile feelings, their aftermath. And something deeper, that came through now in the roughness of his velvet voice. "If you ever tried to hurt yourself, sweet girl, I don't know what I'd do."

A lump formed in her throat, and she looked back down, curling her fingers together. "I didn't mean to scare you. I should have explained more...but I was so tired, and embarrassed and surprised that you knew. That day I did that...the day the gun went off..." She sighed, closed her eyes. "You know they say women do poison or something like that, something that won't destroy their face, because we're vain, even in death. But at the time, all I thought was that I wanted to destroy my face, because even that wasn't pleasurable to him anymore. Or to me. I saw a mother who wasn't a mother, a wife who wasn't a wife. I thought, 'I'll just destroy it all'."

She shook her head. She could feel his increased concentration, the fierce emotions her words were stirring in him, but he stayed silent, let her say it. "It was soon after my son's death, and I was…in despair. But whatever angel guided that bullet, told me I still I wanted to live."

Taking a deep breath, she lifted her attention to his face. What she saw there—anger, compassion, love—nearly stole her voice, but she had to say the rest. "You know what the best day of my life was? I was at the beach with my son. He was two. I played in the surf with him, sat in wet sand and dug in it with a little plastic shovel. He painted my calves with splotches of it while sand got into our swimsuits. I cherished every move, stored every laugh in my heart." She paused, swallowing the ache. "I brought our chair down to the tide line and held him in my arms while he fell asleep against my neck, and I dozed with him, amazed that Cole and I had created this perfect thing, to house this precious little soul…"

She stopped. There was no way she could go from there to what had happened to that perfect creation, that precious soul, but fortunately Jon knew, and she could leave it. But her mind wouldn't. She remembered Kyle's soft baby hair, and the horrific moment at the funeral home, when his body had been delivered there in the sealed casket. She'd screamed at Cole, beaten on him because she wanted that casket opened and he didn't. She had to see his body, no matter how mangled or decomposed, so she could stroke that soft hair from his forehead one last time. They'd both cried, even as Cole held her at arms' length, not able to bear holding her, even then.

"I know I'll never be that happy again, I'm sure of it…" She swallowed against the far too familiar dull pain in her heart, tasting her tears on her lips. "When I finally realized that, I could accept all the rest. It didn't matter. And I knew I'd never try to take my life again."

Jon cocked his head, his blue eyes bright with pain for her, but his mouth set in a determined line she knew too well. "And yet, despite your acceptance of that, I not only feel your body yearning but your heart and soul as well. There's more, Rachel. There's more and you're not giving it to yourself, because no mother who loses a child thinks she ever deserves happiness again."

She shook her head, more vehemently. "There's a rhythm, a natural energy that moves through us, a natural order, and you see it around us all the time. I feel it when I do a particularly good yoga session. But it doesn't mean we're special or unique in the universe, magnified under some cosmic being's glass. It just means that life goes on, and you can make the most or the least of it. Your choice. There isn't a grand scheme. What you get is what you get."

"But you haven't chosen." His voice was soft, but relentless. "You can't not choose, Rachel."

"I'm afraid of any more choices." Her voice cracked. "I've made all the wrong ones. I have to just stay...on the same track, you know?"

"Remember that day I had you close your eyes and tell me the age you always feel, no matter what you see in the mirror?" At the reluctant lift of her shoulder, he took a step into the room. "Close your eyes now. And when you do, I want you to imagine the type of woman you think would suit me best. Who do you see, Rachel?"

She couldn't resist the edge of command in his tender voice and he knew it. Just as he knew when she closed her eyes, she couldn't see him with anyone but her. She could tell herself that merely meant her mind was being a willful child, refusing to let go of the candy the adult part of her knew wasn't good for it. But if she tried to see him with someone else, like one of those girls at the coffee shop, it wasn't only anger and jealousy that made it hard to envision. It *felt* wrong.

When she opened her eyes, he was taking a seat that mirrored her lotus position, sliding up so that his knees touched hers. Laying his hands there, palms up in invitation, he met her gaze, that powerful connection she couldn't deny. "Close the circle, Rachel. Let the energy flow between us. You know as well as I do, when we meditate, things become clearer. Let's go to that place together and see what we find."

"I don't think I can. My mind is too scattered."

"Let's try. Let me help."

She gave a bitter half-chuckle. "You're the reason it's like that. You're so persistent, and eventually you'll win, but it won't work, Jon. I'll make you miserable, and I won't be able to bear seeing it happen. Why don't you understand that? Let me live my life like this, with yoga and physical therapy, and don't make me take things to places I can't control."

"Lay your palms in mine, Rachel."

She complied with a sigh, because in all truth, she couldn't keep herself from touching him. He shifted one of his hands so her palm was the one facing up, his pressed down on it, the opposite of the other side, so they had balance in the closed circle. The heat of his flesh sent a ripple through her nerve endings, a jolt to her system as if she was an appliance that had been plugged in, brought to life. Fear constricted in her chest. He had so much power over her.

"Control is the whole point, Rachel." His eyes locked on her face, holding her still. "As I told you in the beginning, you need a Master who won't *let* you take control. I'm him. And you can keep fighting it, but I won't give up. When I put that collar on you the other night, you knew you were mine. It was why you tried so hard to tear it off. Because Cole made you feel like an utter failure, and you thought you didn't deserve what I was offering. Like a lot of other things, that ends now as well."

The steel took over now. "I'll never allow you to think that about yourself. When you grieve for your son, I'll give you my arms, my comfort, and I'll grieve with you, because he's a part of your soul, a large part of who you are. But he's in a place where he can understand now, where his father's disappointment and anger can't poison him. He knows, as I do, how much you love him. And how hard you tried to love his father. And because he knows, and loves you, he doesn't want you in that grave with him."

Their palms lay flat together, not gripping, yet still connected. Her gaze rested in the light clasp of his, her heart full of both uncertainty and longing, the way he so often made her feel. "It's in yoga you found your peace," he said in a low voice, his thumb making a gentle pass over her palm. "A way to accept the good and the bad, to have it make more sense. And as much as I enjoyed the club, *this* is where you need to accept me as your Master, in that delicate balance between the tragedies of the past and the possibility of your future. Breathe with me, Rachel. Just breathe with me, and let's see what happens."

He closed his eyes then, drawing that first deep breath, his hands loosening further so that their palms had room for some heat between them, that energy transfer. She watched him breathe, watched his chest expand, the lift and fall of his shoulders, the pulse at his throat.

His lips curved. "Close your eyes, girl, and breathe with me."

She shut her eyes and began the *pranayama*. As the silence settled over them, their breathing started to align, and she was sure their heartbeats would as well.

They stayed that way for some time. Though attuned to Jon's stimulating presence, her body integrated it, made it part of the calm center the breathing was expanding inside of her. Some of the sick fear and throbbing want started to ease, to slip away. As much as she wanted to deny it, she knew his presence was responsible. He helped bring her balance.

His hands left her palms, gracefully turned and curled around her wrists, a loose circle that slid back along her forearms, then forward once more as she kept her hands outstretched, both palms facing downward now, so when he came back he met them again, making them vibrate with the strip of heated space between them. Her wrists were tingling from his caress. Three more breath cycles, then he did it again. After nine repetitions, he spoke. "Keep your eyes closed."

Using the pressure of his hands, he guided her to her feet with him. He faced her away from him, his touch falling to her waist. "Lift your hands above you, bending back toward me, arms overhead."

She did, feeling the stretch in her spine, his shoulder beneath her head as she went into the second step of the sun salutation cycle. He slid up her rib cage, palms molding her there, holding her. "Tree pose."

Sole of her foot pressed against the opposite thigh, knee bent, her hands adjusting to a pointed fold above her head. He took down her hair, combing it out with his fingers, and she held her balance with effort. "You are so beautiful," he said, his voice a sensual rumble in the quiet room. "All mine."

She trembled, but he steadied her, holding her in the pose. "Next phase. Forward fold, then to Down Dog." When she folded forward, he was still holding her hips, fingers in the bend between hip and thigh, his body against hers. She let out a tiny sound as he pressed his groin against her through the narrow space between her legs. His cock was hard enough to make her mouth water, but he sounded entirely calm, placid as a lake.

"Keep your mind in a meditative state. Let the arousal take you where you need to go. Just let it happen, Rachel."

He shifted so she could stretch her legs back into *chaturanga*, Plank, then she lifted her hips to lean back into Down Dog, taking the stretch to her shoulders, the back of her legs. He ran his hands along her buttocks now, down over the long muscles in her thighs.

"One day, I'll make you hold this pose while I slide inside, let you feel how my cock buries into the very heart of you." His fingers trailed over her dampening crotch panel and her arms quivered harder. But now he bent over her, his arm around her waist, steadying her as he dropped a kiss on the bump of her spine in the center of her back. "Have you ever done the *camatkarasana*, Rachel? The Wild Thing pose?"

She shook her head. She'd seen it of course, but maybe because of what it symbolized, a celebration of personal power and freedom, she'd avoided it.

"Well, we're going to do it now."

It was a very advanced position. From Down Dog, it took a lithe lift of hips, swinging one leg over so she'd go to a backbend *asana*, where her right leg would be straight out to the floor, foot rolled on its edge, while her left leg stayed bent, foot flat on the mat. One arm reaching up and out, off the mat, the other braced, then she'd arch her back farther to complete the pose.

He backed off then, but stayed close enough to spot her. "You can do it, Rachel. I want to see you do it. Do it for me. And for yourself. Deep breaths, feel what it means. Prepare yourself for it. Embrace it. When you're ready, go."

She breathed, closed her eyes, felt the thrum in her muscles, the energy flow through her. She'd found peace in yoga, balance, but she hadn't become whole, because she'd hidden there, instead of treating it as a sacred sanctuary. Hiding meant that a person stayed out of sight of the good as well as the bad. A sanctuary had windows to see the world, a door to invite it in, because there was nothing to fear there.

She lifted her hips, giving herself the momentum she needed to do a slow turnover. Then she was there, him over her. He didn't touch her, but his energy was close, ready if she slipped. Letting her make the step, but providing her the courage to give all of herself to it. That focus and attention of his was there, radiating on her even as he straightened, moved back, and let her finish it under his satisfied expression. She could see herself in the mirror, and it was an extremely sensual and feminine pose, the body reaching out as if it was flying backward through the clouds. The short name was apt, but she was also aware of another translation for *camatkarasana*.

The ecstatic unfolding of the enraptured heart.

"God, you're gorgeous." His fervency was impossible to deny, as was the passion that was starting to swell in her body in this thrown-open wide pose, all under the heat of his gaze. Her hair brushed her fingertips. He bent then, and she drew in another breath, feeling that energy surge through her as he pressed his mouth to her arched throat, his hand passing over the curve of her breast, her distended rib cage and stretched abdomen, coming to rest over her mound, and lower, cupping her pussy and pressing on her there.

"Hold the pose, sweet girl. Just hold it. Feel what this does to the energy."

It spiked it like a rubber ball through her body, but there was a contained focus to it that let her hold the position, the energy so dense she was helpless and yet exuberant in its grasp. He was taking her to that place she kept denying existed, that she refused to accept for herself. And she knew he was right. Her acceptance was irrelevant. She belonged to him.

He'd make a Master's decisions for her, because he'd never let her hide from her own desires. And there was a freedom in that type of bondage impossible to explain, but it was something her heart had understood for a very long time.

"To give yourself to me, you have to believe in your power and freedom, Rachel," he said, his eyes very close. He was squatting next to her, trailing his hand along that open line of her body, as if admiring a sculpture, too tempting not to touch. "I believe in your courage, even if you don't. I'm not afraid of your pain and memories. You can trust me with them, know that I'll help you with them." He held her gaze now, showing her the truth of it. "And I promise I'll love you all the more, seeing what you've endured, yet what you're becoming when you let yourself love again, let yourself be the submissive you've always known yourself to be."

She shuddered at the idea, wanting so badly to believe. To hope. Her arms were starting to tire. He straightened and slid his arms under her, taking her weight when she began to falter. She abandoned the pose entirely, wanting to touch his face. Reaching up, she traced his temple, his jawline, and he caught her thumb in his teeth, nuzzling it with his tongue.

"Give yourself to me, Rachel," he repeated. "Tell me you're mine, just once, and I promise to be with you, no matter what you need. You just have to be willing to try, to trust me." That intent expression filled up her entire universe. "Do you love me, sweet girl?"

She couldn't lie to him, not here, not like this. And though the pose was broken, the feeling wasn't. He was right. This was where she'd found her truth, her center, when she'd had to put her life back together. And now she found she was no longer alone in that center. She swallowed. "Yes, Jon. I love you. I love you so much."

His eyes deepened to that midnight blue color. The energy that came from him went through the soles of her bare feet, pressed into the mat. It almost made her smile, made her want to laugh. To cry. To celebrate and yet be held, quiet and still, in his arms. Joined with him in the most intimate way possible.

He was holding her in one arm, and as if reading her mind, he now slid the other hand back over her mound, caressing her. She gripped his biceps, held him harder. He lowered her to the floor but gave her the unspoken direction to keep her legs closed together with the pressure of his hands on her thighs. Then he slipped her yoga pants off her legs, stroking her thighs and calves, the soles of her feet. He took the panties with the pants. Then he removed her snug tee, making her arch her body and stretch her arms back. He closed his hand over both of her palms, pressing her knuckles to the floor to keep her arms over her head.

Rising, he stripped as well. Her gaze devoured every inch of him, down to his aroused cock, and the lean ropes of thigh muscles that he would use to thrust into her. When he turned and bent, pulling something from his backpack, she savored the delectable view.

"Close your eyes. I don't want you to see this for a moment, and I want you to feel everything."

She obeyed, heard a metallic tone as something was laid near her head. But then her attention was pulled from that when he brought his body fully down upon hers, naked flesh to naked flesh. With his hands on her hips and upper thighs to remind her to hold her thighs closed together, he positioned himself so that his cock slid into the narrow opening between her thighs, slowly finding the moist path to full penetration.

In this position the angle was higher and yet somehow deeper. It was a Tantric position, one she'd seen before in her studies, where the lovemaking was prolonged and more excruciating, because it was a helpless position as well, everything concentrated in one narrow section of their connected bodies. She made a soft, inarticulate sound that had him curving his hands against her head, tangling fingers in her hair.

He thrust in, rotated, and slowly drew back, then went back in, seating himself as deeply as the position allowed, making her groan of need deepen. "That's it, sweet girl. You're so wet for me. I wanted my cock deep inside of you when I did this. You remember I told you that velvet collar wasn't your permanent one? I finished the permanent one. Open your eyes."

She did, immediately. He propped himself on one elbow, breast to chest with her, and showed her a choker of sterling silver wire, yoked at intervals by vertical supports made of gold. Several strands of the silver wire had been twisted into a decorative band running horizontally through the center of the collar, flanked by the simple straight lines of the others. A sapphire pendant, bound in a sinuous pattern of silver wire as a setting, was attached to one of the gold supports.

"It has a screw-down lock in the back." He lifted it to show her, his weight resting on his arm so he wasn't crushing her. As he did, he moved inside of her, making her catch her lip in her teeth. But her eyes didn't leave the collar as he spoke again. "Once it's on, only I can remove it, with a tool I designed specifically for the lock. On the gold support closest to it, I've etched the Sanskrit word for "owned", because I saw how you responded to that at the club. You want me to own you, heart, body and soul." His eyes delved into hers, pinning her soul in truth. "And that's a good thing, because it's what I fully intend to do."

"When did you do this?" she whispered. The collar, his words, the proximity of his body—all of it was a barrage on her senses.

"I started working on it a few months after I met you." His lips twisted. "I knew it was wrong, because at the time I still thought you were married. Even if I never gave it to you... Well, I didn't want to send any energy your way that would disrupt your marriage. But I made it anyway. I guess I know why now." He gave her that look of mild reproof and heated passion that had her pussy muscles constricting around him. He made a movement, one slight press against her leg, a flex of his thigh muscle, and he settled in deeper, making her gasp.

"Like that, do you?" His voice was almost a growl, but he brushed the smooth metal against her cheek, continued in a deceptively milder tone. "The velvet collar gave me the exact measurement I needed, and so I adjusted it yesterday and put it on a mold to test it for scratching or pinching. I won't say I want the fit to always be comfortable," his eyes gleamed, "but I want you to always want to wear it."

The problem wasn't wanting to wear it. She wanted it so badly, she could already feel it on her throat. But still she hesitated. In response, he shifted again, laying the collar next to her. He settled his hand in its place, letting her feel the fingers press there. She lifted her chin instinctively and he registered it, with a flare of desire in his gaze. He slid back out, just an inch or two, then back, slowly compressing her clit, sending a ricochet of reaction through that area and deep into her womb. He was so deep and shallow inside her at once, it was maddening.

"You already know it when I put my hand at your throat, Rachel. Don't deny the truth. Tell me you're mine, and I'll put this on you. After that, you won't ever shake me." His fine ebony brow lifted, his eyes sparkling. "Though, for the record, you're not going shake me even if you refuse it."

He bent now, hand still on her throat, and his mouth paused over hers. When her lips parted, he increased the pressure of that restraint, keeping that barely there distance between their lips. "You know I'm gentle and patient, but I'm also a Master. I'm not going to let you run from me, or yourself. I think you want and need that. Almost as much as I want and need you."

She wet her lips and glanced toward the collar. He'd been working on it for months. This wasn't a whim. It was...everything to him. It was in his face, his intensity. She was afraid, but how could she possibly turn her back on what might happen, what could be offered here?

Will you refuse your Master, Rachel?

He was her Master. She knew it. Who was she kidding? She was going to have to trust him, no matter her fears.

"Yes," she said, her voice barely over a breath, but she found the courage to meet his gaze. "Yes. I'm yours, Master."

That sculpted jaw tightened further, his brow drawing down as he moved, made her gasp. "This is mine? This pussy?"

She nodded, her cheeks heating a little at the directness of it. He bent, kissed the top of her breast, then dipped to suckle her nipple, giving it a sharp nip that drew a little cry from her as his cock thickened, shifted. "These breasts?" he asked, ruthless.

"And the heart beneath them," she promised. "Every part of my body, my heart, my mind, my soul. Goddess help me, it's always been yours, Jon. Please, don't let me...don't leave me alone."

"I won't." He moved again, that slow, small thrust and withdraw that was building to such a painful pressure in her lower belly. "The way you ran from me the other night? That won't happen again."

"No, Master."

"And you'll accept punishment for it."

Gladly.

His lips quirked. "You squeezed around me like a fist, sweet girl. You need the punishment, don't you? Ask for your collar, and your Master will give you everything you need."

She swallowed. "Please, let me wear your collar, Master. I'm sorry I took the other one off."

His expression softened then, his fingers brushing her cheek. "I'm sorry that evening got ruined. I expect we'll have to do it again, give you plenty more memories to erase that one."

Thinking of how many times since then her mind had returned to everything that occurred *before* Cole appeared, she thought she might not want all of it erased. But...a different sensual encounter with Jon and the Knights? If he needed to feel better about it, then the least she could do was help.

Since her lips were trembling against a smile, he didn't have trouble reading her mind. He gave her a narrow look, but there was a warm humor in his eyes that added to the mélange of positive feelings building in her — love, arousal, happiness.

"You might be an even bigger monster than Dana."

She wanted to chuckle, but he was done playing. He did that deep press again, trailed the collar down her sternum, teasing the pendant over her stiff nipple, then he replaced it with his mouth, a firm lick there, a quick press of lips over the nipple to pinch it into his mouth, give her moist heat.

"Jon..." It was a long, breathy sigh, and her legs pressed together, squeezing him inside her. The desire surged up in her, impatient and not wanting to be banked any longer. Her gaze fastened on that collar. "Jon, please. Master. Please put the collar on me so I can be yours." *So I can be free.*

"I like hearing you beg." He slid it under her jaw and she lifted her chin again as he brought the clasp together at her nape. It fit snug and perfect on her throat, sending a spiral of reaction down from the contact point. As he'd said from the beginning, it was no light, barely there collar. It had the weight and significance she craved, that she'd always wanted. It stiffened her nipples further, tightened her lower abdomen, pulled at the muscles in her thighs and curled her toes.

The sapphire rested at the base of her throat. As he bent, he placed his lips above it, so she tilted her head farther back, arching the rest of her up to him. "Mine now," he said, his voice thick with emotion and fierce resolve at once. "My slave. My love."

"Yours," she whispered, and hoped for it, with all her heart.

Yes, she might not survive losing this, having her belief betrayed, but the truth was, as much as she feared that, she simply wasn't strong enough to give him up. She had to be his, and had to trust that he would love her forever, just as he said. But for now, she would settle for each day because that was all she could handle. Trust would grow slow, but if she believed, the rest might come.

He folded himself over her now, arms on either side of her, hands beneath her, their bodies flush together, every naked inch. She could feel her arousal not only lubricating his path but trickling between her thighs. It took quite awhile to come this way, and the pleasure of it became unbearable, an excruciating sweetness to every stroke. He didn't falter, keeping it slow and easy as the position required, though his shoulders and back began to be slick and gleaming with the perspiration of withheld release.

333

His muscles flexed beneath her hands as she held his shoulders and he coiled around her the same way, their bodies one writhing animal, moving in a rhythm that connected to the earth. The sun beams coming through the rice shades had angled so they were in her eyes, and she buried her face in his throat, feeling his collar on her, his fingers sliding along it, touching and pulling it, confirming its presence and meaning, increasing the restraint at her throat and her arousal at once.

She was crying out now, every stroke like a tiny orgasm, but still not quite there. His. She was his. His slave, his submissive. She would do everything to give him pleasure, follow his will, his desires, and find her own, have the courage to grip them again. This acceptance was the true Wild Thing pose, for she found the strength in this moment to embrace that power and freedom, to believe this *was* her birthday, a chance to renew all the dreams she'd had and believe in them again, as if she'd been given a cake with the candles of all the birthdays, past, present and future.

"God, you're so tight and sweet." Keeping up that movement, he lifted enough to claim her breast again, suckling the nipple as he laid his hand over the collar, stretching her neck up farther, increasing the reminder of his possession, his claim. It knocked her over.

"Please...I can't... May I..."

"Come for me."

It rolled up hard and slow, like the richness of molasses, and when it took hold, it was so powerful he had to hold her still, keep her legs down and clasped together, making it that much more incredible. When he released at her pinnacle, it pushed her higher, so much pleasure at once. He captured her fierce cries in his mouth, his tongue plunging hard and deep like his cock. She clung to him, rocking with his body, making noises of need and yearning into his mouth, tugging on his hair as her body convulsed on his and the world changed irrevocably.

* * * * *

Coming down was as slow a process, for he kept kissing her mouth, her throat, her breast, moving inside her, though he let her legs slide outward to cradle him. That movement alone brought on an intense final spasm that had her clinging to him an extra, gasping moment. Lesser aftershocks continued for a long time afterward, as he cleverly kept drawing them out. While he did his sorcerer's magic on her body, his gaze rarely left her face, that total attention she'd envied Dana for having with Peter. It was now a gift she'd won as well.

"You're crying." He placed open-mouthed kisses over every tear, nuzzled her ear, the line of her jaw. "Don't cry, sweet girl."

"They're good tears, I think." She reached up, traced his face. "You know, when other girls were dreaming about careers as veterinarians or dancers or equestrian jumpers, I only had one dream."

"Tell me what it is, and I'll make it happen."

She smiled at that, even though it made her eyes brim again. "The big adventure I dreamed about was falling in love with someone and loving him with all my heart and soul, for the rest of my life. It was all I ever wanted."

When those blue eyes filled with pleasure for her, his mouth a sensual curve, she saw what Dana had been trying to say. *They only pick one.* By some miracle, she was it for him.

"Part of the problem with trust is that you're a fairy tale, Jon," she whispered. "It's hard to believe you're real, when I've longed for you for so long, and convinced myself you're a delusion I had."

"I'll change your mind about that." He gave her buttock a pinch, hitching her leg more securely around his back. Her heel rested on his upper thigh, his firm ass beneath her calf, flexing as he shifted their bodies. "I'll be the fairy tale *and* the reality. Shining armor one moment, underwear dumped outside the hamper the next. The best of both worlds."

It made her smile, as she was sure he intended, and he framed her face in his hands, tender affection in his expression. "I believe there comes a time when, no matter what else has happened, your soul is ready to give yourself something you want, and you're ready to accept it, your appreciation of it deepened by experience." His serious blue eyes caressed her face. "I also believe that sometimes you've suffered enough, figured enough things out, that you earn something wonderful in this life. You don't have to wait for it. You get your taste of afterlife now, full of everything you've always wanted. On the karmic scale, it means you've been very, very good."

She closed her eyes, clasping his strong forearms. "Or it means God is very, very merciful." She hadn't believed that, not after Kyle's death, but somehow, the love she was finding here told her she might find that faith again. Human tragedy might have taken her son from her, but he was in Love's hands now. Maybe, wherever he was, he was happy and at peace. And maybe she could find the same in Jon's hands.

"Oh, sweet girl." He slid from her at last. Just as he'd done a remarkable few days ago, he turned them and curved around her, protecting, sheltering and caressing her at once, holding her pain and happiness in the same capable hands. "I'm here. And whether whatever we call God is merciful or not, I'm not going anywhere. You deserve everything I can give to you, and I want to give you the world."

"I only want you," she said softly. "If God lets me have that, then I won't ask for more."

The End

Also by Joey W. Hill

 හ

eBooks:
Afterlife
Board Resolution
Chance of a Lifetime
Choice of Masters
If Wishes Were Horses
Make Her Dreams Come True
Nature of Desire 1: Holding the Cards
Nature of Desire 2: Natural Law
Nature of Desire 3: Ice Queen
Nature of Desire 4: Mirror of My Soul
Nature of Desire 5: Mistress of Redemption
Nature of Desire 6: Rough Canvas
Nature of Desire 7: Branded Sanctuary
Snow Angel
Threads of Faith
Virtual Reality

Print Books:
Behind the Mask *(anthology)*
Enchained *(anthology)*
Faith and Dreams
Hot Chances *(anthology)*
If Wishes Were horses

Nature of Desire 1: Holding the Cards
Nature of Desire 2: Natural Law
Nature of Desire 3: Ice Queen
Nature of Desire 4: Mirror of My Soul
Nature of Desire 5: Mistress of Redemption
Nature of Desire 6: Rough Canvas
Nature of Desire 7: Branded Sanctuary
The Twelve Quickies of Christmas Volume 2 *(anthology)*
Virtual Reality

About the Author

ھۂ

I've always had an aversion to reading, watching or hearing interviews of favorite actors, authors, musicians, etc. because so often the real person doesn't measure up to the beauty of the art they produce. Their politics or religion are distasteful, or they're shallow and self-absorbed, a vacuous mophead without a lick of sense. From then on, though I may appreciate their craft or art, it has somehow been tarnished. Therefore, whenever I'm asked to provide personal information about myself for readers, a ball of anxiety forms in my stomach as I think: "Okay, the next couple of paragraphs can change forever the way someone views my stories." Why on earth does a reader want to know about me? It's the story that's important.

So here it is. I've been given more blessings in my life than any one person has a right to have. Despite that, I'm a Type A, borderline obsessive-compulsive paranoiac who worries I will never live up to expectations. I've got more phobias than anyone (including myself) has patience to read about. I can't stand talking on the phone, I dread social commitments, and the idea of living in monastic solitude with my husband and animals, books and writing is as close an idea to paradise as I can imagine. I love chocolate, but with that deeply ingrained, irrational female belief that weight equals worth, I manage to keep it down to a minor addiction. I adore good movies. I'm told I work too much. Every day is spent trying to get through the never ending "to do" list to snatch a few minutes to write.

This is because, despite all these mediocre and typical qualities, for some miraculous reason, these wonderful characters well up out of my soul with stories to tell. When I manage to find enough time to write, sufficient enough that the precious "stillness" required rises up and calms all the competing voices in my head, I can step into their lives, hear what they are saying, what they're feeling, and put it down on paper. It's a magic beyond description, akin to truly believing my husband loves me, winning the trust of an animal who has known only fear or apathy, making a true connection with someone, or knowing for certain I've given a reader a moment of magic through those written words. It's a magic that reassures me there is Someone, far wiser than myself, who knows the permanent path to that garden of stillness, where there is only love, acceptance and a pen waiting for hours and hours of uninterrupted, blissful use.

If only I could finish that darned "to do" list.

I welcome feedback from readers—actually, I thrive on it like a vampire, whether it's good or bad. So feel free to visit me through my website www.storywitch.com anytime.

Joey welcomes comments from readers. You can find her website and email address on her author bio page at www.ellorascave.com.

Tell Us What You Think

We appreciate hearing reader opinions about our books. You can email us at Comments@EllorasCave.com.

Why an electronic book?

We live in the Information Age—an exciting time in the history of human civilization, in which technology rules supreme and continues to progress in leaps and bounds every minute of every day. For a multitude of reasons, more and more avid literary fans are opting to purchase e-books instead of paper books. The question from those not yet initiated into the world of electronic reading is simply: *Why?*

1. *Price.* An electronic title at Ellora's Cave Publishing and Cerridwen Press runs anywhere from 40% to 75% less than the cover price of the exact same title in paperback format. Why? Basic mathematics and cost. It is less expensive to publish an e-book (no paper and printing, no warehousing and shipping) than it is to publish a paperback, so the savings are passed along to the consumer.

2. *Space.* Running out of room in your house for your books? That is one worry you will never have with electronic books. For a low one-time cost, you can purchase a handheld device specifically designed for e-reading. Many e-readers have large, convenient screens for viewing. Better yet, hundreds of titles can be stored within your new library—on a single microchip. There are a variety of e-readers from different manufacturers. You can also read e-books on your PC or laptop computer. (Please note that Ellora's Cave does not endorse any specific brands.

You can check our websites at www.ellorascave.com or www.cerridwenpress.com for information we make available to new consumers.)

3. *Mobility.* Because your new e-library consists of only a microchip within a small, easily transportable e-reader, your entire cache of books can be taken with you wherever you go.

4. *Personal Viewing Preferences.* Are the words you are currently reading too small? Too large? Too... ANNOYING? Paperback books cannot be modified according to personal preferences, but e-books can.

5. *Instant Gratification.* Is it the middle of the night and all the bookstores near you are closed? Are you tired of waiting days, sometimes weeks, for bookstores to ship the novels you bought? Ellora's Cave Publishing sells instantaneous downloads twenty-four hours a day, seven days a week, every day of the year. Our webstore is never closed. Our e-book delivery system is 100% automated, meaning your order is filled as soon as you pay for it.

Those are a few of the top reasons why electronic books are replacing paperbacks for many avid readers.

As always, Ellora's Cave and Cerridwen Press welcome your questions and comments. We invite you to email us at Comments@ellorascave.com or write to us directly at Ellora's Cave Publishing Inc., 1056 Home Avenue, Akron, OH 44310-3502.

ELLORA'S CAVE
Romanticon

Annual convention
for women who
refuse to behave

WWW.JASMINEJADE.COM/ROMANTICON
For additional info contact: conventions@ellorascave.com

*Discover for yourself why readers can't get enough
of the multiple award-winning publisher*

Ellora's Cave.

*Whether you prefer e-books or paperbacks,
be sure to visit EC on the web at
www.ellorascave.com*

*for an erotic reading experience that will leave you
breathless.*

CPSIA information can be obtained at www.ICGtesting.com
Printed in the USA
LVOW122034020112

262082LV00001B/137/P